DAUGHTER

OF THE

KATSURA

Part One of Michiru's Tale

PHIL BARLOW

First Printing; 2018

ISBN 978-0-6483823-0-0

www.philbarlow.com.au

Steel is not made in a bathtub. It requires a furnace.

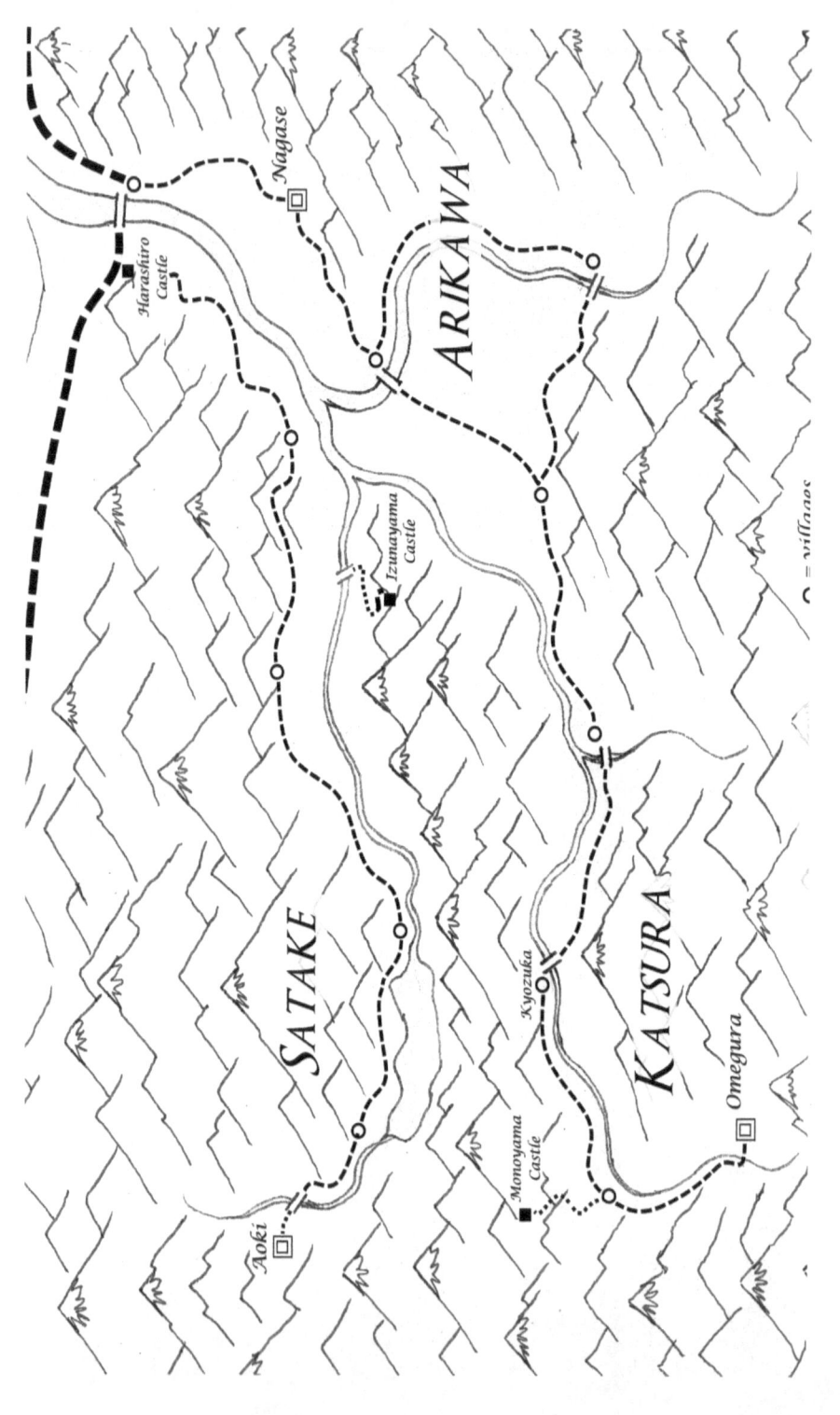

KATSURA CLAN

Lord Kosei	Michiru's brother
Lady Michiru	Kosei's Sister
Yoshioka Shuji	Senior Katsura samurai
Oba Hirakazu	Katsura samurai lieutenant
Kikuchi Masahide	Katsura samurai lieutenant
Keiko	Michiru's lady-in-waiting
Namika	Michiru's maid

ARIKAWA CLAN

Lord Sojiro	Michiru's groom
Tamuro Yatsuhiro	Arikawa samurai captain
Shigemori	Arikawa samurai
Ōmono	Ashigaru from Yatsuhiro's command
Hatoyama Toichi	Arikawa clansman, Sojiro's uncle

SATAKE CLAN

Satake Kiyomori	Head of the Satake Clan
Teshiga Isao	Commander of Doshiyama Castle
Utaemon Katsuo	Satake councillor
Oseku Toyonari	Satake emissary

SOME TERMS USED IN THIS BOOK

onsen	hot springs, often with bathing facilities and/or an inn
hakama	loose fitting trousers
kami	Shinto spirit or god
naginata	spear-like polearm with a long curved blade
tatami	woven straw mats of a standard size used in most houses
miko	young women that serve at Shinto shrines
norimono	formal fully enclosed palanquin used too carry dignitaries
hime	title roughly meaning "princess" or "great lady", also used as an honorific
-san	honorific added to a name to show respect
-sama	a greater honorific used for important persons
sensei	a title used for a teacher
ryokan	an inn
ashigaru	a lightly armoured footsoldier, usually a peasant
taisho	a title used for a leader
ronin	a samurai without a lord to serve through misfortune or disgrace
ojin	uncle or old man
ryo	a gold piece of around 15 grams in weight
koshukin	ryo minted by the Takeda from the purest gold
shoji	a sliding lattice screen covered with rice paper
teppo	matchlock muskets copied from Portuguese imports
seppuku	ritual suicide to regain honour

HAKONE – WINTER OF 1652

Lady Arikawa Michiru stared at the once scarred and battered box in front of her. Like her, it had seen much and travelled far. Now, only she knew of its scars. Made from deep coloured rosewood and bound with bronze fittings, it radiated quality. She remembered when a spear had broken one corner. The box had saved her from a broken back. She scrutinised the repair her husband ordered done. She could see none of the damage, especially not in this light and with her old eyes. However, she knew. There had once been a furrow of a bullet across one edge. She ran her fingers over the wood where the groove had been. The repairs were masterful. The scars were gone.

For her, the box was a source of memories, of people and places, a token of respect, dignity, and honour. It was not the box that was important now. No, this was about the gold. She leaned forward to open the box, wincing at the sudden pain in her thigh. The old arrow wound ached worse in this cold. It was partly why she came here; To get some relief from the hot waters of the spa and warm her tired old bones.

The builder of this onsen had made it possible to heat parts of the inn from the natural hot waters. They even added private baths to the more expensive rooms. She had decided she would happily pay for that. *Money can buy almost anything nowadays. Can it buy peace of mind? What about forgiveness?*

She lifted the lid. The rich crimson silk lining was decorated with a repeating pattern of four black diamonds arranged in a diamond; The Takeda crest. The glistening gold ovals nestled in neat rows, tied into stacks of ten with ribbons of stark, white paper. Except for

1

one. The odd stack bore the character for nine. She recognised her husband's writing in dark ink on the paper. She touched the stack and smiled. Running her fingers over the rest of the treasure, her smile faded. *So much wealth for one person. So much pain and death. What am I to do with it?* The maid slid the door open and Michiru closed the box.

The young farm girl had little grace about her. Michiru had overheard that the headman of her village had recently managed to get her a job here. *Well, she has a lot to learn.* Shivering as a waft of chilled air reached across the room, she grumbled. 'Come on, girl. You are letting the cold in.' It had been snowing for three days now and the chill was really beginning to take hold.

The young maid scurried across to Michiru. A clumsily arranged tea service sat on the tray from which she proceeded to make her tea. The old lady came close to interrupting more than once, making the girl even more nervous. Taking a sip of the proffered cup, her mouth pulled in tight in dissatisfaction. 'This tea is cold,' she scolded.

'Oh, I am so sorry, my lady.'

She did not mean to be difficult but some things she would not tolerate and cold tea was one of them. 'There is no excuse,' she snapped again at the mortified maid. 'All you have to do is boil water. You can do that can't you?'

'I am so sorry, Lady Michiru. Of course my lady.' She bowed repeatedly as she backed out of the room with the tray of offending tea. Tears clouded the girl's eyes. Michiru saw the fear in her as she backed out of the room. Obviously, the last thing the girl wanted was to lose her job for offending such an important guest. Especially with the weather was so bad. The inn had precious few paying guests at the moment. Many of the current residents were travellers trapped here by the early snow.

Michiru remembered the stories that Chika and Ōmono had shared with her about the lives of serving staff. The petty tyrannies, injustices and cold-hearted abuse. She thawed a little. 'Calm down, girl, it is alright,' she reassured her. 'Do not rush or you will break something and then you really will be in trouble.' She waved her away. 'You may take your time with the tea. I have much to think about.'

The maid bowed deeply relieved that there was a warm side to this scary samurai lady. 'Thank you, hime-sama.' But the old lady did not hear her. Michiru sat, staring at the wooden box in front of her, engrossed in her own thoughts.

CHAPTER ONE - SPRING OF 1581

Michiru looked at the ground and scowled. She clenched her teeth, fuming with frustration. *I am going to kick Kosei between the legs. Not too hard, but hard enough for him to remember. Then I will run for it.* Darting a glance back towards the main house she saw the old samurai Shuji watching her. With a pout, she decided against it. *I do not need another lecture on "lady-like" behaviour.* She stood waiting, her well-worn bow in one hand, an arrow shaft twirling between impatient fingers of the other.

Kosei bent his bow to its full extent, the string pulled back past his ear. He let out a slow breath, adjusted his aim a fraction and let the arrow fly. The solid wooden thunk told him that he had hit the target. A closer look showed the arrow had only nicked the edge of the black circle painted on the wood. *My aim was right the first time.* He snorted in exasperation. The bow was not his favourite weapon.

He spun to look at Michiru, a frown creasing his forehead. 'You will be going to Nagase tomorrow,' he growled. She glared back at him through the strands of glossy black hair that had escaped her ponytail. *How can someone so beautiful be so infuriating?* He always thought their family blessed because of her angelic appearance. Now she looked more like a vengeful witch, lips clamped in a tight line and eyebrows lowered. He half expected ominous clouds to roll in over the mountains, echoing with thunder.

He sighed. *I wish Father was still here to deal with her. Since Mother died, she has managed to get away with so much. Like wearing men's clothing whenever she is outside the house. Hardly dignified for a samurai lady. Well, the time for indulging her is well and truly past.* Steeling himself for the objections he knew that Michiru would throw at him, he put on his "Lord" face. *I cannot let her sway me on this.* Kosei loved his sister without reservation. *But I am head of this clan now, and I require obedience.*

'This wedding will take place, Michiru. Everything is ready. Soji-ro-sama writes that all the preparations have been made. Shuji-san will escort you to Nagase tomorrow and I will be there in a week's time for the wedding. The weather is good and the omens favourable. There is no reason to delay.'

Michiru remembered the day of her betrothal to Lord Sojiro. She had been fourteen. The marriage ceremony had been planned to be the following year. It had seemed such a long way into the future then. When the time came, Father had postponed the wedding saying she was not ready yet. That was three years ago. *Now father is dead and Kosei is the head of the family. I do not know who is keener for the marriage, the Arikawa or my brother.* All she knew was she did not want to marry yet. She was not ready to give up her life to become a quiet and obedient wife.

Kosei was firmly committed to the idea, considering how uncertain these times were. The neighbouring Satake clan, were gaining strength, thanks mainly to their gold mine. They threatened to cut the Katsura lands off and isolate them in their valley. The Arikawa clan were the Katsura's ancient allies. They held most of the decent farmland in the lower valley as well as the control of the river crossings. Having such large areas to defend was straining Arikawa resources. They were a tempting target for the Satake. The larger Arikawa clan needed the alliance with the Katsura as much as the Katsura needed them. *If the situation were more stable, I might wait a little while longer. But. Seventeen is a good age.* Besides, if nothing else, he would honour his father's agreements. His father organised this match, so the matter was already settled as far as he was concerned. Kosei maintained his mask-like visage.

'Very well, Brother.' Michiru stiffened, adopting a formal posture. 'It will be as you order.' Her tone hovered on the edge of outright disrespect. Letting her eyes fill with tears she continued melodramatically. 'I'm sure mother would be proud to see you casting me out into the world.' In her heart, she knew the futility of protesting. But the chance to get in a barb at her brother was too tempting.

How far can I push Kosei? Could I get him to postpone the wedding again or even cancel it altogether? Maybe I could run away. I could sneak off at night and disappear into the countryside disguised as a peasant. A series of improbable fantasies flitted through her mind as she fixed Kosei with a steely glare.

'Michiru!' he said gruffly. 'Don't pull that face at me!' He handed his bow to a waiting page. 'Father arranged this marriage and he expected you to honour that agreement. I ask you not to make this difficult.' Kosei's "Lord" face slipped. 'I could not agree to the marriage if I did not think this match would be right for you. Sojiro-sama is a good man,' he asserted with genuine feeling. 'He respected Father and I am sure he will look after you.' His expression lightened, breaking into a lopsided smile. 'I know you will love being the boss,' aiming for what he thought of as her weak spot. 'Just think. The only one who can tell you what to do will be your new husband and you will have him spellbound within a week.'

Michiru's head bowed, her expression surly.

Kosei took a hold of his sister's shoulder and lifted her chin. 'It will be alright,' he reassured her as he looked into her eyes. 'You will have lots of good advice and help from councillors that you can choose yourself.' He added playfully, 'And if anything goes wrong, you can blame them.' Michiru tried to stifle a grin as he chuckled. In a serious tone he added, 'You have grown into a fine young lady. You are the daughter of a lord of a small but respected clan. You are samurai and we are proud of you.' He let go of her shoulder and stood back, 'But now, you must leave us and start a new life with your husband. We will see you again from time to time. But we will always think of you.' He offered her a deferential bow.

A chill ran up the back of her arms. *He sounds just like Father.* The scent of Kosei's sweat mingled with the sharp tang of the rosin from the bowstring caught in her nostrils. The familiar floral undertones and fragrances of the garden she had grown up in stirred her memory. *It feels strange that Father is not here anymore. I miss him so much. Losing Mother was bad enough.* She winced at the unexpected wave of sorrow. *I know that wishing he was still here is selfish. Father is somewhere better, maybe already reborn into his next life.* Like a wisp of wind-blown cloud, his shade moved on and the moment passed. Once again, it was her brother in front of her, reassuring her. She took in his whole face. She knew it so well. His slightly crooked front tooth and the sparse beard. But there was also a strong even nose and intense eyes. *Does he want the best for me, or the clan?*

He did not come right out and say that she was behaving like a spoilt child. But she knew she was. She saw it in the retainer's faces. Especially Shuji. *Well, I see have little choice. I have to trust you and Father.* Michiru could not give Kosei a total victory. He was her brother after all. She looked at him and sniffed. 'I still don't want to go.' Raising her bow, she snapped off a shot in one fluid movement. The high-pitched zing of the arrow's flight ended with a sharp wooden thunk. Kosei looked at the target and laughed.

*　　*　　*

Michiru stomped along the veranda. *I am glad I wore hakama. Stomping would have been harder in a kimono. I do not want feel feminine. I am angry.* A furious scowl distorted her delicate features. Her bottom lip protruded like a spoiled child on the edge of a tantrum. The echo of her mother's scolding words intruded into her petulant self-absorption, "Pull that bottom lip in or you will trip over it!" Her eyes grew hot with tears. Whether it was from the perceived injustice of her brother's decision or remembering her mother, she could not tell.

She stopped outside the door to her room and looked at her sandaled feet. *They would understand how upset I am if I walked in with them on.* Her leg twitched, almost taking the step, but years of conditioning intervened. 'Nanny!' she called. To stop and engage in the mundane task of removing the sandals herself risked losing her anger's momentum. 'Nanny!' she yelled again, feet firmly planted, the bow still gripped in one hand.

Michiru's nanny slid the screen aside and bowed to the fuming girl. Hisa, was old. Old enough to remember Michiru's grandfather, who some said she had served as a concubine. Dressed in a simple dun coloured kimono, her grey hair was tied up in a tight bun. 'Ohh, Mi-chan. whatever is the matter? What's wrong? Did you hurt yourself again?'

Seeing her standing there expectantly, Hisa understood the problem immediately and hurried to her thankless task.

'Baka!' Michiru cursed.

'Oh, I'm sorry, my lady,' said the old woman in a pained tone as she fumbled with Michiru's sandals. 'I am getting clumsy in my old age.'

Michiru felt a slight pang of remorse for her rudeness, but it was soon burned away by the smouldering heat of her indignation. 'Not you, Nanny! Kosei!'

'Oh?' *I know perfectly well what the problem is, girl. There are few secrets in this house.* She had taken care of Michiru since she was a baby and knew her well enough to let her have her rant. 'What seems to be the problem, deary?' she asked.

Freed from her footwear, Michiru stepped onto the tatami matting of her room. 'He's still insisting on this stupid marriage to the stupid Arikawa.'

She almost flung the bow into the corner in frustration. But Shuji had trained her too well for her to disrespect the kami of her bow, or the craftsman who had convinced it to reside there. She placed it on its stand with reverence and tried to calm her turbulent mind. She heard the bow's spirit laughing at her childishness. *Do I deserve the kami's blessing if I act like this? Is this the behaviour of someone of noble birth?* She sat down, her shoulders slumping dejectedly.

Sit up straight, my lady,' the old woman said, as she had many times before. Michiru corrected her posture without thinking. The old woman sucked in her cheeks, empathising with the young girl. *Sorry Kitten but it's the real way of the world. You are better off than many your age.* Hisa thought of all the other girls from her youth. Not many had made it to forty. *Most women can only get work as servants, labourers, nuns, or prostitutes. Unless there is a man to marry.* 'Mi-chan. You must get married. It is the way of things for a woman.'

'I don't care,' she pouted.

Hisa tried to soothe her. 'Come now, Mi-chan. It is the same life whether we spend it laughing or crying. And your brother has decided. He is head of the family now.' *And that should have been the end of the matter. Young people these days. No sense of duty.* Michiru's young maid, Namika, came in from the hallway. The old woman shooed her back out. 'Go get the Lady some tea, girl.'

'But what about Sojiro-sama's family?' Michiru whined, knowing she was clutching at straws. 'What about his mother? She could be a mean mother-in-law who pinches me or beats me. What if his retainers are rude? What about his consorts? How many does he have? What if he lets them be mean to me and won't punish them? What if I make a bad mistake and ruin everything?' In her nervousness, she was working herself into an undignified state.

The old woman came to stand behind her, lifting her gently to her feet. 'Shhh. Let's get you changed, hmmm? It always feels better to be dressed in nice clean clothes, yes?' She turned to one of the concealed wardrobes, taking out a folded kimono from its wrappings. 'How about this lovely blue one with the waves. You like this one don't you? It was your mother's favourite colour too.'

Michiru silently complied, shedding her clothes with resignation. *I always knew I would have to get married. I just did not want it to be now.* Michiru had overheard other women talking about their marriages. About painful sex, sleepless nights with drunken husbands, undeserved beatings and long, agonising childbirth. It all scared her.

It was not that she had no experience of what happened between men and women. Living within paper walls she could not help but hear much of what went on. She had spent time exploring pleasure with one of the young pages, but she had never let it go too far. He had been as inexperienced as she was, and he was not a man. Her maids had told her men were usually insistent, rough and uncaring.

Most of all, Michiru dreaded having to suffer through pregnancy and then childbirth, only to have to do it all over again, until she either died or could not quicken with life any more. *Mother died in childbirth. She died delivering her fourth child.*

Michiru had learned many of the things that she needed to know to run a samurai household. But being responsible for everything worried her. She was to be ultimately responsible for the smooth running of her husband's household. However, everyone who served them would be relying on her as well. *I do not know if I can do it. I will ruin everything.*

Dressed now in a more feminine manner, she knelt down to allow the old woman to comb her hair. Hisa released it from the cord that held it up. She combed Michiru's glossy black hair with a cherry wood comb anointed with camellia oil. 'Such lovely hair,' she reminisced with a sigh. 'I used to do your mother's hair like this, you know. She was so proud of how long it was. Long and beautiful like a Fujiwara princess.'

Michiru relaxed under the old woman's tender ministrations. The anger drained out of her as her thoughts turned to the parents that had given her everything they could. *I owe it to both of them to make the best of this marriage. Hisa is right. I should accept my karma with dignity. I must put away my fears and selfishness.* 'I wish they were both still here, Nanny,' she said quietly.

'They are here, sweet one. They always have been. And they are so proud of how beautiful you have grown,' she smiled, believing it in her heart. A single tear slid unnoticed down her cheek.

*　　*　　*

The next morning Michiru sat in her room as they carried out the last of her chests, packed with all the necessities of her wardrobe. Sunlight, muted by the translucent screens, shone across the bare room. Dust motes danced in the golden sunlight as if alive. Her eyes took in all the little details of this room where she had grown up. The shoji that led out to the garden had been custom ordered for her by her mother. The screen-maker had layered ferns, wildflowers and wispy tendrils of vines into paper of the lower panels.

Michiru knew every one of them intimately. She had stared at them on countless rainy days throughout her life, gently tracing the outlines with her fingers.

She took a last lingering look at the carved cedar wood frieze above the door. Tiny wooden birds darted through the intertwined branches of two cypress trees. She had spent hours watching them move in the flickering light of the lamp. She loved the way the craftsman had made new details appear whenever you looked at it from a different angle. It was masterful work.

The final items taken were her naginata, which rested in their wooden brackets on the wall in the entrance. They were not only weapons. They were a symbol of a samurai woman's resolve to fight to protect her home, her family and herself. Michiru went to her own plain weapon, the one she had used for years and practised with every day. Above that was the heirloom given to her on her fourteenth birthday. Its haft gleamed with rich warm wooden tones bound in aged iron and bronze. It had belonged to her maternal grandmother and was made in an older style. The blade was wider than a sword with a more pronounced curve at the end. *This is mine now. In time, depending on fate, I will pass it on to my own daughter.*

She ran her hand along the shaft. Her fingers traced the circled three heart-shaped leaves of the Katsura crest inlaid with silver into the wood. Michiru lifted the naginata from its mounts and felt its reassuring weight. With practised precision, she spun it full circle once. She cut from side to side, feet shifting to adjust the balance of weapon and wielder. Becoming one. Her heart swelled in pride at her control of the ancient weapon. With a sigh, she sheathed the blade. 'This is the last item, Keiko,' she said, handing it to her lady-in-waiting. Keiko accepted the heirloom with deep reverence, serious as always. She carried out the naginata to be loaded with the rest of Michiru's trousseau.

Michiru watched the young woman carry away the weapon. *I still do not know much about Keiko.* The daughter of a local samurai, she had come to serve as her lady-in-waiting six months ago. *I do not think I have ever seen her laugh. Maybe I should get her drunk one night. That might loosen her tongue.* She was a slight girl, not quite as tall as Michiru but around the same age. She had a melancholy about her, which made her seem older. *I wonder why she is so sad all the time. All I know is that her family are poor samurai, little better off than peasants.* When Keiko first arrived, Michiru had hoped that they would become friends. However, the young woman had maintained her distance and her reserve.

She watched her maid, carrying Michiru's own naginata, scurry out behind Keiko. *At least Keiko is not as talkative as Namika.* Father had employed Namika two years ago to serve as her maid. Michiru knew more about her. She always had something to tell. *Hisa is constantly hushing her up. I am sure that girl would talk all the way to Nagase.* She had already told Michiru all about her family's orchard and bee-keeping dramas. She also mentioned her grandmother's strange preference for radishes and the gas it produced, and that she would be leaving behind two hopeful paramours.

Michiru returned to her room to wait. She knelt and tried to calm herself. Closing her eyes, she breathed in the scent of her home. The cedar wood beams, the straw of the tatami mats and the burnt oil in the lamps. In the background was the turmoil of floral fragrances from the courtyard garden outside. Hints of other smells wove through the air. Camphor wood from her closet, camellia oil she had spilled in the corner when she was ten. All these things took her back to moments throughout her life. *I wish I did not have to leave.*

So absorbed was she in her own thoughts she did not notice Kosei standing on the garden veranda watching. 'Sister,' he said quietly. 'It is time to go.'

She was brought back to the moment by the sound of her brother's voice. *I must go. Others are expecting me. And it is a long way to Nagase.* With a calm that belied her turmoil, she made a slight bow. 'I apologise for keeping everyone waiting.' She looked up to see a strange expression on Kosei's face. She could see him struggling with something as he stood outside her room.

After a moment, he gave a heavy sigh and asked, 'Are you ready?'

She hesitated. 'I think so.'

Kosei's hands gripped his fan behind his back, eyes fixed on some detail of the ceiling. 'We will miss you, you know.'

Michiru felt the heat of tears growing behind her eyes. She pressed her hands flat against her thighs, willing herself to maintain her composure. *Now was definitely not the time to start crying. Not just before stepping out into public.* 'Thank you, Brother. I will miss you too.'

'I'm sorry if you feel...rushed.' He twisted the fan in his hands absent-mindedly.

'I understand that I must do my part,' she said, trying to keep her voice under control.

'Yes,' he said, clearly wanting to say more. He stared at her a moment longer, struggling to keep his own thoughts off his face. 'Well. I will see you again shortly.'

He turned abruptly and strode along the veranda to the reception room. The sound of his footsteps receded, leaving her alone. *Last chance. Last chance to get away. Last chance for freedom.* She heard the priests begin singing. *Time to go.* She smoothed her already immaculate white kimono and willed herself to stand.

✳   ✳   ✳

Incense and expectation filled the air as Michiru accepted the blessing. *O kami. Please help me.* The final strains of the priest's intonation faded away. Everyone bowed. The rituals for her protection and well-being were complete. Michiru rose and turned to look out onto what would be her procession. She paused for a moment, taken aback by the sudden realisation that all this was for her. *Everyone is watching me.* She felt a prickling of apprehension along her hairline. She forced a look of demure serenity on to her face. The one she practised for an hour in front of the mirror last night.

In the dappled shade at the edge of the courtyard, a crowd waited in colourful confusion. The chatter of their conversation rose and fell like wash of the tide on a pebbly beach. A black lacquered palanquin stood in the middle of the column of porters, waiting for her. The gilded metal fixtures glinted in the sunlight. The gold of the clan's katsura leaf crest contrasted starkly against the gloss black of the lacquer. The team of bearers, all dressed in fresh new clothes, bowed to the ground nearby.

Two miko, women from the clan's shrine, flanked the norimono also dressed in stark white, their hair done in a simpler, but similar style to Michiru's. Another miko bearing a spear waited to lead the porters. Their singing now took up where the priests left off. They would divert the attention of any spirits that might attach themselves to Michiru as she left. Two bowing samurai waited, holding open the door and roof of the norimono for her. Four more teams of porters carried Michiru's belongings between them on poles. It was all packed into lacquered chests draped with the clan's crest. Behind them another five teams carried boxes containing gifts for her new family. On both sides black armoured foot soldiers waited. Some carried spears, others bore fluttering green Katsura banners.

Michiru frowned. *So I am travelling to my new home carried inside a lacquered box. It has windows and a door, yes, but it is still a box. What am I, a piece of porcelain?* She had never particularly enjoyed travelling by litter. It was not that she did not like being spoiled. But sitting in a cramped little box, feeling every bump and jolt always made her head ache and stomach churn. *I wish I could ride instead.*

Her father let her ride along with him sometimes. One hour of calligraphy for each hour of riding had been the price. *"There is a cost for everything,"* he had told her. Shuji had maintained that deal, so she still rode whenever she could. Michiru spotted four horses under a nearby tree, tails flicking and coats twitching. A pair of young pages held their reins, waiting for the samurai officers. She smiled to herself. *A nice horse on a sunny day. That would be much better. I will pester Shuji until he lets me get into the saddle.*

On one knee before her was the veteran samurai, Yoshioka Shuji. A solid man in his fifties, he wore his grey hair folded in a helmet-cushioning topknot. He wore a black coat over his dark lac-

DAUGHTER OF THE KATSURA

quered armour, a circled katsura leaf in white on the back. The helmet tucked under his arm bore his own crest, a right granted to him by Father. On the front of his helmet, three comma-shaped whorls swirled inside a gold circle; A symbol for Hachiman, the warrior God. Shuji was the clan's senior councillor and most valued retainer. Now he served Kosei as he had Father. He was also Michiru's teacher, the one who taught her to ride, how to fight with a naginata and to shoot a bow. He began instructing her at the age of ten, at her father's insistence. 'I will be accompanying you to Nagase, my lady,' Shuji informed her with a bow.

She returned his bow, as correct as she could manage. She knew he would be her escort commander, but the situation called for formality. *I am glad that Kosei is sending Shuji with me. At least I can feel safe on this trip.* In her best formal tone Michiru responded, 'Thank you, Yoshioka-san. I look forward to your company on this journey.'

Waiting behind him were two other samurai officers. Both wore the clan's green coats over their black armour. Although she knew them well, Shuji introduced them as etiquette required.

'Your other officers are Kikuchi Masahide-san,'

The dark-eyed samurai bowed in response to the introduction. 'My lady.' His armour enhanced his normally lean frame, and there was no mistaking the serious expression on his long face. It was rare that Masahide actually smiled, but she had spoken with him on many occasions. *I just wish his replies were more than a single word.* He had an intense gaze that generated a strange feeling in her. Over the last few months, she had toyed with the idea of making him her first. He was discreet enough to have not made it general knowledge, and she trusted him not to hurt her.

Shuji gestured to a broadly smiling samurai, 'and Otō Hirakazu-san.'

'My lady,' he answered with enthusiasm, snapping off an energetic bow. He was half a head shorter than his comrade but nowhere near as good-looking. He filled his armour in such a way that left no doubt of his strength. His broad cheeks seemed to fill his helmet and provoked a stifled smile from Michiru. She had seen him visit Namika more than once. Despite his lack of pure physical attractiveness, Hirakazu had no shortage of women interested in spending time with him. *Probably because he is so much fun. This could be an interesting journey.*

'It is our honour, hime-sama,' Shuji replied, offering her a hand over the sill. He smiled and whispered to her, 'We are all tremendously proud of you today, my lady.'

She blushed a little, uncomfortable with the praise yet revelling in it, as any girl would. She broadened her smile for the crowd. Her own excitement was growing, swept up in the mood exuded by those around her.

Shuji watched her absorbing the attention. *It all hinges on you, girl. Our strongest ally needs a son. Even if you were a giggling idiot you could give him that. But I wonder if Sojiro-sama realises just how much of a gem he is getting. Oh yes, I know you are a raw stone, uncut, not yet tested for hardness. But what I have seen gives me confidence in the future of our clans.*

Michiru secretly felt pleased that this was all for her. She looked around the crowd, the whole household lining the area, along with faces she recognised from town. *They are coming to see me off. Smiling. Happy for me.* She swallowed hard. *They are my family too. I see them every day. They are part of my home. Part of my heart. And now I have to leave them.* Michiru tried hard to hold back her emotions. *No crying! Tears would be most undignified.* Gathering her composure, she remembered her mother's words and prepared for the performance. *"In front of others we perform a role, as if in a play. If people expect a lady then give them the best lady you can be."*

The vibrant green leaves of the katsura trees in the courtyard fluttered in a slight breeze as Michiru stepped elegantly onto the veranda, moving with as much grace as she could. She tried to become the spectacle they all wanted. Descending the steps, she took one last look around the house and grounds of her home before they put her in the box. Michiru tried to memorise it all. *Will I ever see it again?* She looked up to the horizons of her world, the wooded slopes of the valley, with mountain peaks visible in all directions. *Maybe. But now I have to go somewhere strange and make a new home.* Her blood chilled, settling into a knot in her stomach. *This can no longer be my home.* Shuji stood by the norimono, offering her a hand and waiting. With a sigh, she accepted his hand, stepped in and sat on the cushion. With that, the roof and door closed, cutting her off from the outside world.

CHAPTER TWO

They left the town of Omegura and the procession settled into a mindless trudge. The spring day was warm, although the memory of winter's chill still lingered in the shade of the tree-lined ridges. The underbrush beside the road was a lush emerald green, hiding the mysteries of the forest in their search for sunlight. Every piece of flat land in the valley was cultivated, the road snaking along the foot of the ridgeline while the river went where it pleased.

Michiru had enjoyed being the centre of attention. People had lined the road in the first village, calling out their best wishes, but now there were no more crowds. The only people they saw were going about their daily business. Oh, they would wave as she passed, but then went right on doing whatever they were doing. A fleeting distraction from their everyday.

Michiru huffed inside her box. *At this pace, it will take forever to get to Nagase.* Determined not to put up with this for the whole journey, she began her campaign against Shuji. *If it all goes according to plan, I will be riding a horse before the end of the day.* She slid open the door. 'Namika! Tie this door back, I want it open.'

Namika hesitated. The peasant girl was unsure if someone would chide her for letting the lady do something out of the ordinary. 'But, my lady, the dust will get all over you.'

'The dust is getting in anyway.' Michiru whined in pouty tone she had been practicing. She tried to find the exact pitch to work on the old samurai. *He should be catching on to the problem shortly.* 'The air inside is full of dust!' she said, coughing loudly as she worked her fan.

Riding back to Michiru's litter, the Katsura captain leant down. 'Is there a problem, my lady?' asked Shuji from the back of his horse. *He makes an impressive figure mounted on his caparisoned steed, dressed in dark armour. He looks every bit the samurai captain.*

'As a matter of fact, there is,' she said. And so she began.

* * *

Hirakazu rode up from the rear of the column, stopping next to Masahide, who sat waiting patiently. 'Ah. I should have known.' He stood up in his stirrups and craned his neck, trying to see past Shuji to the head of the column. 'So she hasn't won yet?'

Masahide maintained his impassive expression. 'No.'

They sat on their horses and watched the opening exchange. The samurai captain had the natural advantage. He was a man, he was mounted on a horse, and he was fully armed and armoured. But his opponent had her own advantages. She was a young woman, she was seated leisurely in the norimono, and surrounded by her own guards. And she outranked him. It would be an interesting contest.

Hirakazu turned his helmeted head skywards, squinting his eyes against the sun. 'It shouldn't be long then.'

'What?'

'I expect Michiru-hime will be on horseback before midday,' he said, turning to his friend with a grin.

Masahide adjusted his helmet cord. 'You are mistaken.'

'She'll wear him down. You'll see,' he replied with confidence.

'Yoshioka-san is too patient. She will ride when he decides. Not a moment sooner.'

They watched the two opponents circle each other verbally, relying on excessive politeness to avoid outright refusal and causing offence. But every time Shuji tried to politely deny her "request", she succeeded in heading him off, keeping the contest alive.

Hirakazu laughed. 'I think you underestimate the Lady. I think you always have.' His horse skittered sideways to avoid a nip from Masahide's horse.

Masahide shot a glance at him, lips firming into a hard line. 'What?'

He settled his horse. *Surely Masahide knows that Michiru-hime has an eye on him. Does he truly not realise?* 'Nothing,' he said with seeming innocence. Changing the subject quickly to avoid a potentially embarrassing discussion, he continued, 'Well, if you are so sure, put up some silver.'

'You will lose.'

'It should be easy money for you then.'

Masahide regarded him sideways. 'By Midday?'

'Yes. Before midday. One silver.'

'Two.'

Hirakazu chuckled and turned his horse around. 'Oh, big spender. Very well, two it is.' He laughed as he rode back to his post at the tail of the column.

One corner of Masahide's mouth lifted into what could loosely be described as a smile. *I am two silver richer. It is not that I underestimate Michiru-hime. It is you who underestimate Shuji-sama.*

Despite a valiant attempt, Michiru could not outmanoeuvre her teacher for long. Shuji closed the matter by stating that nothing could be done until after the midday break, so, with respect, she would just have to wait. He rode off happy. Michiru pulled a face at his vanishing back. She looked around and saw Hirakazu ride off laughing. Even Masahide had a half smile. *Well, I hope they are laughing at Shuji rather than me.* She slammed the door and crossed her arms in frustration. The norimono lifted up and the rocking began again. She tried to think of arguments she could use to avoid getting back in the palanquin once they halted. In the end, she realised that most solutions were quite unlady-like. She would just end up embarrassing herself.

*　　*　　*

By the time they stopped, she vowed to herself that she would not make the whole journey to Nagase in the box. Yet she was so relieved to be sitting on a futon laid out for her under a persimmon tree that she forgot to complain until it was time to go. She stood and looked at the captain with an up-turned chin. 'Shuji-san, there is no reason why I should not ride. Prepare a horse for me, if you please.'

'Hime-sama,' he replied with a reluctant shake of his head. 'You are not dressed appropriately to ride. I am afraid that your fine clothes would get ruined.'

With a mischievous grin, she reached down and lifted the front of her kimono to show her legs all the way up to her thighs. Shuji gave her a wry smile, seeing the riding clothes underneath. With an appreciative chuckle at her efforts, he relented. 'Alright, go pick a horse and talk to him for a while.'

With an undignified whoop, Michiru unwrapped herself from the confining layers of her kimono. Underneath she wore a pair of loose men's pants and a long pale yellow jacket with a wide brown and green sash. She left Keiko and Namika to retrieve her garments. She dashed past a smiling Masahide, who was collecting something from a disappointed looking Hirakazu, and headed towards the horse line. Michiru's eyes found the little mare she had picked out earlier this morning. *This one will be more easy-going than the other horses.* After a whisper and a quick pat of the mare's nose, she leapt into the saddle.

"Talking to the horse" was a practice Shuji had taught her to use because she did not have her own mount. She would take the horse for a ride so that they could get to know each other. First at a walk, then at a trot, they went around in circles. While the horse was getting used to her weight and signals, Michiru learned the horse's rhythm and gait. Revelling in the fluid movements of her mount and sheer joy of riding, she lost track of time. It was with a sinking feeling she noticed everyone else making their way back to their places. *Ah well. It was good while it lasted.* With a sigh of regret, she returned to the road as the procession started moving on.

She rode up and back along the column twice before settling the mare into a walk next to Shuji. Her eyes sparkled with excitement and her skin had a healthy flush. They settled into a comfortable silence. Michiru took in the sunlight, raising her face to catch its rays. She took in the natural beauty of the river, feeling some inexplicable appreciation of the scene. Its banks were overgrown with lush green reeds and grasses. Deadwood gathered around scattered rocks and collected their own islands of debris. The ever-changing surface of the river itself mesmerised her with its sound and movement. She waved away a buzzing fly and the real world came back into focus. She feared that moments like these would be fewer and further between as her life changed from daughter to wife and eventually to mother. *Will I still be allowed to ride after the marriage?* 'Thank you, sensei,' she nodded, grateful for the chance at freedom, no matter how brief.

'That's quite alright, Michiru, but you did not need to ask my permission.'

'What?' she sat bolt upright. 'Then why did you object?'

He looked sideways at her. 'I was just advising you,' he explained. 'You made the decision not to ride.'

'Another lesson?' She slumped her shoulders and rolled her eyes. *He tricked me into learning, again.* 'And on such a beautiful day,' she shook her head in mock sadness. She did not mind that much. At least she had a chance to ride.

'Yes, and why not, Michiru?' He waved away a persistent fly, one of those ever-present companions around horses. 'Why did you not take one of the mounts and ride right from the start?'

It felt like a trick question. *No matter what I say, it will be wrong.* She answered tentatively, 'Because everyone was waiting for me, expecting me, to get into the norimono.'

'Yes. You did it because other people wanted you to.'

'But what else could I do? That was what I was supposed to do, was it not? You even helped me in.'

'Could anyone have stopped you walking to the horse and getting on?'

Frowning, she rubbed the mare's neck. 'Someone might have.' *I am sure someone, may be Kosei, would have...would have what?* She felt cheated, duped. It took some of the shine off the day.

'Yes they might, but the point is much of what we do is because of what other people expect and what they will think of us. That is what custom is. We honour customs and traditions so we can live together harmoniously, so that we know what to do. So we know what to expect. You chose not to ride, you decided to stay with tradition and to be carried. But you had made the decision to break with tradition once you were out of sight of home, did you not? By hiding riding clothes under your kimono.'

Michiru had not thought of it that way. The more she considered it, the more she saw how much other people's expectations drove her daily life. Even her choices in clothing style were to please or impress others. *It all seems a little bit crazy, when you think about it.* She did not want to say anything yet, until she had the chance to think about it some more. *I do not want to sound foolish. What? Wait a minute. Isn't that exactly what he means?* She shook her head.

'Another thing I wanted to talk to you about is councillors,' he continued. 'Many people will try to give you advice, tell you what you should and should not do. Some will try to use custom and tradition to make you feel powerless, to make it seem like you have no choice. In the end you have to make the decisions and you are responsible for them.' He looked across at her, shifting his seat in the saddle. 'Even doing nothing is a decision.'

She was unsure how to reply. She patted the mare's neck, breathing in that wonderful horse scent that made riding so special for her. *He has never spoken to me like this before. He is my teacher, yes, but what he is telling me now was not like anything he has taught me before. Has he given Kosei the same talk?*

Riding on in silence for a while, they passed through one of the valley's many farming villages. Neat houses lined the road, pressed up against the slopes of the surrounding ridgelines. All the level ground held crops. Everything else must fit wherever it could. The peasants and their children gawked at the rare sight of their procession. Michiru waved, pleased to get responses from them, feeling less alone in the landscape.

As they rode along at an easy pace, she contemplated the things Shuji said. *These are things Father might have said, if he were here. Considering how short our remaining time together is, it would be worthwhile to keep Shuji talking.* 'Sensei? How do I tell between good councillors and bad ones?' she asked.

'We will talk more about that later,' he promised, one arm resting on the hilt of his sword. *There would be plenty of time on this journey for lessons. No point scaring or confusing her with too much.* 'For now I just want you to remember that some people will try and manipulate you. They will try to intimidate you, play on your fears, and even romance you.'

She considered herself smart enough to tell when someone was trying to manipulate her, until she remembered her sensei did it all the time. *As did Father.* 'But I will be married. Why would anyone romance me?' *I think it is unlikely that a samurai would try to seduce the wife of the head of his clan.*

'To shame you, to blackmail you, to embarrass your husband. Oh there are many reasons, Michiru.' He decided to lighten the tone of the conversation. 'Then there are all the young men who will become infatuated with the new lady. Wife or not, they will barely be able to contain their poetry.'

They both laughed, but she dreaded the thought. *The last thing I need is having to fend off love-sick paramours.*

'Listen, Michiru. I only tell you these things so that you can be wary. You may not always be able to trust those around you. Keep the good ones as close as you can. But remember that even good councillors have their faults.'

'Thank you, sensei. I will think on what you have said.'

'Well, you will be able to do that back in the norimono.'

'What?'

'You can't ride all the way. This is a wedding procession. We have to preserve the dignity of the clan.'

'Ah, now you are testing me, right?'

'No.'

'Well, I have learned my lesson,' she stated. 'I will ride the rest of the way, Shuji-san.'

'No, you are not. You are going to be carried in the norimono.'

In her confusion at this sudden betrayal, she fell back on her childhood protest. 'That's not fair! We just discussed this and you said...anyway, you can't make me,' a defiant frown marring her delicate features.

'It won't be me kicking and screaming as I am tied, gagged and thrown into the box.'

'You would not dare!'

'For the honour of the clan, I certainly would.'

*   *   *

By the time they arrived at the border town of Kyozuka, the sun was disappearing behind the heavily timbered ridgeline. Shadow filled the floor of the valley and the day's warmth retreated up the eastern slope with the sunlight. Grey timbered houses crowded against each other in whatever space was available. The smell of dust and horses covered everything, but under it all was the ever-present human odour. As the procession approached the outskirts of the town, Michiru grew impatient to be out of the norimono. She watched the last of the day through the window of the palanquin, glad that the tedium of travel was almost over. The few people she saw outside as she passed, stopped and bowed.

The town of Kyozuka owed its existence to the river crossing. Father had said that there had always been a bridge here. The family had stayed here once before while Father supervised the rebuilding of the bridge. She and Kosei had spent most days exploring the river and the woods. *I remember how unfair it was that I got in trouble for staying out all day and Kosei did not.* As the houses crowded in on the road, she saw people packing up their wares for the day.

The inns on both sides of the river were assured of good business throughout most of the year. But it peaked during the rainy season, when everyone wants to find somewhere dry to stay with a hot meal. Shuji chose the inn on this side of the river, being the larger of the two, as more suitable for the dignity of the occasion.

The inn was a grand old structure, solid and well made. Sculptured trees peaked over the tile capped, whitewashed walls that surrounded it. From the outside, the considerable thatched roof was all that one saw of the building itself. Once through the gate, you were in a carefully designed world, a world of craftsmanship and skill. Even the living, growing things were organised, arranged and trained into ideal forms, placed just so. *I hope there is a decent sized bath here.*

Lanterns came out in the failing light as the party filed through the large wooden gate into the courtyard of the inn. The porters huffed as they set down their loads, shaking their arms and legs to loosen their tired muscles. Michiru heard the relief in their voices that mirrored her own. *How long must I wait?* She was so cramped and uncomfortable in the box that she wanted to explode out of it and run straight to the bath.

The inn was alive with the sounds of drinking and laughter, with most of the guests sounding like they were settling in for the night. Michiru's mouth watered at the thought of the dishes she could order. She loved the elaborate banquets put on at ryokans, with the multitude of dishes that were as much art as food could be. It reminded her of those journeys with her family, sitting up to eat with Father. *He would pass me choice pieces from his bowl and say, "Eat. You are too skinny."*

She watched the bustle around her through the tiny window. Shuji directed the crowd with a commanding tone born of experience. 'Hirakazu-san,' he called, 'get the luggage locked up in the inn's storehouse. Masahide-san, set the guards.' She hoped they would hurry up. 'You two, go get some water.' The smell of the food wafting through the palanquin's grill made her tongue slick with saliva.

The teishi, master of the house, greeted Shuji, his slight frame bowing constantly, as she watched through her grilled window. 'Welcome, welcome, noble guests.'

26

His great wide smile exposed the most awe-inspiring teeth she had ever seen. *They are so white, and perfect. But so much larger than they should be.* She could not take her eyes off them.

'This way, this way, if you please,' he beckoned, scurrying out of her sight to lead them in. The norimono lurched up once more to follow their bobbing host through large doors that led into the depths of the inn. He guided them through a passageway to the back of the building. He simpered as they made their way through, 'We have set aside the guest house for her ladyship. I hope this will be to her satisfaction.'

The dim interior of the passageway had a damp earthy fragrance. Sounds from outside echoed in the wood lined structure, before receding behind the shuffle of the bearer's footsteps. *This was considerate of them, providing a way to get to one's room without having to walk through the interior of the inn. Quite discreet too.* A strange rising feeling caught her by surprise as the norimono was lifted onto the wide wooden veranda at the back of the inn. At last, they finally put her down.

Shuji waved the scurrying maids back and opened the doors for her. 'My lady,' he bowed with a smile, offering her a hand. She unfolded herself as he helped her out of the norimono.

'Welcome to our humble ryokan, my lady,' bowed the innkeeper. A select delegation of staff was arrayed behind him with heads to the floor.

She stood, blinking, taking a moment for her legs to become capable of movement, glad to have Shuji's arm to hold. She smiled and nodded to everyone, looking around at the garden wonderland on display. The building itself was sparse of decoration and the materials quite plain. Yet everything looked well-made and in good repair. A deep array of sculpted shrubbery and artfully random trees filled the back garden. A few steps led down from the veranda to a flagstone path that meandered across the garden to a formal teahouse tucked away down the back. Another building was just visible behind the left side of the landscape. 'These are our humble gardens, which look much better first thing in the morning, I can assure you.' Michiru suppressed a smile at his gushing welcome.

'This would be a most serene space at the right time of day,' she said, as she tried to stop her eyes settling on his astounding teeth. He looked like he was hoping for something more flowery and effusive. Maybe a discussion on plant choices and the changes in colours at the different times of year. But she wanted a bath and something to eat. It had been a long day and her kimono was stifling. *The first time Mother made me wear the layered kimonos I complained. Mother said, "We all have our loads to bear. Be thankful that you only have to wear clothes. If you were a boy, you would be wearing armour. That would be more uncomfortable."* She shifted the weight on her shoulders. *But now I am wearing this riding outfit underneath as well.*

The little man's smile faded a little as he waited for her to continue. Looking disappointed when nothing further was forthcoming, he forged on. 'Our guest house is this way, if you please,' gesturing to a walkway off to the left. Willing strength into her legs, she tried to mask her caution by attempting to glide. Around the corner, the veranda turned into a wooden path. It led between mossy boulders and judiciously placed trees to a separate house, sheltered from the inn itself by the garden. 'We keep this for our important guests,' intimated the innkeeper, 'to allow them some privacy.'

Two maids knelt on the veranda, bowing. The screens stood open to reveal a reception room of elegant simplicity. Lantern stands radiated their glow from the corners of the room. *All I want now is for them all to leave so I can relax.* 'Thank you, for your welcome,' she said through her fatigue as she mounted the steps.

Still unsteady from the constant rocking motion of the cramped ride in the norimono, she stumbled on the second step. She let out a cry as she fell. The hem of her kimono tripped her and she came down hard on one knee. The palms of her hands hit the timber of the veranda with a slap, breaking her fall and only just avoiding breaking her nose. Everyone ran to her aid, fussing and clamouring, trying to help her up. Embarrassed, she cursed her weakness under her breath. *Can't I even get up three stairs without falling over?* The fussing staff gently ushered her into the main room of the guesthouse. They sat her down, brought tea, hot towels, cold towels, food and even sake.

'Are you alright, my lady?' a concerned Shuji asked.

'Yes, thank you, Shuji-san,' she replied. Taking long deep breaths to calm herself, she regained her equilibrium. *Silly to trip like that in front of everyone. I will have to be twice as careful in the future.*

'It was quite understandable, my lady. You have been cooped up in the palanquin all day.' He tried to soothe her bruised ego. 'It was my fault, my lady. Please forgive my lack of foresight. I should have waited until your legs were steadier before coming to the room.'

'No, Shuji-san,' she replied, knowing that he was just being polite. 'I am not a baby anymore. I should be able to walk on my own two feet.' Her equilibrium slipped a little. 'Especially now.' *What if I trip like that when I arrive in Nagase. I will have to slit my throat on the spot from the shame.*

He smiled at her. 'Don't be too hard on yourself, Michiru. Everyone needs a little help now and then.'

She looked up at him. 'Yes, sensei.' *With Shuji everything is a lesson. Well, I have had enough for one day.* 'Shuji-san, I would like to take my bath now, if you please.'

'Of course, my lady. I will see to it.' With a quick nod and a wave of his hand, everyone cleared from the room in a flurry of swishing fabric. 'Also, the captain of the Arikawa escort has arrived,' he added. 'I will bring him to you after your bath.' He gave her a nod and left. Namika closed the screen behind him, shutting out the world for a moment.

Michiru exhaled and slumped. In the back of her mind, her nanny told her to sit up straight. She responded without thinking. *Still one more thing to do. Meet the new captain. I hope that he is at least a tolerable sort of character.* Her imagination conjured up a stocky greying old samurai without a sense of humour who grew red in the face when he was angry. She sighed heavily. *We will be stuck with each other until we get to Nagase. Well, in reality, we will be stuck with each other for good if he is Sojiro's captain.* A grin spread slowly across her face. *I will be the new Mistress of the House. If he gives me a hard time, I could make his life very difficult.* She sighed. *Maybe I should not antagonise the man though.*

We wouldn't want him to have a stroke now, would we?

Michiru stood wearily, heading towards the main bedroom. It had been a long, tiring day and tomorrow would be the same, with the added strain of the welcome at the end of it. *I am not looking forward to tomorrow at all.* Keiko helped remove the layers of her clothing and replaced them with a lighter robe.

Thankfully, the guesthouse had the added luxury of its own bath at the end of the veranda. It was compact but serviceable, simple lanterns filling the room with a warm yellow glow. A pair of bath attendants waited by the steaming tub, grinning as they bowed to the honoured guest. She sat on the short wooden stool and let them do their work. One of the girls scrubbed away the dust and sweat of the journey, the other rinsed her off with warm water. Once they were finished, Michiru climbed into the sizeable wooden bathtub, letting out a quiet sigh as she settled into the steaming water. After travelling most of the day in a cramped box, Michiru relaxed in the glorious, soothing heat. The water worked its magic on her tired muscles. In a steamy haze, she admired the patterns in the dark grain of the rustic timber posts and beams. All too soon, Keiko motioned to the attendants, who helped her out of the bath and dried her off. *I would love to stay in for longer. But I suppose I should not annoy this new captain by making him wait.*

As they wrapped Michiru in a fresh, clean robe, Keiko spotted a folded slip of paper poking through between the door and the frame. 'My lady,' she said, plucking the note and offering it to her. 'Somebody stuck this in the door.'

Michiru took the piece of paper and looked at both sides, hoping for some clue as to who sent it. *Why anyone would be sending me messages, I don't know. Is it a love note?* Her mind whirled at the prospect of some romantic adventure. *That would be most inappropriate, considering I am on my way to get married. No. It is more likely to be from someone wanting an audience.*

She opened it warily, torn between curiosity and fear. Written in tiny women's letters, she had to tilt the paper towards the lamp to make out the meaning. Reading the note with a growing sense of disbelief, a chill ran up her arms. *"Lady. Men hiding in town. Dan-*

ger." There was no name. Her hair prickled at the nape of her neck. Keiko, worried by the expression on her face, asked, 'What does it say, my lady? Who is it from?'

Michiru felt her own questions rising inside her. *Who was the letter from? Who could these men be? What do they want? Why warn me?* A score of scenarios whirled through her head, none of which ended well. *Whatever it was going on, I am not so sure I even want to know about it.* Sensing the curious stares of the bath attendants, she tucked the note away and left the bathhouse as casually as she could.

Stopping in the doorway, she whispered to Keiko, 'Fetch Shuji-san, now.' Biting her lip she added, 'But act calm.' Michiru watched as she reined in her curiosity with a frown and left to find the captain. With Namika's help, Michiru dressed quickly as her mind raced through the possibilities. She ate a few mouthfuls of food, promising herself more later. After a few deep breaths to calm herself, she sat down in the reception room and waited for the samurai to arrive. Reading the note again, she tried to decide how to broach the subject with Shuji. *Should I trust this new samurai captain?* She placed the folded note inside the blades of her fan and clamped it shut. Bursts of merriment from the inn punctuated the gentle sounds of the night outside. The racket made its way, oddly muted, through the surrounding garden.

Keiko's voice outside the door interrupted her thoughts. 'Yoshioka-sama and the Arikawa captain are here to see you, my lady. '

Michiru stared at her fan. 'Ask them to join me, if you please.' She rearranged herself on the cushion. *I hope Shuji will catch on to my signal.*

Michiru made her left hand into a fist, placing it on her hip with the thumb extended. Her posture mimicked the swordsman holding the scabbard of his sword whilst using the thumb to push the guard up, sliding the blade clear, ready to be drawn. Her other hand, with the closed fan, she held up in front of her mouth. She held that pose until the screen opened. Shuji, now changed out of his armour, frowned as he read her pose and nodded.

31

Kneeling next to Shuji on the veranda was a samurai dressed in a crisp grey green kimono, his hair pulled back in a neat queue. The night-time shadows accentuated the hollows of his cheeks, making his jaw seem oversized. The two samurai bowed and entered the room, the Arikawa samurai moving with the fluid precision of a swordsman. *He carries himself like Kosei.* Keiko closed the screen behind them as the two men took their places.

'Michiru-hime, may I introduce Tamuro Yatsuhiro-san, Captain of your Arikawa clan escort.'

Yatsuhiro bowed. She noticed a crooked scar on the side of his neck, near the edge of his collar. *So is he a man of action or was that an accident?* As he rose she took in his features. The tanned skin of his face already had lines forming around his eyes. Those eyes were dark and intelligent. But the face was a mask of politeness, betraying nothing of the thoughts behind it. 'I bring greetings from Sojiro-sama, Michiru-hime.' His deep voice was quiet and comforting. Michiru felt a small leap in her chest that caught her by surprise. As he looked up his eyes locked on hers, 'He hopes that you are well and that you will enjoy the journey to your new home. My lord looks forward to seeing you and asked me to give you this.' From his sleeve, he took a folded sheet of paper, a white peony tied to it with a red ribbon.

Poetry and flowers. *It looks as if Sojiro-sama is trying to woo me.* She accepted the presentation, watching Yatsuhiro for any sense of his character. Michiru could not read anything untoward in his expression. His solid, even demeanour gave nothing away. Her mind buzzed with questions as she tried to calm herself. *Can I trust him? Could he be a conspirator? Why would he be involved in a plot against her?*

'Thank you, Tamuro-san,' she said, feeling a little flustered for some reason. She removed the flower and inhaled its gentle fragrance. The petals were cool and uncrushed. *It must be from the inn's garden. So, the flower was from Yatsuhiro.* 'Such a lovely gift,' she said modestly as she peered at him over the flower. He made an imperceptible bow in acknowledgement of her thanks. Turning her attention to the letter, she slid the ribbon off and opened the wrapping. In precisely brushed characters Sojiro had inscribed;

If breezes on Inaba's peak

Sigh through the old pine tree,

To whisper in my lonely ears

That thou dost pine for me,

Swiftly I'll fly to thee.

She admired the choice of the poem, written over five hundred years ago by the poet Yuki-hira. She smiled, folding the letter and putting it away to think about later. She looked back up at the Arikawa captain and felt herself pinned by his watching eyes. Words disappeared from her mind like dry leaves scattering before a sudden gust of wind. His head cocked slightly as he waited for her response. Again she found herself unable to construct a sentence that sounded mature. *What is wrong with me?* Her skin prickled as the silence became uncomfortable. Finally she stammered. 'I ... I look forward to meeting your ... your lord and I welcome your company on this journey.'

CHAPTER THREE

Through the gaps in a shuttered window nearby, sullen eyes watched the Katsura guards. They stood, bored, in the flickering lantern light outside the gate. The watcher scratched the stubble on his cheek. He had put a month into this job already and it could still all go wrong so easily. He frowned in concentration. He looked back down the street. *Come on old man. What is taking you so long?*

The watcher glanced over his shoulder to where five scruffy warriors leaned against the wall. Although dressed in stained and frayed clothing, they gripped well-kept weapons in their hands. Gathered from the surrounding areas, these ronin, once samurai who had been dismissed from service or whose lords had been killed, had been hired for their skills not their appearance. They had hidden in here for half the day, crowded into the small storeroom. One of them let go an audible gust of wind, provoking muffled laughter from the men either side of him. The watcher rolled his eyes and turned to the man next to him, a bulky savage-looking man. In the dim light, he could see the terrible scar that ran from the corner of his left eye to his mouth, giving him a permanent sneer. They exchanged a flat look, the scarred man shaking his head wearily.

Just as well the guards will be drugged. Otherwise I would not even contemplate what we are about to try. At least not without more men. Another gust of wind broke out behind him followed by more snickering. A stench was starting to fill the confined space, resulting in groans and hushed complaints from the other men. And more snickering. The watcher sighed and ran over the plan again in his mind, looking for faults and flaws.

His mind drifted towards the prize. The whole reason he was

about to risk his life. Gold. Enough gold to set himself up in a town-house, with servants, for a year or two. Even longer if he could find paying work. He could dress well, go out on the town and stay out all night. *Just as long as you do not gamble. Otherwise you will just end up back here. With all that gold I will never have to work with these barn rats again.* The stench wafted past him on its way out of the window. *How I hate working with common ronin.*

*   *   *

Michiru, now more composed and feeling the foreboding return, glanced across at Shuji. She held up her fan, flipping it to show him the slip of paper in its ribs. The old samurai frowned. She pushed the fan across the tatami towards him. He plucked the note from the fan and scanned it.

'I believe we can set aside formality for the moment,' said Shuji as Keiko poured them all tea. He handed the folded note to Keiko and signalled her to give it to Yatsuhiro.

Michiru watched him carefully for his reaction, but found herself staring. *Wake up girl! This is serious!* She saw the Arikawa samurai look back at Shuji from under his eyebrows. Shuji held his gaze. Yatsuhiro took a sip of his tea and read the note, his lips firming into a tight line. He looked back up at Shuji. 'I must alert my men.' He said quietly. 'We will set up a perimeter.'

Shuji picked up his long sword and rose to his feet, 'Yatsuhiro-san, join me in the other room, if you please?' The Arikawa captain bowed and followed him. Michiru also stood, with every intention of going with them into the other room. *There is no way they are going to discuss this without me.* Yatsuhiro looked over his shoulder, giving her an unreadable look. If he was surprised or disapproving, she could not tell. Not that she cared either way.

The three of them gathered closely in the inner room, the tension palpable. Michiru listened nervously as Shuji took the lead. He looked straight at Yatsuhiro. 'Before we go spreading alarms and giving away an edge, I need to find out as much as possible first. Are there any immediate threats that you know of?'

Yatsuhiro shook his head, unconsciously biting on his lip, betraying a crease in his seemingly calm demeanour. 'None.'

'Do you think they are bandits? Or ronin?'

'Bandits would not worry me, Shuji-san. We could handle them easily enough.' Yatsuhiro ran a hand over his head, smoothing his hair. 'Ronin would be more of a concern. Someone will have hired them, or else they have an ambitious leader. Whoever they are, I can order scouts out and send for reinforcements. I believe it would be best if we remained here until they arrive.'

Michiru frowned, 'But who is behind this?' She was desperately hoping Shuji would turn them around and head home. *I would be fine with that.*

Shuji massaged his forehead with his fingertips. 'There are three main possibilities. First, someone in the Arikawa Clan does not want this marriage to take place.'

'Unlikely,' stated Yatsuhiro. 'It surely would have come to light in the years since the betrothal.'

'It is still a possibility that someone was biding their time, hoping for some other circumstance to end the marriage,' he speculated, twisting his sword hilt to rest his arm on it. It had never been considered that anyone might object.

Yatsuhiro shook his head. 'I cannot see anyone in Nagase being involved, if that were the case.'

Michiru asked, 'The second, Shuji-san?'

He looked her intently. 'Someone among the Katsura intends to prevent the wedding from taking place.'

Michiru could not recall anyone being in the least bit worried about sending her off. *I thought they were all disgustingly pleased with the arrangement.* A gnawing unease grew in her mind. What Shuji was saying was starting to sink in and she knew she was not going to like it. 'And the third, Shuji-san?' she murmured, not sure if she wanted to hear his response.

'Satake clan,' he stated ominously. 'Arikawa and Katsura united lock the Satake in their valley. They want control of the pass, all the way down the north side of the valley. They are the logical choice, in my opinion, my lady.'

'Unfortunately, I think Shuji-san is right, my lady,' said Yatsuhiro. 'It would be a bold move, on their part, but it makes sense.'

*   *   *

The old sake peddler made his way up the street, the young woman behind him carrying a lantern to light the way. He wore a jovial smile as he chuckled quietly in between talking to himself. 'Yes, yes. A wonderful night. Auspicious times. Heh heh.' He moved with a strange bouncing gait, legs bent and feet pointed outwards. A cask rode on his back, the contents sloshing rhythmically with each step. His companion wore a light pack, stacked with cups and bamboo flasks. The lantern advertised his trade as it bobbed at the end of the bamboo pole in her hands. He continued to chuckle. 'Drink of the gods. Spirits from the spirits. Heh heh.'

The guards watched him approach, a distraction from the boredom of their duty. A pair of street vendors was hardly a threat to the Lady's security. One of the guards straightened up and pushed himself off the wall. 'Don't even think about it, Hiroji,' said one of his companions.

'The woman might be pretty,' he answered over his shoulder. 'She may even be willing to earn some quick coin.' The other men smiled, familiar with their comrade's weakness for women. Any women.

'I'm not going to cover for you while you disappear around the back.'

'The old man is selling sake,' he pointed out. 'I'll buy you a round.'

'Knowing your luck, that is just when Yoshioka-san will pop his head out of the gate to check on us.' The other guard folded his arms. 'I'm not getting in trouble for you again. Not after last time.'

Hiroji's shoulders slumped dejectedly as the odd pair reached them.

'Evening, evening, good sirs,' the old man bobbed as he took the lantern from the young woman. She removed her pack and took out a tray and some small cups.

'Sorry, ojin, but we can't sample your wares tonight. We're on duty,' Hiroji said as he peered closer at the woman, unable to resist assessing his chances.

'Oh ho, tonight is your lucky night, then sir. Tonight you must have a drink. Heh heh.' The woman deftly filled the cups from the spigot of the cask on his back.

'What?'

'Those Arikawa soldiers nearly emptied my cask. Heh heh.'

One of the other guards jumped into the conversation. 'You're not making sense, ojin. What are you talking about?'

'Didn't I say? Oh, so sorry. Heh heh.' He waved the woman forward with her tray. 'Already paid for by the captain. A toast to the Lady's good health and happiness. For the marriage or something. Heh heh. Go on, Yuki. Give them gentlemen their drinks. We still have to go inside so the rest of the men can toast as well. Eh heh heh.'

She smiled suggestively at each of them as she offered up the tray. 'Please. A toast to the Lady.'

Hiroji tried out what he considered his most irresistible look on the young woman as he took a cup. 'To the Lady, then.'

'To the Lady,' they replied as the guards downed the sake.

*　　*　　*

'When you talk about them stopping the wedding,' Michiru queried, 'what do you mean?'

Shuji and Yatsuhiro looked at each other for a moment. It was Shuji who spoke, 'They will either try to kidnap you or kill you.' Yatsuhiro watched her carefully as the heart of the matter was revealed to her. He was most interested to see what her reaction would be. *Will she faint?*

'I see,' said Michiru hollowly. Her world spun. *Why me? How did this turn into something that could cost me my life? I did not even want to be married.*

'There is also this to consider,' added Shuji as he turned and opened a hidden door in the base of Michiru's travelling wardrobe. From inside he drew out a flat box skilfully crafted from a deep red wood, fitted with brass corners and a small pair of handles. By the way he was handling it, it seemed quite heavy. He slid the box across the floor and opened the lid.

'Ohh,' sighed Michiru and Yatsuhiro together. Inside the red silk lined box were neatly stacked rows of flat oval gold coins. Rarely used or even seen by most people, they mesmerised Michiru with their magic. It made her feel like a real princess to have such a treasure, like something from a fairy story. *Is this for me?*

She took one of the ovals from the box. It was thinner than she first thought, with a slightly irregular shape. Three encircled heart-shaped leaves, the Katsura mon, was embossed on the top half of the flat metal and below that, other stamped marks giving the weight.

'This is your dowry, my lady,' said Shuji reverently. 'One thousand gold ryo. One thousand koshukin, minted by the Takeda using the purest gold from their mines in Kai. All I know is they were put aside for you on the day of your birth. It is a gift worthy of a princess.' He closed the box. 'If anyone has guessed the value of the dowry, or that we even have it with us, it would provide plenty of reason for someone to attack you.'

Her mind reeled as it dawned on her how much more likely it was that she was the target of these skulking marauders. Inside, she was horrified and felt a rising tide of panic threatening to overwhelm her. She looked at Shuji and felt some of her confidence return. He was the one person she knew she could rely on. *If anyone can deal with this enemy and keep me safe, it is Shuji. He will take command as he always does.* With a deep breath, she pushed the panic away.

*   *   *

The leader of the ronin squinted at the sentries through the bars of the storeroom window. He watched impatiently for any sign of the drugs taking effect. If they did not work as promised the whole plan was ruined. The four guards stood, backs to the inn's wall either side of the gate. The low murmur of their conversation carried across the street, slowly petering out as they lapsed into silence. First one then another started to slump, sliding slowly down the wall. A third guard turned to rebuke his fellow's drooping postures but his legs lost their strength and with a sound of dismay, he collapsed sideways. The fourth man's head tilted back as he toppled to the ground with a groan.

The ronin smiled in satisfaction, relieved to see that the drugs had been worth their price. Thrilled that the waiting was over, he clicked his fingers. 'Go.' They all slipped out of the storeroom and into the street. More men appeared silently from other hiding places and followed them toward the gate. The leader waved groups of ronin to move to their pre-arranged places. There was no turning back now.

He nodded to two of his men who returned the gesture and ran for the wall. With a hand from his friend, one of them scaled it and disappeared over the top. Two more raced over to put out the lanterns. The leader quietly drew his sword as they walked up to the gate and waited. He turned to his men and hissed, 'Remember. This is not a free-for-all. Understand? Stick to the plan or I will kill you myself.' He glared at them until they all nodded. The gate rattled and opened a crack.

*   *   *

The sound of the front shoji sliding and rapidly approaching footsteps had both men in front of Michiru with hands on swords in an instant. Namika appeared in the doorway to the bedroom, registered the scene in front of her and dropped to her knees with a gasp.

Bowing deeply, she said in a hushed and shaky voice 'My Lady!'

Michiru stepped past both captains. 'What is wrong, Namika?'

'Oh. My lady. I was in the kitchen. The guards. I tried to wake one,' she sobbed. 'He wouldn't answer.'

'What about the guards? What about my men?' asked Yatsuhiro with growing disbelief.

'I don't know, o-samurai-sama. I came straight here. I think they are all dead.'

'All of them? But that's impossible.'

'What will we do?' she hissed in terror. The girl was shaking, nearly hysterical.

Michiru tried to reassure her, despite her own trembling inside. 'Shhh, Namika. It's all right. We will be fine,'

She grabbed Michiru's sleeve, her eyes wide with fear. 'The staff are all hiding.'

Michiru shot a glance at the old samurai. 'Shuji-san?'

Yatsuhiro turned to Shuji. 'I have fifty men outside. I will slip out and attack them from behind.' The tension in his pose was visible. Michiru was entranced. An unfamiliar feeling stirred deep inside her. She saw a power within him, tensed like some dark tiger, ready to strike.

'With respect, I think it is too late for that. The Lady is the priority for both of us now. We must assume the worst and keep her safe.' He stood, tying back his sleeves with a cord. 'We don't have much time. Where are your men?'

'At the end of the street,' he replied, the realisation that he may now be a captain without a command finally sinking in. 'All my men,' he said, turning a shocked face to the older samurai. Michiru could see the urgency drain from him as his shoulders slumped, his eyes squeezed shut. Her heart went out to him as she watched him struggle to get a hold of himself.

'Yatsuhiro-san,' Shuji said firmly. 'We know nothing for certain yet. But first we must look to the Lady's safety. Agreed?'

He took a deep breath. *Of course. We know nothing yet. First, protect the Lady.* 'Yes, Shuji-san. You are correct.'

'Wait here.' Shuji stepped out onto the veranda, sheathed long sword in his left hand. His eyes scanned rapidly. Shigemori, the solid young samurai who arrived with Yatsuhiro, stood poised outside the door with the four Katsura guards. With hands on sword hilts, they all faced the main building of the inn. The nervous tension was palpable. 'Anything, Hirakazu?'

'Nothing, taisho,' he answered.

'Masahide. Go get the others from around the back,' Shuji ordered calmly.

'Yes, sir,' he replied with a quick nod before running around the corner of the guest house.

A crash of crockery came from inside the inn, followed by thuds and muffled voices. Shuji fought the instinct to rush to the source of the disturbance and confront the danger. He saw his men flinch as well. 'Steady,' he growled quietly. 'We are guarding the Lady, not looking for a fight.' Masahide returned to Shuji's side with four more Katsura samurai. 'You men stay here. Hirakazu. Go and find out what is going on. Quietly. Report to me when you are done.' As he went back inside he said to the guards, 'Stay alert.' He closed the door and crossed the reception room with hurried strides. 'We have to run,' he said, his lined face mask-like in the lantern light.

'Don't we have enough guards to hold them off?' Michiru asked nervously.

'These men have a plan, my lady. They have taken our guards into account and found a way to neutralise them. We must assume that the greatest danger is to stay put and wait for them in the hope that we can defeat them. Fleeing is our best option, I believe. The men will cover our escape and buy us some time.'

'Can we afford to leave a rear-guard?' asked Yatsuhiro with an apprehensive glance at the women. 'Won't that leave the Lady too vulnerable?'

'We have no choice. There is little time. We will stand a better chance in a small group.'

Michiru eyes opened wide as she looked at him in shock. 'But they will die.'

'Yes,' he replied gravely. 'But we will have a better chance thanks to them.' He knew better than anyone just what he was asking these men to do. Shuji stared at the wooden box containing the gold, a frown creasing his forehead. He paused and looked around. Michiru could see his mind working furiously. He turned suddenly and searched through her travelling wardrobe and hurriedly pulled out Michiru's silk scarves and underskirts. He laid four of them out on the floor and put a quarter of the coins on each. She watched fascinated as he created improvised money belts by rolling the coins in layers of the expensive silk, tying them off with knots at each end.

Hirakazu entered silently and went straight to Shuji's side. They shared a quick whispered conversation before Hirakazu left again, giving Yatsuhiro and Michiru a brief nod from the doorway.

There was a rattle from the closet. Michiru leapt back, fumbling for the small dagger hidden in her kimono. *They are here already!* Shuji's short sword flashed into his hand as he moved between her and the closet. Yatsuhiro stood at her back and covered the doorway. There was another rattle ending with the clunk of wood amongst a string of muttered curses. Using the tip of his blade, Shuji slid the closet door open, revealing the embarrassed smile of a cheeky looking peasant, his head sticking out of a concealed trapdoor in the floor.

'Hello, o-samurai-sama,' he said brightly to Shuji, adding a respectful nod before talking past him to Yatsuhiro. 'We've got trouble, taisho.'

At the sound of that voice, Yatsuhiro turned around, 'Ōmono?' he hissed. 'What are you doing here?'

'Is he one of yours?' Michiru asked, still focussed on the intruder, dagger poised.

'I'm afraid so.'

'Thank you, taisho,' the little man said in a hurt tone. 'We should go. How many are you bringing?'

'Five plus me. Aren't you supposed to be on leave?'

'We really should go. I was coming here anyway. The niece of my old village's headman works here. We should leave now, taisho,' the man said, now signalling frantically with one hand.

Yatsuhiro knelt next to the trapdoor, 'There is a good chance that they know about this tunnel.'

'There is a door here in the side of the tunnel. It opens under the house,' the ashigaru pointed out. 'That's how I got in.'

'How did you find out about that?'

'I told you, taisho, the niece of my old village's headman works here,' he stated matter of factly. 'She's waiting to take us to the edge of town. We go out under the house to the inn's back wall, follow the wall behind the shrubs and out the back gate.'

Shuji looked at Yatsuhiro and nodded. After a brief moment he said, 'My lady. You and Namika swap clothes, if you please. Underclothes as well.' The women stared at him uncomprehendingly. 'Quickly please,' he added.

Michiru hastily removed her outer kimono. *I hope he knows what he is doing. I have to trust him.* It was a beautiful piece of work. Katsura leaves of varying maroon and orange hues had been incorporated into the design with rich greens and contrasting yellow tones, highlighted with delicate golden thread. While the men retrieved travelling sandals from the alcove, she and Namika hurriedly stripped down and exchanged underclothes. When Michiru saw the difference in quality of make and material, the need for this level of deception became clear. Keiko helped the young maid dress in the fine clothes, while Michiru put on Namika's much simpler garments. Michiru shivered slightly, feeling a little exposed in the lighter material.

While they changed, he outlined the plan. 'There is always a tunnel in these remote guesthouses.' After receiving blank stares from the women, he explained, 'For lovers to come and go without being seen.' He said to Namika, 'I want you, dressed in the Lady's clothes, to hide in the tunnel. If they find you, pretend to be Michiru-sama for as long as possible. If you are still here in the morning, get changed and return home. Let Lord Kosei know what has happened. Yatsuhiro-san and I will try to get the Lady Michiru to Nagase.'

Namika tried to keep the fear off her face. Shuji had tried to reassure her with his matter-of-fact tone but Namika's chin quivered all the same. *I am no hero, I am just a maid.* She nervously adjusted the unfamiliar garments. *I am lucky to have had Michiru as a mistress. Or else I would still be back working in the orchards with Mother. More likely I would have gone to work in some rich household or inn, where the master would try to seduce me and the jealous mistress would beat me. Or I would be thrown out if I displeased either of them, or I would be pregnant.* She looked at Michiru standing there in her poor clothes. *I owe Michiru-hime a great deal. In truth I am more worried about her. It was her they are after, not me. At least I will be hiding somewhere safe.* Gathering her resolve, she bowed, 'Hai'.

'Thank you, Namika. Thank you. Everything will be alright,' Michiru said. 'You will see. Please tell my brother, when you see him, that I am alright and Shuji-san is looking after me. Everything will be fine.' Michiru grabbed the hem of her borrowed kimono and tucked it into the sash, leaving her legs free. She re-tied her hair at the back of her head and slid her dagger into her sash. The rosewood box, now empty of its treasure, caught her eye. *Father had this made for me. I cannot just abandon it.* Impulsively, she grabbed one of her sleeping robes from the wardrobe and wrapped the box in it.

Shuji watched her with a strange expression as he and Yatsuhiro tied money belts underneath their kimonos. With a shrug he tightened his sash and turned to survey Namika's appearance. *She might fool them if they are in a rush, but a careful examination will spoil it.* 'You might want to put some make-up on,' he suggested to her. Turning to Yatsuhiro he said, 'We need two more men. We should take young Shigemori with us. He is the one you brought with you, is he not?'

'Yes, Shuji-san. Thank you. I will bring him in.'

'Ask Hirakazu to come in as well, if you please.'

*　　*　　*

Seven shadows detached themselves from the tangled silhouette of the shrubbery, slipping silently towards the back corner of the garden. The moon illuminated the area in a ghostly, bluish glow, as the figures followed the narrow path along the wall. A chaotic chorus of frogs emanated from the river nearby, creating a drone punctuated by solo performers, repeating their routines. The combination of fresh scents from the trees and the garden's sweet fragrance would normally have delighted Michiru. Now, she was so tense that she barely noticed the breath-taking beauty of the night.

Following the dark shapes of the samurai toward the gate, she glanced behind instinctively, looking for any sign of pursuit. Keiko followed close behind her, a knotted bundle in her arms and a light-framed carry case strapped to her back, holding the only possessions the two women now had. Each of the samurai wore an improvised money belt under their clothes, carrying a quarter of the gold coins each. Michiru had the empty rosewood box wrapped in a robe and slung over her back.

Behind them shouts broke out from the house, followed by the screams and crash of combat. Without an order they all quickened their pace toward the gate. A silent pause brought Michiru's heart into her mouth. In that moment the faces of the men left behind to cover her escape flashed through her mind. *I grew up among those men in there.* Her eyes welled with tears of shame at leaving them to die. She fought back a sob. *Enough weakness! They are samurai.* The sounds of fighting continued as they approached the back gate.

'Mono-chan?' queried a hushed voice from the darkness.

'Hai. It's alright, Ki-chan,' replied Ōmono as he groped carefully into the shadows of the corner. He drew out a small woman, dressed like one of the inn's maids. Despite the sparse moonlight, Michiru could still see the fear on her round face. The little man turned to the samurai, 'Kiku will show us to the edge of town.'

'Alright,' said Shuji, 'I hope everyone's sandals are tight.'

Yatsuhiro opened the gate a fraction, scanning the street in both directions. Seeing no-one outside, he gave a silent signal and they filed out of the gate. Her eyes wide and pulse thumping in her ears, Michiru pressed herself against the wall, Keiko huddled behind her. Shuji moved silently up against the dark timbered building on the other side, looking down the cross street for any sign of danger. The street was bordered by the high plastered walls of the inn on one side and the dark timbers of poorer houses on the other. A small roofed shrine stood at the other end of the street, its white paper charms fluttering gently. *This is the critical moment. If we make it to the edge of town without being spotted, it will give us a crucial head start on any pursuers.*

He looked inquiringly at Kiku, who pointed to the street on the right. The samurai waved her forward, indicating that she should lead. Michiru saw her hesitate, before gathering the courage to move away from the wall. To the maid's credit, rather than sneaking around like a burglar, which would have aroused suspicion if anyone saw her, she walked out into the street like she was heading home. Once Kiku was around the corner, the remainder of the party followed, hugging the walls of the buildings as they trailed behind her. Yatsuhiro and Shigemori led the group, while Ōmono, a short spear gripped loosely in hand, guarded Michiru and Keiko in the middle. Shuji and Hirakazu brought up the rear, checking behind them as they went.

The sound of rushing feet brought Michiru's heart into her mouth. She spun around, the hair on the back of her neck on end. She saw five men in dark hoods and facemasks rushing from their hiding places around the shrine, running towards them with swords drawn. Michiru nervously gripped her dagger. She had been taught how to use it, but seeing these men charging at them with such purpose, she felt of little use against a swordsman. She recalled her mother's words when she had given her the blade and showed her where to cut. *"A lady can never let herself be captured. This blade is to protect yourself and your honour, or if necessary, take your own life." Is this where it will happen? I have barely begun my life and now I must end it?*

Shuji looked over his shoulder and hissed 'Run!' as he and Hirakazu drew their long swords.

Still moving down the street, Kiku looked back, 'This way! This way!' she said as loudly as she dared, frantically waving for the others to follow her towards the next intersection.

Shuji and Hirakazu turned back on their pursuers, cutting down the first two enemies in a split second flash of blades before swiftly turning back to follow. Kiku made for the street on the left, but before she could disappear around the corner she was gripped by a pair of strong arms. A masked man stepped out from around the corner, holding the frightened maid.

Four more men, faces covered and swords drawn, appeared out of the shadows of the cross street to bar their escape. Kiku, gasping with effort, furiously struggled to break free from the tall man holding her. Yatsuhiro dashed forward and sliced diagonally upwards, cutting through the tall man's arm and opening his torso. Kiku tumbled to the ground with a cry as the mortally wounded man toppled backwards, spraying blood on his way down.

Ōmono, spear in hand, ushered Michiru and Keiko up against the timber front of a building, constantly checking in both directions. Hirakazu and Shuji paced carefully backwards up the street, facing the three men following behind them. The tense scene seemed to freeze momentarily under the ethereal moonlight.

Yatsuhiro broke the tension. *Time is not on our side.* He leapt at the men blocking the intersection. Feinting and parrying with practiced skill, Yatsuhiro pushed forward, keeping the two men facing him off guard. But this was Shigemori's first real combat. His opponents came at him from two sides. He coiled and lunged at the man on his left, forcing him to dodge out of the way. He reversed direction to parry the other attacker's blow but the tip of the parried blade sliced through the young samurai's shoulder. Shigemori hissed with pain.

The two Katsura clan samurai were locked in a frantic combat with the three masked men pressing in from behind. Ōmono rushed to assist the struggling Shigemori, as Yatsuhiro, also seeing the young samurai in trouble, changed the direction of his attack. He pulled back momentarily, making another upward sweeping cut. The masked man brought his sword down to block the blow, but as soon as the blades touched Yatsuhiro reversed the stroke with blinding speed, his sword sweeping around to come hissing down from above, cutting through the man's clavicle and opening his heart and lung in a shower of blood. Yatsuhiro ripped the sword from the corpse and stepped back before his other opponent could react.

Shigemori tried to press his attack but his wound robbed his blows of strength and the masked man held him off easily. His second opponent, seeing an opportunity, came in behind him with a slashing blow that cut through the young samurai's neck, unleashing a torrent of blood. Ōmono, rushing to the aid of the doomed Shigemori, plunged his spear into his killer's side, but too late. Michiru gasped in shock, appalled at the furious violence and death. She had never seen the damage that steel does to flesh and the brutality of it sickened her.

Ōmono freed his spear from the masked man's corpse as the other attacker slashed at him. But as he attempted a backward leap out of the way of the blow, Ōmono tripped and fell backwards, slamming down hard, his head bouncing off the earth with a sickening sound. His spear skidded across the ground to stop in front of Michiru, who, not knowing what else to do and in desperate fear for her life, picked up the unfamiliar weapon.

She knew she was out-classed. She had never used a spear, only a naginata. *It is a basic weapon. Stab your enemy. They are trying to capture me. I must win or make them kill me.* An inexplicable fury flashed in her mind from somewhere deep down. She could hear her samurai fighting to protect her, at least one had died already. His precious lifeblood was soaking into the dirt of this backstreet. *I will not stand helplessly to be captured.*

Michiru stepped further out into the street to give herself more room, levelling the spear at her rapidly approaching enemy. Light headed and shaking, she tried to summon whatever gods or spirits might help her. Shuji cried out from behind her, 'No!', but she was too focussed on the man in front of her to hear. Hirakazu redoubled his attacks against the last remaining attacker facing him to allow Shuji to break free from the combat. Yatsuhiro cut down his last opponent and turned at Shuji's cry. Both of them were too far away to help, but neither could resist the urge to try.

Keiko dove towards the stunned Ōmono, pulling free his short sword from its scabbard. Michiru's first thrust was knocked aside contemptuously by the masked man. He parried the second thrust, lunged in past her spear point and punched Michiru in the face. She fell, stunned by the blow, eyes watering. Standing over her triumphantly, he rested the tip of his sword on her throat, 'Stop right there or she dies.'

With a gasp of surprise, Michiru's attacker stiffened in pain, letting out a gurgling growl of frustration as Keiko plunged Ōmono's short sword through his back and into his heart. His sword fell from his lifeless hand as he dropped to his knees and toppled onto the dazed Michiru. Shuji and Yatsuhiro skidded to her side, pulling the dead man off her. Keiko stood immobilised with shock, mouth hanging open, visibly trembling.

Hirakazu finished off the last attacker and hurried to Keiko's side, taking her arm and leading her to the corner. Kiku, who had stayed on the ground during the fight, rushed to Ōmono. Blinking rapidly and shaking his head, the little ashigaru sat up. 'Hello, Kiku-chan. Did I ever tell you how beautiful you are?' he slurred, his eyes unfocussed.

'Come on,' commanded Shuji, as he and Keiko pulled the still dazed Michiru to her feet. 'Let's get out of here before more of them turn up.' Kiku helped Ōmono up and handed him his spear. Yatsuhiro knelt next to the body of Shigemori.

'Farewell, my young friend,' he whispered tenderly. He cut the improvised money belt from the body, gathered up the young man's two swords and hurried to join the others.

Winding through the cheap houses on the outskirts, they made it to the edge of town. They all stood panting, taking cover in the shadows of the last house before the open fields. Yatsuhiro used a scrap of cloth to stem the flow of blood from a cut on his jaw that spoke of a close call. Ōmono shook his head and blinked repeatedly, trying to clear his head. Michiru was still unsteady on her feet, Keiko beside her, shaking and breathing rapidly. Shuji approached Kiku, the young maid panting nervously. 'Thank you for all that you have done for us,' he said.

Yatsuhiro added, 'It may not be safe for you here anymore.' Taking his purse out of his sleeve he handed it to her. 'Get your things and go to the temple outside of town. Ask to see Goryo. Tell him "Tamuro Yatsuhiro" sent you and show him the purse. He will recognise it. Ask him to pass along "The Lady escaped capture" to both families. He will look after you until things are safe again.'

'Thank you, O-samurai-sama' she replied, bowing shakily. She accepted the silken pouch with a deeper bow. She turned and hurried back down the street. About half way to the corner, she stopped and opened the door of her tenement. She looked back, bowed again and disappeared inside, closing the door behind her.

Chapter Four

Utaemon Katsuo, Lord Kiyomori's senior councillor, hurried down the corridor to the audience chamber. The gloom of the dark timbered corridor deepened the samurai's foreboding. *I hate taking Kiyomori bad news.* He straightened his hastily donned surcoat. *Especially when it is a result of his own bad choices. And this is bad news.*

Sweat trickled down his spine. He knew they should have used experts. He had suggested hiring a team from Iga, but Kiyomori did not want to spend that much. "A simple job," he had said, "Ronin should be sufficient." *Well, maybe not.*

Passing between the four grim guards in the ante room, he entered the presence of his lord. Satake Kiyomori, Lord of Aoki stood looking out through the barred window, attention fixed on the courtyard below. The midmorning sun etched the outline of a middle aged man too fond of his food and drink. Especially his drink. Despite the great care Kiyomori took with his wardrobe, he looked haggard in the sunlight. *The drugs are taking a toll on him. I warned him they would.* Katsuo knelt just inside the room, reluctant to approach within easy striking distance of his lord. He held a deep bow, waiting, delaying the inevitable even if only for a moment.

Kiyomori turned from the window, 'Ah, Katsuo. Tell me about our guest. Is she comfortable?' His full-lipped mouth twisted in a smile.

Katsuo sat up. 'Yes, lord,' he said, clamping his mouth on anything further.

'Yes what?'

'Our guest is comfortable.'

'And?'

'I'm sorry, my lord. What do you mean?'

Kiyomori looked at the old councillor with one eye and scolded him, 'I swear I want to stab you sometimes. I know you well enough now to tell when you don't want to tell me something. Now, what is going on?'

Taking a deep breath Katsuo said, 'It's not her, my lord. Not Katsura's sister.'

Kiyomori lowered his head, rubbing his temples with his fingertips. 'Oh, by all the gods,' he moaned. He sat down on his cushion, gritting his teeth in frustration. *Why am I surrounded by idiots?* Blood thudded behind his eyes. He knew if he did not get control of himself he was going to kill someone else for no good reason. *Like the last time.* He breathed deeply until the fire in his mind subsided. *It is wasteful. It will not fix the problem.* He rested his head on his upraised fingers. 'We have a fine, well-dressed young lady, brought here by the ronin, who are telling me this is the one they were sent to get. Yes?'

'Yes, my lord. She may look like the Lady Katsura, but it is not her.'

'What do you mean it's not her? Have you met her before?'

'No, my lord, but this is no samurai lady. I suspect she is a maid or servant.'

Kiyomori's head rose. He glowered at him from under his sparse eyebrows. 'And precisely what makes you think that?'

After a nervous gulp Katsuo explained, 'A number of minor inconsistencies, my lord. Hair, skin, especially around the eyes, nails, feet. The way she sits.'

'Did you question her?'

'I tried, my lord. For a long time she said nothing. But now she just keeps rambling on and on.'

'We could make her tell us the truth,' Kiyomori growled.

The councillor winced. Torturing young women for information was not beyond Kiyomori. With great delicacy he said, 'She is a decoy, my lord.'

'A decoy? How in the nine hells could they know about the kidnapping? How did they find out? You don't just have a spare decoy on hand.'

'I don't think they knew, my lord.' he said. 'Yoshioka Shuji was commanding the escort. This is something he would do.' Katsuo frowned. *Once again, Yoshioka Shuji has managed to interfere with my plans.* 'He has dressed up a maid to throw us off the scent.' Scenarios started running through Katsuo's mind and he went quiet, Kiyomori momentarily forgotten.

'Then how did they escape?' he shouted. 'I thought there was a plan. Did I not pay for a plan?'

Katsuo snapped back to the present, 'I do not know what happened, my lord. It seems that Yoshioka set the decoy then managed to get through our men and escape.'

'Our men? I thought you said they were ronin?'

'Yes, my lord. That's what I meant. Sorry, my lord.'

Kiyomori hunched over with suppressed tension. 'Well I hope they realise that they'll get nothing if they don't catch them,' he muttered darkly.

'I am sure that they are pursuing them and are hot on their trail, as we speak, my lord.'

Kiyomori glared at the sweating councillor. 'What else?'

'I'm sorry, my lord. Could you repeat the question, please?'

'What about the gold? Did they bring the gold with the girl? Did they find the koshukin?'

'No, my lord.'

'No, of course not,' he fumed. He stood up and went to the window, gripping the grill with both hands. 'No prisoner, no gold, no idea what happened.' He turned around, his self-control strained. 'Well, somebody better find them, don't you think!' he snarled.

'That may prove difficult, my lord. Yoshioka is smart.'

'I don't care!' he roared. 'Don't you understand? I need that hostage by the time Harashiro castle falls. Holding that castle is the key to hobbling the Arikawa. With her locked up in that castle, they would not dare try and take it back. If Arikawa takes any action that leads to her death, he offends the Katsura and risks them turning against him.'

'Yes my lord. The ronin will catch them,' he assured him, trying to project confidence. 'I don't think I can guarantee what condition she will be in when they return her.'

'As long as she's alive, I don't care. If I have her, I'll have something to negotiate with. If I had those koshukin I would have something to negotiate with.' He advanced on Katsuo, hands spread. 'Do you know how many guns I could buy with a thousand ryo? Do you realise what I could do with a thousand ryo right now? My gold mine is nearly mined out!' His hands clenched into fists as he bellowed at the councillor, 'What have I got? Nothing!'

Katsuo's head went all the way to the floor in mortal fear. 'I am sorry, my lord. Please forgive me.'

'You'd better sort this out, Katsuo,' he said in a menacing tone, battling to get his rage under control. 'Otherwise you will have nothing. I'll take your two swords, give them to your sandal bearer and you can sleep in the stable!' He fumed. *How dare they fail? How was he going to carry out his plan now? He could not afford a protracted fight.* He turned on Katsuo and fixed him with a glare. 'Get the girl and the gold and I will think about forgiving you. Now get out!'

*   *   *

The day had dawned grey and overcast. Yatsuhiro laboured up

the densely wooded slope. He picked his way through the rocks and boulders wherever the trees allowed it. The smell of pine and decaying vegetation was thick in the air. The buzz of insects created a constant background noise, interrupted on occasion by an episode of bird drama.

He stopped, panting, to look back at the others. They all sweated heavily, dust thick on the damp patches of their clothing. Ōmono had given Michiru his spear to use as a staff to pull herself up the hill. The ashigaru had convinced Keiko to give up her load, leaving the little man carrying almost his own weight on his back. Keiko was scrabbling to grasp at whatever handholds she could find to pull herself upwards. She seemed on the edge of panic.

The two Arikawa clan samurai, Shuji and Hirakazu, followed. They turned around at random intervals to scan the trail behind them for signs of pursuit. The group had pushed on roughly north, heading up the slope away from the town all morning. Their vision was limited, but at least the trees hid them from unfriendly eyes.

Yatsuhiro pointed the struggling Michiru diagonally up the slope. 'Take the slope at an angle, my lady,' he urged. 'We should stop behind that rock outcrop for a while.' Not having any breath to spare, she just nodded and pushed herself on in the indicated direction.

He watched her labouring up the slope, a little surprised that she was still going. *I thought that she would have collapsed weeping, sobbing and complaining of the impossibility of going on.* That would have ended with them all taking their own lives. He nodded to himself. *So far, she seems to be a worthy bride for the Arikawa.* He frowned as he took a sip from a water flask. *Her safety has already cost the lives of a number of good men. If I can get her home, it would not only bring honour to my family, but also the bolster the Clan's morale and reputation.*

Shuji came up and stood beside him. He scanned their back trail as he caught his breath. 'They don't know exactly where we are, thank the gods, but they know we are here,' he mumbled.

'How many, do you think?'

The older samurai scratched his face with his sword hilt. 'Twenty, maybe thirty behind us.' He squinted at the woods around them, visualising the lay of the land. 'There's probably ten or so over to the west and the same to the east. They are expecting us to double back west, or head east.'

'They are the only ways we can go. We have to stay on this side of the mountain.'

Shuji looked to the east, squinting as he rubbed his chin with his hand. He turned to follow the others. 'Come on,' he said with a pat on Yatsuhiro's shoulder. 'Let's get everyone reorganised.'

After a last look behind, he followed the older man's lead.

*　　*　　*

'So what are our choices, then Shuji-san?' Michiru asked, once they had flopped down in the shade of the rocky outcrop.

'Cutting our way through their line is not practical,' he declared, as he inspected and retied Michiru's sandals. 'If we head west towards home, we will have very little time to escape. There is a good chance that they will cut us off. Even if they don't, they will still be on our heels all the way.'

'And to the east?'

The old samurai paused, seemingly concentrating on her sandals. 'The same, my lady.'

Michiru stared out over the valley. A verdant sea of trees rolled up the foothills to wash the slopes of the mountains and ridges. Cloudbanks that had hovered around all morning were thinning and breaking up. Patches of blue peaked through here and there, letting the golden rays of the Goddess touch the earth.

The shriek of a falcon echoed nearby, drawing her attention to an unfolding drama. A stooping peregrine had missed its prey and was frantically fighting momentum to change direction. The falcon set after the bird, spiralling in hot pursuit, its wings pumping. She watched as the escaping bird zigzagged and side slipped, diving into the cover of the trees. It left the overshooting falcon to screech in frustration. Michiru burst into a smile and clapped her hands in excitement at the bird's escape, feeling hope for the first time since last night. Offering up a silent prayer of thanks to the Goddess for the sign, she decided. 'We go north.'

'That is Satake territory.' Shuji replied. 'I don't know what outposts or patrols they have along this part of the border, but it will be guarded. The deeper we go into their lands the harder it will be to stay hidden.' *Once we cross that ridge there is no turning back.*

'So they won't expect it, will they?' she said with a thin smile.

He did not want to dwell on all the things that could go wrong. He knew that he might be coming across as quite negative to her. Everything he had said so far, in fact. He looked at her sceptically. *Yes, it is important for me to warn her but I suppose I should be supporting her as well. Especially when she is handling this so well.* Shuji stood, tightening his own sash and adjusting his swords. *She has a good point. They will not expect them to go this way.*

'Do you disagree?'

'No, my lady,' he sighed, 'it seems to be our best choice.' He offered her his hand. *Now it is definitely a race. If we can shake our pursuers, we will stand a much better chance of making it to Nagase.* He looked up at the remaining slope. *I hope these women can handle the pace. How far could we carry them on our backs if we had to? Would that be any faster?* The soreness in his legs reminded him of his age. *Maybe on the other side.*

Taking Shuji's hand, Michiru pulled herself to her feet, dreading the gradient in front of her. Her thighs and calves burned from the exertion of the climb, her lower back ached as well. She spoke to Yatsuhiro in a nervous voice, 'I believe that you are also carrying Shigemori-san's load of the gold.'

'Yes, my lady.'

'I ask that you let me carry that burden,' she blurted out.

'Are you sure, my lady? It is not too much for me, there is no need for you to worry.'

'I have my reasons,' she said sombrely. She would not mention her feelings about Shigemori's death, or of her shame at being the only one of them not carrying a load. 'But the most important is that you may need to fight,' she said, looking up at him, 'and the extra encumbrance puts you at a disadvantage.'

He gave her a lop-sided smile, intrigued at such tactical thinking from a young woman. *She is proving to be quite an interesting young lady. Shuji must be an excellent sensei.* 'A good idea then, my lady,' he replied with a nod. *I will watch her with great interest. Everyone will be sure to ask for my observations when we get home. If we get home.* He eyed off the ridge above with distaste.

He started to remove one of the bundles tied around his waist but Michiru interrupted him with a weary motion of her hand. 'If you do not mind, could it wait until we get to the top? Please?'

The two captains shared a grin. Yatsuhiro replied, gesturing upwards, 'Of course, my lady. After you.'

She nodded her thanks, willing herself to start moving again. *The only way to go is forward and that means climbing the ridge.* With a deep breath of resignation, she hitched up the box on her back and trudged up the slope.

*　　*　　*

By the time they reached the ridge-line mid-afternoon, Michiru was crawling. Despite the box on her back being empty, it felt like it was full of rocks. Every time the box shifted, one of the metal corners dug into her back or hip, rubbing raw patches under her clothes. So many times she wanted to throw it away. It was just a damn box after all. But it was a connection to her father, something he had saved for her, so she endured.

She eased herself down beside Keiko and Ōmono, panting from the exertion of the climb. The samurai remained standing. They scanned back down the slope for signs of their pursuers. With a pained expression on her dirt-streaked face, Keiko removed her backpack and set to repairing her sandals. Michiru glanced across at her with tired eyes, then at her own tattered sandals, and set to work removing them.

Ōmono shuffled across to her, still on two knees. 'How about we roll some rocks down on these dogs sniffing at our heels?' suggested Ōmono as he rummaged in his pack.

'I would rather leave them wondering where we are,' said Yatsuhiro. 'We should take advantage of our lead and either find a safe hiding spot or try to get more distance between us and them.'

Triumphantly brandishing a loop of cord drawn from his pack, Ōmono set to repairing and reinforcing Michiru's footwear. She looked closer at the cord and saw was made from strips of fabric torn from a rag and plaited together. It seems that nothing went to waste with Ōmono around.

Shuji held his side, troubled by ribs that had been broken too many times and a grinding torment in his neck. He breathed deeply and mastered the pain. *I am not ready for a monastery yet.* 'We still need to decide which direction we are going.' he said, sitting on a handy log. 'We could head for Monoyama fort, but it is likely they would cut us off first. Between the border patrols and our pursuers, we would be lucky to make it, but at least we would be in friendly territory.'

Yatsuhiro's brow furrowed as he drew out the extra roll of gold from inside his clothes. Dark smears of Shigemori's blood marred the silk. His jaw clenched at the thought of the young man's death. *Someone must pay for this loss. Too many men lost.* He took a breath and put the pain aside for later. *There is no doubt that our situation is precarious, but we have a chance.* He offered the money belt to Michiru.

Michiru stood reluctantly to take it in both hands. It was heavier than she expected. She spotted the bloodstains, her eyes locking with Yatsuhiro's. She saw a pain in his eyes that mirrored the sudden icy stab in her heart. She too had lost. Men she had known most of her life had died so that she could escape, one face in particular appeared in her mind. *Masahide.* Michiru looked away as Keiko helped her secure the treasure around her waist.

Yatsuhiro turned to Shuji, pretending not to have seen the pain on her face. 'I think Michiru-hime was right with her idea of taking the most unexpected option.' He cleared a patch of dirt, and using a stick, started to draw a rough map. He sketched the mountains, marked Kyozuka village and the Satake border. 'Once they top this ridge, our pursuers will come down this side quickly. We should do the same. When we get to the lake,' he drew in the lake between the mountains, 'we make for the eastern end and cross the river.'

'There is a good chance that they will be at our backs the whole way. I did not want to have to turn and fight when we are outnumbered five to one.'

'It is the only way we will get to Nagase. Once we cross the river we have a better chance of losing them.'

'We are going to run out of light soon. Stumbling around in the mountains in the dark is never a smart thing. We should take the time to conceal ourselves and let them pass us by in their haste. Then we can return to the road and seek help.'

Michiru had an urge to keep moving, to stay well ahead of the pursuing enemy. 'I think we have little choice in the matter.' She stood wearily, looking at Shuji as Ōmono finished lacing up her repaired footwear. 'I think Yatsuhiro-san is right, sensei, we must head for Nagase.' Seeing disapproval on the old samurai's face, she added, 'I do not intend to risk being captured whilst hiding. We have no time to debate or plan. We must move now if we are to stay ahead of them.'

Unaccustomed to the tone of command in his student's voice, Shuji bit off a rebuke. *Haven't you been training her to command? But she is just a girl. Isn't she too young? No. Let her learn by doing. She could be the last defender of her House. She needs to test her limits. But is now the right time?*

Yatsuhiro noted the startled expression on Shuji's face as the old man watched Michiru helping Keiko to her feet. When the old samurai looked back at him, Yatsuhiro smiled and raised his eyebrows, 'Shall we get going?'

'I guess we shall,' he said. 'I hope you don't mind trotting for a while.'

'Not a problem for me, ojin,' he laughed.

* * *

They made good time downhill through the woods, reaching the lakeside as the sun's disc dipped behind the mountains. The last colours of the day reflected here and there, the setting sun touching the higher reaches of the landscape with its fire. An orchestra of wildlife filled the twilight with a chorus of natural song, but the magical vista was lost on the fatigued figures passing in the gloom. Aching muscles, sore feet and chaffed skin had already overwhelmed their sense of wonder. Whirling clouds of insects rose from the reeds to bite and sting, increasing the misery of the weary party as they skirted the edge of the lake.

Shuji grew concerned as the darkness deepened and their pace slowed. 'We have to find somewhere to stop.'

'No,' Michiru groaned, 'We must push on.'

'Not now, my lady,' Yatsuhiro said. 'We risk injuries stumbling around in the dark. We should find somewhere, at least until the moon rises. Our pursuers face the same problem. They will most likely stop when they get to the lake's edge.'

'I think I can hear the river,' Hirakazu added.

'Very well.' Shuji said, 'let's get across that and then rest.'

As the sound of flowing water became clearer, they spotted the lights of what Michiru guessed was a mill, sitting on the far bank of the river. They crossed the river downstream, giving the building a wide berth. Ōmono took the lead, feeling his way through the water with his spear. Forming a chain, they each held on to the sash of the person ahead of them.

'If there is a mill there will be a village nearby,' hissed Hirakazu from the back of the line. 'Up on higher ground.'

'Let's steer clear of any villages for the moment,' Shuji replied. 'We'll make our way downstream a little and see if we can find some shelter.'

Michiru gritted her teeth against the icy burn of the water as she struggled through the current behind Keiko. *I hope we find some shelter soon. I don't know how much further I can go on.* Her legs barely responded to her commands. Pain and exhaustion threatened to immobilise her, but fear pushed her forward.

CHAPTER FIVE

At the foot of a bank cut out of the valley by some massive flood long ago, they stumbled upon a broken house. Little remained of the walls and part of the roof had collapsed, but enough survived to give them some cover. Debris piled up the corners of the sad little building and stumps of broken rafters leant against the walls. Mustiness fogged the shell of the house that spoke of damp, mould and rot.

Michiru slumped against a wall and massaged her cramped legs and burning thighs. Ōmono cleared a space in the old hearth. She watched as the ashigaru clapped his hands, showering sparks into a twist of straw. He conjured a dancing flame with his breath, feeding it bone dry twigs and kindling, keeping it smokeless. She was fascinated by the ease with which he created the fire. *I have never seen it done so effortlessly. He made it look like magic.* He grinned at her as he held up his hands, revealing the flint and steel.

'Not much point having a fire when there is nothing to cook,' pointed out an unusually sour Hirakazu. He sat down next to the hearth, his sheathed katana gripped in both hands. *I knew I should have grabbed something to eat before we left the inn.* He grunted to himself, disgusted that he had broken one of the cardinal rules of guard duty. *Eat while you can.* 'No point boiling water if there's no rice, is there?'

'Always handy to have a fire,' Ōmono quipped. 'If nothing else, you can make tea.' He held up a kettle he found among the debris with unfeigned pride.

Yatsuhiro chuckled, familiar with the ability of the ashigaru to

64

find useful things anywhere. He had known Ōmono for years now and yet the little man never ceased to amaze him. *If only he showed a bit more respect and did not take off every time we get near an inn.*

Shuji stood in the doorway. 'Hirakazu is right, though. We need food. And water. And clothes. Something less conspicuous,' he plucked at his fine but soiled kimono. 'We all look out of place. The less attention we attract, the better.'

Yatsuhiro followed Shuji as he went outside. He stood by the door and peered through the gloom, scanning for movement while Shuji walked around and checked to see if any light from the fire escaped the ruined house. 'That village should be to the north-west.' he said. 'There will be a road to it from the mill.' Yatsuhiro looked back at the two women and tried to gauge their fatigue. *I doubt that they can go much further. We need to find a safe place to hide and rest up.* 'We have to go in that direction tomorrow, anyway. A quick look around might be useful. I would rather avoid villages,' he said to Shuji as they went back inside the decrepit house. 'But I don't think we have much of a choice.'

Shuji looked at Michiru. Propped up against a ruined wall, she was trying to repair a sandal while Keiko tightened the other. They were both clearly worn out. *They are young and healthy, if maybe too soft for this kind of journey. I know Michiru has never had to sustain this level of effort before. Some hot food and a good sleep would help their spirits, if not their aching bodies.* 'Hirakazu and Ōmono stay here on guard. Yatsuhiro-san, please go back and try that mill we passed. Food, clothes, water bottles. Sake if they have any. Offer to pay. Do you have any silver?' Shuji reached into his sleeve.

'No. I gave mine to Kiku back in Kyozuka.' Yatsuhiro accepted some coins, stashing it in his sleeve before kneeling to tighten his own sandals. 'If you are heading for the village, you should take someone with you.'

'I am. I will take Keiko with me.'

Everyone looked at him, then at her. None were as surprised as

Keiko herself. She looked around, unsure what to think. *He must be joking, right? What use am I going to be?*

Shuji knelt in front of her. 'Keiko-san,' he reassured her. 'We are going to be creeping around a village. That is all.' He could see how exhausted she was, both physically and emotionally. The terrifying events of the last day were taking their toll. He put a hand on her arm and spoke in a gentle tone. 'I know you are tired and afraid. I am not asking you to wield a blade tonight. All I need is for you to be careful and quiet. That is how you are all the time, is it not?' he smiled at her. 'I will be nearby, watching out for you.'

Keiko could feel everyone's gaze. She looked up into his eyes and nodded, 'Hai, Shuji-sama.' *This I can do.* She preferred to remain unseen and unnoticed anyway. *And if Shuji-sama is protecting me everything will be alright.* Taking a deep breath, she pushed down her doubts and nodded again with more conviction. She set her delicate eyebrows in an uncharacteristic scowl. *I will not shame Father with my weakness.*

Ōmono, kneeling by the brazier sighed and drawled, 'Well, it wouldn't be a bad idea to take this, Keiko-san.' From the small of his back, he produced a simple aiguchi, a needle pointed dagger with a dark skin hilt and black sheath. He offered it to her as if it were a sword, with one fist on his hip and the other holding the dagger straight towards her.

Feeling somewhat bemused, she asked, 'Are you making fun of me?'

'No, not at all,' he replied. He stammered at being misunderstood and tried to explain. 'We...we are on the road. The normal rules don't apply for us. We are like...' he paused, trying to think of an appropriate phrase, '...a temporary family, and we have to watch out for each other.' The expression on the little ashigaru's face, with the big smile and the concerned eyes, made Michiru realise the size of his heart.

Keiko darted a glance at Michiru, who was grinning and nodding. Shuji was sitting back on his heels, smiling. The others stood watching with interest. She did not mention that she already had a dagger, one that belonged to mother, given to her by her father before she entered Michiru's service. Even so, she took the offered blade, appreciating the thought. She bowed nervously, 'Domo ariga-to gozaimashite, Ōmono-san.'

He smiled, convinced yet again of his powers with the ladies. 'Do itashimamashite, Keiko-san,' returning her bow.

Shuji stood. 'All right, let's get going.' Turning to Ōmono, he said, 'Do you still have that lantern of yours? Set it up about thirty paces out, if you please. Leave a pointer under a stone.'

'Yes, taisho.' Looking at Shuji with a nervous smile he said, 'It won't be very safe, though.'

'I know, but it will have to do. We should have some moonlight tonight,' he said scanning the sky. 'If not, we have to be able to find you again.' Clapping the little man on the shoulder, Shuji motioned to Keiko and they both headed off into the darkness.

*   *   *

Hirakazu stood watch in the remains of the doorway, looking out across the dale, senses strained for anything out of the ordinary. Ōmono gathered up the water bottles, tying them together by their straps. He bowed to Michiru as she sat by the back wall massaging her aching legs. With the bundle over his shoulder and the kettle in his hand, he headed off towards the river.

She could scarcely believe that they had stopped. Michiru stretched and yawned. *Now I can take this box off my back.* While it had not been a heavy load, it was uncomfortable. She stood up and fumbled with the knot. Hirakazu came to her aid. 'Here, my lady. Let me help you with that.'

She looked up to thank him. A spear blade erupted from Hi-rakazu's chest, spattering blood across Michiru. His face distorted with a mixture of pain and surprise, Hirakazu grasped at the spear point as laughter rattled out of the darkness behind him. Michiru watched in shocked silence as the spear blade disappeared from his chest with a gruesome scrapping sound. In the flickering light of the fire, his face looked like a tortured soul from hell as he slumped to the ground.

An unkempt ronin dressed in frayed and faded clothing approached her, bloodied spear levelled and a distorted leer on his face from the frightening scar that ran from the corner of his left eye to his mouth. Behind him stood an older ronin, sword held loose in one hand, the same leer on his face. 'Oh my, my, my!' chortled the older ronin, trying to see past the spearman. 'What have we here?'

Michiru spun around to flee through a gap in the back wall. But there was a lean ronin, sword drawn, stalking in through the opening with an evil chuckle. She made a desperate lunge and grabbed Ōmono's spear, whirling it around her head to stall a rush. Feeling a deep anger and frustration welling up inside her, Michiru brought the spear down with a snap into a low point guard.

The ronin all laughed. 'Oooo! Little flower has a thorn!' said the lean ronin. 'I think maybe you should do the disarming, Bunyo. I'll catch her if she tries to run.'

Eyes darting between her assailants, Michiru frantically tried to think of a way out. The sweat on her back chilled as her pulse raced. *If I can hold out for long enough, someone might return in time.* Her skin prickled as a doubt rose in her. *Three experienced fighters could make short work of me. If I can take one of them out immediately, my chances of surviving will be much better.* Michiru gritted her teeth and tensed.

The spearman, with obvious contempt for her skills, made a weak feint before attempting to disarm her. She needed more room before trying to take on the spearman, and as long as he remained in the doorway, the older ronin could not attack. She stepped to her right, away from the feint, thrusting the spear with one arm out to its full extent, into the face of the lean ronin.

Surprised by the speed and direction of her attack, he tried to twist out of the way. The tip of Michiru's spear sliced through the bridge of his nose, into the eye and took out a shard of bone from the edge of the socket. The lean ronin shrieked in agony as he spun around. Gripping his ruined eye, he fled howling into the night.

Growling obscenities, the scar-faced spearman turned his disarm into a swinging blow that smashed into the box tied across Michiru's back. She crashed into the wall and collapsed in a heap with a groan, Ōmono's spear pinned under her body. As she struggled to get up Michiru heard the older ronin scolding, 'Take it easy on the goods, idiot! She's not worth as much dead.'

The spearman slammed his spear point into the floor, pinning her down by her kimono. With a grunt of satisfaction, the smirk returned to his face as he grabbed her by the shoulders. In a surge of sheer panic, Michiru pulled an arm free, slid her dagger out of her sash and rammed it up under the spearman's jaw. His hot blood ran down her arm. He collapsed on top of her, immobilising her with his bulk and overwhelming her with his stench.

Suffocating under the dead man's weight, Michiru found no escape from the panic. She felt a scream rising up inside her as she kicked and bucked, pushing with all her strength to try to free herself. When the weight suddenly lifted, she sucked in a lung full of air. Before she could shout, a blow to her stomach slammed her breath back out again. 'You just settle down, hmm?' the older ronin said, resting the tip of his short sword at her throat. 'Now, I don't want to have to slap you around, but trust me I will.'

Gasping the air back into her lungs, Michiru looked around in desperation. 'My men will be back at any moment,' she snarled at him, her head pounding. 'And you will die!' She felt none of the bravado that she was flaunting. Inside she was frantic with fear, her mind racing, searching for a way out.

'Oh, I don't think we need to worry about being interrupted,' said the older ronin, a wicked grin twisting his features. 'There are at least a dozen more ronin out there looking for you. The nice fat reward on offer is making you very popular. Your friends are probably dead already.' Keeping his blade at her throat, he reached down to open her kimono. Michiru gasped, pulling away from him. 'Ah, ah, ahhh!' he said. 'We can do this the easy way or the hard way. I'll tell you what though,' he chuckled, 'I'm going to keep you for a week at least before I hand you over. And thanks to your wonderful blade work, I've got you all to myself!'

Understanding what would happen if she did not escape him, Michiru's hands scrabbled around beside her, seeking anything she might use as a weapon. 'Oh don't bother trying anything,' he hissed at her as he knelt down. 'Give me too much trouble and I'll just slit your throat and collect the cash, anyway.' He groped inside her clothes for her breast. When he found her nipple he pinched it hard, making her cry out. Panting heavier now, he tried to rip open her kimono with one hand. With a howl of desperation, she swung a fist at the side of his head. The ronin caught the blow easily, gripping her forearm. He put down his short sword and slapped Michiru hard across the face.

Her head rang from the blow and blood dribbled from her nose. Michiru saw nothing for a few moments, lost in a haze of red. As reality came back into focus, she felt the man's hand between her thighs. A jolt like a lightning strike passed through her. With a growl that grew into shriek she shoved him away and leaped to her feet. Spinning to face the startled ronin, she drew the long sword from the spearman's corpse.

Michiru leapt straight back to the attack with a slash across his body. With a speed that surprised her, the ronin went to one knee, drew his long sword and deflected the blow in one blurred movement. He made a returning slice that left a stinging cut across her thigh. His eyes were pinned to hers the whole time. Her heart sank as she realised she was hopelessly outclassed.

He looked at her without emotion, 'The hard way it is.' He stood up and went into a high guard.

A blade flashed out of the dark towards the poised ronin. The returning Ōmono appeared from the side, slashing at her attacker's leg. The ronin must have sensed the attack or seen Ōmono moving out of the corner of his eye. He spun around and deflected the ashigaru's blow. However, the momentary distraction gave Michiru the opening she needed. As the desperate ronin tried to reverse his swing, she released all her fear and desperation in a furious 'Kiai!' She struck him a two handed blow that opened his neck and spun him around to crash on the floor, choking on his own blood.

Michiru gasped, not believing that she was still alive. She stood, shaking, still holding the dead spearman's sword. Her head buzzed. All she could hear was her own breathing. This was worse than the flight from the inn. Others had done the fighting for her. Michiru had fought this battle by herself. The whole time she had been terrified to the verge of panic. Now, she was frozen, her mind roiling as she tried to make sense of it all. *How was she still alive?* Ōmono stood there holding out a water bottle and saying something, but she could not comprehend. The sword, dark with blood, dropped from her hands as she sank to her knees, releasing a shuddering sigh.

CHAPTER SIX

Yatsuhiro returned from the mill to a scene from a nightmare, lit by the flickering of the brazier. Ōmono knelt on the floor in front of Michiru with a worried look on his face, trying to calm the distraught girl. Her blood-spattered clothes were in disarray, shuddering sobs racking her body.

His jaw clenched with anger at the sight Hirakazu's lifeless body sprawled on the ground. He checked the wound. *Through the back.* He closed his eyes. *Another good man lost.* With a gentle touch to Hirakazu's chest, he made a silent prayer. *Find peace my young friend.* Bringing himself back to the moment, he went to Michiru, anxiously looking for signs of wounds. 'Are you injured, my lady?' he asked her, smoothing the tangle of hair back and staring intently at her face. She looked back at him with wide eyes but struggled to find words and looked down at her trembling hands.

Seeing her still wracked by sobs, Ōmono spoke instead. 'She's been knocked around,' he said in a low voice. 'She has a bloody nose, and maybe a black eye, but nothing broken.' He continued to shush her, rubbing her back and cooing, as one might try to comfort a child.

In an icy tone Yatsuhiro asked, 'What happened?' He tried to take in the carnage and make sense of what he saw. Ōmono explained how he had gone to the river for water, leaving Hirakazu on guard and how he had run back when he heard the howl of the injured ronin.

'I heard him too. He ran off into the dark.' He checked the bodies of the ronin to see what he could learn, 'If I heard the scream, somebody else will have too. There will be more of them about. We'd better move.' He retrieved Hirakazu's swords and the money belt that held his load of Michiru's gold.

'What about Shuji-san and Keiko-san?' the ashigaru asked.

'We know where they've gone. We'll follow and wait outside the village for them.' Finding out nothing of particular use from the bodies, he picked up the ronin's spear and lifted Michiru up by the arm. 'My lady. We must go. There could be more here soon. We must leave. Now.'

Michiru looked up at him with startled eyes, mouth open in a silent gasp. She blinked a few times, sniffed and rubbed the tears from her eyes, 'Y...yes.' Gathering her resolve, she took the spear from Yatsuhiro. She gingerly pulled her dagger from the dead ronin, cleaning the blade on his clothes before replacing it in its sheath. She stared at the body for a moment, unsure of how she felt.

'Hime-sama,' hissed Yatsuhiro. 'We must leave.'

'Yes,' she replied in a hushed voice. Michiru took the ronin's sheathed short sword and pushed it into her own sash before turning to face her two remaining companions. She decided to leave thinking and feeling until later. 'Lead on, Yatsuhiro-san.'

*   *   *

They waited for Shuji on the outskirts of the village. They chose a clump of trees next to the road and crouched in the dim moon shadows, waiting. Michiru's head and legs ached, her nerves jangled at every noise from the village. A raised voice, the cry of a child, the bang of a door. Michiru was beginning to shiver by the time a pair of dark shapes detached themselves from the outlines of the village, and came down the road. When the figures drew close to their hiding place, Yatsuhiro hissed twice. Shuji, followed by a laden Keiko, silently left the road to join them amongst the trees. 'What are you doing here?' he whispered.

'I'll explain later. For now, we need to find a place to hide,' Yatsuhiro said. 'Did you find anything suitable in the village?'

'We found a house that looks deserted. Let's head for that. It's worth a closer look.' Shuji noted Michiru's slumped posture and Hirakazu's absence. Clearly, something had happened. 'Are you alright, my lady?' he asked.

'I am fine, Shuji-san, thank you,' she said unconvincingly.

He could tell, even in the dark, that she was not alright. *This is neither the time nor place to pursue it further.* 'Very well, let's go then.'

Shuji led them along the boundary of the village, moving from shadow to shadow. The moon threw enough light for them to see the shapes of individual buildings but little in the way of detail. Vegetable plots took up most of the open ground, narrow paths dividing them into a haphazard maze. Most of the villagers had retired for the night, the glow disappearing from the gaps of the last few houses as lamps went out. Shuji spotted one of the hulking storehouses found throughout the countryside. They were also the only fireproof buildings and the tallest structures in a village.

Staying close to the wall of the storehouse, they moved up to the corner. Shuji signalled, 'Wait here.' He headed for a dark house across the street. Michiru tried to block her nostrils to the miasma of mould from the storehouse and the human odours of the village. Risking a peek around the corner, she watched Shuji creep around to the back of the house and disappear. She shivered and turned back to Keiko. 'How safe is this place?' she asked.

Keiko leaned against the wall, her silhouette expressing the same exhaustion Michiru felt. 'I don't know. It seems all right. It's just a farming village,' she replied in a whisper. 'There is no garrison that we could see.'

Yatsuhiro tapped them on the shoulder, motioning to the house. She could just make out Shuji at the back corner waving them over. They tiptoed through the abandoned clutter around the house to where Shuji held open a gap in the timbers of the wall.

The gloom inside was cut by the moonlight seeping through the gaps in the shutters and walls, some even making its way through the attic. Ōmono opened his shielded lamp and scanned around the interior. Woven baskets and farming implements stood in haphazard stacks, taking up half of the interior space. A ladder led up to the roof space. The pungent tang of rodent and mouldy straw filled the interior, along with another, ranker smell she could not identify. The occasional gentle creak of shifting timbers was the only sound.

Shuji came in, checking behind him as he ducked through the gap. 'Clear a space behind all that stuff,' he hissed. 'Pile some of it between here and the door.' They soon created a nest against the back wall.

Michiru watched Shuji as he went to peer through the gaps in the front shutters of the house. She followed him across the room and stood with him. 'what happened to Hirakazu?'

Michiru closed her eyes, Hirakazu's final moments flashing through her mind. 'He died protecting me from ronin,' she managed to say. She took a breath to say more, but the words would not come. She fidgeted with the unusual sensation of having a sword in her sash. 'What now, sensei?'

Shuji face set like stone. 'Bind our wounds as best we can and get some rest. Keiko and I found some food and clothing, but not enough.'

'How long can we stay here?'

'Farmers are early risers. We should be out of here well before dawn,' he said, shifting around to look further up the street. 'Otherwise we will be stuck here until late tomorrow night.'

'I wonder if we could stay undiscovered that long,' she muttered to herself. She moved over to lean on the wall, looking through the nearest gap.

'It would be risky.'

Yatsuhiro came to stand next to her, peering through the gaps in the shutters. 'Enough time for a short sleep,' he said in a soft voice. 'Then head up into the trees and hide for a day or so.'

His breath on the back of her neck sent a tingling down Michiru's spine, a warmth spreading to her loins. Her face flushed in response to his unexpected closeness. Shocked at her own body's response at such a time, Michiru tried to concentrate on the matter at hand, stammering a reply and hoping no-one noticed her reaction. 'We were just discussing the wisdom of staying here until tomorrow night.'

'I would rather not, my lady,' Yatsuhiro said. 'Once those ronin you killed are found, this village is the logical place for our pursuers to look first.'

Michiru's scalp prickled, as the tension of being hunted reasserted itself. 'Maybe we should not stay. Gather what we can and find somewhere else, out of the way.' Her eyelids were becoming increasingly heavy. *I wish we could just find a place to sleep. Even if I could just close my eyes for a moment.*

Yatsuhiro and Shuji both turned to look at her and froze. Michiru blinked in confusion. Now they were both watching the ceiling, lowering themselves into crouches. Their hands were creeping towards their short swords. She could sense that something was wrong and spun around, but no matter where she looked, she could see no threat. Following their eyes, she watched with rising fear. A faint trace of dust sprinkled from the ceiling above, illuminated in the thin light of the lantern. She backed away as another line of dust fell.

Shuji used hand signals to indicate he was heading to the manhole. Yatsuhiro moved Michiru behind him. She fumbled for the short sword at her own waist, unsure of whether she should draw it yet. Shuji flattened himself against the wall, sliding along it like a shadow, eyes riveted on the entrance to the loft.

The top of a matted head of hair peeked through the hatch, followed by a pair of eyebrows. When the eyes appeared and registered the people's attention on him, the owner shrieked. He dropped to the floor and made a bounding leap for the exit in the back wall. Shuji, unprepared for the speed of the ragged man, was unable to intercept his flight.

Ōmono stepped out from behind a pile of cane baskets and swung a bucket in a graceful sweeping arc to crack the scrabbling figure on the side of the head. The dark shape fell to the floor in a pile against the wall. 'Ohh! That's going to hurt,' the cheeky ashigaru whispered to Michiru. Despite herself and the tense situation, she almost laughed.

Ōmono opened his shielded lamp wider as they gathered around the prostrate figure. They were all simultaneously repelled by the most offensive reek imaginable. Even Shuji made a face, trying to wave the stench away. The figure on the floor was dressed in tattered remnants that failed to cover his limbs. Often-repaired straw sandals and a bulging carry bag completed the outfit. Yatsuhiro bound his hands and feet quickly before dragging him to the corner and propping him up. Ōmono stuffed a rag in the man's mouth and tied a gag around his head. A dark rivulet of blood ran from his split eyebrow where Ōmono's bucket had hit.

Shuji made to go up the ladder, his short sword drawn. 'Get ready to leave and then see if you can wake him up.'

Michiru picked up the fallen carry bag, which did not smell much better than its owner. It seemed to contain various packages, odd-ments and vegetables. Unwilling to put a hand in there, she placed it down against the wall. She heard Shuji moving around in the roof space. She looked around the interior again. *Who used to live in such a small house? How many lived here? Who slept upstairs? Was the place like this when people lived here or is it only this run down because they have all gone? Why did they leave?*

Climbing down the much-repaired ladder, Shuji interrupted her thoughts. 'No one else up there. A few odds and ends that he prob-ably stole from the locals.' Looking at the unconscious man he said, 'I would say he is a sneak thief who has been hiding in here, living off whatever he can steal.' He sneered at him, 'Parasite.'

As they gathered near the exit, Michiru could make out the strain on all their faces in the faint light of the lamp. *I just want to stop, or soon I will have no choice.* A headache had started behind her eyes, making her frown. Rubbing her temples helped a little but the ache was still there. 'Let's get on with it please, Shuji-san. The sooner we move, the sooner we can sleep.'

Shuji shook the prisoner and poked his shoulder but he gave no sign of consciousness. He patted the man's cheek and the vagabond's eyes fluttered, unfocussed and struggling to open. He placed the point of his short sword against the man's belly, raising a vague unease in Michiru's mind. *I hope he would not kill a bound prisoner in cold blood right in front of me.*

As the thief's senses returned, he winced from the pain of his wound and took in his surroundings. The one good eye grew wider, darting around looking for escape. He panted through the gag, becoming more agitated. Shuji spoke in a low and deadly serious tone. 'When we take the gag off you will not scream, yell or shout. You will keep your voice down or I will cut you open, understand?' He prodded him with the sword to emphasise the point.

The cringing thief made promissory noises through the cloth binding. Ōmono removed the gag and clipped him across the ear, 'Sorry, thief.' The man glared up at him and pulled a face. Michiru took an irrational dislike to him as soon as she saw that expression.

'Stinking thieves!' he hissed. 'Give back my things. Give me back my bag.' He craned his neck, peering around them for the carry bag.

'What did you hear?' Shuji growled.

He reached for his bleeding eyebrow with his bound hands, hissing in pain at the touch. 'Enough to know I got to get away from here. You lot are trouble, you are.' He gingerly assessed his injury with his grubby fingers, adding mournfully, 'You've spoiled a good setup.'

Michiru tried hard to understand his thick speech. 'We are leaving, anyway,' she said, wondering if he was touched in the head. It would certainly explain some things about him.

'Doesn't matter now! People will be looking for you.' The thief flexed his jaw from side to side. 'Time for me to go somewhere else, I reckon.'

Shuji prodded the grubby figure. 'Well, we could kill you and leave you here.' The man shivered and shook his head.

Michiru added in a hushed voice, 'Or we could leave you tied up, with all the things you have stolen. We could leave a note for the villagers to find and tell them to work you like a slave for a year to make up for your stealing.'

'No! No!' he pleaded, waving his tied hands. 'I know a place. A place you can hide,' the frightened man volunteered. 'A place no one goes anymore. I can take you there!'

*   *   *

They hurried along the road leading out of the village and turned off into the woods, following a path that it seemed only their guide could see. Branches slapped at them as they pushed through into the murkiness of the forest. The path wandered up the slope before turning back to the east, ending at a small clearing in the surrounding forest. In the gloom, Michiru could just make out a low wooden building perched next to a small pond fed by a gentle waterfall.

'You be safe here,' said the thief, grinning. 'No one comes to this place anymore. No one even remembers it's here.' Michiru sensed the tension in him and hoped he would not try to run. She had to admit it seemed like an excellent hiding spot, if they could believe him.

'Do you trust him, sensei?' Michiru asked Shuji.

'No, not really,' he replied. 'I'm afraid we do not have many options.' Looking around the edges of the clearing, he continued, 'That's why we are going up into the trees a way. We can take a better look at this tomorrow.'

They made their way deeper into woods, heading upslope of the clearing. Only once Shuji was satisfied with their distance from the little house did he call a halt. 'Alright, we will stop here,' he said, to everyone's relief. While they all cleared a space, Shuji reapplied the thief's gag. The man rolled his eyes and groaned. 'Nothing from you, do you hear?'

'Hhnm hnn,' was his reply.

Shuji bound his hands and tied him to a tree a short distance from their camp. 'You wait here,' he whispered.

'Hhn, hn, hnm,' he muttered at the old samurai through the cloth of his gag.

*　　*　　*

Ōmono's ingenious portable brazier was soon boiling water, well shielded from the clearing. Shuji insisted that they share tea together and have something to eat before getting to sleep. He passed around some tacky rice balls, which they devoured wearily. As they shared a warming tea from chipped cups, they grew silent in contemplation and exhaustion.

'We nearly lost you tonight Michiru,' mused Shuji.

She stared at the light of the fire, embarrassed to be such a burden. Michiru looked up at the old samurai. 'I apologise, sensei, for not being a better student.' She bowed her head with remorse. 'I wish now that I had made greater effort to become more proficient.'

Yatsuhiro and Shuji exchanged a smile, remembering their own feelings of youthful inadequacy. Yatsuhiro looked at her with an intensity that increased her nervousness. 'You should never have had to defend yourself, my lady. That is our duty, as samurai,' he said. 'We should not have left you. We failed you.'

Michiru noticed the hardened lines of Shuji's face as he nodded in agreement. 'You have not failed,' she replied, unsure of where this might lead. 'I am alive and unharmed, thanks to all of you.' She bowed again, grateful for everything they had done to help her stay alive.

'That is only through the favour of the gods, my lady,' said Yatsuhiro. 'It could have easily turned out different.'

Shuji stirred the coals with a stick. 'We have managed to stay ahead of our enemies so far. For now we should stop and gather our strength. Our only concern should be getting you safely to Nagase. If the gods are with us you will not need to fight again.' He looked hard at Michiru. He could see she was spent. He had seen it before in young samurai after their first battle. *She would sleep for half a day, more if I let her, then the aches will set in.* It was her state of mind rather than her body that he was most concerned with. 'But just in case, we should spend time practicing, when we can.'

'If you think that is best, sensei.' she said, thinking that there was no way she could ever learn enough.

He stood, 'But now, my lady, you should get some sleep.'

Michiru was so exhausted after the strain of their escape and the fight with the ronin that she needed no convincing. The side of her face was swollen and sore, her legs and feet ached, and she felt like a horse had trampled her. Michiru had never felt so tired. She lay down on some straw matting salvaged from the abandoned house, falling asleep before Shuji covered her with a jacket.

*　　*　　*

The old samurai sat back down next to Yatsuhiro, signalling Ōmono to have a seat as well. 'The Lady has trouble handling a spear, it seems,' observed Yatsuhiro.

'She has never picked one up,' said Shuji, blaming himself for the gap in Michiru's training.

'She should be able to use one in roughly the same way as a naginata, surely.'

'Excuse me, taisho, but when was the last time you used a naginata?' Ōmono interjected.

'Oh,' he said in realisation. 'Never. My father wanted me to concentrate on sword and spear. He didn't even want me to "waste time" with the bow.' Yatsuhiro frowned, 'Has she learned the sword, Shuji-san?'

'No. I made her spend time with the naginata. The bow she has used more. She enjoys the bow,' he reminisced for a moment, recalling the earlier attempts by her father to discourage her. 'She has only a passing familiarity with the sword. An experienced swordsman could easily overwhelm her. Besides, now is not the time for her to take up something new.'

'What's your favoured weapon, Yatsuhiro-san?' Ōmono asked.

'Short spear,' he replied. 'I find it can deal with anything.'

Shuji explained, 'When you get past the point of the spear, it is no longer a weapon but a hindrance.'

'Not so for a skilled warrior,' stated Yatsuhiro firmly.

'Maybe so, but for many novices, it is.' He picked up the spear, running his finger from the tip of the spear two hand spans along the shaft. 'With a naginata you still have all that edge to deal with. And the leverage of the long haft means it can cleave like a great sword. The blocks and butt strikes of the short spear are also possible with the naginata but need to be done in a flowing movement, because of the extra weight.'

'Well, if the lady is familiar with naginata,' said Ōmono, 'maybe she will be more confident if she has one.'

Shuji looked flatly at the ashigaru, 'We have none for her to use, Ōmono. What do you have in mind?'

Ōmono picked up the spear taken from the dead ronin, looking at the shaft with one eye. He then turned to Yatsuhiro with a slight bow, 'If I may have Shigemori-san's short sword, my lord, I can make one. Maybe his spirit will guide her hand and he may yet protect her.'

The two samurai looked at each other. After a moment, Shuji nodded. 'A spear's shaft is round, Ōmono. A naginata needs an oval shaft, so that you can feel which way the blade is facing. How do you propose to deal with that?'

'I have a temporary solution for that, my lord. I can make a better one from scratch in a few hours, if you can get me some decent wood,' he replied with confidence. 'In the meantime, it will take me an hour or so to put something together.'

'We should get some sleep first.'

'I would like to do this now, if you don't mind, taisho. Just in case'

Yatsuhiro stood, shaking each leg to loosen the muscles. 'I will take first watch and keep Ōmono company.'

'All right, then,' mumbled Shuji, making himself as comfortable as possible against a log. He was more tired than he cared to admit. *I'm too old for this*, he thought, feeling all his aches and pains demanding attention. 'Wake me at dawn, if you please.'

* * *

Ōmono fetched a handsaw from his backpack and disappeared in to the dark. He returned shortly with a pair of saplings about as thick as his little finger. Setting himself up next to a log, he pulled his backpack over and laid out a selection of items; a spare pair of bamboo chopsticks, a small ceramic pot with a lid, a ball of hemp cord and a flat tipped metal spike mounted in a wooden handle. He clasped his hands together and closed his eyes for a moment, mumbling a prayer over the tools.

He stripped the saplings with his knife, measured them against the spear shaft and cut them to size. With great care, he split one down the middle and put the two pieces aside. Taking the spear, he looked it over before clamping it against the log with his foot. Sawing through the shaft just below the bindings for the head, he removed the spear point, tossing it into his backpack. 'You never know when you'll need something like that. Always handy to have a bit of steel.'

'Not to mention the fact that you can get a good price for it,' added Yatsuhiro with a smile.

'That, too,' he replied without any shame.

Using his knife, the little ashigaru cut a guide notch in the flat end of the shaft and down both sides for about a hand's span. Holding the shaft against the log with his foot again, he cut two slots, close together, in the end of the shaft. Switching back to his knife, Ōmono trimmed the waste from between the two slots, making it wide enough to house the tang of the short sword blade.

Putting the shaft aside for the moment, Ōmono reverently picked up Shigemori's short sword, drawing it from its sheath. He turned the blade in the glowing light admiring the lustre of the polished steel. He nodded in appreciation, 'I am always impressed by the craftsmanship that goes into working steel like this.'

'It is a wondrous thing, turning raw iron into such an object,' agreed Yatsuhiro. He watched in fascination as Ōmono continued his work.

Once again, Ōmono offered a prayer, this time over the blade, asking Shigemori to help defend Michiru-hime. With his metal spike, he removed the pins that fixed the handle to the tang of the blade, sliding it free and putting the hilt to one side with respect. With the blade held in a piece of folded cloth, he removed the hand guard and placed it with the hilt.

Pulling the spear shaft onto his lap, he lined the tang of the blade up with shaft and marked two holes on either side. Handing the blade to Yatsuhiro, he asked, 'Would you mind holding this please?' Working against the log, he bored two holes through the shaft with the flattened spike. Taking a bamboo chopstick, he whittled the end of it down to a tight fit into the holes. From the resulting dowel, he cut two pegs, a little longer than the thickness of the shaft.

'Will that hold the blade?' asked Yatsuhiro.

Ōmono scrutinised the modified spear shaft. 'It will be lighter than normal,' he said, 'and she probably shouldn't try to chop with it. But it should hold together once I'm done.'

Taking back the blade, Ōmono replaced the hand guard and fittings. He fitted the tang into the slot in the shaft, tapping the bamboo pegs through the holes until they just came through the other side. Splitting the other chopstick in two, he tapped the slivers of bamboo into the slot on either side of the tang. He shaved the ends of the pegs and the slivers down with his knife until they were flush with the shaft and looked at his work. 'Not bad. Not great, but it will do.'

'What about the shaft? I thought it was supposed to be oval.'

'Ahh. Watch and learn, mighty captain.'

He opened the small ceramic pot, added a few drops of sake and stirred it with the remains of the bamboo chopstick. Applying a small amount of the resulting glue to the sides of the shaft, he tied the sapling strips into place with the hemp cord. Once secured, he applied more glue to the undersides of the strips, tying them in place at regular intervals down the shaft. He applied more glue onto the shaft for about four fingers below the hand guard, and then bound it with more cord. Once he had secured the shaft in the same way at both ends, he bound a few more evenly spaced sections, coating them with glue as he finished each one. Finally, he repeated the binding once more for a hand's span below the guard.

Standing up and stretching his legs, Ōmono checked the heft and balance of the weapon and nodded to himself in satisfaction. 'There we are, taisho. Surely not fit for a lady, but good enough for the moment.'

'Ōmono,' he said with a slight shake of his head, 'I would like to see what you could do in a proper workshop.'

'So would I, but a workshop is hard to carry around,' he said with a smile.

* * *

Michiru's mind climbed out of an abyss of darkness into consciousness. Her world rocked as someone shook her shoulder, her name battering against eyelids that refuse to open. Pain came rushing in as her body protested her first movements. She groaned.

'Hime,' Keiko whispered again. 'We must move now.'

'What?' she croaked through her thick dry lips. She opened her eyes but immediately squinted at the sudden brightness. 'Oh.' Levering herself up, she shaded her eyes and looked around. The moist smell of early morning held the acrid tinge of the charcoal from the brazier. The others were nowhere to be seen.

'Shuji-san said to let you sleep. I have cleaned up the little house by the pond,' she explained, 'and I have set up a bed for you. He said you should sleep for the rest of the morning.'

Rising painfully to her feet, Michiru noticed the young woman's puffy eyes and drawn features. *She looks how I feel. Until now I had not realised how much I rely on her. She has certainly been my constant companion.* Michiru looked at Keiko with a new clarity. *She maybe the closest thing I have to a friend.* 'I think we should both get some sleep. Come on, Keiko-chan,' she said, taking her arm. 'Let's leave the men to sort things out. Maybe we can even get them to heat us up some water for a wash.' As she willed her aching limbs to move, she moaned, 'It is a pity we don't have a bath tub.'

CHAPTER SEVEN

Michiru ran as hard as she could, gasping from the exertion, unable to get a full breath. The air was dark and thick with the smell of blood. The chilling sounds of lewd laughter came from the murkiness. Every time she tried to look behind, unbound hair flew in her eyes and her feet stumbled on the uneven ground. The laughter grew louder as she careered through the trees. She must keep moving, pushing on, her legs made of stone, no time to stop for air. Lunging through the trees, cruel branches reached out, whipping her in the ribs, stomach and face. She could feel hands grabbing at her clothes and pulling her hair. She caught a foot in the tangled underbrush and felt herself fall. The leering voices laughed louder in her ears as she toppled. She screamed in terror, clawed fingers gripping her flesh. Her shriek echoed on.

She sat up, breathless, her body full of aches. She sobbed, remembering every blow. Her clothes were sodden and twisted around her. Keiko was kneeling at her side, a look of concern on her drawn face. 'Hime-sama, it's alright, you are safe. It's just a dream.' She offered Michiru a water bottle, smoothing her hair back off her face. Michiru closed her eyes, trying to stifle her sobs.

Running footsteps grew louder. The door slid open with a crash as Shuji and Yatsuhiro burst in, swords drawn. 'My lady! What's wrong?!'

She took a deep shuddering breath and reined in her emotions, wanting to appear stronger. 'Just a bad dream,' she said in an attempt to salvage some dignity. 'Thank you, gentlemen.' She fumbled with her clothing, still not fully awake, trying to make herself more presentable.

'My lady,' Yatsuhiro nodded as he sheathed his sword. He watched her for a moment, trying to read her mental state. *Is she unravelling under the strain? Considering what she had been through, a nightmare or two is perfectly natural.* 'We will be just outside,' he said gently and with a bow turned and walked out, shutting the door behind him. Shuji also sheathed his sword, but he came and knelt in front of Michiru, his concern clear on his face. Keiko helped her change in to a fresh kimono while Michiru tried to recover her calm.

After a while, Shuji asked, 'Do you feel better now, my lady?'

Still not able to look at him directly, she gave a silent nod. She glanced at Keiko and gave her a nod that meant she should leave them.

Keiko bowed, 'I will fetch you something to eat, my lady,' she murmured, getting up and leaving them alone. Michiru shifted stiffly, arranging her clothes, still avoiding eye contact.

'Will you tell me about the dream, my lady?' he asked softly. As her sensei and her captain, he worried that she might not be dealing with the trauma of recent events. *No one could blame her for her reaction. She is not a warrior, just a girl. This was not what she was trained for.*

'It was nothing, sensei. Just a nightmare.' She smoothed her already neat clothing.

'Very well,' he nodded. It was not worth pushing her about it; she would talk when she was ready. 'I think we should find you and Keiko some men's clothing for the remainder of the trip. After all, our pursuers are looking for a group with women in it.'

'So now I must travel in disguise? So much for my wedding procession,' she said with a hint of bitterness.

'If necessary, yes,' he snapped in reply. 'We must outsmart our foe and choose the right moment to head for the border. We will be travelling at night most of the time, but we may have to make a run for it. I don't want you two tripping over all the time and getting snagged on everything.'

'I do not want to run anymore,' she looked away, ashamed of the tears building in her eyes.

'Then be prepared to sneak, crawl and hide,' he snapped. 'If you think this has been hard so far, think again, young lady.' He huffed and regained control of his irritation. 'We do what we must. Simple. We have been quite lucky,' He leant toward her, holding her eyes with a fierce gaze. 'We have escaped the enemy's trap, but we are still a long way from safety. You must push on.' He clenched his fists on his thighs, wishing he did not have to frighten her more than she already was. 'If you give up now, that decision, my lady, it will affect other people's lives. When you make your choices, others will also suffer the consequences. That is your burden and you must bear it,' he said. Sitting back and sighing, he added, 'As your father and mother did.' He cracked his neck with slow tilt of his head to the left. There was another pop as he made a slow nod. Tension eased between them and he felt her submit to her duty. He cleared his throat and adopted a calmer tone. 'You took a real risk fighting those ronin, Michiru,' he said.

She recognised him once again as her teacher and accepted his criticism. *Yatsuhiro and Ōmono must have told him the details of last night's encounter.* 'I sought to reduce the odds, sensei,' she offered.

'You gambled.'

'The other ronin was less alert. The big one was already aiming at me. I thought I could dodge away and attack the other one at the same time.'

'You took your eye off him and tried to pull off a fancy move.' Shuji added with disapproval. 'Combat is no place for flashy blade work. Not you. Not now.' With a firm command he said, 'Stick to the basics. Remain on the defensive.' He looked at her from one eye, making her shift uncomfortably.

'Yes, sensei.'

'Yoish,' he said, nodding with finality. Turning toward the door he called out, 'Ōmono!'

The door opened and the ashigaru came in, placing a long

bundle wrapped in plain cloth on the floor in front of Shuji. She watched Ōmono, but she could read nothing from him as he bowed and left. Shuji unwound the bundle with reverence, revealing the improvised naginata. 'Your own naginata is with the baggage we had to leave behind at the inn,' he said. 'Ōmono has constructed this honourable substitute for you from Shigemori's short sword. This must serve until we can get yours back.'

Michiru's eyes widened in surprise. *He made this for me?* She bowed low, 'Thank you, sensei,' not trusting herself to say more.

'It seems the gods bid you defend yourself, Michiru-hime,' he admitted. 'I hope your father is watching over you.' *Because I think we are going to need his help.* Shuji picked up the naginata with both hands and offered it to her with a bow.

Michiru knew that her life was changing but this was unexpected. She could no longer be the girl who left home. *My old life is gone. This is a frightening new reality, a new life. Where failure means death, or dishonour.* She looked at the offered weapon, a blend of the crude and the highly refined. Deadly. *Could I deliberately kill someone again? I must. The enemy has left me no choice.*

She reached out and accepted the weapon.

*　　*　　*

Ōmono grumbled to himself as he trudged up the path to where they had tied up the Smelly Man. He thought it was a mistake to keep feeding their prisoner. He had no time for thieves. *Life is hard enough without the little you do have being taken from you when your back is turned. Someone was going to have to kill the little monster anyway. We cannot afford to leave him behind, not with what he knows.* Even so, it was his job to take him his food. 'Hello, vermin,' he greeted him.

The pungent thief slouched against the ropes binding him to the tree, watching the approaching ashigaru. His eyes flicked between Ōmono's face and what he was carrying. His appearance was worse in daylight. Ōmono untied the gag, to his prisoner's great relief.

'Now, I suggest you remain quiet. That way I won't have to kill you. Yet. Am I clear?'

'Yes, O-sama,' he said in a disrespectful tone.

A slap from Ōmono's open hand rocked his head forward. 'Either you like pain or you are a slow learner.'

'Yeah, brave warrior, beating up on the tied up prisoner. What a hero. Give back my bag!'

Ōmono gripped the wrapped rice ball harder, struggling not to smash it into his grubby face. 'Oh, I'm sorry. The boss thought you might be hungry.' He turned to go with a grin on his face, 'I'll just tell him you didn't want it.'

'No, no, no,' the smelly little man stuttered pleadingly. 'I want the rice. I do. I do.'

The ashigaru looked at him. 'It's wrapped up. How do you know it's rice?'

'I can smell it, genius.'

'I don't know how you can smell anything else except yourself.'

'You stink,' he spat, 'All of you. Especially the women. Now give me back my bag.'

'Sorry to tell you, arsewipe, but that unholy reek is coming from you,' Ōmono corrected him.

'You are thick as well as stinky,' he chuckled. 'The smell protects me from people's smell. But it's wearing off. So give me the bag!'

'What?' Ōmono shook his head and stared at him in confusion.

Michiru had caught the last part of their conversation as she approached. 'I have brought you some water.' She was intrigued now, as well as repulsed. Shuji had insisted that she get up and move around. And while she was moving around why didn't she make herself useful and take some water to the prisoner. 'Shuji said to tie one of his arms back and free the other so he can eat and drink.'

'Personally, my lady, I'd rather not get that close to him.' But despite his protests, the ashigaru retied the rope to allow the thief some extra freedom before tossing the wrapped rice at his feet. The man snatched up the food and devoured it with no manners whatsoever.

Michiru crouched nearby, watching in morbid fascination. *How can anyone be so dirty? I could not stand it. How long has it been since he washed?* 'What did you mean about your smell protecting you?' she asked.

He cocked an eye to watch Michiru as he pushed the last of the sticky rice into his mouth. He chewed it with his mouth half open, watching her with a speculative look. 'Why you want to know?'

'It is just that I have never heard of such a thing.'

'I tell you if you give me back my bag,' he said, sensing an opening.

Michiru looked up at Ōmono who snorted and shook his head. 'Ignore him, my lady. He's just crazy,' he said. 'Time to tie you back up, Ratboy.' The thief locked eyes on her, a faint smile on his face even as Ōmono gagged him and retied his arms.

*   *   *

In the afternoon, Shuji ran Michiru through a brief practice with short sword and spear. 'It is more important that you concentrate on getting used to your new naginata.' They reviewed her defensive techniques and she settled into slowly repeating the movements he taught her. He watched her run through the drills. *Really, I hope that she will have no need to wield a weapon for the rest of the journey. But, I expect that we have at least one fight ahead of us. No doubt the ronin are still searching for us. They will want their payday.*

Ōmono appeared from the woods nearby, dressed in some of the old clothes they had found last night. He was carrying a freshly cut pole over his shoulder, a scarf tied around his head, his spidery legs bare. Once again, Michiru was surprised at the little man. He now looked nothing like an ashigaru. She stifled a laugh with her hand.

He hobbled past an astounded Shuji who caught himself in the act of drawing his sword. *I almost did not recognise him.* He was portraying the character of the yokel porter with masterful mimicry. Ōmono now looked like someone that you might see on any road in the realm. It was an excellent choice for mixing with the locals. *I have to admit that the disguise is perfect. Truth be told, I am glad to have this most capable man with us. Yatsuhiro is lucky to have found him.* 'What are you planning, Ōmono?'

'I thought I might make my way back down the road a bit and trot into town,' he said. 'I can pick up a few things, do some trade. No one will bat an eyelid.' Adjusting the bundles suspended from either end of the pole, he added with a smile, 'I might overhear something useful, as well.'

Yatsuhiro smiled as he leaned against a nearby tree, knowing the ashigaru was the perfect man for the job. 'And I don't doubt you will manage to find something tasty while you are there.'

'I hadn't thought of that,' he beamed innocently and gave a quick bow, 'thank you for the suggestion, taisho.'

'Take Keiko-san with you,' added Shuji

He stopped in his tracks. 'Is that a good idea, taisho?' he stammered, the grin evaporating from his face.

'She will make it more convincing when you buy women's things,'

'I will go with him, Shuji-san,' Michiru volunteered.

Yatsuhiro's face froze as his heart stopped for a moment. He turned to regard the young woman with a pained expression. 'I do not think that is a good idea, my lady.' He was not so sure he wanted to let her out of his sight. Especially here.

'Yoshioka-sama is right, my lady. That could be very risky,' added Ōmono, looking nervously at Yatsuhiro for support. The last thing he wanted was to be responsible for his Lord's bride wandering around a village in enemy territory.

'You may have noticed that I am not actually asking permission from any of you,' Michiru retorted. This would be a rare opportunity for her to see things for herself. It was not just a matter of curiosity for her. She could see the need for her to understand better what was happening in the lives of ordinary people. She had always thought that she was not that far separated from the reality of daily life. She had spent time with her father travelling their domain, administering the various aspects of the estate; road building, farming, forestry and irrigation projects. She had not paid much attention to the details up until now. Shuji's previous lecture about councillors made her realise that she would have to rely on the reports of other people for information about the state of the domain. 'It would be best if I saw things for myself, don't you think?'

'This can go wrong in so many ways,' Shuji said almost to himself. He rubbed his face wearily. He still had not had enough sleep and felt every one of his fifty-odd years. 'We will have to make you as ugly and unattractive as possible, then.'

'What? No arguments?' she asked in surprise.

'I can think of a few.' muttered Ōmono with a fixed smile. 'If you need to borrow any you can have some of mine, Shuji-sama.'

'We could argue about it, if you like,' he said, ignoring the little man's comments.

'No, that is fine,' she replied quickly.

Ōmono sucked his breath through his teeth, nodding, 'As you say, taisho.' Now it would take much longer to work his way through the scrub along the side of the road. *And if some tough, or gods forbid a samurai, took an interest in Michiru and insisted on taking her, they would have to fight their way out. This just complicated a simple job.* It also meant he couldn't sneak a quickie with a farmer's daughter. Ah well, shikata ga nai.

They set about blackening some of Michiru's teeth, mussed her hair and rubbed dirt, soot and crushed leaves on her exposed skin. The kimono she had borrowed from Namika was plain enough but it still required a few modifications to make it truly humble. Keiko sewed on some rough patches and faked a few repairs. By the time they had finished working on her appearance, she looked something like the smelly man's sister.

Ōmono loaded her up and coached her on how to make it look heavier. Learning to imitate the manner of a downtrodden and morose peasant was eye opening for her by itself. 'Try not to smile if you can help it, my lady. And definitely no laughing. You see, it's all about putting yourself into the role. Like acting on stage.'

'Only the audience could kill me if I get it wrong.'

He nodded. 'It's like that in the real theatre, too, sometimes.'

She laughed. 'I suppose you spent some time as an actor.'

'No laughing, remember. For now, acting is a survival skill, my lady,' he said, suddenly serious.

'Yes, Ōmono,' she replied downcast, lips trembling and eyes filling with tears.

'I'm sorry, my lady. I didn't mean to upset you.'

'Hah. Got you,' she said triumphantly.

'Oh, very good.'

Shuji gave them one last look over before he nodded his approval. 'Well you do not look anything like a samurai lady anymore. Best not to speak unless you absolutely must,' he cautioned her. 'Yatsuhiro and I will be on the edge of the village, keeping an ear out for any commotion.'

Yatsuhiro stared at Ōmono, giving him a significant look that left him in no doubt about what would occur if anything happened to Michiru.

Ōmono dug into a fold in his clothes and produced a small bamboo whistle, a child's toy, worn with age and use. He gave it a quick trill. 'Will that do, taisho?'

He shook his head, surprised at the things the man carried. 'Just make sure you don't sell her, no matter the price,' he warned the ashigaru with mock seriousness. 'And don't take too long,' he added as they disappeared into the trees.

By the time they had reached a place where Ōmono felt safe enough to leave the cover of the woods, Michiru was scratched and sweating. The unaccustomed effort of carrying a load through the underbrush and over uneven ground left her aching and panting. Ōmono looked at her and shook his head. 'My, my. You are new to this aren't you, my lady?'

She stared at him through sweat-stung eyes as she caught her breath. 'No need to rub it in...brother.'

Ōmono grinned and checked the road again in each direction before stepping out and hoisting the carrying pole onto his shoulder. 'Well ... sis. Us peasants are used to a life of hard toil and little food. Better toughen up. You make sure you eat like you're hungry when we get the chance. We wouldn't want anyone to get suspicious. We never really know when we will get to eat again. Why do you think most of us are farmers?'

She fell in behind him as he started towards the village. 'What about artisans, tradesmen and so on?'

'Oh, you can sell your wares for coin, but you can't eat copper or silver. And sometimes there is no food to be bought, no matter how much money you've got.' He winked at her. 'Much better to grow your own.'

'What is the worst thing you have had to eat?' she asked, keen to learn whatever she could about this new layer of the world she had discovered. It was also a good way to take her mind off the ache in her legs.

He chuckled as they ambled along the road, the sound of their sandaled feet barely audible over the sighing of the breeze through the trees. 'I could say, my mother's cooking, but I know what you mean. Hmmm,' he pondered. After a brief moment with his head bowed, he replied, 'It would be an even contest between pond snails and grasshoppers.'

She shuddered a little. 'Why would you eat them?'

'It depends on how hungry you are, and how long it's been since you last ate.'

* * *

To Michiru, the village looked nothing like she remembered from last night. In the moonlight, she had not been able to see the refuse in the ditches or collected up against the walls of the buildings. The houses were more ragged and dilapidated in the harsh light of day. There were gaps in the greying wood of many walls and rickety doors and screens barely worth the name. *Doesn't anyone here ever repair their homes?* Dusty children and dogs wandered listlessly, avoiding the adults working inside or stooped in the vegetable plots that took up every available space between the buildings.

'This is nothing like the villages at home,' she said quietly, a little shocked at the lack of pride these people took in their homes. While there was always a stink associated with any dwellings, she could taste the rot and smoke in the air.

'Don't be too quick to judge these people, sister.' Ōmono replied in a low voice as they trudged along the street. 'Sometimes, if the lord keeps demanding money there isn't the time or the energy to clean up like most people would. When food is short and taxes high, people tend not to care. Remember though,' he added, 'you live like this at home.'

She bowed her head and gripped the shoulder straps of her pack, keeping her eyes lowered as she fell in behind Ōmono. As they made their way along the street, he would stop in front of houses at random and call out for the occupants if none were visible. Michiru was envious at the easy way he interacted with the villagers. He bartered, haggled and traded, rarely parting with actual coins if he could avoid it. Before long, they had most of the things they needed, except for food.

'Well, my sister, no one seems to have much food to spare so we'll have to buy it from the inn.'

'What is wrong with that, brother?'

Ōmono grimaced as he adjusted her pack to accommodate the new weight on her back. 'I won't be able to trade, I'll have to pay. We can't buy too much food without raising suspicions.'

'Could we pretend that we are going to sell it on the road?'

He turned her around and looked at her with a new appreciation. 'Yes we could,' he said. 'That's a very good idea, sister.'

'I am learning.'

'So you are, sister. So you are.'

*   *   *

Their packs now full, Ōmono stood outside the inn's kitchen bouncing the last of their coins in his hand. 'Well, sister, I think we've earned ourselves a treat.'

'We do not have much time, brother. We should be getting back on the road.'

'Oh, I don't know,' he said with a sideways grin as they stepped back out onto the main street. He looked around for a moment and spotted something. 'We can afford a short break, I think.'

Michiru followed him along the dusty road, trying to settle the pack. Her shoulders and back were already sore from the unfamiliar load and the padding did little to protect her existing sores. She watched the peasants returning from the fields, implements across their shoulders as they trudged home. They were dusty and sweaty, faces drawn from the day's toil. Their eyes were dull with fatigue and she could see the pain on their weathered faces. 'They all look so tired,' she whispered. 'It must have been a hard day for them.'

Ōmono nodded. 'Hard days are one thing. It's when every day is hard that makes them look that way. Day after day, year after year. That's what wears you down. Ah. Here we are.' They stopped in front of a ramshackle house opposite the hulking storehouse Michiru remembered from the previous night. Her eyes were drawn toward the abandoned house where they had taken temporary shelter last night. It looked even smaller and more dilapidated than she imagined. Ōmono set his carrying pole and its load down and stretched his shoulders with an exaggerated effort.

The house he was facing had an open front, screened off from the rest of the interior. A vastly old woman sat on a cushion fanning herself as a teapot steamed away on a portable brazier. Her skin, stretched and wrinkled, turned brown by thousands of days in the sun. Age hung on her bones with a palpable weight. 'Come and sit for a while,' a croaking voice offered. 'Take the weight off your feet and have a sweet cake.' She held up a tray of the small delicacies with her scrawny arms.

'We'd love to, obaa-san, but ...' He held out his open hands.

With a sly smile, she poured two cups of tea. 'Oh, surely a smart man like you will still have a few coins left in your sleeve. Why don't you and your wife sit a spell and keep an old woman company.'

Ōmono gave Michiru a tired nod. Despite her misgivings at the delay, she removed her pack and sat down with him. *Why is he wasting time here?* They bowed their thanks for the tea and Ōmono placed two copper coins on the tray. Taking a pair of sweet cakes he handed one to Michiru as he munched on the other. 'I'm afraid you are mistaken, obaa-san. My name is Ono and this is my little sister, Keiko.'

The old woman nodded to her. 'I'm sorry for my error. Please forgive me. It is a pleasure to meet you both. Please take another sweet cake. They are two for one copper.'

'Thank you, obaa-san,' he said, picking up another cake from the tray.

'Are you travelling far, Ono-san?' the old lady asked.

'Well, I'm not quite sure, yet,' he said in a disconsolate tone. 'I got tired of working in a kitchen and decided to have a go at being a porter. You know there is always work moving stuff from one place to another.'

'Hmm, yes,' she replied. 'The roads are full these days.'

Michiru turned away and bit into the sweet cake, enjoying the simple food. Her eyes scanned the street, worried that their pursuers might be hiding here waiting for them to show themselves. 'Why are we stopping? We should keep moving,' she whispered.

He bent over to tighten the ties of his leggings. 'We need information,' he hissed back. 'We will spend some time with the old lady and find out what we can.' He stood up and gave the old woman a huge smile, reaching into his sleeve to jingle some coins. 'We should have enough time to share some tea with you, obaa-san.'

CHAPTER EIGHT

It was nearly dark when the pair returned, both carrying good-sized loads. Ōmono even had a sizable wooden box slung on one end of the pole. They all gathered at the shabby little house to hear his news. The porter and his little sister put down their loads, glad finally have finished walking. Keiko brought bamboo water bottles, curious to hear what news they had. 'What took you so long?' Shuji asked as he helped Ōmono untie his bundles from the carrying pole.

'We had to wait for an old lady to finish a story. It took a while to coax the information out of her.' He unwrapped an earthenware jug from one bundle, passing it to Yatsuhiro with a brief bow. 'The ronin are ahead of us,' he informed them. 'Rather than wasting time looking for us, they moved on straight away.'

Yatsuhiro sat down, tugging the straw stopper from the jug and sniffing the contents. 'We will have to move with a lot more caution then. That is going to slow us down.' He took a swig from the jug. *I do not like the idea of enemies waiting ahead of us, but then who would? Better to know they are there than not. Can we evade them all together?* He passed the jug to Shuji.

'I would rather take longer and travel further. I do not want to get into a tangle with ronin right now. Not if we can avoid it. What else?' he asked, accepting the sake from Yatsuhiro.

Ōmono continued to unpack the bundle as he spoke. 'We went into the village along the main road,' he drew a breath with far too much enjoyment. Michiru guessed he was about to regale them with a masterpiece of storytelling.

101

'Just give us the short version, Ōmono,' Yatsuhiro said.

'Oh,' he said, deflated. 'Very well, taisho. We stopped and traded at a few of the house fronts, bought some food at the inn, if you can call it that, had something to eat and left.' With that, he clamped his mouth shut, but could not resist commenting, 'You wanted the short version.' Keiko giggled behind her sleeve.

Shuji passed Michiru the sake, surprising her a little with the informality of drinking from a jug. She accepted it anyway, taking a modest swig of the liquor, enjoying the taste rather than the after-burn.

'So apart from gorging yourself on sweet cakes,' Yatsuhiro said with mock severity, 'Did you find out anything else?'

Michiru saw the guilty look on Ōmono's face, guessing that the sweet cakes were part of an on-going joke between the two men. Yatsuhiro's mouth tilted into a lopsided grin, seeing his jibe hit the mark. They had an easy manner with each other when they were together. Not at all like samurai and ashigaru. She could not help but feel there was something more, something she was missing. *He seems to be a good captain. I wonder if he is the same with all his men.*

Looking around, she could see Keiko watching Yatsuhiro intently. She was momentarily surprised because the young woman's gaze was rarely so direct. Her wide-eyed concentration on his every move, her mouth slightly open, provoked a strange sense of irritation in Michiru. Her brow furrowed imperceptibly into the beginnings of a frown. *Why does Keiko's behaviour make me feel this way? Surely she is not falling for him.* She looked at Yatsuhiro again. *Although it would be perfectly understandable. He was a good man; strong, capable, even handsome in a way. I will have to speak with her later.*

A change in the ashigaru's tone brought her back to the moment. 'The word is...' he began, shifting his jacket uncomfortably, '... that Satake troops have besieged the castle at Harashiro.' They all seemed frozen in that moment as his words sunk in. Into that stillness Ōmono's voice echoed, 'We are now at war with the Satake.'

Michiru's hair prickled. *Why? When had he heard this? What could Kiyomori hope to gain by attacking the Arikawa? How would they reach safety now?* Her mouth was agape, her legs robbed of strength. She almost fell, ending up sitting cross-legged on the ground with Keiko supporting her by the elbow. Letting go of an explosive sigh, she had not realise she had stopped breathing. Her eyes turned to Shuji with a panicked look.

Shuji scanned their little group, his face impassive. *Ready or not.* 'We tempt fate if we remain here much longer.' He took a final swig from the sake jug and replaced the stopper with finality. 'Get everything packed up, we leave tonight after sunset.'

*   *   *

The plan was to get clear of the village before the moon came up. Once out of the vicinity of the village, they could step out on the road and make up some distance. When the moon started to get low, they would search out a spot to hole up for the day. If they could find something with a view of the road, then they could watch the comings and goings during the following day.

While the captains involved themselves with making plans, Ōmono sidled up to Michiru, a bundle in hand. A mouldy stench arrived with him. 'Here is your thief's bag,' he said. 'I managed to find it while you were busy visiting the place of washing hands.' She looked at him in surprise. 'You seemed interested in what the little maggot had to say,' Ōmono shrugged. 'This will open his mouth for you.' Becoming deadly serious, he said, 'My lady, just remember that he is a thief and a liar, and probably more besides. You cannot trust him.'

Michiru knew the ashigaru was only looking out for her, but she was curious and disgusted at the same time. *How did someone end up being such a wretched creature? Was it karma?* She wanted to find out more, so she accepted the bag. 'Thank you, Ōmono.' Knowing what the answer was likely to be, she asked, 'What is going to happen to him now?'

He felt uncomfortable to be the one to tell her. *I wish she had asked either of the captains rather than me. But it will be best for her to know the truth.* 'We will have to send him onward, my lady.' He tried to give a hurried explanation, 'We can't trust him not to blab to someone. He is just as likely to run straight to the nearest Satake samurai looking for a pay-out.'

'Of course,' she said sadly. *Am I to be the cause of yet another pointless death. In cold blood. Despite the fact that he helped us. What sort of karma am I making for myself?* She may not hold the knife, but it will be because of her, to keep her safe.

Ōmono pointed at the bag. 'Well, my lady. Let's go see what the stinkworm has to say for himself.'

* * *

Michiru knelt well out of arms reach while Ōmono retied the scruffy man's bonds, leaving the gag until last. The ashigaru was right about the smell, his aroma had not improved. They had caught his scent before they even saw him. The thief drummed his legs on the ground, clapping his tied hands as they approached.

'My bag!' he had gasped with glee, one clawed hand reaching towards her. Michiru dropped the bundle in his lap. She watched in fascination as he fumbled through the contents before producing a small grubby bamboo container with a sibilant 'Ah ha.' His grimy face was ecstatic.

He gripped the pot in the crease behind his knee and removed the cap. A sharp odour, unlike anything she had ever smelled before, immediately assaulted Michiru. There was a faint fishiness to it but something else lay over it like a steaming cloud of death. Ōmono retched, stumbling further away through the trees. She dared not breathe through her nose and held her sleeve up in front of her mouth.

'Ah,' he said, dipping a finger into the pot and smearing the contents on his upper lip. Blinking rapidly he rolled his eyes and sighed. 'At last.'

'Ugh.' It was such a thick cloying smell that she could taste it. Leaning over to spit out the aroma on her tongue, she asked in horror, 'What is that?' Resisting the urge to run as far away from the stench as possible, she remained stoically seated, trying to retain some dignity.

'This stops me smelling.'

'What?' Ōmono spat, leaning on a nearby tree. 'That is the most disgusting stench I have ever come across. You smell worse now,' holding his sleeve over his face as a mask.

'Not you not smelling me, stupid. Me not smelling anything,' he explained slowly. 'Derh.' To Michiru he added, 'Your boy here is none too bright, miss.'

'Why do you do that?' asked Michiru

He placed the lid back on the tiny pot and put it back in his bag. He looked at her, his head cocked to one side. Wrinkling his mouth from side to side, he seemed to come to a decision. He leaned back against the tree. 'My problem is I smell everything,' he explained. 'Birds, dogs, wet straw, other people.' He blew out a breath of disgust. 'People are the worst. I can tell what they have had to eat. I can tell all sorts of things by the smell that comes off them,' he chuckled. 'Embarrassing for me and for them. Can you imagine how bad a town is?'

Michiru shook her head, still suspicious and mindful of Ōmono's warning. 'Did you grow up like that?'

His eyes dropped to the bag, absently poking around through the contents. 'No. I was just a normal kid. A few years ago, I got smacked in the head by a pickpocket with a club. Hard club. Knocked me out for a couple of days.' Michiru passed him one of the packets of food they brought back. 'Since then, everything I smell is real strong.' He munched into the rice ball, picking out the dried fish and pickled vegetables rolled up in it.

A sceptical 'Hmph,' came from Ōmono. 'Sounds like a tall story to me,' he said with undisguised disbelief.

'But why – that?' she said pointing to the container of ointment, unable to watch him putting his filthy fingers on the food and into his mouth. If that was how he normally ate she was amazed he had not already died from some kind of food poisoning.

'I pinched it from some peddler selling medicines. I pinched a whole heap of stuff,' he said, chewing with his mouth open. 'I was checking them out when I found that,' he said gesturing to the bag. 'When I sniffed it, all the other smells were gone. I couldn't smell anything.'

'Have you always lived like this? By stealing?'

Looking down, concentrating on the food left in his hand, he said sheepishly, 'No. I used to live in town, but it was too much. Too much for me. Too much for everyone.' He met her eyes and squinted. 'I used to work in a bath house,' he chuckled, on the verge of tears. 'How's that for a joke. Around stinky people all the time. I couldn't stand it. Couldn't even stand my own mother. I knew she was sick before she did. I smelled that too.' He stopped, shovelling the last morsels into his mouth. 'It was too much so I left,' he finished, chewing noisily, just to be offensive.

Trying to draw the story out of him, Michiru kept on, 'Is that when you started stealing?'

He looked at her angrily now, 'No. I went into the hills, to get away from people smells. Sat in an old shrine for a week. But I needed food. At first, I stole enough and went back up into the hills. But then,' he shrugged, 'Why go back if I can hide?'

'Because that stench would give you away,' interjected Ōmono, showing little sympathy for the man.

Moisture filled Michiru's eyes, threatening to spill over as she contemplated his fate. It may have been naive, but she saw the ultimate injustice of his situation. Through someone else's actions his life was ruined, changed beyond recognition. Nothing could ever be done to put it right. *What he is now is not his fault. To kill this man now might seem a mercy, considering his plight. It may have been his karma, but what would her karma be if she allowed Shuji to kill him? Maybe a kuzushi, a medicine master, might be able to help him, or know of someone who can.* She looked at Ōmono. 'We must take him with us,' she declared.

Ōmono sucked in his breath, 'Ooo, I don't think that wise, my lady. Don't fall for his lies. He would tell you anything to get your sympathy. It's just a story.'

'Nah. You should listen to her,' the thief told Ōmono, 'You should take me with you.'

'Quiet, you, or I'll slap you into next week.'

'Would you do that? In front of the young lady? Oh, shame on you.'

Michiru stood between them, 'Quiet, please, or Ōmono will put your gag back on. And you,' she pointed at Ōmono, 'control yourself. Keep your noise down, remember?'

Shuji arrived, asking, 'What is going on here?'

'We have to take this man with us,' she answered, 'Ōmono has some objections.'

'As do I, my lady.' Shuji felt that this was something they did not have the luxury of debating. 'Would you like to explain your reasoning?'

'Captain,' she said with care, remembering his earlier lessons about councillors. 'I have thought this through carefully.' She knew she was treading a fine line. Shuji could bundle her up, delivering her bound and gagged just as easily as her enemies would have. Would he allow her to assert what little authority she had? 'This man is a tragic figure. I mean to help him. We will take him with us, bound and gagged if necessary, and once we reach safety we will give him food and coin and send him someplace where he can get some help.'

'You realise the risk you are taking with all our lives, but more importantly, your own?' he asked. *This is no time to get soft heart-ed.* He was angry with himself that this had come up at all. *We could have just slit his throat as we left. It would be a sound tactical decision.* 'My lady, we are in enemy territory.'

'But he is not my enemy,' she said with conviction. 'He helped us.'

'He helped us to save his own neck. We cannot trust him, my lady.'

'The alternative is unthinkable.' Determined to hold her ground, she squared up to Shuji. 'I have decided, Shuji-san. He will come with us.'

There was nothing else for it. She had given him an order. 'Yes, hime-sama,' he bowed. He was proud of the way she was willing to stick to her convictions, wishing she had not chosen this matter to assert herself.. He clenched his jaw. *She will have to exercise authority in her own house, and over a whole domain, in her husband's absence.* He knew that he had just seen his young student's first steps as a true princess. 'As you command.' He bowed.

She turned to the thief. 'What is your name, please?'

He blinked twice, momentarily taken aback. *It has been so long since anybody spoke my name.* He stared hard at her for a moment. 'Haru.'

'Haru. In return for your help, I will give you a chance,' she said with deep solemnity. 'You heard what I said to my Captain?' He nodded slowly. 'Do you understand what it means? It means that until we reach safety, this man here will have my permission to kill you, should you endanger us in any way. Is that clear?' He looked at Ōmono, whose face slowly twisted into an evil grin. Haru swallowed hard and nodded his head again. 'Now, as I have saved your life,' she looked meaningfully at Ōmono, then back at Haru, 'all I ask is that you do the right thing by me and co-operate. You will remain tied up, because I still cannot trust you completely. But you will wash.' He opened his mouth to object but she interrupted him before he could say anything. 'You will wash twice, and you will clean yourself up. You will wear clean clothes and remain quiet. Is that clear?'

Haru squirmed, clearly uncomfortable at the thought of bathing. But Michiru did not let up. She kept her eyes fixed on his, eyebrows raised, waiting for his response. Varied expressions flicked across his face, his mouth opening more than once, but closing again upon changing his mind. After a few moments his shoulders slumped, 'Yes.' He quickly added, 'My lady,' with a wary eye on Ōmono, who had moved towards him menacingly at the omission of the basic courtesy.

Shuji motioned to Ōmono, 'Untie him from the tree and bring him to the waterfall. But fix a line around his waist. I want to hang on to him while he bathes,' he said with apparent distaste at the thought. 'Haru and I will have a little talk.'

Michiru turned and headed back towards the pond, its bank overgrown with grass and reeds. Shuji walked silently by her side, giving her time to choose her words. She felt relieved for some reason. Lighter. 'You think I made a mistake keeping him alive, don't you sensei.'

'It does not matter what I think, Michiru. I gave you my advice. The decision was yours.' He turned to look at her. 'As will be the responsibility. I hope you realise that. But the decision has been made. Nothing can alter that now.' He clasped his hands behind his back. 'Do not worry about things that cannot be changed.' He stopped where the rough path forked off to the waterfall. 'I must say, I do not understand why you think you can help him.'

Michiru took a deep breath, savouring the sweet smell of the cedar trees. *Do I really know myself? Maybe if I try to explain it to him, I will understand it better.* 'You said yourself that we were lucky to have made it this far. I felt that it would be ... ungrateful... to repay that luck with an injustice. Wherever luck comes from, the gods, Buddha or my ancestors ... I don't know. What I do know is the idea of killing that pitiful man felt wrong. It just seemed like ... good karma to help him. For us to help him.'

'Well, I hope you are right, Michiru.'

'So do I, sensei,' she said, bowing slightly and continuing on to the house.

*　　*　　*

Seeing Yatsuhiro and Ōmono seated on a log outside the little building, sorting through packs and bundles, she walked over and knelt down in front of them. 'There is something that has been troubling me, Yatsuhiro-san.'

'How can I help, my lady?' he asked, welcoming the opportunity to learn more about what was going on inside her head. More than anything, he needed to know if she was up to the next stage of the journey. The possibility of a confrontation with the ronin was in the forefront of his mind. *If she is going to fall to pieces, I need to know.*

Fiddling with the knots on one of the bundles, Michiru asked, 'When I left home, I gave up my family. So, I am not Katsura anymore. However, I am not Arikawa until after my marriage. What am I now?'

He was startled by the question. It was not something that he had ever thought about, let alone heard of. After considering it for a moment, he replied, 'You are my lord's betrothed. It is not important which clan you come from, my duty is to protect you.' He gave her a confident smile, feeling he had dodged that one well.

'And I thank you, but that did not answer my question,' she pointed out with a shrewd grin. She looked to Ōmono, who gaped at her in confusion, before he turned to stare helplessly at Yatsuhiro.

Silently struggling through the logic, Yatsuhiro failed to find a satisfactory answer. 'I will be truthful, my lady, I do not know. I imagine that, legally, you would still be Katsura, because that is what you were born. But your duty now is to the Arikawa.' He shook his head as the arguments tumbled through his mind. The more he thought about it the less sure he was. 'It could be said that you belong to neither, and yet owe obligations to both.'

Ōmono laughed. They both looked at him in astonishment.

Sure that the impudent ashigaru had something interesting to add, Yatsuhiro asked, 'What is it?'

'It is moments like these I'm glad I'm just a peasant,' he chuckled. 'Sorry, I meant no offence, but my life is much simpler.'

Michiru sighed. 'I imagine that is part of the price of being samurai. Thank you anyway, Yatsuhiro-san.' *There is probably no real answer to my question. If I walked away from this marriage Kosei may not take me back, but maybe then, I could do as I please. I would be without a family, without obligation but also without protection. It seems that I will never be as free as I am now. I would be all alone.* She gave the bemused captain and his grinning ashigaru a nod and left them to get her gear from inside the little house.

Yatsuhiro shook his head as he watched Michiru enter the ramshackle building. 'Did you understand any of that?'

Ōmono smiled sagely. 'Only another woman understands a woman's mind.'

Yatsuhiro turned his head slowly to look at the silently chuckling ashigaru. 'Remind me again why I brought you along.'

'Because I live to serve you, my lord,' he said, smiling widely.

*　*　*

Entering the gloomy interior of the hut, Michiru found Keiko packing a final few oddments into a bamboo basket. She was dressed in the same tough peasant wear of loose jacket, tight fitting pants and straw sandals. Two wide straw hats and an extra backpack leant up against the wall.

'I see we are all packed up and ready to leave.'

'Yes, my lady,' she said in a quiet voice. Michiru looked closer and noticed the young woman's downcast eyes and quivering chin.

'Keiko-chan,' she said as she knelt down next to her. 'Whatever is the matter?'

'I ... I am scared, my lady,' she said reluctantly.

'It is alright to be afraid,' she said, placing a hand on her arm. 'We are caught up in something frightening. I am scared, too.' Having suffered from her own fears, she sympathised with what Keiko was going through. However, for Michiru, the new lightness in her spirit had all but banished that nervousness. 'You should not worry too much. We have good men looking after us.' Reminded of her earlier observations, Michiru broached the subject that had given rise to her uncomfortable irritation. She sat up, folding her hands in her lap, nervous at exposing the young woman's feelings. 'I noticed you watching Yatsuhiro quite intently.'

'You must be mistaken, my lady. I would never...'

'It is alright,' she said reassuringly. 'It is quite natural. He is a strong, handsome man, though, is he not? And a captain, no less.'

'Yes. Yes he is,' she replied, smiling thinly, almost sadly. She shook her head. 'He is much too important a samurai to ever notice me.' Keiko's shoulders tensed. 'But you, my lady, he watches you all the time.'

Michiru gasped. 'It is his duty.'

'No, my lady, I think it is more than duty.'

'But I am to be married.' she protested. 'It could never be.' *Can it be true? Do I want it to be true?* She knew with a heart-wrenching certainty that such a thing could only bring pain and heartache.

'Of course, my lady. You are correct.' Keiko looked up at her, but because they were alone and Michiru was the closest thing she had to a friend, she risked speaking her mind. 'But marriage is not about love. Love grows for its own reasons.' She stopped, suddenly fearful of overstepping her bounds.

Michiru was intrigued and wanted to hear more. Not only because this was the first time that Keiko had opened up to her. She desperately wanted to talk about the feelings she had been experiencing ever since Yatsuhiro had given her that flower. She did not know if it was love. She had no experience of such things. 'Go on, Keiko-chan.'

'Do you love him?'

There it is. The question she feared even to ask herself. Michiru bit her lip, 'I do not know. How do I tell?'

Keiko smiled, looking down at her hands. 'I'm afraid I can't help you, my lady. I think that if you both feel love for each other it would be a tragedy not to let him know. Nobody can know what the future holds, Hime-sama.' Nervous at having spoken so candidly, a short laugh escaped her and she lowered her eyes. 'I am sorry, my lady. Please excuse my silly talk of love. It is nothing.'

They sat silent for a while before Michiru answered. 'Nothing can happen before we arrive in Nagase. And then I will be married.' Her voice sounded hollow in her own ears. *Will I ever know love? Will I love Sojiro? If Yatsuhiro loves me, what will he do after the wedding?* She shook her head, took Keiko's hands in her own, and changed the subject. 'We have other things to worry about right now. The road ahead will be very dangerous. Nagase is on the other side of the border and we are at war now. We may have to fight our way through. Can you use a sword?'

'No, my lady.' Her head bowed in remorse. 'I apologise for my inadequacy.'

'But you did kill a man who had his sword at my throat, with one of these.' She pulled the short sword from her sash and offered it to her. 'Keiko-san. You saved my life. I thank you. In return, I give you the right to carry this blade at all times, or until you decide to put it aside. I will get Shuji to show you how to use it.'

The astonished Keiko dropped down into a deep bow, 'Oh thank you, my lady! I don't deserve such an honour! Thank you, Michiru-hime!

'Also, I promise that I will supply you with a dowry when you marry, and your children will be samurai.' She smiled as Keiko sat up, took the short sword and pushed the scabbard through her sash.

'I swear I will use this blade to protect you.' she said, touching the hilt.

'You must also protect yourself, Keiko-san. Promise me that. I want you to live. I need a friend. Can you promise me? Will you be my friend?'

'I promise, Michiru-hime.' She bowed deeply again. 'I would be honoured to call you my friend.'

'Well, then,' Michiru said as she stood. 'Let us make an appearance.'

CHAPTER NINE

They pushed on down the road away from the village for most of the night. The soft glow of the partial moon highlighted the landscape. The road showed as a pale ribbon leading into the dark, leaving everything else in ink black shadow. A chorus of frogs and the rustling breeze through the trees covered the sound of their passing. Thick scrub prevented them from leaving the road for most of the way, but Yatsuhiro and Ōmono travelled well ahead of the rest, ensuring they did not have any unexpected encounters. Shuji prodded the freshly washed and gagged Haru ahead of him, hands bound behind his back and a harness of straw rope around his torso. Michiru could still smell his musty odour but it was nowhere near as eye watering as it had been.

As the moon lowered in the sky, Ōmono came trotting back down the road. They all tensed involuntarily, huddling closer together, not knowing if his appearance meant danger or not. But the ashigaru's grin flashed in the growing dark, alleviating their fears. 'Yatsuhiro-san said he has found a good spot for us to stop,' whispered the little man. 'He is waiting around the next bend.' When they reached him, he signalled them off the road and up the slope. He had found a rocky outcrop that presented a good view of the road and plenty of cover. Gratefully, they curled up on the opposite side of the rocks. Shuji volunteered to take the first watch while the rest tried to get some sleep.

He woke Michiru once the sun was up to take her turn as sentry. Rumpled but rested, she set herself up on a log, one foot propped on a rock, eating an apple in the dappled sunlight as she gazed out along the valley. She pushed her jacket off her shoulders and down around her waist, tying her hair back with a loose cord. The gentle breeze was warm and comforting. She closed her eyes and sighed. Feeling the touch of the Sun Goddess across her skin, she offered a silent prayer of thanks. She kept watch on the road below all morning. A column of Satake soldiers filed down the road around midmorning. She estimated around a hundred, with ten mounted samurai leading them. Since then, only groups of porters had followed at irregular intervals, escorted by relaxed ashigaru.

Around noon, a rumpled Ōmono came and stood next to her, stretching his arms over his head with a groan. 'Aarrghh!' He sniffed, scratching his side. 'Good day, my lady.'

'Good day, Ōmono.'

'Has there been much movement below?' he asked, watching a pair of porters labour along with a large box slung on a pole, carried between them. He took a long drink from a water bottle and ambled over to where Haru was tied to a tree.

'A hundred troops earlier this morning. Just porters, now.' She finished off her apple in silence.

After giving the bound thief one of the packages of rice and some water, he re-tied his bonds and joined her at the log. He sat down with a sigh and enjoyed the sun's warmth for a moment. Ōmono knew he should take this opportunity to talk with her. *Now was as good a time as any.* He stared at his hands. 'Can I speak plainly with you, my lady?' he asked.

'Of course, Ōmono. What is it?' she said, intrigued by his seriousness.

'Shuji-san asked me to teach you what I could to help you stay alive and in one piece.'

'He told me he would. Do you mind?' she asked him, unsure of where she stood with the ashigaru since her decision about Haru.

He gave her a crooked smile, 'I suppose I can help you out.'

She laughed at his off-handed manner. 'You are not like other peasants, Ōmono.'

He chuckled, 'Oh I've been many different things, not all of which I'm proud of.' He rummaged around in his satchel and retrieved a small packet. As he unwrapped it, Michiru caught the wonderful scent of honey. Images of sunny days at home fluttered through her mind as the smell triggered memories of her childhood summers. 'I used to sell these, in one of my other lives,' he revealed. They shared the delicious sweet, savouring every morsel. 'Honey is truly a gift from the goddess,' he acknowledged with satisfaction.

'What do you mean?'

'Well, if you think about it,' Ōmono explained, 'the Goddess shines her light on the plants and flowers, and they grow. Then the bees come along, they must be some kind of kami, and they collect the essence of the Goddess' light to take back to the hive. The hive must be magic too. In the hive that essence is made into honey.' He held his hands out wide, believing his point proven. She smiled and bowed to his logic.

He picked up a water bottle and continued his tale. 'After growing up on a farm, I drifted around for a while and saw a bit of the world. I did all sorts of work. Anything to make some coin. One day, two patrols clashed in a village where I was staying and I ended up an ashigaru for one of them, the Arikawa.' He folded up the wrapping and put it away in his ubiquitous satchel. 'Did you spend much time with the peasants at home, my lady?' he asked out of curiosity.

'People would wave to me and call out when I went for a ride,' she replied. 'Sometimes I would stop and talk to them,' she added, feeling a little defensive. She realised that she had never thought much about them, spending most of her time focussed on herself. 'I suppose it was mainly the servants at the house that I spent time with.' Michiru admitted. 'We used to travel a lot, when I was young. But since my mother died I spent most of my time at the mansion in Omegura.'

'You are lucky. You have a good home. If the rest of your clan's samurai are anything like Shuji-san, it would be a good family to serve. He's a true captain.'

'Yes,' she said. *Both Kosei and Father said the same thing.* 'What about Yatsuhiro?' she asked. 'What is he like to serve under?'

'He's sensible, fair and ... honest,' Ōmono said. 'Some samurai can be ... difficult.' He leant over to confide in her. 'I've served under some samurai who I had to run away from.'

'What? What about loyalty?

'Oh, that kind of loyalty would have got me killed,' Ōmono responded without remorse. 'Make no mistake, my lady, the last man I served was a swine, samurai or not. It was just as likely he would have killed me himself.' He looked at his hands and took a deep breath.

He tried to explain, 'A peasant's final option when things are bad is to run away. To go somewhere else. If you leave the decision too late, you die. Whether it comes from a blade or slow starvation, wild animals or sickness, you should have been somewhere else.' For Ōmono, this was an obvious truth. It had been proven to him too many times to question it. 'Of course you could ignore all that but one day you will find yourself about to die and you will realise you should have been somewhere else, and you missed all the signs.'

The logic was inescapable. Michiru found the man's honesty discomforting. *My world has been so different to his, yet here we are together, our fates intertwined. If he had not come to show us a way out, I would more than likely be dead or captured.* If they had not risked going over the ridge. If he had not distracted the ronin. If they had not found Haru and thus the little house by the waterfall. *So many possibilities.* Michiru felt her world spin a little, and she realised she was standing somewhere very different to where she had started from.

'Real loyalty,' he added definitively, 'is staying. Staying when you know you should run. And most of the time, you won't know until the last moment if someone is truly loyal.' They shared a sober silence for a moment before Ōmono declared, 'I should become a priest.' At which they both chuckled. After offering Michiru some water, and drinking some himself, he became more serious. *I suppose I had better get on with it.* 'Things are going to get a lot more dangerous, my lady. We will likely be facing soldiers at some point. And samurai,' he added, trying to think of how he was not going to frighten her too much.

'You have spent time in the dojo, and in the training yard, yes?'

'Yes. Shuji saw to that.'

'Well it's nothing like that,' he said. 'As you found out fighting off those ronin.'

Now that she had fought against real enemies, men trying to capture or kill her, the prospect of more combat weighed on her mind. She remembered the surging panic of trying to kill your enemy before he kills you, when you don't know if all your strength will be enough. Michiru felt unsure if she could go through that again.

'In training, you have time and space. You have a good idea of what's going to happen and you can start again if things go wrong. You know no one is trying to kill you.' He took a deep breath. 'Your fight against the ronin was so dangerous because it was in a small space and you couldn't get away from them. Most of the time, it is a bad idea to put yourself in a tight spot. You should try to have as much space around you as possible. It gives you room to avoid the enemy, even to run away if necessary. Don't put your back to a wall, otherwise they can pin you to the wall and ...' he finished with a thumb gesture across his throat.

He saw no point in sweetening the truth. *It is better for her to realise from the start. The risk of talking openly with samurai depends on how touchy they are. At least she is willing to listen.* 'You will be outclassed, my lady, in any combat we end up in with samurai.'

'Thank you for your confidence, Ōmono,' she said without humour.

'I said I was going to speak plainly, my lady. Let's be honest. You are not ready for a career as a warrior. You must keep them at a distance,' he advised her with a stabbing gesture. 'Don't make fancy moves. Stick to quick thrusts if you can. Make your enemies dodge. Go for the face, the chest and the stomach. While he is avoiding your attacks, he is not attacking you. But beware of feints.' He was talking faster now, 'if he gets too close, you have to switch to a knife and stab him. Stab him fast and stab him again and again. Stab him in the chest. Stab him in the stomach. In the side. If you get hit, stab him back. Stab him until he is dead, then stab him again to make sure.'

He paused, seeing the expression of horror on her beautiful young face, realising that he was overwhelming the young woman. He took a deep breath. *Maybe I got carried away.* Ōmono tried to think of something he could tell her that might lift her spirits. He forced a smile, focussing on the ground. 'You should know, Shigemori-san would be proud that you carry his blade.'

'Did you know him well?'

'Yes, I did, my lady,' he said with a touch of sadness in his voice. 'He was a good man, but young and inexperienced. His father is one of the clan councillors, so a lot of expectations there.' He grinned as he started to share details of the young samurai's life. 'His mother was desperate to find him a bride, so he always got nervous about going home. He knew his mother would have a selection of girls for him to meet, discreetly of course.' Ōmono smiled, staring at his hands. 'He already has a son, with a girl who used to work in the Household. He was always frightened his mother would find out,' he laughed. 'For her he tried to make out that he gambled or wasted his money, but he paid for everything for the mother and his son. He had a younger brother and two sisters, he taught them to catch crickets.' Ōmono stopped. He felt a rising sadness threaten to choke him. He exhaled heavily, dispersing the emotions that filled his chest with pain. After a deep breath, he mumbled, 'I should get back to the point, my lady.'

'Combat is dangerous. People die, sometimes at the moment of victory. Please be careful.' He was on his knees now, bowing low. *I want her to survive, to have many babies and live a long and healthy life. Otherwise, I will end up on the road again. She is the future of the Arikawa and everything depends on her safety.* 'Please forgive my rudeness.'

She smiled at his sincerity, thinking that she would like a hundred of him in her service. *How can I reward him for everything he has done? What could I possibly give this man? I will have to consider that carefully once we get to Nagase.* 'Thank you for your concern, Ōmono-san. We could not have made it this far without you,' she bowed in return.

Shuji walked up, a water bottle in his hand. He looked at her with a critical eye. The rest seemed to have soothed many of Michiru's hurts, as far as he could tell. He was still reluctant to push too hard though. *If we are cautious there would be much less chance of an ambush. I know the ronin are out there, somewhere, but how many of them is the big question.* He took a long drink, tossing the empty bottle to Ōmono. 'How are we all feeling after our little walk, hmm?' he said in mock cheerfulness, rubbing his hands together. 'I hope we are ready for some more tonight.'

Michiru's face fell. Her pain remained. Her legs, her back, everything was still sore from the unaccustomed exertions of the last few days. Her face still had a lump from the ronin's blows and, despite washing under the little waterfall, she felt dirty. Fear of what lay ahead was a tight knot in the pit of her stomach. She frowned, angry with herself. *Enough whining! You are your father's daughter. You must be strong. You are samurai.* With a deep breath, she summoned her strength. *You must face the world and whatever it brings. You must not fear death, only dishonour.* 'I think I will ride this time,' Michiru stated imperiously.

'You need a horse before you can ride, my lady.'

'I am surprised you have not yet found one for me, Shuji-san.' She shook her head with mock sadness. Then she brightened up as if with a sudden thought. 'I could always ride on the back of a faithful retainer.' Rising to her feet and pulling the jacket back on over her shoulders. 'How about you, Shuji-san?' Michiru asked.

He bowed, 'I'm afraid I would have to slit my belly, first, my lady.'

*   *   *

They stood, packed and ready to go, waiting for the light to fade. Michiru thought they all looked much better prepared for what might lay ahead. They were fed and rested, and had weapons and supplies. Even Haru seemed calm, although he was constantly screwing up his face, undoubtedly from the smells assailing his senses. She felt their chances were much better than they had been a few days ago.

Shuji pointed to Izuna-yama, the hulking mountain that divided Satake lands from the southern part of Arikawa territory. 'After speaking with Haru, I think it would be best if we cross the border over that eastern spur.' He ran his finger from the peak eastward halfway down the slope. 'There. Our chances of meeting up with a patrol are small. It is unlikely that there are any posts up there.'

Ōmono feigned relief, 'Oh good. I was beginning to feel that we hadn't done enough climbing. Thank you, oh Merciful Buddha.'

Shuji ignored the quip. 'We can slip over the river, and up over the mountain's shoulder. We should have a good moon for it,' praying for Tsukiyomi to make it so.

'We should find a spot close to the river crossing before day break, if we can,' suggested Yatsuhiro.

The terrain opened up from here, as the floor of the valley widened out. They moved parallel to the road where possible, staying in cover or moving through dead ground when they could find it. Even though it meant their progress was much slower, they stopped often to scan ahead from cover. Shuji decided that it would be better to be careful and conserve their energy. *We may have to sprint for the border. Better to be fresh as possible for such an eventuality.*

By the time dawn grew near, they were approaching the river at the base of the spur. Michiru tried to make out details of the river in the gloom but it was cut too deep into the valley floor and the moonlight was almost gone. All she could be sure of was that the water was splashing around boulders and rocks. That she could hear that clearly. The bank was steep here and smelled of wet dirt and vegetation. She could not see far along the bank in either direction. After a few pokes at the crumbling lip of the bank with the butt of her naginata, she turned to Shuji. 'What now, sensei?'

'We will scout around for a crossing when it is lighter,' Shuji replied. 'For now, let's go back a bit and find somewhere to sleep.' They turned around and trudged back towards the tree line. Michiru was glad that they would be stopping soon. Weariness dragged at her feet. The sound of Keiko's scuffling walk betrayed how tired she was as well. Sleep would do them all some good.

As they approached the tree line, a deep voice spoke from the gloom of the woods. 'Well, I am glad I have finally managed to catch up with you, my lady.' A line of dark figures emerged from the trees, spreading out on each side.

The sound of swords sliding from their scabbards sent a chill up Michiru's spine. A hint of pre-dawn light flashed on the moving blades. Swallowing hard, she glanced at her two samurai. There were a dozen or more ronin spread out in an arc in front of them. A primal panic rose up in her belly, her body already moving backwards.

She tried to calm her thundering heartbeat. *One long, deep breath and exhale.* Keiko stood at her right side, dropping her load and drawing the short sword Michiru had given her. Ōmono on her left, holding the bound Haru in front of him, spear at the ready. She heard Haru struggling, muffled protests coming from behind his gag until Ōmono quietened him with a jerk of his bindings. Michiru felt her companion's closeness and pulled herself back from the edge of panic. She could not run and abandon them to fate. She gripped the naginata with both hands, twisting the shaft for a better grip. *One long, deep breath, and exhale*

Shuji stepped forward, squinting to see better in the growing light. 'Who are you?'

'That hardly matters, old man.' A tall ronin, dressed in scraps of armour stepped forward. Even though most of his face was shadowed, the stubble on his face picked up the light, putting his scruffy appearance at odds with his cultured voice. 'We are going to take the girl with us. Now, you can either step aside,' he shrugged, 'or I will cut you down.'

A few of the ronin snickered. A lean ronin, a dirty bandage across one eye, shouted, spittle flying from his lips, 'We're going to get you this time, girl!' pointing at Michiru with his sword. 'You won't be getting away from me again!'

Michiru's stomach churned as she recognised the man whose eye she put out at the ruined house. She widened her eyes as much as she could to improve her vision, glad that she was more prepared this time. Her head lowered as she took a fighting stance, looking out at the ronin from under her lowered brow. *If he comes any-where near me he will lose more than an eye.* She twisted her feet into the dirt, to get a firmer footing.

'Enough.' The leader turned and pointed his sword at the one-eyed ronin. 'You do nothing until I say so.' The scrawny man flinched back nervously.

'I am Yoshioka Shuji, Captain of the Katsura Clan.' Drawing his sword with deliberate calm, he took up the classic Seigan stance, sword gripped in both hands, its tip at eye level. 'Just walk away. None of you have to die today.' This was a fight he would rather not have and he would rather not gamble with Michiru's life. *But by the gods I will slaughter them if they come within my reach.*

Yatsuhiro stepped up beside Shuji, drawing both of his swords, 'I am Tamuro Yatsuhiro, Captain of the Arikawa Clan. You should listen to him. This won't be as easy as you think.' He was counting on their greater numbers being a hindrance and them getting in each other's way. *Now is as good a time as any.*

The ronin shifted nervously. 'I don't like this, Sanzo,' muttered one.

The leader slashed his sword, 'Silence!' They all stilled. 'There's only five of them. We get the girl and then we get paid. Isn't that simple enough for you?'

A stocky ronin, his hair bound up like a tea whisk, mumbled 'I'm still not so sure I trust Kiyomori to pay us.'

'I said shut up!'

An idea exploded into Michiru's mind. With a desperate hope opening up before her, she stepped forward. 'If you capture me and surrender me for the money, what then? Do you think that silver will change your life?

You will still be ronin,' she gambled, sensing an opportunity. At least it would be an opportunity if she was right, and if they listened.

'That's enough from you I think, young miss,' the leader, Sanzo, said condescendingly.

'No, you be silent!' she shot back, pointing her naginata at him. A murmur and few chuckles rippled through the group of ronin. With as much bravado as she could muster, she said in her deepest voice, 'I have already killed two of you, and taken this one's eye.' She swung the tip of her naginata to aim at the one-eyed ronin, who stood trembling with barely suppressed rage. She felt light headed, suppressing the urge to turn and run.

'What are you doing?' Shuji hissed out of the side of his mouth at Michiru.

The tall ronin's face darkened as he made to advance on her. Yatsuhiro angled to block his way, sword levelled at his chest, 'How about we let her speak, hmm?' he said with a barely contained threat. He decided this one must die first. But he wanted to hear what she was going to say, so he held back the blow that would end the ronin's life.

Seizing her chance she let her idea unfold. 'You men are ronin. No home. No honour. No place in the realm.' She stared directly at each man in turn. 'If you get your money, what will it change for you?' she asked, hoping she was right. 'Maybe you can drink yourself senseless for a few weeks, waste it all in the brothels.' Some of the ronin shifted uncomfortably, confirming her suspicions.

'I will make you a counter offer.' She paused, looking from side to side. 'Serve me. Regain your honour and a place in a clan.' The ronin muttered amongst themselves. This was a rare opportunity for a ronin. Redemption. To be offered another chance.

Shuji turned to her, 'My lady, if I might have a word.'

'Not now, Shuji-san.'

'Not all of us want to serve, you know.' The ronin leader pointed out. 'Why should we want to be at your beck and call? To throw our lives down for you?' A few of the men voiced their support for his view, but the rest seemed more thoughtful. 'I would rather stay my own man.'

'How is that working out for you?' interjected Yatsuhiro, with a smile. Some of the ronin nodded, one snickered. 'Listen. The Arikawa are at war with the Satake now. We could use good men. You know what is expected, and how to fight. Join us. Swear loyalty to Michiru-hime and you will be samurai again.'

Looking at their faces one by one, he urged, 'Think about what you have seen her go through. The fight in the backstreets of Kyozuka, ten dead. The fight near the mill, two more, by herself! She has come all this way through enemy territory. Is this not a mistress you can serve?'

Michiru looked up at Yatsuhiro, locking eyes with him for a moment. Her breath caught in her throat and she blushed at his words. He twitched his eyes towards the ronin. She pulled her thoughts back to the present, realising that he had guessed what she was doing. With shoulders back, she took a deep breath and turned to them. 'What do you say?'

As the daylight grew, the ronin weighed up their options. First one and then another came forward, until most of them stood in front of her. They were grimy and tattered but they were healthy and skilled. Michiru hoped that they would take her seriously. She needed these men loyal to her if she was going to make it to her new home in one piece.

'You're not going to bow to her are you?! screamed the one-eyed ronin. 'You arsekissers! He shook, his face contorted with hate. Turning to Sanzo and dancing on the spot with fury, he shrieked, 'You said we were going to make her pay! Now you're going to let her go?!

Sanzo looked at the man with undisguised contempt, 'Get a hold of yourself, you fool.'

The frantic ronin spun on them, snarling through his teeth. 'Where's the gold! Hand it over!'

Shuji and Yatsuhiro exchanged glances. If they found out they had Michiru's koshukin on them they would tear into them like wolves. Even a handful of coins could last a ronin for a year. With this much gold it would be the last man standing who claimed the treasure. Considering the ronin's edge in numbers both samurai would die before they could defeat the ronin.

'I know there's a treasure! Hand it over!' he looked at the grimacing leader with undisguised malice. 'Ha ha. You thought none of us knew, but I knew, I heard. I want my share and I want revenge for my eye.' He pointed his sword at Michiru, fixing her with a glare from his one good eye.

'You really are thick aren't you,' snarled Sanzo. He gestured at Shuji, 'This man is a clever old badger, he doesn't have the gold. Otherwise I would never walk away, you idiot.' He looked at Shuji's passive expression, waving a finger at him. 'No. He's hidden it somewhere, I think he stashed it at the inn somewhere. Somewhere we will never find it.'

The crazed ronin snapped. 'Nyaahh!!' He leapt towards Michiru, howling in fury.

Yatsuhiro's sword whistled as he took one pace forward and cut the ronin horizontally, across the waist. He fell screaming, a great gash through his torso leaking blood onto the ground, his legs unresponsive. He made one last convulsion of rage and was still, his thin lips pulled back from yellowed teeth in a final snarl.

The remaining uncommitted ronin stepped back, on guard and ready. Michiru stretched a hand out towards them. 'Wait! It is alright,' she said to reassure them. 'Wait a moment.' They glanced at each other and lowered their weapons. Despite the fact that these men had been hunting her, she thought it a bad idea that they should walk away with nothing. They may decide to betray them to the Satake, or worse, follow them and slit their throats in their sleep. She did not dare reveal that she was carrying gold, especially not this gold. 'If you go to my brother, Lord Katsura in Omegura, and tell him you helped me, he will pay you,' she offered.

'How can we prove it?' asked one of the ronin.

The leader's eyes narrowed, suspicion now part of his nature as a ronin. 'He may not believe us. He might decide to have us tortured and executed instead. That is something I would like to avoid.' He knew that without some sort of proof they would just as likely slam the door in his face. Most ronin discover sooner rather than later, that samurai don't like parting with money, especially to those they despised. Collecting from Kiyomori was always going to be the riskiest part of this job.

Michiru saw the crux of their problem. She wracked her brain trying to think of some token she could give them. Something that could not have been stolen. Some sort of proof. Her mouth shifted into a grin once the answer occurred to her. She handed Keiko her naginata and approached the ronin leader. 'Sanzo, would you hand me the scabbard of your sword, please?'

He blinked and cocked one eyebrow. Seeing no reason not to, the ronin obligingly handed her the scabbard. Everyone was curious to see what she was up to, not just the ronin.

She untied the sageo, the multifunctional cord wrapped around the scabbard. She re-tied it in the practical kakucho pattern, but she made a deliberate mistake. It was the same mistake that she had made the first time Kosei let her tie his. Some of the samurai watching nodded, realising what she was doing. 'Show this to my brother,' she told him as she handed back the scabbard. 'He will understand.'

Sanzo was amazed. In one fell swoop, she had stolen his men and given him an opportunity to still get paid. Even though he had the edge on the samurai captains, nothing was certain in battle except that men would die. *I lost the fight the moment the girl started talking.* True, capturing her had not been personal on his part, so it would be easy for him to walk away. He did not really care if Kiyomori's plans succeeded. However, crossing a daimyo like Kiyomori was dangerous, so it would be prudent for him to make himself scarce. He chuckled quietly. 'You are a surprising young lady, Katsura no Michiru.'

'Thank you, Sanzo-san.' Once more she made her offer to the uncommitted ronin, 'Will none of you agree to join us? What about you, Sanzo-san?' she asked the ronin leader. 'I can always use talented men.' Shuji started coughing.

Sanzo sheathed his sword, 'Thank you, but no. I detest civilised society,' he said with a dismissive wave of his hand. 'I have too many undesirable habits to be comfortable serving in a palace. I'm more suited to a different lifestyle.'

'Sanzo is right,' said the ronin with the tea whisk hair. 'I doubt whether I would fit in either.' A few of them chuckled.

The four ronin bowed, 'Thank you, lady.'

As they turned to leave, Sanzo said, 'Good luck to you, Michiru-hime. I am afraid you are going to need it. Kiyomori is willing to go to any lengths to stop you. He has worse tricks up his sleeve, I think.' He waved and walked away.

A tight-lipped Shuji came up next to Michiru. 'What are you doing?' he said with deceptive calm.

'We need men, now we have men,' she pointed out, heading back towards the remaining ronin. 'You always told me a single arrow is easier to break, sensei.'

'We know nothing about them!' he fumed as he followed after her. 'Besides, you're doing it all wrong. You can't just make men samurai on a whim!'

'This is war, Shuji-san! We can worry about formalities later.' She stopped and turned to face him. 'I want you to be Captain.'

He blinked. 'Captain of what?'

'My Honour Guard.'

'What are you talking about?!'

'I command you to take these men and form a guard to protect me. Does that not make sense?'

'This is highly irregular, my lady.'

'I know, but I am learning,' she said, striding off again.

He shook his head as he followed her, 'I don't know from whom.'

Shuji signalled each ronin forward, calling on him to state his name and make his oath of loyalty to The Lady Michiru. Each man added his name to the document, drawn up on a sheet of paper provided by Ōmono, and imprinted his thumb next to his name with a drop of his own blood. When all of them had done so, Michiru thanked them. 'You are no longer ronin. You are samurai.' They all bowed low, moved by the seriousness of the occasion. She kept her hands hidden so that no one could see them shaking.

CHAPTER TEN

After midday, Yatsuhiro took two men and reconnoitred ahead. The remainder slept, ate and rested. Most of them wore clothing so frayed and tattered that it was barely holding together. It looked as if some of them had not been eating too well, either. Shuji, still not convinced of Michiru's solution, took the opportunity to talk to the new men and find out more about them. 'It will take a few weeks or more for them to get into condition, but they will do,' he reported to Michiru. 'We are in need of some supplies. Especially food, but some new clothing would be a good idea.' He fidgeted with the hilt of his sword. 'They will feel more like samurai once their shirts are not falling off their backs.

Michiru mentally chided herself. *Mistake number one. More men require more food.* 'We do not have that far to go,' she told him,' and if necessary, we can go without for a day or so. There will be plenty for them once we are safely in Arikawa territory.' She looked up at the slopes of the mountain. She realised now that command brought a completely new set of problems. 'Maybe the scouts will have some luck. Instead of resting, maybe we should be hunting?'

'No, my lady. Let them rest for now. They have had less sleep than we have.'

*   *   *

Michiru's new samurai lay in a loose group under the shade of a stand of cedar trees. Sleep eluded them as they contemplated this new turn of events in their lives. Two of them lay on their sides, surreptitiously watching Shuji and Michiru talking as they pretended to sleep. 'Are you awake, Muneto?' whispered a stocky man with huge forearms.

'Yes,' he replied in a low voice.

'Can you hear what they are talking about?'

'No.' Muneto rolled onto his back, He had a long face. The beard he grew since becoming a bandit made it look longer. He interlaced his fingers across his stomach and sighed. 'Why do you care, Takuro?

Takuro, rolled onto his stomach, propping his square jaw on his calloused hands. His brow furrowed in frustration. 'I just want to know what's going on. Don't you want to know?' he asked in his characteristic stilted speech.

Muneto had always thought he sounded a bit slow, like he was not all there in the head. 'No,' he replied flatly. 'All we have to do is follow orders. That's the new game now. Do what you are told and they will look after us.'

Takuro frowned. He twisted to look at the ronin lying on the other side of Muneto. 'Don't you want to know what's going on, Tano?'

One of the figures propped up against a nearby tree, opened an eye to look at him. 'We'll find out soon enough. Don't worry about it, Takuro. Get some sleep.'

'I can't. I'm worried.' He crossed his arms, laying his head down on them. 'She called us samurai. We have to be samurai now.' His voice had an edge of concern to it.

'So what,' mumbled an unconcerned Muneto.

'So, I don't know how to be a samurai. I wasn't really a ronin, just a bandit.'

Tano pulled himself up onto one elbow with a grunt, his wild unkempt hair falling over his eyes. 'All you have to worry about right now is staying alive and protecting the lady. Do that, and everything else will work out. Now get some sleep.' He lay back down with his hands behind his head. 'It will be nice to get paid regularly again.'

'It would have been better to find the gold Ichiro was talking about,' said Muneto, his eyes watching the swaying branches above them.

'I'm not sorry he's dead,' Takuro said drowsily, his eyes finally closing. 'He was always mean to me.'

'Well he won't be mean to you any more, will he,' murmured Muneto as he stared vacantly in to the upper reaches of the tree, wondering where the old samurai had hidden the gold.

*   *   *

The scouting party returned shortly before sunset. The looks on their faces was less than encouraging. They all gathered around to hear the report. Yatsuhiro cleared a patch of dirt and sketched out the terrain features with the tip of a stick. 'First. There is now a fort on top of that spur.' Everyone was silent as he added it to the map, the implications for their original plan sinking in. 'We had no clue they were building this. It looks like the earthworks are complete. For now, it's made up of wooden towers and palisades. The garrison is around a hundred, with about the same number of convict labourers in a cage outside the front gate. There is a village, of sorts, at the base of the hill. Tradesmen and their families, I would imagine. Needless to say, sneaking over the spur is now going to be much harder.'

He sketched a zigzag from the fort to the river. 'They are using the prisoners to construct a road and stairs. They are also quarrying stone blocks for castle construction.' He looked at everyone's face. 'From the point of view of the Arikawa clan, this is bad news. This fort is a bridgehead across the mountain and the river, into the heart of our domain. If they turn it into a castle here, with storehouses, stables, a bridge and such, the Satake could seize the Kajigawa valley and drive a wedge between us and the Katsura.' Yatsuhiro stood, gripping his sheathed katana, 'If we can't do something about this,' he warned, 'the Satake can weaken both our clans considerably.'

'If that valley becomes a battleground, half of this region's crops will burn, or be carried away, and there will be a famine,' predicted

Shuji, twisting his scabbarded sword in both hands.

'So what do we do now, sensei?' Michiru asked, a sinking feeling settling in her stomach as yet another obstacle was thrown in her path.

The old samurai sighed. A breeze tugged at the grass. *Yes, there is a choice.* But Yatsuhiro and he now had conflicting priorities and he was unsure they would agree on a united course of action. It risked splitting their group, and there was no telling how their new recruits might react to that. Shuji scratched his jaw. *Let Michiru make the choice.* It was a suitable compromise, as long as Yatsuhiro was willing to abide by her decision. That was the true difficulty; whether the Arikawa samurai would surrender to her judgement. He was in no way obliged to, but it would go a long way to cementing the loyalty of the men. 'Michiru-hime. I think the best thing to do is for you to make the decision. We will advise you, but you must decide.'

Her jaw dropped, dumbfounded at his statement. Once over the initial shock, she protested, 'Why me? I do not have the experience or knowledge for this decision. Please excuse me, sensei,' she said bowing low. 'But please do not ask me to do this.'

'Yes, why should she have to make a decision, Shuji-san?' asked a perplexed Yatsuhiro. 'There is no question about our course of action. You must cross the spur in the early hours of the morning and take Michiru-hime to Nagase. I will stay and scout the fort. When I return with the information we can devise a plan of attack.'

'You would abandon Michiru-hime before you have delivered her to safety?'

'In this case, I think yes.'

Michiru asked, 'Did you have a different plan in mind, Shuji-san?'

'There are a number of options open to us, my lady,' he said, 'of which Yatsuhiro-san's is a good one. One we may want to keep it as our best choice,' giving the Arikawa captain a nod. 'But we have a rare opportunity that we are in a position to exploit. Yes, it is important to get you to Nagase,' he said to Michiru, 'but I am sure you understand what this new development could mean for both Houses. We have a chance to get someone inside, to get much better, more accurate information. We also have a chance for sabotage.'

Yatsuhiro shook his head straight away, 'We cannot put the lady in that much danger. It is too risky.' He knew their situation was tenuous enough without deliberately gambling with the very person they should be protecting. *I want to burn this fort to the ground. But it is more important to get Michiru to Nagase in one piece.* His chin jutted out stubbornly as he crossed his arms.

'We need not involve her in the mission itself,' Shuji responded with a calming gesture, 'We locate a defensible hiding place, send out scouts, and watch. We watch for opportunities. We can head for the Kajigawa bridge at any time.'

'Every day we are here we risk detection and capture,' Yatsuhiro pointed out.

Michiru could see he was becoming quite agitated. She had not seen him talk to Shuji in this way before. There was anger boiling below the surface. The dark tiger she had seen in him earlier began to emerge, the growl in his voice almost audible. It worried her that her two captains might end up antagonising each other. She realised that her decision might be the only way to settle the issue.

'A day or two delay now could be worth it in the long run,' Shuji countered

'One who chases after two hares will catch none,' Yatsuhiro shot back in an irritated tone.

She interrupted what was starting to degenerate into a pointless argument. 'Captains,' she pleaded. 'I think it would be best to do as Shuji-san suggests, but I need to know more. I need your advice and guidance.' *I do not want to make the decision. I do not know what to do. How could I?* But she did understand that her new samurai might abandon them, or worse, if she did not take decisive action now.

Shuji smiled to himself. *Good girl.* 'We will keep you as safe as we can, hime. I am sure Yatsuhiro agrees that something must be done about this fort, for all our sakes.' He turned his gaze on the Arikawa captain.

Some of the heat drained from Yatsuhiro. *We must be united to keep these ronin on our side.* His shoulders relaxed as he regained control of his emotions. 'As you wish,' he said begrudgingly.

Michiru breathed a deep sigh of relief. 'Well, it is probably worth making some tea and having something to eat, because this could take a while.'

*   *   *

They talked late into the night, discussing the possibilities and answering Michiru's questions. She decided that they should at least look for a safe place to hide and watch. The next morning the group relocated to a patch of rocky ground screened by scattered trees and clumpy bushes with a good view of the surrounding terrain. Shuji laid out their camp and continued his interviews of the new men. Haru, who had so far remained compliant, was untied and taken down to the river for yet more scrubbing.

Ōmono walked through the makeshift camp with a bundle, passing out rice balls to everyone. 'Eat up. Might as well. It'll all be gone soon.' He observed wryly, 'I don't suppose anyone has bothered to check if there are fish in this river.'

'I am surprised you did not look yourself as soon as we set up,' remarked Shuji.

The little man looked hurt, 'I can't be expected to do everything you know, Shuji-sama. Why I did everything except grow this rice,' holding up the last rice ball. 'I washed it, cooked it, made it into balls.'

Knowing he was playing it up, Michiru asked with a smile, 'Did you not buy them back in the village?'

He looked to one side. 'Well I watched while the woman at the shop washed it, cooked it and made it into balls,' he muttered before proclaiming, 'but I carried them, didn't I.'

'Yes you did,' the old samurai chuckled.

Within the hour, Yatsuhiro came jogging back into the camp leading two of the new samurai. He accepted a water bottle from Ōmono before strolling over to where Michiru and Shuji sat. 'Two very important things,' he said, his breathing heavy but not laboured, waving the men off to the campfire. 'A column is coming up the road. Thirty odd prisoners, ten guards.' He paused and took a long drink.

'Don't keep us in suspense,' prompted Shuji, 'what is the other important thing?'

'An opportunity, but we would have to act fast.' He knelt down close to Shuji and Michiru, speaking low so that only they could hear. 'Take the fort.' They both stared at him, stunned. 'Not as stupid as it sounds. We ambush this column, take out the guards. We recruit or bribe the prisoners, put on the guard's equipment. We march into the castle mid-afternoon, take the garrison by surprise and lock the gates. We can then at least burn it properly.' He sat back on his heels and waited for their reaction.

'You were quite against anything so hazardous last night,' Shuji said, clearing a space in the dirt with his foot.

'Do not misunderstand me. It is a big risk. But it does achieve a number of things.' Ticking off with his fingers, 'We get the most reliable information, Michiru-hime will be safer inside the fort than out in the open and we can burn the fort, all its buildings and stores when we leave.'

Michiru's brow furrowed in doubt. *It sounds impossible. It is insane. Aren't there a hundred men in that fort?* She looked at Yatsuhiro, wondering if he was being serious. He had been the one insisting on avoiding danger. Shuji did not seem to be as doubtful as she was. He looked as if he was considering it. 'Sensei. How is it possible to take a fort garrisoned by one hundred men with thirty?'

Rubbing his stubbled chin, he replied thoughtfully, 'Not everyone in a castle is on duty at once, unless an attack is likely. Usually, up to half, or even two thirds of a garrison will be off duty at any one time.' He grinned. 'Some soldiers manage to run quite successful businesses in their spare time.'

Yatsuhiro added, 'Those on duty will be spread throughout the fort, manning as much of the perimeter as possible. If they're using prisoner labourers, some troops will be outside guarding them as well. We will be walking in through the main gate. As long as they are outside the fort itself, they will have their hands full enough without bothering us.'

Shuji made some marks in the dirt with the end of his scabbard. Michiru assumed that he was making some sort of calculation, although he was not forthcoming with any explanation of what he was thinking yet. 'There is a good chance that some ashigaru will run for it. Especially the ones outside. That will help the odds. There is also a good chance that the prisoners will take the opportunity to escape once the commotion starts. A lot will hinge on us taking down the Satake samurai.' Curious as to how far the young captain had thought this through, he asked, 'What about Michiru-hime? What will she be doing while we are taking the fort?'

'We can work that out later,' he said quickly, sure that he and Shuji could find some way of keeping her safe during the attack, whether she liked it or not. 'The lady will need to be there with us, or at least nearby.' Yatsuhiro looked hard at Shuji. 'It all depends on how far you trust your new samurai. Using them as guards while crossing over the border was one thing, but now ...' He sniffed and gave a lopsided grin of derision. 'Do you really expect them to back you up in such a desperate fight?'

Shuji continued to make marks in the dirt with his scabbard, eyes fixed on his work. 'I have spent a little time talking to them. I think I have their measure, for the most part. The two brothers, the one's from Kai. They will work well together. Keep them as a team.' He made two marks in the dirt. 'Also, the young fellow Tendo and his friend Misao are keen to make a new life as well. The one with the sideburns, Renji, is a bit opinionated but I think he might be a good man.' He added new marks for each man as he gave his assessment. 'The others, seem to be mostly bandits with little experience of battle. How they will react in a stand up fight, I don't know yet. Whether they can be trusted ...' He looked at Michiru.

She sighed. Trepidation ran up her spine like an icy snake. Michiru had been hoping to avoid any more fighting. She had been feeling a bit smug about how she had dealt with the ronin. She thought it was a good solution for everyone and it had saved bloodshed. But now, this talk of going into combat deliberately. She shuddered at the thought. 'Do you think it can be done, sensei?'

'Do you wish to take the risk, Michiru?'

'That is the point, is it not?' she observed, resting her chin on her hand. 'We could attempt to sneak through, which would be safer. No doubt about that.' Nobody could blame her for taking the safe option. In fact, it would be expected. 'If we try this plan it will be all or nothing. I would be risking not only myself, but everyone else as well.' Michiru looked between the two samurai. Their expressions were firm, Yatsuhiro watching for her reaction, Shuji focussed on a spot on the ground.

She fidgeted under Yatsuhiro's unflinching gaze. She felt exposed, as if his eyes could see straight to the secret turmoil in her heart. As if he could see the conflicting emotions that left her lost and bemused. She was afraid that if he guessed how she felt, he would laugh at her foolish infatuation. She tried desperately to push it all down into the dark where he could not see. *Concentrate on the matter at hand.*

She knew that Shuji was right. They needed to do this if they wanted to spoil the enemy's plans. Yatsuhiro was naturally concerned for her safety. His was a great responsibility. It might cost him his life if he turned up in Nagase without her. But Shuji was talking about the bigger picture and she trusted his experience. If it is important, she must put her own misgivings aside and act for the good of her family. Both her families. 'I think we must try. That fort should be destroyed.'

*　*　*

While they were talking, Shuji drew a map in the dirt based on Yatsuhiro's description of the approaching column. He called the men over and they all gathered around the diagram. It represented the thirty or so prisoners surrounded by ashigaru spearmen, archers and mounted samurai. Shuji's gaze travelled around their small band. 'I will take three men and cut up the head of the column. Yatsuhiro-san, take three men and cut up the tail.' He pointed to the leaf on the map that stood for a mounted samurai, 'You two,' he said to the Kai brothers, 'take him down.'

Next, he indicated dark pebbles on the map, at each corner of the column. 'These are archers. Take them first.' His gaze swept across the new men, 'Any of you that can use a bow, pick one up straight away and target him.' He touched another leaf on the other side of the rows of marching pebbles. 'He will be wearing armour so kill the horse and chase him down. Two of you only! Everyone else, once the guards are down, keep control of the prisoners.' He looked around the circle of faces. *I am gambling on these men. Gambling that they are committed to Michiru and they will be worth their swords. I pray that the gods keep them safe too, because I will need every one of them when we try to take the fort.* 'Any questions? No? Go get into position!' He stood and turned to Michiru, 'I don't suppose I could convince you to stay back, could I?

'It would not take much, sensei. I am so scared!'

'Good. I would have doubted your intelligence if you were not.'

Her expression grew firm. *Now is not the time to be timid.* 'I must do this.'

'Very well, my lady. Your task is to take out this guard in the middle and then turn around to help Ōmono and Keiko with the captain.'

Ōmono and Keiko both gasped at the same time. 'Are you sure about that, Shuji-san?' the ashigaru asked reluctantly. He did not mind the odds, three to one against an armoured and mounted samurai was the best way to take one down, but usually one attacker would die. Putting the women in the attack could lead to one of them being killed.

'Surprise will give us an advantage. All you need to do, Keiko, is distract him. Slash your sword around in front of the horse. Make it back up. Be ready to dive out of the way if it tries to bolt.' Turning to Ōmono he said, 'While Keiko backs the horse up, you concentrate on the rider. Stab at his face and under the arm if he tries to raise his sword. If you can't put him down, keep him occupied. Lady Michiru can attack him from behind.' Looking around at them he said, 'Are there any questions? Right! Let's go.'

As Shuji tightened his sash, Michiru beckoned to him, 'Sensei.'

'Yes, my lady?'

'What about the prisoners?'

'What about them, my lady?'

'Well, what do I say to them?'

'I don't know,' he shrugged. 'That is up to you.'

'That is not very helpful, sensei.'

He smiled, tying on a rough headband, 'You might want to think of some way to appeal to criminals.'

She gave him a flat stare for his helpfulness. 'Why thank you for that, Shuji-san.'

* * *

The tension of waiting in hiding, while the enemy passed close by, was unbearable. Michiru felt certain that they could see her among the grass and low shrubs, and were even now coming towards her, ready to attack her crouching form. She fought the urge to spring to the attack, her nerves twitching at the tension. The moment dragged on. Her sense of panic grew as she imagined something had gone wrong.

Yatsuhiro's shout took her by surprise, even though she had been waiting for it. Leaping to her feet with a yell, Michiru charged her first target, the guard in the middle. To her left, Keiko and Ōmono rushed the mounted samurai officer. She heard other shouts off to her left and right but kept her eyes on the startled ashigaru in front of her. Michiru's heart thundered in her ears as she focussed on her target, her hair prickling as she rushed to get her blade within range.

The guard gaped at her in surprise, trying to bring his weapon to bear. With his spear a forearm longer than her naginata, he had a longer reach. But speed and surprise allowed her to get in close while he was still confused. His mouth hung open and his eyes were wide in fear as she sprinted towards him. She could see his uneven teeth and scraggly whiskers in fine detail. Her training under Shu-ji kicked in, making her moves almost automatic. Michiru caught his swinging spear with her blade, levering it up over her head and stepping forward inside his reach. Slipping her weapon from under his, she pivoted the naginata around her hand to slash his neck. Continuing the sweep through a splash of blood, she spun on her foot to face the direction of the horseman, desperate to help her friends. She heard the guard drop to the ground behind her. *I killed him.* She shuddered. But Keiko and Ōmono needed her, so she shoved the heartrending remorse aside.

She took in the combat with a glance. The mounted samurai captain had caught Ōmono's spear in one hand, and the little ashigaru was trying to wrench it free. Through the dancing struggle of the two men, she could see Keiko had managed to grab the horse's bridle. She was holding on for dear life as the nervous animal's jerking head pulled her off her feet. A hot wave of panic washed over Michiru, threatening to root her feet to the ground. She only had to take half a dozen steps.

She watched in growing fear as the samurai raised his sword, aiming a blow at Keiko, jarring Michiru free of her paralysis all at once. She leapt forward, screaming as she drove her naginata in to the samurai's lower back, just below the waist of his armour. The blade cut through the layers of fabric underneath and plunged into his lower torso with a sickening feeling, transmitted along the shaft to her hands. He screamed, his body arcing backwards, toppling to the side. His twisting fall threatened to wrench the naginata from her hands but she held on to the weapon with the grim strength of desperation. Ōmono's makeshift fixtures could not hold against the wrenching force of the falling samurai's body. The weapon snapped, leaving her gripping the wooden shaft while the blade remained buried in her enemy. Through hot eyes she saw she was too late. The samurai had already struck his blow, sending Keiko reeling backwards, a shocked look on her face.

She tossed aside the useless shaft and dodged around the still skittering horse. Keiko lay sprawled on the ground, a dark stain from her neck to the centre of her chest. Michiru dropped to her side, heart breaking as she saw blood spattered on the young girl's pale face. 'Keiko!' she cried, her growing tears blurring her vision. She tore off her headband and tried desperately to stem the flow of blood.

Ōmono skidded to a stop beside her, 'Oh no' he moaned.

This is all my fault! She cursed herself silently, wishing she could take it all back. Tossing aside the blood-soaked headband, she took her friend's hand. 'I'm sorry. I'm sorry. Please don't die. Please,' she begged, welling tears of remorse blinding her eyes. Keiko's breathing was shallow, her eyes unfocussed. Michiru was surprised at how much the young woman had come to mean to her. Despite their different upbringing, they had become friends. Her only friend. And now she lay here dying because of Michiru's decision. Her throat tightened in anguish. 'Please don't leave me.'

Ōmono furrowed through his satchel, pulling out a clean cloth. He inspected the wound with trembling fingers, before exhaling with relief. 'It's only shallow,' he told her. He staunched the bleeding with the cloth, applying a gentle pressure to the vicious gash. 'He only caught her with the tip of his sword.'

While they were fussing over Keiko, Shuji and Yatsuhiro rounded up the prisoners and posted guards. They had done well, taking the Satake completely by surprise. Shuji set two men to stripping the armour and clothing from the guards. After an uncomfortable moment, standing, holding the horse's reins, he put a hand on Michiru's shoulder. 'My lady. Now is the time,' he whispered. 'Keiko will be safe for the moment.'

Michiru was frightened of letting the young woman go. Without her she would be alone, never able to be herself, condemned to forever wear a mask. She looked up pleadingly, unable to hold back the tears streaming from her eyes. 'Please?'

'I am sorry.' His voice was grave but firm. 'Get on the horse.'

She hung her head, gripping Keiko protectively. She knew Shuji was right. Gathering her will for what she must do, Michiru let her go, caressing her face as she stood. Ōmono took her place and started binding Keiko's wound. She dashed the offending moisture from her face with her sleeve and took the reins from Shuji. He boosted her up into the saddle.

Michiru tried to focus. She could now see that the prisoners had been carrying crates slung on poles between them. 'It looks like there are supplies here for the fort,' she said to Shuji in a strained voice, trying to distract herself from Keiko and focus on what she must do.

'We'd better get everyone out of sight first, before we go poking around in boxes, my lady.'

'You are correct, of course, Shuji-san.' With a deep breath, she tried to summon that part of herself that had spoken to the ronin. The part of her that was not trembling in fear. She looked down at the dusty and haggard men, lined up on the road. Faces full of doubt and self-pity, fear and astonishment, resignation and dejection.

Her mother's voice echoed in her mind. Without understanding why, Michiru launched into the scolding manner she remembered from her childhood. She fixed them all with a fierce gaze, leaning forward on the skittish horse. 'You are all criminals!' she shouted, with a sweeping gesture of her hand. 'Maybe some of you are victims of circumstance,' Michiru said looking from face to face, 'but some of you are evil and deserve to die. Liar, thief, robber, rapist, drunkard, oath breaker, murderer!' She sat back up in the saddle. 'Condemned by the law of this land, you have been sent to die. But before you do, Lord Kiyomori will take every day of back breaking labour he can get out of you!'

'How can I let men such as you back into the world? I should kill you all now,' she paused to let that sink in. She wanted them to understand. Because this time, unlike with Haru, she would not stay Shuji's hand. *Why should I? If Keiko dies, why would they deserve to live?* 'I want you to consider your karma, because this is the last stop before Hell. Are you ready to stand before the Judges of Meido?' They all slumped. Michiru took heart at their reaction. She was getting through to them. There was a glimmer of hope. Everything that she had been through. Everything that had happened. The deaths. The pain. *Could she lead them? Would they follow?* She pointed to the wooded mountain, in the grip of her role now, 'Ahead of you lies a half built castle. The Satake want to work you to death to complete it. However, I have other plans for you. Your lives are mine! And should I wish it, I can send you back to the gates of hell where I found you.'

She turned the horse sideways, proclaiming, 'I am Lady Katsura no Michiru, sister of Lord Kosei of the Katsura Clan. The men who have freed you today are my Guardsmen. I give you the choice. Follow my orders, help us in our mission and I will release you. Or you can die, here, now. You can leave this life behind and hope your next one will be better.' If they had any sense they would realise they were being given a rare chance.

'Should any of you want the opportunity to earn back a place in the world, to become men again, you can serve me as my ashigaru. For now, follow my men's orders and you will get food and water.'

Michiru was surprised by the ragged cheer that broke from the dusty figures on the road. The horse shied away from the sudden noise. *Did it work?* She looked at them as she settled the horse. Their plain, ordinary faces were the same as ones she might see at home. What clothing they had was dusty and threadbare. None wore sandals. She doubted if Kosei would think these ragged criminals fit to be Katsura ashigaru. *I guess we won't know until they are put to the test, as Ōmono would say.* Drained and dizzy with relief, she looked back towards Keiko. The horse sensed her desire and turned that way without direction.

'Shuji-san! I will leave you in command.'

'Yes, my lady!' he replied, watching her ride away without waiting for a reply. *The sooner we are back in cover, the better. The last thing we need is to be caught out here in the open.* He called to one of the new samurai, 'Your name again, if you please.'

'Mutugabe Renji, taisho.'

'Good. Take two men and collect our gear. Meet us over in that grove,' he ordered. Yatsuhiro set some of the prisoners to work and cleared the road, erasing traces of the fight. Others stripped the bodies and dumped them out of sight in a nearby gully. The dead horse they covered as well as they could, but the carrion birds would draw attention before long. They bundled up the looted armour and equipment and carried it all along with the crates towards the trees. The dusty criminals kept looking around nervously, unsure of what would happen next, still not believing this sudden turn of events.

Michiru rode back to Keiko, sliding off the horse to kneel at her side. The young woman was shockingly pale. The bloodstain darkening on her clothes contrasted with the fresh bandage Ōmono applied. 'You will be fine, Keiko-chan,' she said, forcing a smile. 'You have to be alright. I still have to find you a husband.' She forced a smile as she ran a hand down Keiko's clammy face. Her eyes crinkled at the corners as she tried to keep her emotions in check. 'Remember? I promised.'

Ōmono, who had bullied four prisoners into assembling a makeshift stretcher, touched her shoulder. 'My lady,' he said, 'we have to move her.' He knew these first hours were important in surviving such injuries. They needed to get her safe and still. Movement risked opening the wound and Keiko had already lost enough blood.

Michiru drew in her strength and stood. She knew she could not do anything more to help. Ōmono was the best one to look after Keiko now. Maybe she would be better off helping Shuji with the new men. 'I will leave her in your hands, Ōmono-san.' She threw herself up into the saddle and galloped off after her new recruits.

Going deeper into the woods, they made a fire and cooked up some of the rice they found in the crates. Washed down with copious amounts of fresh water from the river, the meal was welcomed by the tired men. Michiru watched them as most of them laid down, sighing with contentment. Others huddled together in twos and threes talking. She could not imagine what they were talking about but knew that some of it would be nefarious. 'I want these men questioned, Yatsuhiro-san,' she said, fearing she may have released some real villains.

'A sound idea, my lady. However, we should let them sleep first, while we figure a few things out,' he suggested. He knew that not all of these men could be relied on. They would be lucky if half turned out to be worth their rations. He would pick the best he could while the others slept, allowing him to form something resembling a reliable core. Without doubt, some would try to make a run for it. 'I will post some guards,' Yatsuhiro said. He strolled off toward the prisoners. On the way, he collected some of the new samurai, scanning the resting prisoners with a discerning eye.

Shuji leaned negligently against a tree nearby, watching. A dull ache pressed on his ribs after the exertion of the last skirmish. *I need time to think.* He drew in long deep breaths until the pain subsided. This plan was launched without much time for discussion or refinement. They were making it up as they went along and that was usually the most dangerous way to do anything. He was impressed with Michiru. She was proving most inspiring, something her father did well, too. However, where her father had built up a core of highly proficient samurai, Michiru had vagabond ronin and convicts. *I have my doubts about this, but I also know we have little choice. It has to work.*

CHAPTER ELEVEN

Michiru knelt next to Keiko as Ōmono cleaned and dressed her wound. He made gentle noises and spoke soothingly as he worked. Michiru wondered if he might be more than a little interested in the young woman. After all, she supposed men might find her attractive. And she knew Ōmono had a thing for the ladies. In spite of her concern, Michiru grinned. She remembered Shuji saying that there was nothing like a crisis to bring people's true feelings out into the open. It was unfortunate that she would have to disappoint Ōmono. Keiko would be marrying a samurai someday.

She looked at Keiko's grey face, achingly aware that it could have been her lying there, waiting for her wounds to either heal or kill her. Keiko looked up at her, trying to smile. 'I'm sorry, my lady,' she said thickly, her lips and tongue sticking together as she tried to speak.

'Hush now, Keiko-chan,' she said, smoothing Keiko's damp hair back. 'You rest easy. It will be alright.'

Once she was quiet again, Michiru asked, 'How is she really, Ōmono?'

He put on a good face, but she could sense his worry. 'She will be fine, my lady,' he said with a slight incline of his head. 'We need to keep the wound clean and keep her still. The sword nicked some of her bones, that is the most dangerous part. She must rest, so as not to open the wound.' He looked down, knowing there was not much chance of that in their current situation. He looked up with an apologetic expression that tore at Michiru's heart. 'I have applied a soldier's treatment for sword cuts, made from narcissus root and flour paste. That will help for the moment. But she needs a real doctor, my lady, with medicines, if we want to be sure.'

Shuji, who had been standing behind Michiru, tapped her on the shoulder and walked towards a nearby boulder. 'We cannot take her with us, Michiru,' he said once she joined him. 'You must realise that.'

'So what, do we dispatch her?' retorted Michiru, surprised at the heat in her tone. 'Leave her by the side of the road?' She knew he was right. Again. They were fleeing for their lives and Keiko must be left behind. *Oh merciful Buddha! How can I do that to her?* She clenched her jaw, staring defiantly back at Shuji. *She deserves better than that.*

Yatsuhiro stood politely out of earshot with one of her new samurai by his side. The Arikawa captain watched her with a look of concern on his dusty face. But there was something else there, in his eyes. Her heart tumbled in confusion. *Could it be that he has feelings for me?* She was still unsure of her own feelings. But, of all the things to happen now, she did not need that on her mind. Michiru tried to clear the emotions from her face and turned to acknowledge his presence. 'Is there something you wish to say, Yatsuhiro-san?'

'Excuse me, my lady. It is about Keiko-san,' he said. 'Misao-san here says that he has some doctoring experience.'

Misao smiled and nodded. He looked young to be a ronin, without much of a beard on his oval face. His slight build was nearly half a head shorter than Yatsuhiro but his stance was firm and well balanced. *I wonder how he came to be with those ronin?* His eyes watched her carefully, plainly still a little in awe of her and unsure of their relationship.

'Where did you learn this, Misao-san?' she asked, not daring to hope yet for Keiko.

'My father sent me to a temple when I was younger. I stayed as long as I could, but I really did not fit in.' He gave a nervous laugh. 'I must tell you that I only have some basic skills, my lady. Keiko-san will still need a proper physician. I cannot guarantee that I can help her, but I will try.' His voice trailed off self-consciously.

'What I really need right now is to be able to move her. Can you at least make her safe enough for us to carry her?'

'I think I can improve that a bit,' he said, indicating Ōmono's makeshift stretcher, 'and dress her wound well enough for a short journey.'

'Thank you, Misao-san,' she said with some relief, 'I am sure you will do the best that you can. Thank you.' The young samurai smiled, bowed to Michiru and Yatsuhiro and walked over to see to his new patient.

'I hope that helps, my lady,' Yatsuhiro said, watching the ex-ronin with a speculative eye. 'At least she will get some treatment. And carrying her into the fort might be that little bit more convincing.'

'Yes,' she murmured. Turning to Yatsuhiro she asked, 'What happens once we reach the fort? How will she get home?'

He scratched his chin, choosing his response with care. 'What does that matter, my lady? The most important thing is that you get to Nagase.' With a sharp intake of breath, she looked at him. 'Now, please do not get offended, my lady. I am speaking the truth, just between us at the moment.' He moved closer, holding her gaze with determination, 'We all care for Keiko-san, but she is your servant.' He let that sink in as he saw Michiru bite off the objection she was about to make. 'You are the most important one of us and the one who must go on.' He waved a hand around their party, 'We all can fall by the wayside, as long as you,' he said, pointing to her chest for emphasis, 'make it to safety.'

Michiru looked down, her mind in turmoil. She had not considered things in such a cold light, and she had come to think of Keiko as a friend rather than a servant.

'You must think like a leader if you are to hold this group together. The ronin swore their oaths to you. The prisoners believe you are in charge. Even if I wanted to, I could not take command. Nor could Shuji. We all have our obligations and duties and we must honour those above our personal wants and feelings.' Sensing the turmoil she was going through, he responded with a gentle hand on her shoulder. 'My lady.' She looked up, eyes threatening tears. 'We must make what arrangements we can for Keiko and move on. We will do our best for her, but time is running out.'

After a moment, Michiru straightened up with resolve, 'You are right, of course, Yatsuhiro-san. We shall do just that.' With a quick turn, she left him standing with a bemused look on his face. 'Ōmo-no-san! Misao-san!' she called before turning back to Yatsuhiro, 'Well, Captain, are you coming?'

*   *   *

Renji looked at the pile of mismatched armour and then up at Michiru.

'It only needs to be light,' she said to the frowning samurai. 'I need to be able to run, if necessary. Or ride.' She glanced sideways at Shuji, watching for a reaction, grinning as he closed his eyes and shook his head. 'Well, Renji, what do you think? Can you do it with what we have here?'

'It will take a bit of re-lacing, my lady.' He knelt to pick through the pieces in front of them. 'There are a couple of pieces that should do, but they will all need to be ... adjusted, because of your ... size,' he stammered, wiping back his hair with an unconscious gesture.

She stared flatly at him. 'What do you mean?'

He was a little flustered, wary of offending her. 'Well you are not as ... bulky as the men who wore these pieces, and you are some-what ... shorter too.' He grinned nervously.

Shuji huffed. 'Just try to manage it without too much in the way of padding, Renji.' He turned and left, trailing a cloud of annoyance.

Renji exhaled, rolling his eyes, before picking up a chest plate and examining it critically. 'I don't think he is keen on you wearing armour, my lady.'

She frowned at him. 'Do think I will be safer without it, Renji?

The normally confident young man blushed, 'Yes, my lady. I mean no. I mean...oh.'

After an hour or so, he was back, laying out the adjusted pieces before her. Her first look at the assorted oddments gave her doubts about the idea. She had been most concerned about the extra bulk of the armour. She had never worn armour, let alone practiced in it. Now she was considering fighting in it. She knew that fatigue might be a real concern for her.

'They may not match but they will serve,' he promised. Improvised padding was visible on some pieces, sewn on to the lining with quick, coarse stitches. Michiru stood, dressed in her travelling clothes, to let Renji fit the armour.

He picked up a bundle and unrolled it. 'I had to pad these shin guards to fit your legs,' he said, wrapping a flat panel around one of her lower legs. It had metal splints sewn to a background made from layers of grubby looking, dark green cloth. Red cords tied around her ankle and behind her knee to hold it in place. 'Luckily, I found a pair with good knee protection,' he pointed out. A semicircle of layered cloth backing to cover the kneecap topped the shin guard. Hexagonal metal plates were sewn on in an interlocking pattern. The armour's black lacquer was chipped and worn but still serviceable. He fitted a shin guard to the other leg in the same manner.

Satisfied with her leg armour, he moved to another bundle, unrolling it on the ground and picking up what looked like a long bag with metal splints fixed onto the dun coloured fabric. He held one end out for her, 'Now for the armguards. Slide your arm into this, please, my lady.' Michiru obliged, and he pulled it on, all the way up to her armpit. A stench of sweat, dust and mouldy fabric wafted into her face. Michiru coughed and blinked her eyes. 'Wow!'

He grinned as he tied the two attached cords, one under the opposite armpit and the other over the opposite shoulder. The metal splints covered her forearm and upper arm, with a small roundel on her elbow. A contoured plate covered the back of her hand, and another covered the base of her thumb. Her second and third fingers went through a loop of cord that held the plate in place, with a similar loop for the thumb. 'I found the smallest pair of sleeves I could, my lady. Unfortunately, they smell a bit ... manly.'

'Yes, they do,' she commented sourly. He put the second

armguard on the other arm. She vowed to either wash or replace these at the earliest opportunity. So far, the armour felt comfortable enough. She tested the fit and feel by holding, loading and drawing an imaginary bow.

'That was the easy part,' he said, standing back to see the effect. 'That should give your limbs some protection against cuts and slashes.'

He bent down and picked up a simple chest and back plate constructed from two thin metal halves hinged together. Green laced shoulder straps hung from the back. Suspended from the bottom edge of the chest and back plate hung six rectangular thigh guards, attached by a row of green cords. Each one consisted of four overlapping curved plates laced together. The inside of the chest plate was lined with thick leather

'I managed to pad this piece enough, I think. Let's see how it feels.' He fitted the armour around her torso, inserting the locking pins and tying the waist cord. He draped the straps over her shoulders tying them to the rings on the front and stood back to assess the fit. 'I could fit more pieces, my lady, but I think that would make it too heavy. It is all about layers, you see. You can cover all the weak spots, but you also stack on the weight.'

Michiru looked down at herself, feeling cocooned in the snug fitting armour. For someone not used to wearing armour it was an unusual sensation. She moved around experimentally. Despite the extra bulk, it was not as bad as she first thought. It was a bit stuffy, but in a strange way, it was also comforting, being encased and protected. She looked at Renji, feeling a little foolish, like a child playing dress-ups.

'It may feel restricting at first, but you'll get used to it,' Renji offered, scratching at his sideburns. 'I don't think that a helmet is a good idea, but I did find this.' He held up a light metal facemask that covered the forehead and cheeks. 'It will help protect your jaw, my lady, if nothing else.'

Michiru took the proffered facemask and inspected it, unimpressed by its appearance. 'They call them Monkey Cheeks,' he told her. With an apologetic shrug he added, 'It is better than nothing.' While she tied it on and added a headband over the top of it, Renji wrapped a long sash around her waist, tying it and tucking the ends in. He picked up a pair of daggers, and slid them into the front of her obi, one on each side, angled inwards.

'I have never fought with a knife, Renji,' she told him. 'I doubt whether I can use a pair.' *All this is a lie. I am no warrior.* She clenched her fists, tears threatening to undermine her dignity.

Renji gripped the hilts of the daggers and gave them a slight shake and stared into her face. 'My lady!' Michiru returned his gaze, surprised at his manner. 'Anyone looking at you would not know if you can use them or not! You have to make people think twice when they face you. Sometimes, that's all you need.' The samurai grinned. '"All warfare is based on deception," remember? Knives are for close quarters. When you get in close, whip these out,' he said, touching the daggers, 'and stab like you mean it, twice if you can. That should put your enemy down. Then you get space.' He stepped back, making sweeping gestures with both hands. 'We'll practice later, if you wish, my lady.'

She nodded. 'Thank you, Renji-san.' Although she doubted she would ever have time to learn enough.

Shuji walked up, his sheathed katana held loose in his left hand. He paused as she turned to face him. Michiru bit her lip, feeling guilty at wearing someone else's armour. He walked around her, checking the armour over, head tilted to one side as he stalked. He stopped in front of her, gripped the chest plate by the armholes, lifting it up and down to check the fit. 'Jump,' he barked. She complied, still unsure whether he approved or not. Parts of the armour shifted a bit as she landed. 'Good. It is light enough I suppose. A bit of tightening up to do here and there, but well done, Renji,' he said, nodding to the nervous samurai.

'Now you must convince anyone watching that you are used to wearing it. That you are comfortable in it. Do you remember the story of Tomoe Gōzen?'

'Yes, sensei,' she replied sheepishly.

'Oi!' Shuji growled, tapping her on the forehead with the hilt of his sword. 'You must bring her to life.' In deep tones, he recited the description of the legendary samurai woman of a bygone age. '"Tomoe was a warrior worth a thousand ordinary men, ready to confront a demon or a god, mounted or on foot. Yoshinaka would send her out as his first captain, with strong armour, a sword, and a bow. She performed more deeds of valour than any of his other warriors."' He glared at Michiru. 'You must find her spirit and convince those who see you that you are just as fierce.'

He stepped back, eyes still fixed on the young girl. 'Pull your shoulders back. Lift your chest. You are samurai! Be proud! Tighten your stomach! Drop your chin and lift the crown of your head to the heavens. Now scowl. Like you are disgusted by what you see.' Michiru tried to follow all of his instructions at once but she could not make them fit together. 'Every time you stop moving, adopt that pose. Relax and walk around the room.' She did as he ordered. 'Now, stop! And stand.' She added an insolent tilt to her head and a faint smile. *I feel ridiculous. Like a cross between an insane maniac and a stage actor*. It was a good thing she could not see the size of the grin on Renji's face.

He sighed, wishing that he had more time. *How could I have known? Her father wanted her raised as a lady, not a warrior.* He looked at her standing there in the looted armour. *It is just as well she had been so active growing up. If she had been like other girls she might not have made it this far.* 'Well, we will work on that.'

CHAPTER TWELVE

The two captains matched pace for a while, falling into the familiar rhythm of the march. Yatsuhiro's easy stride belied the tension in his face. Shuji looked at the younger man, smiling to himself, 'You seem concerned, Yatsuhiro-san. Is there something worrying you?'

'Sorry, Shuji-san,' he said, darting a quick glance back at Michiru, walking, head down, ten or so paces behind them. 'I will guard myself more closely,' he said with a slight nod.

'If there is something that concerns you, I should know,' he stated matter-of-factly. He tried to settle the unfamiliar helmet better, retying the cords with practiced ease. 'As a fellow captain, you understand this, I am sure.'

After a deep sigh, Yatsuhiro looked out towards the surrounding countryside, scanning for tell-tale movement, shape or shine. 'We have been lucky, Shuji-san. We are on the wrong side of the border and now there is open war.' He looked directly at Shuji as they walked. 'We are more than likely being hunted. What we are about to attempt is risky enough under the best circumstances. I just feel that we may be pushing our luck. Should we not find an approach that does not put Michiru-hime in so much danger?'

'My lady has made her feelings known on that subject,' he replied, making his own visual scan of the surroundings. 'Anyway, was it not your idea in the first place?'

He grinned. 'It does not mean it was a good one.' After a quiet moment, he asked 'Will she hold up under the pressure?'

'You cannot always predict how someone will react. She has

done surprisingly well so far. My concern would be how all this will affect her in the future.' *It was a pity that Fate took both of her parents before she was grown.* Turning to Yatsuhiro he added, 'Michiru-hime spent a lot of time with her brother. She is like him in many ways.' He grinned, recalling the rivalry between the two siblings. 'You know, she is a better shot than he is,' chuckling at the thought.

Shrugging to settle the unfamiliar armour better, the older samurai reminisced, 'Her father was a good lord. But when the good lady, his wife died, he left Kosei-sama to manage young Michiru at home. He probably should have sent her off to learn how to be a lady.' He sighed. 'She is learning. If she can get through all this and hold it together, she will do well, I think. Especially with your guidance.' He smiled knowingly.

'I hope I am up to the challenge. It would be better if you could stay to help her for a while,' Yatsuhiro admitted.

'I already have a lord to serve. After this, I will leave her to you, my young friend.'

Yatsuhiro glanced over his shoulder at Michiru and saw the determined set of her features as she trudged along behind them. *How much easier might a man's life be with a dull wife?* He imagined that Nagase would become a more interesting place once Michiru arrived. 'There has been much speculation at home about Michiru-hime.' He turned again to survey the road behind before continuing. 'Mostly family politics and women's intrigues,' he said dismissively. 'They are all expecting a hako-iri musume, a daughter in a box.'

Shuji laughed. 'Well now, aren't they in for a surprise?'

*　　*　　*

Michiru was sweating inside her armour. However, not all of it was from the exertion of the march. *I am so scared. But I cannot let anyone see it.* As part of the ruse, a piece of rope was wrapped around her wrists to give the appearance of having her hands bound. In reality, she held the ends of the rope in her hands, allowing her to free them quickly. They were staking everything on this ruse. Death or capture would be the consequences of failure today and it would all happen before the day was done. She blinked the sweat out of her eyes and tried to calm her breathing. Michiru insisted on taking a central role in this mission despite the objections of both her captains. Shuji's proposal had been to pack her in one of the crates and keep her hidden. Once again, someone wanted to put her in a box. Yatsuhiro suggested that she hide in the tree line outside the fort until the fighting was over, but she did not like the idea of being so far from Shuji, who was still her most valued protector.

So, she would be the bait. While the enemy's eyes were on her, they would not notice anything that might give away their deception. Her insistence had not been out of bravado, a desire for action or any silly ideas about adventure and glory. She meant to remain with her guards, untested or not. She wanted loyal men around her. She felt that it was as safe an option as any other was. Michiru remembered her father reading from ancient Chinese texts about generalship and gaining victory. He taught it to Kosei and she had helped her brother with his practice. Learning to be the Sage Commander. She had not understood most of it, but her father had thought it important and he studied it all his life.

She had never thought much about what she had heard in those days. In fact, she had forgotten most of it. That was until she found herself in a situation where it had made sense. One passage leapt to mind when she found herself watching the released prisoners. "Bind them with deeds; do not command them with words. Assemble them by fellowship; make them uniform by the martial." Father had used it to explain to Kosei why he must fight alongside his men. She trusted that her father was right and decided to follow his example.

Armoured men hedged in Michiru. Renji and another ronin in front, with Misao and a wall of a man called Tanzo behind her. He had been one of the prisoners they had liberated but here he was, armed and armoured as one of her guards. Shuji had surprised her when she recommended this man to stay by her as an escort. He was taller than most of the other men, with broad shoulders and a flat face framed with a course stubble. His thick eyebrows sat low over his dark eyes and broad nose. However, his frame was sparse, eaten away by prolonged hunger. She had been a little afraid of him at first, but Shuji assured her he had questioned him extensively and he was satisfied enough to give the man a weapon. If nothing else, she trusted Shuji.

She looked back over her shoulder to where Keiko lay on the stretcher, carried by four of the prisoners. Her face was still pale, teeth gripping her bottom lip at the discomfort of the movement. Fresh blood stained the dressing on her chest. Michiru's fear for her friend, lying there helpless, gnawed at her heart. Ōmono walked beside the stretcher leading Haru on a rope, still gagged with his arms tied back over a short pole across his back. She was beginning to regret the necessity of keeping him bound in this way, but it was better than the alternative and it would not be long before they could release him. The rest of the column snaked out behind them. Dusty prisoners carried the crates of supplies while some of her new samurai positioned themselves as guards at the rear.

They crossed the river and began their way up the winding road to the fort. A jumble of rough houses lined the road for a short way. The acrid smell of a smithy hung in the air with the metallic ring of a pair of hammers working. Once past the village, a mixture of fragrant pines and cedars crowded the road, throwing welcome patches of shade across their path. Piles of debris from the felling of trees and construction of the road were pushed to the downhill side, showing the haste with which the work had moved on. The slope grew steeper and she began to catch glimpses of the first outposts of the fort. A dozen bare-backed carpenters toiled away at improving the first stages of construction under the eyes of spear wielding Satake ashigaru.

'This part of approach would be difficult enough to attack if they had only a few of missile troops to defend it,' Yatsuhiro commented to Shuji, as he ran a professional eye over the roughly constructed defences. 'See the latticework fences lashed between the trees?' he said without looking. 'They have covered them with branches and shrubs. Give it a few months and it will be a tangled mess. Outflanking this position would be noisy and time consuming for sure.'

Shuji grunted, 'I hate attacking fortifications. I would rather surround them and starve them out. Assaults are usually such a waste of men.'

'Sensei,' Michiru called. Shuji fell back between her escorts. 'If this fort were properly garrisoned, how many men would you need to attack it?'

For a moment, he did not reply, 'Part of the problem, my lady, is that when you are attacking you really have very little idea of what is up ahead. Even with good reconnaissance, the defender can still have a surprise or two for you. That's why spies are so useful.' They continued to trudge up the steepening dirt roadway. 'Assuming a garrison of one hundred men, I would want three to five hundred men to take this place.'

'Really?' she asked, surprised at the figure, 'Why so many?'

A faint smile pulled up the corner of his mouth. He pointed to the partially constructed building at the upcoming hairpin turn. 'See this position here? When it is finished, the troops stationed there will be able to fire on attackers as they come up this road.' He pointed up the slope to where the road continued back in the other direction, 'More troops can fire down on attackers from up there as well. Before you can continue up this road, you must take that building. The defenders will pull back, up to the next corner, where the process must be repeated. All the time, they will be firing down on you from positions further up the hill. And you have not even reached the fort itself yet.'

Michiru looked at the foundations of the fortifications off to the left and right, where the earth was cleared and posts dug in to the slope. Low wooden walls of logs lay between the posts, giving cover from missile fire and presenting enough of an obstacle to deter attackers from frontal assaults. She began to appreciate the difficulty of trying to take such a position.

'What about those guards up there?' She indicated with a twitch of her head the half a dozen men stationed at various places up the slope, watching their progress up the road.

'Each of those positions should give you an idea of where the other defensive works will be built. If the Satake continue to develop this fort all these temporary structures will be replaced by more substantial walls and towers. For the moment, there is no real threat from this side of the mountain, so there is no need to expend the effort here. This is why castles are often built on hilltops, my lady. It gives the defenders a natural advantage and presents your enemy with problems to deal with while you are shooting at him.'

'So, would a thousand men take it easier than five hundred?'

'No, my lady. Greater numbers do not always help. The terrain and obstacles like fences narrow the approaches, so you can still only attack with a fraction of your men. The extra troops do allow you to send in additional waves, after the first attacks are repulsed.' He swallowed hard, remembering his own nightmarish experiences, grisly scenes of hellish torment that still haunted him. 'Attacking over the bodies of your comrades will affect the men's morale.'

'What about attacking at night? Would that not be better?' she asked.

'Not if the defender rolls burning bales down the hill. Or any one of a dozen other tricks that warriors have devised over the ages.' He lapsed into silence. As she took in the view back down the way they had come, Michiru began to understand Shuji's desire to destroy this fort before it was finished. Trying to take this place once it was finished would cost many lives.

They continued past the outer defences, towards the main fort itself. On one side, a collection of low buildings lined a narrow street that curved around the slope. A wooden cage crowded the slope below the fort, a few sick men littering the inside, only the occasional twitch of movement showing they were still alive. Near naked prisoners, covered in dirt and bruises, trudged up the dusty road from the quarry. They struggled along with fresh cut stones slung between them on poles, presumably for the foundations of the new castle. The tick and chink of hammers and chisels came from somewhere further around the curve of the slope, where the stone must have been coming from. Ashigaru guards were scattered around the area, lounging against walls and posts, appearing quite relaxed.

Coming up the final hairpin bend, Michiru felt let down at the sight of the wooden palisade and buildings. Sharpened logs stood, planted upright around the enclosure, lashed together to horizontal bracing at about knee and head height. What surprised her most was that each log had a gap of about two fists between it and its neighbours. She expected something more solid and imposing.

'Shuji-san! That is not a wall, it's a fence!' she said in hushed surprise, 'Why is there no wall?'

'It is not a fence, it is a palisade,' he corrected her. 'Remember, this is a fort not a castle. A palisade is quicker to put up but as hard to get over as a solid wall. Especially, when the defenders are shooting at you and stabbing you through the gaps.'

'Alright, my lady,' he said finally, 'we are getting close to the gate now. It's time for you to be a prisoner.' He quickened his pace and resumed his position ahead of the escorts.

The tension within the group was palpable now. Everyone tried to look casual, except the prisoners. It was quite natural for them to look scared. She realised that she was the focus of every man within sight. She could feel their eyes on her. The gate guards were so curious about her that they ignored the rest of the column. She clenched her teeth, fearing that at any moment some minor detail might give them away. She was having no trouble acting like a nervous prisoner. A platform surrounded with a low wall, pierced with arrow slits topped the solid timber gate. Ashigaru watched lazily from the cover of their position.

They wound up through the gate and into the lower bailey. Simple wooden buildings bordered the open space. The inner fortifications loomed up at the further end where the path continued up along one side of the slope. An armoured samurai waved them towards the next gateway. 'Might as well take all this straight up to the storehouse,' he said.

'Thanks,' Yatsuhiro said, stopping to take a swig from his water bottle. 'Who's in command at the moment?' he asked casually as the column trudged past.

'Teshiga-sama,' the samurai said, sucking his breath through his teeth. 'He arrived two days ago in a fine mood. I have never seen him that happy,' the samurai intimated with a smirk. 'He probably found a silver coin in his shit bucket.'

Yatsuhiro gave a polite chuckle in return, waving as he trotted back to the head of the column. Michiru found his assured performance impressive. *How is he remaining so calm?* Judging by the friendly banter, the guards suspected nothing. Looking up at the inner fort, she muttered a fervent prayer to her ancestors, 'Please, kami. Blind my enemy and sharpen my eyes. Guide my hand and shield me from harm. Strike fear into my enemy's heart and give me the strength to stand firm.'

The inner gate, constructed in the same fashion as the outer one, loomed over the roadway into the final bailey. The curious faces of Satake ashigaru watched her intently from the top of the gatehouse. Two of them shared a crude laugh. She glared up at them, hating them for whatever the disgusting joke was. Her fears started to smoulder into resentment and anger. She had held some reservations about getting involved in more combat. Now she wanted to put arrows into those two. The realisation shocked her. She was unsure if she liked the change in herself.

The path turned right inside the gate and led up a ramp into a flat open space, with rough timber buildings on two sides. A wooden watchtower sat opposite the gate, rising to three times the height of the palisade. Michiru's scalp prickled at the thought that they might have seen everything from up here. The attack on the column, the hiding of the bodies, everything they had done. The enemy might know exactly what they were up to and Michiru and her men were walking into a trap. Panic surged in the pit of her stomach. She darted frightened glances around the bailey, looking for imaginary armoured samurai emerging from their imaginary hiding places with weapons drawn.

However, there were none. Ashigaru stood idly at their posts, chatting with their comrades or watching the column file into the courtyard. A knot of samurai congregated around the veranda of the main house, some coming or going from the other buildings. Only a pair of guards at the front of the house wore helmets or held spears.

Between the guards stood the commander of the castle, resplendent in his glistening jet-black armour. He had a proud face, dominated by a large hooked nose, topped with a freshly shaved pate and oiled hair. He stood out amongst his subordinates in their plainer dress and accoutrements. She looked down at her mismatched and travel stained clothing, feeling grubby and ragged in comparison.

'Teshiga-sama!' Yatsuhiro called to the commander, making a perfunctory bow.

'You are late,' the well-dressed samurai said imperiously.

'Apologies, my lord. We came across these ones hiding near the river. They fit the descriptions of the fugitives that we were warned to be on the lookout for.' Ōmono shoved Haru forward, using his spear on the gagged man's shoulder to press him down onto his knees next to Michiru. Keiko's stretcher was placed on the ground behind her. With seeming nonchalance, her samurai crowded around them, forming a protective cordon. Shuji and the Kai brothers flanked Haru while Yatsuhiro, Renji and Tanzo crowded along Michiru's left side.

'I believe there is a reward for this one in particular.' Yatsuhiro said with an air of satisfaction, grabbing Michiru's ponytail unexpectedly and tilting her head back. 'Ten gold ryo, if I remember correctly,' His actions were so unexpected, so out of character, that she squealed. The Satake samurai laughed. Her faced burned with shame and anger. No one had ever handled her in such a way. She twisted her head free of Yatsuhiro's grip and shot him a look of pure venom.

Teshiga Isao gave Yatsuhiro a grin as he stepped off the veranda. 'Yes, I heard about these fugitives.' Michiru watched him amble towards her with the confidence of a man assured of his power over everyone within his sight. The smirk on his face made her shiver. She took an involuntary step back, only to be brought up short by Yatsuhiro's grip on her arm. She glanced rapidly at Shuji, catching his scowl under the visor of his helmet before fixing her eyes back on Isao. None of her skittishness was pretence. She hugged her daggers tight with her bound hands.

'Well, I will have to make sure that these are the ones first. May be then I will let you have two ryo.' The Satake samurai gathered around the front of the main building grinned in anticipation of an argument. Teshiga Isao's miserliness must be well known among his men.

'I would be quite happy to let you have half of the reward, my lord. But two ryo is not fair,' he complained.

Isao stopped and turned to look at Yatsuhiro, 'I suggest you be happy with whatever I give you,' he said dismissively, 'or you may find you get nothing at all.'

A sober faced samurai standing at the foot of the stairs spoke up. 'Remember Teshiga-sama, she must be delivered unharmed to get the full reward.'

'Oh I won't break her skin,' he said, almost to himself. He walked up to Michiru, inspecting her outfit with a sneer. 'But I will have to interrogate her'. He tapped her chest plate, 'First we will get you out of this shell, hmmm?' He gripped Michiru's chin, turning her head from side to side. 'Take her to the cell.'

Michiru shivered in disgust. Her heart pounded in her ears. She blinked, the terror of her fight with the ronin flashing through her mind. A rage ignited deep inside her. She wrenched her face out of his hand, fixing his eyes with a look of pure hatred. 'You will not touch me again.' Releasing the rope wrapped around her wrists, she slid a dagger out of its sheath with her right hand and slashed the blade across Isao's throat. He stared at her with wide eyes, his mouth a silent "O" as the blood drenched his immaculate armour. Her fury burned out as quickly as it had taken hold. Isao sank to his knees with a thud and she realised what she had done. This was not the plan. She dropped the dagger. Everyone was frozen, aghast at this sudden turn of events.

Everything around her exploded into action. Yatsuhiro pushed her backwards with a hand on her chest. He lunged forward, his sword whistling from its scabbard. Her men took their cue from him and rushed the shocked Satake samurai. Tanzo dragged her back towards the cover of the first crate. She glanced back over her shoulder to see Yatsuhiro leading a charge that crashed hard against the defending Satake. Ōmono picked up Keiko off the stretcher and rushed into one of the nearby buildings. She was numbed. *What have I done? Did I ruin our chances?*

She flinched as an arrow buzzed past her shoulder. Tanzo shook her shoulder, a desperate edge to his voice. 'My lady!' Her mind snapped back to the moment. She fumbled with the ropes binding the first crate. The large shields that had made up the sides of the box tumbled loose. Michiru grabbed the bow and quiver hidden inside. Tanzo lifted up a wooden shield, covering her from the arrows cutting the air around them. Misao grabbed another shield and protected her back.

She peeked past Tanzo's shield. The prisoners had charged furiously in all directions, motivated by desperation. They fell on the startled Satake garrison, catching many of them by surprise. One defender fired an arrow that dropped one of his attackers but two more overwhelmed him in a flurry of blows. Everywhere she looked knives and clubs rose and fell. The prisoners took up weapons from their victims and turned them on the remaining defenders. The viciousness of the combat was frightening, her mind repelled by the bodies writhing in pain. One defender fled, pursued by three men. They disappeared through the gate, but she heard his dying shriek. The bodies of men, friend and foe alike, were strewn across the bailey, some bristling with arrows, others gashed or stabbed by spears and swords. Michiru covered her nose and mouth with one hand as a gust of hot wind blew dust tinged with the smell of blood and faeces across the bailey.

She had no time to see how Yatsuhiro and Shuji were faring against the enemy samurai. Her mind registered the sounds of combat behind her. But Shuji had given her a task. With Misao at her back and Tanzo shielding her, she readied the bow. She sent three quick shafts whistling into the enemy ashigaru above the gate. Resistance crumbled and the prisoners swamped the gatehouse. She swung her bow around to the tower. An ashigaru leaned over to take a shot but slumped out of sight with one of her arrows in his neck. A second man appeared, looking for a target. Her next shot struck the wooden railing close to him. She ducked down behind Tanzo, cursing in frustration. His attention drawn by the near miss, the ashigaru swung his bow towards her. Snatching an arrow from the quiver, she stood, fixing her eyes on the target. Michiru saw him draw and aim at her.

In a single swift movement, she placed the arrow on the string, drew back, and released. Their missiles passed each other in the air. Michiru's arrow hit him under the arm, driving deep into his lung. The surprised guard clawed at the arrow as he stumbled backwards out of sight. His shaft impaled itself in Michiru's right thigh and sent a jolt of heat through her leg. The heat turned into searing pain and she dropped the bow, grabbing her leg. Gasping in shock, she fell to the ground.

Misao turned at the sound of her pain, kneeling beside her in concern. 'Tanzo! The lady is hit.' He laid down the shield and gently moved her hands aside. 'My lady. Let me deal with this.'

Her mind, focussed on the pain, barely heard his words. She could not trust herself to speak. With her blood now leaking around the arrow, Michiru clamped her lips together and nodded. Fear crept into her heart again. Drawing his knife, he cut the leg of her pants open to expose the wound. With a critical eye the samurai examined the wound and breathed easier, 'Not too bad, my lady. At least it missed the bone.' He held up his knife, 'This might hurt a little.' He grasped the arrow about a palms width from the surface of her leg and ran the blade around the shaft. Steel claws of pain raced up her leg every time the arrow moved, making her tense instinctively. 'Sorry, my lady,' he said apologetically as blood welled around the wound.

From the ground, she could see out past Tanzo's shield. She watched in a haze of shock and pain as the victorious prisoners picked up bows from the fallen guards and shot down into the lower bailey. Their fire was returned by Satake ashigaru still occupying the outer defences. One of the prisoners fell backwards, an arrow lodged in his eye. Another scuttled up to the body, picking up the bow to continue harassing the enemy. Some of the return fire overshot the men at the palisade and scattered around the bailey, decorating the area like bizarre flowers. 'What is happening? Tell me.

What is going on?' she croaked, her throat dry and constricted.

'The Satake samurai are down and their ashigaru are on the run, my lady,' Tanzo replied. 'Yatsuhiro-sama is organising the prisoners and locking the gates.'

Have we done it? With the prisoners holding the gate and the Satake samurai defeated, it looked as if their crazy plan had worked. She closed her eyes and started laughing but it turned into crying within a few breaths. An unlikely band of fugitives had defeated an enemy three times their number and taken the fort. However, she still did not know if enough of the men were left on their feet to hold it. Michiru began to feel nauseous.

Ōmono appeared at her shoulder, dropping his blood-stained spear to help prop her up. 'Shuji-sama is coming, Michiru-hime.'

She turned at his familiar voice gripping his hand. 'Keiko-san?'

'She is safe, now,' he reassured her.

'I'm sorry, my lady,' Misao apologised, staying focussed on his task. 'There is no easy way to do this, I'm afraid.'

'Please, do your best,' she said through gritted teeth.

Having scored around the shaft, he gripped it close to her thigh and prepared to snap off the fletched end. 'This is really going to hurt,' Misao warned her. He snapped the tail off the arrow with a splintering crack. Hot needles of pain shot through Michiru's body, wrenching an explosive cry from her parched mouth. Fresh blood ran across her leg. With as much care as he could muster, he wrapped a cloth bandage around her leg and the remains of the arrow. 'That's all we can do for the moment,' he said, sitting back on his heels. 'We should get you inside before we try and remove the rest of it.'

The lights stopped flashing in Michiru's head, leaving her gasping for breath. A dusty and blood stained Shuji stood in front of her, cleaning his blade with the tail of his sash. She looked up from the ground into his disapproving face. 'I told you to stay behind cover,' he scolded.

167

'Yes, sensei,' she said shortly. 'Can we discuss this later?'

'As you command, my lady.' He signalled for the guards to pick her up, 'Take her to the barracks for the moment.' As Renji lifted her up by the elbow, Michiru saw that two samurai still faced the door to the commander's house with their swords at the ready.

'What is going on, Shuji-san?' she asked, two samurai supporting her as she hobbled along.

'One of the Satake samurai fled the combat and shut himself in the house.' Shuji removed his helmet and wiped his face. 'I imagine he is preparing to commit seppuku, if he hasn't done so already.'

'Take me there,' she ordered, favouring the wounded leg.

Shuji put out a hand, 'Wait, my lady. He is still armed.'

'Then be ready,' she snapped, regretting the rudeness as soon as it was said. It may have been the pain talking, but Michiru felt such sense of exasperation that she was beyond caring about manners. 'Samurai!' she yelled at the house. 'Show yourself!'

'Give me that spear,' she said to Renji, who handed over his weapon. Using the spear as a staff, she hobbled to the veranda's edge. 'Listen to what I have to say!' she yelled at the unresponsive house. The two guards still stood, swords ready, watching the door. 'Samurai, answer me!'

Michiru felt strange. It was as if the world was slowly tilting to one side. The blood trickling down her leg was starting to soak into her sandal. She gripped the spear shaft tighter.

'Samurai,' she said in a tired voice. 'I need you to take a message to your lord!' Her own voice sounded hollow to her, echoing in her ears. She did not know how much longer she could hold herself up. She took another grip on the spear. Still, she heard nothing from inside.

'Shuji motioned to a samurai to open the door. With sword in hand, the samurai slid the screen aside. She recognised the man who had spoken to Isao, warning him that she should not be harmed. He had removed his body armour, setting it to one side. The hilt of a broken katana lay on the mat in front of him, its blade buried deep in the wooden pillar at his back. He sat, focussed on the dagger in his hand, resting the point on his bare midsection. His weary voice croaked, 'I cannot do what you ask.'

'I offer you the chance to live, samurai.' Michiru said sadly. She was sickened by the waste of the day. A deliberate death now, seemed insane. 'You do not have to die today.'

He ignored her, looking instead at Shuji, 'I am Mino Masato of the Satake, second in command of this fort.' He bowed.

Shuji also bowed, replying, 'I am Yoshioka Shuji of the Katsura. Captain of Michiru-sama's Bodyguard.'

'Would you do me the honour of being my second, or must I slice myself open now to stop you from capturing me?'

'You will have to ask the Lady about that,' he replied. 'I am at her command.' With that, he turned and bowed to Michiru.

She felt nothing like a Lady. Unsteady on her feet, using a spear to stay upright, she dripped sweat and blood on the hot dusty ground. It took a few moments for it to sink in exactly what they were asking. They waited. Michiru sighed, 'Has there not been enough lives lost, Masato-san? What would one more achieve?'

'But my lady, the failure is mine. My lord entrusted me with command and I failed,' he said. 'If I returned home he would order me to commit seppuku, if he did not choose to execute me instead.' He looked at Michiru and bowed deeper. 'Will you please allow me an honourable death to erase the shame of my defeat?'

Michiru could not think. *Damn them all.* Her leg throbbed and burned, the darkness pulsing behind her eyelids. Trusting Shuji, she nodded to him. Her eyes closed and she lifted her head, feeling a cool breeze wash over her. A sense of relief flooded through her body. *At last!* The chilled air quenched the fire and took away the pain as she fell. She did not feel Yatsuhiro catch her and carry her inside.

CHAPTER THIRTEEN

Michiru woke with a start, her right leg burning. A woman knelt nearby, absorbed with her task. Michiru raised herself up on her elbows and looked around. The room was simple and dry, the tatami worn in places. The clothes she had been wearing and the pieces of her armour, were folded and stacked in one corner. Two lacquered chests sat against one wall and a lamp stand stood near the door. A rustic brazier smoked gently beneath an iron kettle, letting out a vague tendril of steam. Keiko lay nearby sound asleep. The woman was a thickset, plain-looking peasant in her early twenties, dressed in well-worn clothes. She occupied herself with sewing a new lining in Michiru's armoured sleeve. Her rough hands worked expertly with the fabric, exhibiting a dexterity Michiru envied as she watched her work.

'Ah, lady. You're awake,' she said in surprise, putting her work aside and bowing to the floor. 'My name is Chika. I'm to look after you and Keiko-sama.' The woman stood, bowed again and left through a side door without another word. As the footsteps faded, Michiru made a rapid assessment of herself. She was dressed in clean clothing, her leg elevated on a padded block of wood, the thigh wrapped in fresh bandages. Judging by the smell of herbs and alcohol, she guessed that someone had removed the arrow while she was unconscious, for which she was extremely grateful. She had no illusions about her tolerance for pain. At least she seemed to be otherwise unhurt.

When Chika returned with a tray laden with tea and food, she asked, 'How long was I unconscious?'

'It is mid-afternoon now,' she replied, her manner straight forward. 'Your captain wants to see you. He asked if you feel up to a visit.'

'I suppose I had better talk to him.' She stirred into a sitting position, accepting a cup of fragrant tea.

Bowing, the plain woman replied, 'I'll go get him then.'

Michiru smiled as she left. She assumed this woman had not spent much time at court. She chuckled at the picture that flashed into her head of Chika in an expensive kimono, eyebrows plucked and redrawn, teeth blackened and hair dressed in a courtly style. The image of herself dressed in the same fashion made her laugh, reawakening pain in her leg. She tried to stifle the laughter, and found herself on the verge of crying. She managed to compose herself by the time Chika returned with Shuji.

Shuji bowed. 'I hope you are feeling better, my lady,' he said, indicating to Chika to open the house up. 'The men need to see that you are alright,' he explained.

She looked out across the bailey. The bodies and debris were gone and the prisoners now stood watch dressed in the looted armour. It was surprising the difference that food and a victory had wrought on their bearing. A pair of the newly equipped ashigaru lumbered past with a load of water, sneaking a peek on their way. Michiru glanced at Shuji. 'You have been busy.'

With a bow, he came over and sat by her. Chika offered him tea, which he accepted with a smile. 'Well, there were many things to be done, my lady. Not the least of which was setting up a screen around the bath.' he remarked. 'Chika here was keen to serve you when we asked her. I hope she is looking after you.'

'Thank you, Shuji-san. That was most thoughtful.' The words came out so smooth, the bow automatic. What she wanted to do was run straight for the bath. She needed to scrub the smell of dust, sweat and armour off and soak away the events of the last few days. Unfortunately, Misao said she must keep her leg out of the water, so she was not allowed to have a full soak.

'It seems that Teshiga Isao left you a good sized tub.' He smiled and raised his teacup in salute. With his gaze fixed on the activity in the bailey, he asked, 'How do you feel about dining with the samurai tonight?'

'Is this one of those things that I have to do?' she asked biting her lip.

'No,' he replied. 'But your father did it. And it usually involved lots of sake,' he said with a slight smile. 'I think it would be a good idea for you as well. Take the opportunity to honour their efforts.' Michiru looked across at the sleeping form of Keiko. Shuji saw her concern and reassured her. 'She is well. Misao drugged her with some poppy juice from Haru's collection. He thought it best she sleep, so she will mend better.'

'What about the prisoners, Shuji-san?'

'Three fled before we got here and eight were killed or badly wounded during the fighting. Six more prisoners came up from the lower defences to join us. You now have twenty-four ashigaru in your guard. I have equipped them with armour and weapons taken from the enemy. They all wear green head and armbands to avoid confusion.'

'What about our samurai?'

'Two were killed during the combat. One died of his wounds an hour ago.'

She feared they had lost more. Yet how could she be happy? She felt lost. 'How can I sit down to dinner with these men? What can I say to them?'

Chika refilled his tea. He looked at her thoughtfully. 'Thank you, Chika. You can go and prepare the lady's bath now please.' She bowed and collected some clothes from one of the chests. He sipped his tea in silence until she left. Once they were alone he continued. 'Trust to your instincts, Michiru. They fought well today. Thank them. Everyone appreciates being noticed when the job is done well. Especially if you use their name. But don't get carried away,' he waggled a finger at her and frowned. 'You are starting to develop a disturbing taste for theatrics.' He looked at her earnestly. 'These men were ronin. Not much different from those prisoners. Just with better skills and a touch more pride. They will respond well to recognition. But you cannot reward them yet, so do not make any promises.'

She sighed, 'I owe them a great deal.' However, she also realised that she dare not let the men know about what they were carrying. It would be too much of a temptation. 'They can't find out about the gold, can they?' she murmured.

'No, my lady.' The ronin were a real problem as far as Shuji was concerned. It seems as if most of them have taken Michiru's service seriously. *But they are still ronin. I will not take my eye off them yet.* 'Ronin live treacherous lives. Some may find it hard...to break old habits. Today was a good test. But believe me Michiru, they have yet to truly prove themselves.'

'Thank you, sensei. Thank you for your guidance. We would not be victorious today had it not been for you.' She bowed, feeling the weight of responsibility. 'If you please, can we go over the names of our new samurai?'

* * *

Before the sun had fallen behind the mountain tops, Michiru spoke with the prisoners, informing them that she now considered them as her ashigaru. She assured them that once they reached the Arikawa domain they would be free to choose whether to remain in her service. Food was distributed and a guard rotation set up for the evening. Shuji chose a young samurai called Tendo to be the watch captain, who, along with Ōmono as his first spear, supervised the new ashigaru for the night.

She dined with her samurai at dusk. As they sat down to dinner, the men seemed uncomfortable at first, even in this informal setting. She congratulated them on the victory and thanked them for their bravery and valour. They all toasted her. Once the food was served, it was not long before the men started to relax, thanks partially to the supply of sake handed around. Of course, it would be impolite to tell of one's own actions, so they began to volunteer descriptions of each other's feats. Yatsuhiro encouraged them by delivering his own account of the Kai brother's teamwork.

Throughout it all, she noticed Tanzo remained subdued amongst the toasting and tale telling. Leaning closer to Shuji she asked, 'Why is Tanzo so quiet, sensei?'

'He is not a ronin,' he replied in a hushed tone. 'He is not one of them and probably feels very much out of place.'

'You have not yet explained why you chose him?'

'Apparently he was arrested for attacking a samurai who was thrashing an old man. He beat the samurai senseless and fled. Once they finally captured him, he was sentenced to hard labour.'

Michiru gaped at him. 'I am surprised he was not executed on the spot. How did that make him suitable to protect me?'

'I spoke to the man. Asked him about why he did it and so forth.' He took a measured sip of his sake. 'I judged that he was a good man at heart and given the chance he would prove himself at least a stalwart defender of our gentle princess.' He bowed slightly to her. 'If nothing else his size should be enough to give an attacker pause. Do you feel I was mistaken, Michiru? Are you dissatisfied with him? Would you like me to dismiss him?' He made as if to stand.

She motioned for him to stay. 'No sensei. You are correct. Please forgive me for doubting your judgement,' she replied with a small bow of her own. A wave of fatigue rolled over her convincing her of the need to sleep. She decided that she had done enough and signalled Shuji with her fan.

*   *   *

Muneto stroked his beard, wondering if he should shave it off now that he was a samurai in service. Would he stay in service was the larger question. Takuro, the ex-woodcutter, ex-bandit laughed heartily at Renji's mimicking of the final look on Isao's face as Michiru opened his throat. Muneto frowned at his half-witted friend's snorting laughter. 'Keep it down, would you?' he said testily.

'Aww, don't be such a wet rag, Muneto. Have another drink.' His voice was slurred and his motion shaky as he slopped more sake into the bearded samurai's cup.

Muneto grimaced as he shook the overflow from his hand. *Dullard. We are not out of the woods yet.* He had not believed that they would succeed and had waited for a chance to slip away unseen in the confusion of combat. However, by the time he had cut down the Satake samurai that stood between him and his escape route, the fight was over. He looked around at his comrade's faces. The Lady Michiru had already withdrawn and left them to finish off the last of the drink. They all seemed cheerful and pleased with the way things turned out.

Tano from Kai called out to the others, 'You should have seen Muneto cut down one of the Satake. They touched swords for a bit, stepping and sliding around each other and then Muneto drops his shoulder to the left, totally bluffing the other man. And then, swoosh, uppercuts him in the belly and, whack, across the neck. Dropped him like a sack of rice.' Appreciative comments and laughter flowed from around the room. 'But then he looks around all surprised cause there was no one left to fight.' Tano mimicked the look to the great amusement of the men, who laughed again and raised their cups to Muneto's ferocity.

Muneto smiled wanly, raising his cup in recognition of their salute. *Fools. Somehow, I will find out where the old man hid the gold. And it will be all mine.* He drained his cup and smiled, holding it out to Takuro to be refilled. 'One last cup and then I must go on guard duty.'

On the opposite side of the room, Renji's eyes watched him carefully over the rim of his cup, sipping his sake thoughtfully.

*   *   *

Michiru called Shuji back after the dinner was over. She felt light headed from the sake, of which she had two cups too many. Worn out and ready to collapse, she steeled herself for one more thing. She looked down at the tatami. 'Shuji-san, I would like to see the gold, if you please.'

He bowed, and went to the chest by the wall, laying aside the top layers of its contents. Lifting out the heavy brass-bound box, he opened its lid and displayed the coins. Michiru stared at them. The glossy ovals of gold picked up the flickering yellow lamp light and kept for its own. The dark wood of the box contrasted with the bright red silk nest that cradled these precious objects.

Enough to feed a thousand families. Enough to arm and equip hundreds of samurai. Enough to build a castle or a temple. And it is my dowry. Even though it would be handed to Sojiro-sama, it still legally belonged to her.

Thoughts of her impending marriage brought her mind to Yatsuhiro. Every time he was around her she could not help watching him. His eyes entranced her. The way his mouth twisted when he smiled. The power that showed in his face before battle. His gentle attentiveness and the kindness in his voice. All of these things, and others she could not put a finger on, gave her feelings she neither knew nor wanted. She could not feel like this while she was promised to marry Sojiro-sama, Yatsuhiro's lord. No one had taught her what to do if her own heart betrayed her. A hopeless romance was the last thing she needed. It was bad for her, for Sojiro-sama and for Yatsuhiro. She must bury her feelings deep and forget them. But she did not know how to do that. *Why is this happening? It's not fair.* A single tear rolled down her cheek.

Shuji looked on as expressions of hurt and worry flitted across her face. He thought he understood how overwhelmed she must be. The old samurai saw her fragility, the nervousness and fear. She had endured much in such a short time. He knew there was something else she was struggling with and he had his suspicions what that might be. If he could have spared her he would have, but he knew she must find the courage, the inner strength to continue or else they were all lost.

'Hime-sama,' he said quietly. 'I can only advise you. You must make your choices alone. But we will stand with you when you do.'

She was terrified. She knew that surviving the day had been pure chance. The savagery, the dead men bleeding out into the dust, the twisted faces and screams. It all sickened her, making her want to run and hide in some dark place. If this was command, ruling others, she was not sure she wanted anything to do with it. *Can I just run away? Refuse to go to Nagase?* Wounded as she was, she knew she no longer had the option of sneaking off and disappearing anonymously among the peasants. *Can I go on?* She realised more people would die no matter what she did. She stared at the tatami in front of her, seeing every strand, the repeated pattern transfixing her gaze.

Michiru squeezed her eyes shut, more tears flowing past her control. 'All I have done is put others in danger.' She refused to wipe them away, profoundly embarrassed that her body and emotions betrayed her weakness. 'No matter what I choose, people die. I am responsible for so many deaths. I am unworthy of their sacrifice, no matter who I am.'

In a gentle voice, Shuji told her, 'Michiru, people will judge you first on what you are. You are the daughter of a minor lord. First of all, that means you are a woman. For most samurai that means you are less than they are. You are only a woman. The little respect you will get is because of your family. For peasants, it means that you are to be feared. If you are offended or insulted in any way, you can bring ruin or death down upon them. Most samurai women are seen as proud, spoiled, petulant, scheming and overly sensitive.'

'Secondly, because you belong to a relatively minor clan, people may think of you as either an upstart, who doesn't know her place, or the remnant of a faded glory. Many people will be sufficiently polite to your face to avoid giving you a reason to claim insult. Your retainers may resent you because of the lack of glory attached to being in the service of a minor clan. They fear the suspicion that they face, that they were unable to get, or are unsuitable for, service with a more powerful clan.'

She shifted her posture, familiar with the stereotypes of which he spoke. Michiru had always felt that she was nothing like those caricatures, and that others saw that as well, which was why they were polite. That they might be dissembling had not occurred to her.

Shuji risked a moment of intimacy. He had served her family all

177

his life, in truth she was his family. 'Your father experienced this whenever he travelled. What he did get is respect from the people who knew him. The Takeda and Sanada both honoured your father. Our clans fought together and they saw our mettle in battle and on campaign, through the best and the worst.'

'What they didn't see was your mother and the retainers at home. They did not see what your mother did to hold the estate together. They did not see how she ensured that your father's retainers were paid first, how the food supplies, horses, equipment, farmers, irrigation projects and a thousand other things were handled during those difficult years.' He spoke with quiet passion. 'That is why your family's retainers love you.'

'What you are is not something that you have a say in, but "who you are" is within your control. Who you are is determined by your choices. What you choose to do when confronted, what you say, how you treat people, the care you take of yourself and others. These are what shape who you are.'

Michiru looked up, meeting his eyes, surprised at the tenderness and forthright nature of his words. 'Most people will never really know who you are. Oh they will see some things, hear about others. Only your closest family and retainers will have any idea of your true nature. That was your parent's strength. That is your strength. The people who serve you. Without them you are alone.'

'But how can I...'

He shushed her. 'Consider Keiko-san. Her father is samurai, but he is almost blind.'

Michiru gasped, 'I had no idea.'

'Yes. Now, your father could have discarded him, sent him away. Instead, he found room for Keiko in his household. The money her father receives for her service embarrasses him. He asked to be allowed to commit seppuku but Keiko pleaded with your father to forbid it. After that, your father convinced him to shave his head and become a monk. Now he spends his time reciting prayers for your family.'

'I did not know that.'

'He was a good man, your father. He felt that lordship had great responsibilities. Otherwise, why else was he there? Who else should have helped Keiko's father? Other lords may have taken Keiko in as a toy for their bed and left the blind man to fend for himself. Your father always saw it as his duty, before the gods, to look after his people.'

Shuji sat up straight. 'For you to give up now would be selfish. The people who give you their allegiance; samurai, peasants, the ronin, even the prisoners, have thrown everything into serving you, even given you their lives, because they believed in you. They see something in you that they admire and respect. Don't throw that away. Not yet. Not even when all hope is gone. We will all do whatever we can to see you safely to your new home, or die trying. Can you ask more? What will you offer them in return?'

She bowed, as much to stop him seeing her face distorted in anguish. 'Thank you, Shuji-sama,' she said, her voice thick with emotion.

'Don't be mistaken, my lady,' he said in a lighter tone. 'We all want to live. But if a man must die, then he prefers to choose how and when, and what for. Many samurai hope their deaths will make a difference, to be as memorable as Benkei's. To have so terrified the enemy than none dare approach, even when you are mortally wounded. To have served one's House, to have protected it, maybe even to have saved it.' He nodded. 'We honour our ancestors not by our words but by our actions, and by what is in our hearts.'

She looked at him with surprise. This was a different Shuji speaking to her. He had never been this open with her before and it was a rare moment.

As the insects buzzed in the warmth of the night, he added, 'You hold all our futures in your hand. And yes, that is a great responsibility. But this is what you were born to do. You must find the strength. Even if you fail, better to die trying than to give up too soon.' He bowed formally, 'Please forgive my longwindedness and directness, Michiru-hime.'

She bowed low, her head touching the floor. 'Thank you, sensei.' There was nothing else to say.

*   *   *

Renji stepped out of the barracks, ready to take over guard

179

duty from Tendo. As the samurai on watch, he was responsible for checking on the ashigaru sentries to make sure they were awake and keeping a lookout. It would be a poor thing if they took this fort only to lose it to a sneak attack the next night. He strode casually across to the main house, carrying his sheathed long sword loose in his hand, comforted by its weight. Two guards stood at the foot of the steps, spears in hand. He nodded to them. He could hear muted voices coming from within. He recognised Shuji's deep tones and the refined melody of Michiru's voice, now tinged with sadness. It pulled at his heart to think of her suffering. *Ah. She is beautiful. I wish I could be so lucky as to find someone like her for my wife. But ...* He sighed deeply.

He moved on with his rounds, past the corner of the main house, heading for the gate. A dark flutter caught the corner of his vision, bringing him spinning around with his hand on the hilt of his sword. Muneto stood ten paces away, near the entrance to the hastily constructed bathhouse. 'Easy, Renji-san. It's just me,' he said, one hand extended.

'You startled me, Muneto-san.' He frowned in the dark, keeping his hand on his sword. 'It's late. What are you doing out here?'

'I am on my way to bed now. I was just checking out the bath house.' He approached Renji slowly, one hand resting in the front of his kimono, the other stroking his beard. 'I don't know about you, but I need a bath. I was hoping to convince Shuji-sama to let us use it, if we are here for another day or two.'

Renji took his hand off his sword hilt, but kept an unconsciously tight grip on the scabbard. 'I don't see why he would not agree,' he said, the hair prickling at the back of his neck. 'But we will be in Nagase soon anyway. Why not wait to use a bath house there?'

'You are right, I suppose,' Muneto sighed and turned towards the barracks. He strode off with a wave of his hand. 'I am just tired of smelling like a peasant's armpit.'

CHAPTER FOURTEEN

The arrival of a messenger awoke Utaemon Katsuo, senior councillor to the Lord of the Satake clan. Befuddled by sleep, he made his way to his reception room. 'What is it?' he said, yawning behind his sleeve. He doubted it was good news. Good news rarely wakes you up in the early hours of the morning.

The travel-stained rider licked his lips. 'A letter, sire, from Shizuka-sama,' he said, holding out the folded paper.

Katsuo snatched the letter, opening it and tilting it towards the lamp. 'Don't know him. What is his post?' he asked as he scanned the hurried characters.

'The garrison at Izuna-yamashiro, lord.'

He read the message with growing disbelief. 'What is going on? Where did this "attack force" come from? Who are they?' he asked with growing desperation. The fort in question was the new outpost under construction on the flanks of Izuna mountain, part of the long-term plan to cut a path across the ridge into Arikawa territory. Paved, spanned, supplied and garrisoned, it gave them a firm foothold in the pass, but it was a risky strategy, not to mention an expensive one.

He bit his lip. He thought it was secret. *Now we know it is not.* How will Kiyomori react to this news? If his fears were correct, his lord might just kill him on the spot.

'My lord?' the messenger asked, perplexed.

Katsuo waved his hand in annoyed dismissal, eyes re-reading the message, looking for more information, hoping that he had misread. *Can I get away with leaving it until he wakes up? Probably* not. *He would just be angrier. He will be annoyed enough at being woken at all. Will I be able to wake him?* As Kiyomori used increasing amounts of Chinese aphrodisiacs, he had become even more unstable. On top of the copious quantities of sake he consumed, it spelled disaster for everyone. He clapped his hands, 'Suwo!' His secretary, waiting in the adjoining room, opened the door. Most of the household would be waiting to see what news the messenger brought.

'Yes, Utaemon-sama?'

He tried to think of what to do to pre-empt Kiyomori's inevitable anger. 'Get tea and something light for the lord to eat. Have his consorts standing by, and have the jailers get some prisoners ready to execute. Wait for me outside His quarters. We will have work to do, assuming we live.'

'Yes, sire,' he said before bowing and dashing away on silent feet.

Katsuo frowned to himself. Yoshioka Shuji. Oh wonderful. *Why won't you die, you old badger? Is the girl with him? Undoubtedly.* 'What I wouldn't give to see that man dead,' he said to the ceiling. His mind whirled, possibilities meshed. A slow grin spread across his face. 'And now I know where they both are.' *Things might turn out right after all.*

He had just the men in mind for the job. It was risky to send them off without Kiyomori's express permission. *Ah, but I can have them assembled and ready to leave at a moment's notice.* He got up and made his way through the darkened hallways to the watch commander's quarters.

*　　*　　*

Yatsuhiro watched the first rays of the sun peak over the mountains to the east. He stood in the watchtower of the upper bailey lost in his own thoughts. He could not see much else because the trees around the fort and along the ridgeline were still standing. He suspected that the Satake intended to wait until the construction was nearly complete before they cleared the lines of sight. The two guards stationed up there left him to himself as they watched the approaches to the fort, keeping an eye out for any movement on the slopes below.

He could just make out the shine of the river they would have to cross through the tops of the trees. His home would have been out of sight anyway, behind a spur of the ridgeline that jutted out into the valley. Yatsuhiro's eyes scanned around to the north. Smoke smudged the air where Harashiro castle would be. He clenched his jaw at the thought of Kiyomori's betrayal of the treaty with the Arikawa. *We should never have trusted him.* As the light grew, villages here and there showed their own lines of smoke as their day began. The Arikawa captain was distracted from his thoughts by the sound of someone ascending the ladder. He turned to see Shuji's head appear through the manhole. 'Good morning, Yatsuhiro-san,' he greeted him.

'Good morning, Shuji-san,' he replied gruffly, still smouldering over Kiyomori's perfidy.

The older samurai came to stand by Yatsuhiro at the rail, turning to the ashigaru. 'Go down and get your breakfast. You can bring it back up here to eat.' He waited until they had reached the foot of the ladder before turning back to him. 'Two of the prisoners disappeared last night.'

'I suppose it was inevitable that some of them would take off at the first opportunity.'

'The question is did they just make themselves scarce or did they run for the nearest Satake troops they can find?'

Yatsuhiro stared down into the bailey below, watching the morning routine unfold. 'Either way, we should be ready to move quickly.'

'How much longer do you think we have before they try to take the fort back?'

Rubbing his eyes with one hand, he tried to estimate times and distances. 'Kiyomori will have heard about us by now. He will have to send out orders. If they divert troops from the attack on Harashiro, they will be here tomorrow afternoon.' Yatsuhiro gripped the railing with both hands. 'Will the women be fit to move by then?'

'They will have to be,' he replied. 'They will both have to be carried in kagos, at least for the first part. They can use the horses if they need to flee.' Shuji stared hard at the younger man, Yatsuhiro's concern clear on his face. 'You are thinking about getting reinforcements to cover our retreat, aren't you?'

'How did you know?'

Shuji shrugged. 'It is logical. But it is unlikely they could reach us in time.'

'No. I arrived at the same conclusion.'

'Besides, we both know that there is only one person who can go and fetch them. And I suspect you won't want to leave her at this point.'

Yatsuhiro turned to the old samurai. It seemed that Shuji saw more than others did. 'Is it so easy to see?'

He grinned. 'Well, it is really not so surprising. In fact, it is only natural. The real problem is she has feelings for you.' He became more serious. 'I see her watch you. I see her struggle with those feelings. She knows she is to marry Sojiro-sama and it is tearing at her heart.'

Yatsuhiro turned away. 'She will get over it once all this is done. Once she gets to Nagase.'

'You are assuming you understand her. A woman's heart can be a dangerous thing that no man can predict. And she is young, which means her fire burns hot. She is also proud. You risk her hating you. And Sojiro.'

Yatsuhiro walked to the other side of the platform, seething with exasperation. 'How did this become so complicated?'

'I think you know the answer to that, my young friend. However it happened, you have to deal with it, before it is too late.'

*　　*　　*

Michiru awoke with that strange sense of living in someone else's home. She was disoriented, in unfamiliar surroundings full of strange sounds and smells. The door slid open to reveal Keiko, her movements measured and her thin smile fixed. Her arrival brought a flood of relief as she ushered Chika in with tea and food for them all. Feeling the need for company more keenly than ever, Michiru waved for Chika to sit and join them. She realised that the woman would get precious little time to eat for the rest of the day. Chika was wary at first of sitting with the two samurai women, but Michiru overrode her objections. 'Let's all have something to eat first before we open the screens. Then we can worry about appearances in front of the menfolk.' So they had simple onigiri, seaweed wrapped rice balls, and tea, which was really all that was available, while they discussed clothing options for the day. As there was no need for travel that day, and both women were technically convalescing, Michiru and Keiko could afford to wear more feminine attire.

Chika had procured some kimonos and additional lengths of fabric from the tradesman's wives in the village at the foot of the hill. Considering that work had now ceased on the fort, the wives had been keen to make whatever bargains they could to stay solvent and feed their families. Another piece of knowledge dropped into place for Michiru, as she began to understand more about the flow on effect that events had on the lives of ordinary people.

'When did you get these?' Michiru asked her as she unfolded the bundles of cloth.

'Last night, my lady. I knew you would need something more suitable while you and the Lady Keiko were recovering.' She shrugged. 'It doesn't take long to make a kimono, so I went and asked Shuji-sama for some coins to buy the material. Omono-san came with me and we made some good trades.'

Keiko and Michiru exchanged a knowing look. 'I bet he did,' commented Michiru with a smile. 'Did he find any sweet cakes?'

Chika thought for a moment. 'He did go off with one of the tradesman's wives to ask around, but I don't think he had any luck.'

Keiko stifled a smile. 'I am guessing he had more luck than you think, Chika.' A laugh burst unexpectedly from Michiru, which set them all off. The laughter released some of the tension that had knotted Michiru's very soul, bringing her to the verge of tears. Keiko saw how close she was to losing control and rose with a word to Chika. 'Come on, Chika. Let's wash and dry this material so we can make something out of it.'

As the screen slid shut behind them, Michiru let the tears flow, crying quietly into her hands.

*   *   *

The cloth dried quickly in the warm breeze and it was not long before they had it spread out on the floor. Keiko could not do much with her arm in a sling so she supervised Chika's work, advising her on the finer points of fashion as opposed to functionality. Michiru watched from her cushion, adding the occasional comment. Before long, they had two kimonos and obis fashioned from the material Chika had obtained. There was even enough for plain underskirts, although certainly not in fashionable colour combinations.

By mid-morning, Michiru and Keiko were seated in the main room of the house dressed in their new kimonos, their hair combed out and held back at their shoulders with crisp paper bows. Sipping her tea with detached serenity, Michiru gave the order for Chika to open the screens into the bailey beyond. As the daylight flooded in, she saw that it was full of men engaged in the daily routine of a living fort. Guards manned the walls, supplies were being carried to the storehouse, men were mending armour and cleaning weapons, while others drilled and practiced. All eyes turned her way, which was just the effect Michiru wanted. She gave the attention she received a faint smile and continued to sip her tea.

In the centre of the bailey, Yatsuhiro drilled a group of ashigaru in use of the spear. She noticed Tanzo's tall frame in amongst the ashigaru, earnestly practicing alongside the other former prisoners. She imagined he felt lacking in skills compared to her other bodyguards. Yatsuhiro gave his instructions in a clear voice, simple commands delivered with strength but without shouting. Though his actions focussed on the men, his eyes kept flicking back to her. Her gaze appeared to wander around the bailey but it always returned to Yatsuhiro, checking to see if he was watching her.

Shuji stepped down off the barracks veranda, leaving the men to continue their work. Like most of the men, he wore only arm and leg armour, but both his swords were stuck in his sash. He strode across to the main building, stopping at the foot of the steps to give her a bow. 'Good morning, Michiru-hime. I trust you are feeling well today.'

'Yes, Shuji-san. I am quite well today.' She indicated a cushion nearby. 'I understand that you are busy, but we would be most grateful if you could join us for a moment?'

'Thank you, my lady. I would be honoured.' Bowing again, he came up the steps and took the offered seat. Chika brought him a cup of tea, which he accepted gratefully. 'That was very well done, Michiru. Good timing and presentation. You are to be commended.'

She bowed gently in response. 'Thank you, sensei.' She looked out over the bailey, where the men watched her out of the corner of their eyes while attempting to appear engrossed in their tasks. Yatsuhiro walked around the group he was drilling, making corrections or giving advice, but he still fixed his eyes on her at every opportunity. She looked down, unable to look at him anymore without a tightening in her chest. Her old self would have bathed in the attention, but a sense of guilt pushed all that aside. 'How do the preparations go, Shuji-san?'

'We have used what oil we could find to soak as much of the timber as possible. It should burn well. We also found a significant quantity of gunpowder. That should also help this place burn, although I have reserved half of it to blow up the gateway and water cistern.'

'And the men?'

Shuji looked out into the bailey at the men practicing under Yatsuhiro. 'It takes at least a month to make a proficient soldier, my lady. Preferably three months. Even a captain of Yatsuhiro's skill and experience, or myself for that matter, can only do so much. Luckily, we do not need to fight a battle. We have just one valley to cross. Whatever they learn will have to be enough.'

'Have any more run away?' Michiru asked, setting aside her cup. Ōmono approached from across the yard, a sheathed short sword in his hand. He stopped at the foot of the steps and waited.

'Only two. I think the rest of them have decided that their best chance lies with you, my lady. Though few of them will make good soldiers.'

She turned to acknowledge her favourite ashigaru. 'Good morning, Ōmono.'

'Good morning, my lady. If I might have a quick word with you.'

'Certainly. But first, what has become of Haru?'

'Ah.' He scratched his nose, unsure of the response he would get. 'He is locked in the cell at the moment, my lady.'

'Remember, Ōmono. He is not to be unduly mistreated.'

'Yes, my lady. Understood,' he replied with a quick bow.

'Now. I wish to apologise, Ōmono-san. It seems that during the fight to free the prisoners the other day, I broke the naginata that you made for me. I am sorry,' she added with a small bow.

Ōmono rubbed the back of his neck in embarrassment. 'Oh, I would not be too concerned about that, my lady.' He knelt at the foot of the stairs, bowing his head low. 'It was a poor effort on my part. I apologise for it not being sufficient for you in battle.' They both knew that, given the circumstances, it had been the best thing available at the time and she had managed to take out two enemies with it before it broke. However, custom, and their relative social positions, demanded that Ōmono take the blame for the weapon's failure in combat. 'I have searched the fort but I cannot find any naginata blades here. I am afraid they have fallen out of general usage. Soldiers these days are usually armed with spears, bows or guns.'

Shuji interjected. 'It is just as well,' he said. 'The lady will not need a naginata. Now that we have sufficient men to protect her, I would rather she not have one. Maybe then she will not be tempted to do anything stupid.' He looked at her sternly.

Ōmono cleared his throat to distract them from Michiru's possible embarrassment at this comment, and to bring the focus of the conversation back to his original point. 'I recovered Shigemori's blade after the combat, my lady.' With both hands he held up the short sword he had been carrying. 'I replaced its hilt, so that you may continue to use it, seeing that it served you in battle once before. So you need not go unarmed.'

She looked at him gratefully, 'Thank you Ōmono. I would be honoured to carry his blade again.'

He climbed the steps and handed her the sword with great reverence, bowing again as she accepted it. He backed down the stairs and smiled. 'And now, if you will excuse me, my lady, I must continue working on your's and Keiko-sama's kagos, so that you may travel in comfort for the next part of the journey.' He bowed again, having given Keiko an impish grin.

They all smiled at his light-hearted manner, grateful for him making the day a little cheerier. 'Certainly, Ōmono.' She nodded in response. 'Both the Lady Keiko and I thank you and appreciate your efforts on our behalf.'

CHAPTER FIFTEEN

They sat with the screens open all day. Shuji came and spent time with them making polite conversation. She asked him for his observations about the men and suggested distributing bows to at least half of them. After the selected men spent the afternoon training with the bow, she felt much more confident about their ability to deliver an effective volley, at least at short range. Even some of the samurai showed their archery skills and assisted with the lessons. Yatsuhiro remained with the ashigaru all day. He was tireless in his efforts, always ready to step in and make corrections or to give demonstrations.

With the ashigaru dismissed for the day, Chika closed the screens to give them some privacy. 'I will go and get some more tea and something for you to eat, my lady.' Michiru watched her go, glad that she would have a chance to talk to Keiko alone for a moment.

'Keiko-chan, did you see Yatsuhiro watching me?'

'Yes, my lady. He had a hard time keeping his eyes off you. You were teasing him most effectively.'

'I was not teasing him.' she objected.

'You dressed like a lady again, sat up here aloof and out of his reach, speaking to every one of our group except him. You kept your eyes averted as much as possible, pretending that he was not there while he went about his manly duties. I am sorry my lady but that is classic teasing.'

'Oh,' she said, surprised that her natural behaviour could be interpreted that way. 'I did not mean to do that to him.

'You have feelings for him, don't you?' trying to tread carefully, but sensing Michiru wanted to talk about it.

'I do not know,' she said, bursting with exasperation. It all came pouring out, as her doubts and remorse threatened to overwhelm her. 'There is something between us, but I do not know what it is. I do not know how he feels. I am so confused I do not know what to do.'

'I am afraid you must make that decision for yourself, my lady. I can't tell you what to do.' It pained Keiko to know there was little she could do for her.

After a brief moment, Michiru gathered herself, trying to control a flood of sadness. 'Have you ever been in love?'

Keiko sensed her distress. She drew a breath and tried to explain herself. 'There was a girl who lived near me in Omegura. She was a few years older than me. I used to play with her younger brother and sister. I only remember seeing her a little bit. When I knew her, she spent most of her time weaving and dyeing cloth with her mother. One of the boys used to hang around her a lot. He worked as a porter and would carry loads to Nagase and back. Sometimes he would be away for a month, sometimes only a week. But every time he came back he brought her something. Sweets, a comb, ribbons or a nice piece of cloth. He would sneak into her bedroom at night and lay with her. She thought that he loved her and wanted to get married.'

'Soon she was pregnant to him. I don't know if she told him, but he did not come back from his last trip. She waited and worried as her baby grew. She sent letters to Nagase asking him to come back soon. But still he did not return. She got very sick and could not work, so her sister had to help her mother with the work. In the autumn, she had the baby, but it was stillborn. And still he did not come back. Then one day she got a letter from someone in Nagase. It said that he had got another girl pregnant and had left to work in Ueda. She was heartbroken because she thought he loved her. She waited for him to come back and marry her but he never did. She drowned herself in the river sometime during the winter, but we did not find her body until spring.'

191

'So you see, my lady, I try not to think about love. It can be a dangerous thing for a poor girl. But for you. You are strong and have people that care for you. If anyone could survive love, it would be you. The stories say that being in love is a rare and wonderful feeling that makes you closer to heaven. You have a chance at that with Yatsuhiro. Maybe. If he loves you too. But for you, I would help you any way I can. Even if it meant keeping the secret from your husband. But you must decide if he loves you enough.'

'Did anyone ever tell you that they loved you? Anyone that you think might have really been in love with you?'

'Oh, boys will tell you that all the time. But mostly they just wanted to get between my legs.'

'Really?'

'Oh yes. They would sneak into my room at night and say all sorts of sweet things. They would get all excited and try to touch me, telling me they loved me. I would ask them if they would marry me if I ended up with a child, and of course, they would say yes. But I did not believe them.'

'Why not?'

'Because they were in my room at night trying not to wake my father. I always thought that if they really loved me they would say those things to me during the day and maybe even in front of my father.' She shrugged. 'Even then, I may not have believed them.'

'So how do I tell if Yatsuhiro loves me?' she asked in frustration.

Keiko shrugged. 'You already know he would fight to protect you. Maybe even die for you. He is a healthy man and you are a beautiful woman, so you can be sure he desires you. But would he marry you himself? Would he seek your counsel when he is troubled? Would he share his innermost thoughts and feelings with you? Will he be kind and understanding of you? Will his company save you from loneliness and misery? If all you want is to lay with him then it is not love. But what if it is true love?'

Michiru bit her lip, considering the questions she had asked, trying to answer them herself. But no matter which way she thought about it, she always came back to the same answer. 'Oh Keiko. All that does not really matter in the end. My marriage to Sojiro-sama will go ahead if we ever make it to Nagase. I cannot abandon my duty to my family. Not just to my family, but to everyone that relies on me. What would happen to you if I ran away?' She threw up her hands. Hovering on the verge of tears, her lips trembled as she tried to keep her voice down. 'Could we run away together? Where would we go? Would Yatsuhiro be willing to find another lord to serve? Am I brave enough to throw it all away for him? What if he abandons me, like what happened to your friend? I would have nothing and no one.'

Keiko's heart went out to her. The feelings Michiru had towards Yatsuhiro must be real. They were certainly strong. *Maybe their love would make a new life possible for them.* She handed her a handkerchief from her sleeve. 'You would have the gold. You would have the freedom to make your own choices.'

Michiru dabbed the tears from her eyes, exhaling to try and regain her control. 'On this journey I have learned many things,' she said quietly. 'And one of the most important is how many people rely on the head of the clan. Everyone, from the other members of the family all the way down to the peddlers by the side of the road.' She frowned, looking down at the matting. 'The law must be upheld. The domain must be fruitful. The roads and bridges must be repaired. The borders must be protected. Without good order, everything would fall into chaos and ruin, and people would suffer.' Michiru remembered Shuji's lecture last night. She tried to weigh her own desires against her duty, but could not find a balance. 'Whether I like it or not, I have a part to play in holding that together. It will be my responsibility to keep the House in order, determine the fates of maids and servants, cooks and gardeners, and many others besides. From there, maybe a thousand families would be affected by my decisions.' She straightened, looking back up to see her friend's compassionate expression. 'Shuji-san is right. I cannot, must not run away from that.'

Keiko had never experienced the strong emotions that were tormenting Michiru, and she felt the lack of that in her life. She did not want to see her give it up because she knew it may never happen again. 'My lady, you do not have to run off together. You do not even have to lay with him. No child is needed. He can serve Sojiro-sama and still be a part of your life.'

'But do I encourage Yatsuhiro? Tell him how I feel? Can I ask him to betray his lord's trust for my feelings? To make me happy?' The pain in her heart choked her voice. Tears filled her eyes again, blurring her vision. 'And you. Should you help us to meet secretly, your life would be forfeit. My life would be forfeit. Yatsuhiro's honour would be destroyed. All for my happiness.' She shook her head at the futility of it all. 'If this world were different we might have a chance. But, Keiko, I see no hope, no future for Yatsuhiro and I. It would be better if I had not met him.' She gasped at the realisation of what she must do, as if a hole had opened in her soul. 'Wherever this love has come from, I do not want it. It brings me nothing but pain and sorrow.' Exhausted from trying to hold back the tide of her despair, she finally gave in and admitted the truth. 'I just wish I could let it go.' She threw herself into Keiko's arms in a storm of weeping, unable to hold back the tsunami of her sorrow.

*   *   *

Michiru ran through a dark forest, stumbling forward in panic and blood, chased by taunting voices clawing at her flesh, tearing open her leg. So much blood. The pain in her leg woke Michiru, yet again, from one of her sporadic snatches of sleep. The nightmare haunted her whenever she finally managed to sleep. Yet no position was comfortable for long. The cold darkness of the early hours hovered in the air like a mist. She gave a heavy sigh and threw back the blanket in weary frustration. By the time Michiru sat up and shrugged her jacket over her shoulders, Chika slid open the door from the adjoining room and brought in a tray.

'I've got some nice warm food and tea here for you, mistress,' she whispered as she placed the tray down and picked up a most ugly but functional kettle. She filled the cup and sat back, waiting. Michiru looked at the tray, her mouth moistening at the aroma of the steaming porridge. A small sweet rice cake sat next to it along with a steaming cup of tea. She felt drained by the impassioned outburst of the previous night and hoped that a good breakfast might help.

She sat with her wounded leg out straight and made a start on the plain but nourishing breakfast. Chika knelt next to the tray, watching her intently. Michiru started to find it unnerving when, in a nervous rush, the woman asked, 'Will you take me with you, mistress?'

Michiru stopped mid-mouthful, taken aback by her directness. 'Well, I had not thought about it, Chika,' she said in quiet surprise.

The farm girl lowered her head, 'I know that I am a rough, unmannered commoner and not like the fancy ladies that you're used to. But I am here and they are not. I will serve you faithfully, until you get to Nagase and find someone more proper to serve you.' The coarse featured girl looked up at her in hope. 'All I ask is that you take me away from here. I want to make a new start in a town, start a business selling food, or flowers, or making umbrellas.'

Michiru's eyes softened as she heard the tone of desperation and longing in the young woman's voice. 'We may be going into great danger,' she said with concern, knowing that she must refuse Chika's plea. 'We may not escape alive. I cannot ask you to risk that.'

The distraught woman put her head to the floor. 'Mistress. Every day of my life has been dangerous. Ever since I was young, I have been in danger. I have been starved and beaten and treated so badly,' her voice shook with suppressed emotion, 'sometimes I thought I would die.' Michiru shivered as Chika confessed, 'Sometimes I wished I could.' She looked up at Michiru with pleading eyes. 'Please take me with you. I swear you will not regret it.'

Michiru sipped her tea, shifting slightly to ease her leg. Her brow furrowed in thought. She did not need a "lady"-in-waiting right now, but what she could use was someone to watch her back. She considered it for a moment and made the decision. She had been moved to help Haru, so why not Chika? 'Very well then. I offer you a position as my maid. Do you accept?'

'Oh, I do! Thank you … thank you … so much, mistress!' she stammered, bowing even deeper. 'I accept! Thank you! May the Gods favour you always! Thank you!

'Do not thank me too fast, Chika! You may end up wishing you had not accepted.' With a thin smile, she leaned towards her, plucking at the woman's threadbare kimono, 'We will have to get you some clothes. And, I will also have something unusual to ask of you.'

'What's that, mistress?' She frowned.

'Will you be my escort on the road and carry my weapons?'

'Yes, mistress.' Her brow knotted in confusion. 'But I don't know how much use I can be. I've never used a weapon before.'

Michiru's grin widened, 'What about a bow?'

'No, my lady,' Chika smiled back, 'but I will learn.'

*   *   *

Misao came in and checked Michiru's and Keiko's wounds, putting fresh dressings on, while Chika helped them dress in their washed and mended travelling clothes. Michiru insisted on having her arm and leg armour fitted before taking her new maid with her to the barracks. There, amid the curious looks of the men, they enlisted Renji's help in selecting suitable pieces of clothing and armour for Chika. Once fitted out in a similar manner to her mistress, the young peasant woman began to smile. Michiru finished off the outfit by choosing a short sword for her and pushing it into her sash. The smile was replaced by a look of doubt and uncertainty.

'I told you, Chika. I was going to ask something unusual of you.'

She gripped the hilt gingerly and slid the short sword half way out of its scabbard, looking at the blade in fascination and awe. 'I have never had anything more than a kitchen knife,' she said quietly.

'Well, I hope you will not have to use it.' She placed a hand on her shoulder. 'Now help me over to the rack and let us choose our bows.'

Shuji and Yatsuhiro had the men busy preparing the fort for its fiery death by stacking anything flammable under the eaves of the buildings. Taking advantage of what time they had, Michiru coached

Chika in the use of the bow. While the distances she was practicing at were short, the important thing for her was learning the techniques of nocking, drawing and loosing. They were still practicing when a runner came panting through the fort's timber gate and into the bailey, 'Taisho! Message for the Taisho! Where can I find him?!'

Shuji hurried out of the barracks. 'Report.'

'Sentries have seen a column of troops approaching, taisho. It looks like more than two hundred,' he said in a serious tone. 'Some of them are armed with teppo, sir.'

'Gunners,' he said to himself. 'So that is where his gold has been going.'

The messenger, still recovering his breath, added, 'Taisho, there is more.' He looked nervously at Michiru.

'Yes? What else?

'There was a group of cavalry with the column, taisho. They rode off to the east.'

Yatsuhiro cursed, 'They will be circling around to cut off our escape.'

Shuji turned to Yatsuhiro. 'I want you on that horse and out of here now,' he told him. 'They may not reach us in time, but if that cavalry cut us off ... Go!'

Yatsuhiro bowed his head, plainly not keen to leave Michiru in danger. He realised that those reinforcements were her best chance of getting to safety. 'I'll be back,' he said to her with a nod, turning and striding towards the horses.

Michiru looked at Shuji. She was not exactly sure what had passed between the two men, but she knew that she could trust them. 'How long do we have, Shuji-san?'

'We are leaving now, my lady.' Turning to the men in the yard, Shuji yelled, 'Prepare to move out!' The captain's shouted order energised the men into action, who rushed to their pre-arranged places. He turned to her, speaking in a low, controlled tone, 'Be prepared to move fast. We will be pursued by men with guns, Michiru-hime.

I can't protect you from firearms. Our best defence is speed.' He cursed the Satake commander and hoped he would develop some nasty affliction, preferably a painful one. *They will try to get close enough for a stray shot to wound one of us, to slow us down. That will make the cavalry's job easier. It looks like they want to kill us now, not capture us.*

Renji ran up, the tension of anticipated action showing on his face. 'What do you want to do about the gunpowder, taisho?'

'Spread one barrel around the storehouse. I will set fire to the eaves before I leave,' Shuji instructed him. 'By the time it blows we should be halfway down the hill.' They needed to get out of there fast. With Michiru injured, they would need as much time as they could get. Without a good head start, they would be in real danger of being shot down one by one.

Michiru watched Yatsuhiro amongst the bustle of preparations as he led a horse to a gap in the palisade and mounted up. With a red headband, his arms and legs armoured, and a spear balanced in his grip as he handled the nervous horse, he looked every bit the confident samurai. He glanced across at her, their eyes meeting briefly. She broke the contact and lowered her eyes. With a shout at the horse, he kicked his heels to its flanks and disappeared through the gap. She stared at the dust as it dispersed, leaving a void like the one growing in her heart. *Why did I let him leave without a word?*

Looking around at her retinue, she saw that all her samurai now wore armour. They carried themselves with a pride and purpose that they had lacked previously. Even the liberated prisoners were dressed in light ashigaru armour and looked keen. They all, samurai and ashigaru alike, wore red armbands suggested by Shuji to help identify friends from foes. The Kai brothers, Tano and Seibo, took control of the ashigaru and organised them for departure.

A rattle of distant gunfire echoed up from the road to the fort. Michiru turned and said with deceptive calm, 'I think that is our cue to leave, Chika,' With her maid's aid, she climbed into the waiting litter, the dowry box tied across the back of the seat. She eased her leg into the sling Ōmono had added. Shuji appeared from nearby, running his eyes over the preparations.

He spoke to the kago bearers, selected from the least martial of the ex-prisoners. 'Set a good pace, but try to go gently, if you can. Understand?' The men bowed. Two more were ready to relieve or assist as needed. More carried large shields to provide cover against any missile fire. Chika waited nearby, looking uncomfortable in the borrowed armour, carrying Michiru's bow as well as her own. Two quivers of black and white fletched arrows hung over her shoulder. Ōmono led Michiru's horse, with Haru behind on a long rope. He was no longer gagged but his face had an unhappy pinched look to it, undoubtedly from the maelstrom of smells assaulting him. Shuji leaned down to speak to Michiru, 'The men from the outposts will be back shortly. I will set fire to the fort and catch up to you,' he re-assured her. He seemed calm and unflustered, contrasting the turmoil that seethed inside her. She felt helpless, sitting there waiting to leave and appreciated yet again, why her father had chosen him as his captain. 'It will be an uncomfortable ride, my lady,' he told her. ' I am sorry. If the enemy gets too close, get on the horse and head for the border. Yatsuhiro should be along with his men soon.'

'Thank you, Shuji-san,' was all that she said before the bearers lifted the kago and carried her through the gap in the palisade. What else could she say?

CHAPTER SIXTEEN

They started slowly, settling into a comfortable rhythm. A path was already a cleared over the uneven ground, winding down through the woods to the foot of the hill. Michiru could hear the occasional pop of distant gunfire coming from the other side of the fort. The dull thud of an explosion made her turn to look back up the hill. She expected to see pieces of the fort lifting into the sky in a fiery inferno. Instead, all she saw was a haze of smoke through the trees. 'That was not the fort exploding was it, Renji?' she asked the samurai trotting along beside her.

'No, my lady,' he said, looking back up the slope. 'That was only a little explosion. I'd say a small keg.' She saw dark figures running down the slope towards them through the wispy smoke. 'It looks like Shuji-san is coming, though,' he added. 'Do you think you could handle it if we picked up the pace a bit, my lady?'

Determined not to let her weakness slow them down, she replied, 'I think that would be a good idea, Renji-san.' Adjusting her grip on the hand strap, she shifted her weight in the seat, trying to spare her leg some of the jostling. The wound still burned but it did not feel as if it had reopened, as she feared it might. The bearers quickened their pace at Renji's urging.

Shuji and the last of the guards came crashing through the underbrush, followed by the first shots from their pursuers. The bullets snatched through the branches and whizzed overhead with a sound that chilled her blood, followed by random bangs from behind them. Her guards ducked, searching over their shoulders for the danger behind them. 'I hate guns,' Renji said to himself.

Shuji pulled up next to the kago, panting. The old samurai wore a broad grin and the stink of fire. 'Well, my lady. Any moment ...' A horrendous crash that echoed like the hammer blow of an angry god, interrupted the samurai, staggering the bearers enough to make them drop the kago. Michiru spilled out onto the ground, her leg still in the sling. The shockwave made everyone pause and crouch down, looking back up the slope. Debris started to crash down through the branches of the trees. 'Hah!' exclaimed Shuji. 'That will slow them down!' He seemed quite pleased with himself.

Michiru looked up at Shuji. 'Thank you for the warning, Shuji-san,' she said from the ground. Chika ducked around the skittering horse and helped Michiru back into her seat. Ōmono struggled to calm the fractious animal as he watched the fire through the trees.

'I am sorry, my lady,' Shuji said with a smile. 'I think we caught some of their gunners in that explosion. Let's hope that it will give us some time.' Helping Chika to get her settled in her seat again, he added, 'We should push on, my lady. We are not out of danger yet.' He rearranged the guards around the kago, placing the shield carrying ashigaru to the sides and the back of the column. They set off again at a faster pace, jolting along the track, sacrificing comfort for speed.

Gritting her teeth against the pain, Michiru hung on, determined not to fall. Underbrush and branches slapped at her as the cleared track gave way to a trail. She was sweating with the strain, her stomach roiling from the unfamiliar motion. Her hands ached from gripping the strap, and her arms burned from holding her weight off her backside. Every time she tried to sit back down, another jolt threw her up in the air, only to thump her back down again, jarring her whole body. She spared a glance in front at Keiko's kago but could only see the back of her head.

'Not far now, my lady,' said Ōmono, leading the horse alongside her, his helmet hanging on his back by its cord. 'We are near the foot of the hill.' Michiru risked a look, finally catching sight of the flatlands through the trees. Her heart leapt in relief that the torture would soon be over.

There was a now familiar buzzing sound followed by a pop, as a bullet whizzed overhead. Another thumped into a tree as Chika jogged past it. She let out a little squeal. 'Shieldmen!' shouted Shuji, 'Cover the kagos! Chika! Stay as close to the lady as you can.' Bullets whizzed past at an increasing rate. Some went overhead, others hit trees with a splintering thunk. Then came the dreaded moment when one hit. A trotting ashigaru shrieked in pain as a bullet hit him in the small of his back, shattering his spine and sending him crashing to the ground. One man turned back to help him, but Shuji barked, 'Leave him! We cannot stop! He will be dead soon anyway! They want to slow us down.' He waved his drawn sword. 'Keep moving!'

They broke out of the trees at the base of the hill, stumbling into the river that ran along the edge of the woods. Sweating and panting with the exertion of the descent, they paused only briefly before plunging across it. The bearers now lifted the kagos onto their shoulders and carried Michiru and Keiko above the steady current. Their pace was agonisingly slow as they struggled to maintain their balance on the river's smoothed stones. Shuji directed the ashigaru in setting up their shields on both banks, giving the bow-armed samurai cover from which to shoot at their pursuers.

Michiru shrunk down as low as she could, aware of how exposed she was. The bamboo frame would provide little protection from the flying bullets. She felt one tear through the fabric at her side. She bit her lip to stop herself squealing. She was terrified, expecting a deadly shot with every passing moment. She could hear the cries of wounded, the echoing gunfire, the crack of bullets hitting the wooden shields and the ragged breathing of the bearers. Michiru prayed that the archers could slow the gunners down enough for them to get away. Another man went down with a cry.

Judging the right moment, Shuji started pulling back the men across the stream in pairs. The staggered movement allowed the archers to keep up a constant fire against the skirmishing gunners to cover their retreat. Their numbers thinning, the gunners seemed reluctant to move out of the cover of the trees. As Michiru's party put more distance between them, the danger diminished.

Shuji called a halt and set some men to watch for pursuit. He came up beside the kago, shocked at the sight of a bullet hole in the covering. 'My lady! Are you alright?' he asked in a panic. He looked inside to see Michiru dashing the tears from her eyes.

'Yes, Shuji-san,' she sniffed. 'I am unharmed.'

'Good,' he said, relieved. Inspecting the bullet hole, he traced it to where it had gouged a furrow across the end of the dowry box, strapped into the back of the seat. She watched as he followed the path of the bullet, seeing that it only just missed her leg. He stared at her silently for a moment before sighing in exasperation. He looked anxiously to the north and east. 'How would you feel about getting on the horse?'

'Not yet I don't think,' she said. Her body ached enough as it was. She wanted to recover a bit from the jolting ride down the hill before she subjected her leg to a horse. She knew he was worried about the enemy cavalry that was out there, somewhere. 'Please, check on Keiko for me.' He nodded and jogged over to the other kago, waving back to indicate that she was fine. Michiru sighed in relief.

They continued moving out across a valley floor, too unstable and flood prone for farming. Scattered clumps of trees, hillocks and ridges restricted their view, but also gave them some cover. She could see a pall of dark smoke rising from the top of the hill, giving the impression of a waking volcano. The acrid smell of burnt wood clung in her nostrils as the sun sank lower and coloured the world orange through the smoky haze.

Michiru's spirits rose as they moved across the plain. For the first time since they fled the inn, she felt some hope that safety was within reach. Only one bridge to cross and she would be safe. It made her earlier concerns about her future seem pointless and childish. She had a chance to see first-hand the lives of ordinary people, to listen to their stories and the burdens they lived with. Even if it was only for a few days, she felt her eyes were open now. She owed them a duty, to see that the rule of her house was fair and just. *I hope Sojiro will agree. I must make him see this is a sacred responsibility. That is my burden.* She closed her eyes and considered her growing love for Yatsuhiro, frightened that it would turn to stone and settle in her heart.

Shuji's call for a halt jolted Michiru back to reality. She looked out to see what had prompted the stop and her stomach froze. A line of mounted samurai sat on a low rise directly in their path. 'Shuji-san. Are they Arikawa? Is Yatsuhiro with them?'

'Their lack of welcome suggested that they are Satake samurai, my lady.'

She carefully pulled her leg out of the sling. *Damn it, damn it, damn it!* She took down Shigemori's short sword from its ties on the frame. Keiko, already out of her kago, helped Michiru to her feet with her good arm. Michiru noticed the short sword she had given Keiko thrust into her sash. She looked at her friend, sensing a fear that mirrored her own. She smiled at the young woman, trying to be brave as she pushed the sword into her own sash. 'Remember, nothing is certain.' She clasped her hand, giving it a reassuring squeeze. Keiko smiled thinly in return.

Shuji had the shields brought forward and set up in front of the kagos. The few archers they had took up positions behind the temporary wall, waiting for orders. He gathered the remaining spear armed ashigaru and stationed them behind and to the sides of the archers. Tanzo took up a position next to Michiru while Misao stood with Keiko. Renji and Muneto stood further back, armed with long spears.

Ōmono brought the horse around behind Michiru and whispered close to her ear. 'If things start to go bad, climb on the horse and ride, my lady. Lean low over the horse's neck and don't look back.'

She bowed her head as she considered his words. *Can I abandon them if it comes down to it? Is that to be my reward to them for their loyalty?* She bit her lip as she struggled with the dilemma.

'My lady?' Chika's voice broke into her thoughts. She stood there holding out a bow, gripping her own in her other hand.

Michiru gave her a smile, the question answered in that simple gesture. She would stand and fight with them. 'Thank you Chika,' she said softly, taking the bow with both hands.

Michiru stared out at the enemy horsemen, shifting her weight to her good leg. 'Their horses are tired,' she could see that straight away. The samurai looked like they had ridden hard to cut off their escape. She knew they stood a much better chance against a tired enemy. She was surprised that they had stopped and did not charge immediately. 'They don't seem to be in any rush, Shuji-san.'

'Their captain must be sizing us up,' he speculated. 'They think they have us.' He turned to look at Michiru. 'They may be correct, my lady.' *Time is not on our side. Eventually they will have to attack and then, we will fight to the death.* It was not the first time he had been in what seemed a hopeless situation. So far, he had survived, although many of his friends and family had not. *Concentrate on the now.* He narrowed his eyes, staring hard at the distant horsemen. He thought he spotted at least one musket slung from a saddle, and that worried him more than anything. He tightened a shoulder strap. 'Let us hope that Yatsuhiro got through.'

Michiru had not even considered that he might fail. The possibility chilled her heart. She scanned desperately for approaching friendly riders, but she could see no sign of them. Keiko laid a hand on her arm. 'He was riding very fast, my lady. I am sure he was well past them by the time they arrived. Right now he will be gathering men to come to our aid.'

She answered without turning. 'Thank you, Keiko-san. Of course. You are right.' But her eyes still looked out over the flood plain. Her attention was drawn back to the enemy in their path. They were a motley bunch, looking more like ronin than household samurai or soldiers, but they looked comfortable in their armour. They also handled their horses with the skill and confidence of professionals. She had a growing sense of unease as the standoff continued. 'Maybe they think we are being pursued. They could be waiting for sign of their friends.'

Shuji gave her a tired grin, 'Very good, Michiru,' he said. 'You are learning.'

'I don't know from whom,' she quipped.

Shuji harrumphed. He noticed many of the ashigaru were fretting nervously. He knew they would find the prospect of a charge by mounted samurai daunting. 'Stand firm,' he barked. 'If we hold our ground with our spears set, their horses will veer off. We are close to safety, this is our final obstacle.' Without the spears of the ashigaru their chances of holding off the attack were much worse. He offered up a silent prayer. *Please, Hachiman-sama, toughen their hearts and put steel in their spines.*

Michiru noticed their nervousness as well. She looked around at these unlikely soldiers and realised that only half of their original number had survived this far. Once again, her pain at being the cause of so much death threatened to swamp her. She took a deep breath and exhaled, pushing aside her feelings to deal with later. First, she must concentrate on getting to safety. She tested her leg to see if she could put her full weight on it. For a moment, she stood, but the ache grew sharper. *I won't be doing any running then.* Using the bow to steady herself, she leant towards her captain. 'Will they hold, Shuji-san?' she asked quietly.

'We won't know until it happens, my lady,' he replied.

'Ōmono said the same thing.'

She saw that the mounted samurai were now conferring amongst themselves, passing something from man to man. With a growing sense of foreboding, Michiru felt that whatever the Satake men were planning could only be bad for her ragged company. Gripping her bow tighter, she tried to calm her breathing. Glancing across at the peasant woman next to her she smiled, 'Are you still sure coming with me was a good idea, Chika?'

Chika's eyes were fixed on the enemy horsemen. 'I will tell you tomorrow, my lady,' she replied evenly. *Even if I die here today, it would be worth the risk for a chance at a new life.* If she survived, it would have been worth enduring the fear that was now threatening to overwhelm her. Chika knew nothing of wars and battles but she understood that this journey was a rare chance, and Michiru-hime was giving it to her.

All else was driven from their minds as the horsemen spread out into a line, walking towards them at a resolute pace. The sun threw long shadows across the ground, turning the puffs of dust from the horse's hoofs momentarily solid as they reflected the dying light of the day. Michiru took a shaft from the quiver and nocked it. The other archers followed suit, arrows pointed at the ground waiting to draw.

The mounted samurai halted some thirty paces away, a single horseman riding on alone. Shuji assumed he was the leader, come to deliver an ultimatum, demanding their surrender. *Predictable, but merely a prelude to the inevitable attack.* 'Let me speak to him, my lady. You should stay back and remain out of sight. Let's not make it easy for them.'

Shuji looked around at their makeshift army. They were a ragged bunch, more like brigands than any kind of soldiers. How they had managed to get this far was astounding. But he saw resolve in their faces, and maybe a touch of desperation. Satisfied that they were as ready as they were ever going to be, he mumbled another prayer to Hachiman.

The leader of the mounted samurai stopped a few spear lengths away from the shield wall, leaning negligently on the front of his saddle, a smug look on his face. The man was dressed much like the other horsemen, in plain light armour, a simple undecorated helmet held on with white cords. Shuji took a spear from one of the ashigaru and stepped out from behind the shield wall, walking up to the samurai. 'I am Yoshioka Shuji of the Katsura Clan,' he growled. 'Why do you block our path? What do you want?'

The horseman scratched his jaw, making no attempt at any courtesy. 'So. Yoshioka, eh,' he smirked. Michiru thought his lack of manners displayed an excess of confidence. *Why is he so cocky?* She narrowed her eyes, searching for any clue in his appearance. Apart from long stiff leather bags slung either side of the horse in front of his saddle, there appeared to be nothing out of the ordinary. She unconsciously put tension on her bowstring, uncertain of what to expect.

'Someone is willing to pay good money to see you dead, old man.' He lifted the flap on one of the bags and drew out a smaller and more elaborate version of the teppo used by their pursuers. He pulled back a lever on the top of the gun and pointed the muzzle at Shuji's face.

'Nice toy,' the old samurai quipped, readying the spear, 'but you forgot to put the match on your pistol, genius. It won't fire without a smouldering match.' The Katsura only had a few guns, but Shuji knew how they worked. The gunpowder was ignited by a burning match, which was one reason why they failed in the rain and gunners gave their position away. You could smell the match burning, see the glow at night and the smoke during the day. The tell-tale saltpetre stink was there, but then gunners always reeked of gunpowder.

The samurai gave Shuji a wicked grin. 'The latest in foreign weapons, old man. Doesn't need a match.' He pulled the trigger. A metallic whirring sound came from the pistol followed by an explosion. Shuji tried to twist out of the way. There was a sound of metal struck by metal and the old samurai fell to the ground. Smoke billowed.

Michiru instinctively raised her bow and let the arrow fly. A cloud of smoke obscured the horseman, ruining her aim, but her attention went back immediately to the form of her fallen sensei. At the sight of Shuji's still body lying in the dirt her chest spasmed in shock. 'No!' He lay motionless. Groping for another arrow, she searched for the shape of the mounted man through the smoke. She spotted him galloping back towards his men, leaning low over his horse's neck to avoid the shots of the other archers, snapped out of their shock by Michiru's cry. The smoke wafted away, revealing that a single shaft, standing out from the back of his shoulder, had found the mark. The cantering samurai hugged his arm to his chest but managed to keep his seat and re-join his men.

With growing dread, she saw that all but a third of the enemy samurai had dismounted behind the cover of the smoke, each holding a teppo and fitting smouldering matches to their weapons from metal boxes on their belts. The men who remained mounted gathered the horses and fell back, leading them out of the way. The concussion of the gunshot still rung in her ears, the shock of seeing Shuji fall and the sudden danger threatened to overwhelm her. Realising that they were about to be fired on, she yelled, 'Archers, fire!' letting loose her own hurried shot.

The enemy samurai were already kneeling to fire before the arrows finished their flight. All but one arrow missed. She heard ashigaru dropping to the ground around her. Unnerved at the sight of their captain being gunned down, some scurried for the cover of the shields, whimpering in anticipation of the flying bullets. 'Get up! Get up! She shouted around her in desperation. 'Shoot the gunners! Fire again!' Even Chika bent her bow. The desperate archers loosed another volley along with her before ducking behind cover, not waiting to see whether they hit. Michiru bit back a cry of pain as she dropped to the ground. The strain of diving for cover had pulled open the wound in her leg and hot, fresh blood soaked her bandage. She whimpered.

The command from the Satake leader came short and sharp, 'Fire!' The rattling volley of the guns begun before he finished the word. Bullets whipped and whistled through the party, screams and howls telling of the damage done. The wooden shields provided little protection at this range. A jagged splinter buzzed like a hornet as it flew up and hit her cheek, stinging like a cut from a knife. She reached for it instinctively, her fingers coming away wet with blood. Behind her the horse whinnied in pain and surprise, her hooves stamping the ground. From the sound of it, at least three of her men were wounded or dead, but she had no time to check. Painfully, she struggled to get to her feet, only to feel the strong grip of Tanzo lift her up.

'I am here, lady.'

The reassurance of his solid grip gave her the courage she needed. 'Quick! Before they reload! Fire again!' she ordered over the screaming of the horse. She drew and fired another arrow into the cloud of gun smoke. From the corner of her eye, she saw Chika still firing along with the others. She heard Ōmono and Renji struggling with the horse as another volley hissed towards the enemy. This was their chance to reduce the enemy numbers before the gunners fired again.

But the enemy were not reloading. Sinister shapes with drawn swords appeared through the haze, advancing on the shocked party. The horse's screaming stopped suddenly, the thud of its body falling to the ground making its fate clear. There would be no escape on horseback now. An ominous rumbling built in the air, reverberating like an aftershock of the gunfire echoing back from the hills. 'Shoot them down!' she screamed, her voice cracking from the unaccustomed strain. The volley that followed seemed paltry compared to what they had received. Two of the enemy fell, arrows finding flesh. The enemy samurai broke into a run, a growl growing from the looming armoured warriors, readying to hack into the stunned defenders.

This is it, she thought. The enemy is coming. 'To your feet! Stand! Raise your weapons!' She raised her bow, pulling the string back to her ear and releasing, snatching another arrow from the quiver without looking to see if she had hit anything. Horses whinnied in the distance as the enemy samurai began their charge, but the rumbling seemed to have grown louder than the feet of men could produce. She nocked the next shaft and drew back on the bow. Her heart sank, recalling that some of the enemy samurai had remained mounted. The Satake samurai were converging on her. *One last arrow.*

She looked down the shaft of her arrow at the closest charging samurai, a snarl pulling back the lips from his teeth, his sword in both hands, angled across his chest. Dark eyes glowered out from under the peak of his helmet, fixing her with a gaze that spoke of violence. Michiru licked her lips. *I must kill this man before he reaches me or I will be at his mercy.* From his expression, she could see that she would get no mercy from him.

Aiming for the top of his chest, she pulled the arrow back still further, releasing with a fluid motion to send the shaft straight and true. The man sliced the arrow out of the air before it reached him, not slowing his advance in the slightest. In disbelief, she dropped the bow and drew her short sword. She held the blade to her throat as she had been taught, breathing in deeply, summoning the strength to do what must be done. Her blood chilled. Then she saw Tanzo's spear hovering over her shoulder, ready to thrust at the enemy. Ōmono had pulled Chika back out of the way, standing in her place, readying his spear. She heard swords being drawn all around her as the remnants of her makeshift bodyguard prepared to fight for their lives. And for hers. She heard some of her men growl as they prepared to meet the enemy. Something strange surged up from deep within her. Defiance. She pulled the sword away from her throat, her skin flushing with the heat of her rage as she hurled her own roar into the face of the men closing on her. The unmistakable sounds of galloping cavalry intruded into her mind. The enemy samurai heard it too. Everyone turned to the sound simultaneously.

With an ululating battle cry, black armoured cavalry with long spears, thundered over the nearby rise, red banners flying from their backs. They crashed into the shocked enemy. She watched the face of the closest enemy samurai change from menace to terror. An Arikawa lance impaled him, wielded by a rider wearing a red headband. She flinched violently as her would-be attacker was lifted off his feet and thrown sideways, landing some distance away with a crash. The remaining Satake samurai were shocked and disorganised, standing no chance as the Arikawa cavalry drove them into to the ground with their spears and the hooves of their horses. Michiru gasped with relief, her head spinning as she hauled her mind back from the edge of death. There was something she had to do, but her consciousness could not get a hold of it. Her thoughts were drowned out by the rumble and clatter of the milling horsemen. Shouts, screams and whinnying of horses buffeted her senses. From a buzz in her ear, words began to intrude into her bemusement. The familiar voice of her captain, fierce and concerned, echoed in her mind. 'My lady? Are you alright?'

She looked up in confusion, seeing a dusty Arikawa samurai with a red headband, his intense eyes focused on her. Her recognition of him came together in pieces, her eyes growing increasingly wider. Then everything came rushing back at once. She threw her arms around Yatsuhiro, crying with relief. He held her awkwardly as waves of her sobbing washed over him. 'I thought we were going to die,' she stuttered. 'I thought I would never see you again.' The enormity of her words hit her as they came out of her mouth. She looked up into his eyes in mortification, tears muddying her pale face.

Yatsuhiro blinked in sudden confusion. 'My lady,' he stammered. 'I ... Michiru-sama ... we ...'

The swirl of events passed through Michiru's mind again, and another piece dropped into place. The explosion of the enemy's pistol echoed in her mind. 'Shuji!' she gasped, turning in Yatsuhiro's arms. She pushed away from him and staggered to where Shuji lay face down. She knelt beside her sensei, tears flowing afresh. 'No! Sensei,' she cried hoarsely. 'Not now. We won.' She shook him as if he was only asleep. A fresh sob escaped her control. 'Shuji-sama. I am not ready for you to die.'

Yatsuhiro knelt and rolled the old samurai over. Thick blood covered half his face and soaked the armour and clothing of his shoulder. Michiru looked closer. The bullet had hit his helmet where the peak was riveted on. The steel of the helmet was punched in at an angle, the metal of the visor torn and bent down, slicing into Shuji's cheek. 'He's still breathing,' she said exhaling with relief. Yatsuhiro untied the helmet cords with fumbling fingers while Michiru undid the shoulder toggles of his armour. Chika appeared at her side, offering a clean cloth. Ōmono's words repeated in her mind. *A peasant's final option when things are bad is to run away. Real loyalty is staying. Staying when you know you should run.* Michiru turned and gave Chika a grateful nod, 'Thank you, Chika-san. I am glad you are still here.'

*   *   *

Tanzo looked around the battlefield shaking his head. He leaned down and placed a regretful hand on the horses head. 'What a waste,' he mumbled in his distinctive deep tone.

Ōmono, untying Haru's rope from the saddle, turned to comment. 'Nothing unusual about samurai wasting things, my friend. Here, Muneto-san, hold onto this one for me, if you please.'

Muneto took the rope, his face sour from more than just the death around him. 'You should be more careful what you say, peasant,' he grumbled. 'Someone might get offended and take your head off.'

Tanzo exchanged a glance with the ashigaru. Ōmono continued to remove the tack and harness from the dead horse. He nodded as he worked. 'Yes Muneto-san, that is very true. Tanzo, give me a hand with this. But you know, to us peasants,' he said with an emphasis on the last word, 'Seeing a horse that costs about the same as it does to feed a family for a year, killed for no good reason, makes us wonder about the sense of it all.' Tanzo levered the horse up with a kago carrying pole, allowing Ōmono to drag the saddle clear. 'Not to mention all the work that a horse could do, carrying and pulling loads.'

Muneto grunted as he stood watching them gather up the harness, loading it across Haru's shoulders. 'You peasants. Always so lazy. Always trying to get out of doing honest work.'

'I am afraid you are right there, Muneto-san,' Ōmono said cheerfully. 'Now, let's get these kagos sorted out. I dare say the ladies will need them.' He looked over the litters, checking the frames and poles. Muneto, watched the two peasants with barely concealed contempt, until his gaze caught on Michiru's kago. Something that riveted his attention and wiped the expression from his face. Behind him, Renji ushered the bearers back to their positions, but as he worked his eyes stayed fixed on Muneto.

*   *   *

The Arikawa samurai helped collect the wounded, dressing their injuries and making ready to move on before it became too dark. Shuji regained consciousness while Misao was applying the dressing to his cheek. He had already bandaged Shuji's wounded shoulder sufficiently for him to move, but he would need a doctor to remove the bullet fragments. With the aid of Tanzo and Renji, Shuji tottered to his feet. The old samurai rubbed his neck, 'I feel like I was kicked by a horse.' Exploring his torn face with a light touch he winced as he traced the cut, 'I'm getting too old for this,' he said to himself.

'A few days rest and you will be fine, sensei,' Michiru said. A chill was starting to take hold of her body now that the ordeal was over. Her heart was in turmoil. Relief at her survival, joy at Shuji being alive, embarrassment at her open display of feelings for Yatsuhiro and the certainty that she must marry another man. She tried to push it all aside as they prepared to move.

Yatsuhiro had his men light flares and the ragged column headed for the bridge. 'Well, my lady,' he said with a strained smile. 'Which would you prefer, horse or kago?'

'Maybe we should put the old man in the litter,' she tried to joke, 'He has had a nasty bump,'

'My lady. Some respect, please,' Shuji interrupted, looking around at the horsemen. 'I will borrow a mount if you have a spare one, Yatsuhiro-san.' He turned back to him, adding, 'I think Michiru-hime needs it more than I do,' as he pointed at her freshly bandaged leg. He was right. Her leg ached and every step brought fresh darts of pain. She gave Yatsuhiro a weary nod, avoiding his eyes. She swallowed hard but there was a lump in her throat that would not move. She climbed back into the kago, hiding the hot tears that threatened to escape her control.

CHAPTER SEVENTEEN

Michiru released a sigh of relief as they finally crossed the bridge. Torches and lanterns lit the way up the slope into the nearby village, carried by a score of armoured Arikawa ashigaru. Hardly believing that they had made it to safety, Michiru found it difficult to keep from smiling. The column of weary but elated travellers stopped outside a substantial inn on the outskirts of the village. Chika helped her clamber out of the kago as the escorting cavalry clattered past. The inn's welcoming lights and bustling entrance promised a return to something like a normal life. Curious faces peered out of every house as her entourage piled up in the pools of light created by the lanterns surrounding the gateway.

The inn was low lying, a single story building, spreading out on either side and presumably towards the rear. The innkeeper stood bobbing and bowing at the gate, immensely pleased at the honour being done to his inn, and the money he would make from such a large party.

'Well, Chika. I guess this is the beginning of a new life for both of us.'

'I will never be able to thank you enough, Michiru-sama,' she said, kneeling and bowing deeply. *Is this where we part ways? Will she dismiss me now?* Michiru would surely have the local ladies flocking to serve her once they heard where she was. 'Thank you for bringing me with you.'

'You are welcome, Chika,' Michiru replied wearily, using the kago frame for support. 'But I could use some more of your help to get inside. My leg is really hurting.' They shared a smile and Chika rose to lend her a shoulder. She hobbled a few steps towards the inn when Ōmono walked past, still leading Haru on a rope. Michiru sighed heavily. 'Ōmono,' she called. 'Please bring him here.'

'My lady, he can wait until the morning.' He added confidently, 'I'm sure he won't mind.'

She signalled for him to come over. 'Take the rope off him, please and bring him here.'

'Yes, my lady,' he said, sullenly, untying the rope. Haru massaged his wrists and gave Ōmono a scathing look, which he returned with as little grace. Ōmono pushed him down to his knees in front of Michiru.

'Well, Haru. Here we are as promised, safe and sound. Some of this we owe to you,' she said looking pointedly at Ōmono. He avoided her eyes. 'Is Ōmono right? Can you wait until morning or do you want to leave straight away?'

He looked at her strangely for a moment. 'I guess I can wait,' he mumbled. Ōmono slapped him on to back of his head. 'My lady,' he added grudgingly.

'Then I will speak with you in the morning.'

Yatsuhiro rode up sporting a wide grin and dismounted, going down on one knee. 'Welcome to Nagase domain, my lady.'

She realised that they had an audience and played the part for his benefit. 'Thank you for everything you have done for us, Captain. We would not have made it here safely without you.'

He stood and bowed with pride as Shuji and the remainder of the guard also knelt in salute. 'Tomorrow we will travel the final distance to your new home. For now, let us show you our hospitality. There are fresh, clean rooms, food and a bath for you.'

She gave him a grateful but weary bow and turned towards the inn, lured by the thought of a scrub and soak. Chika lent her a shoulder to lean on as she hobbled through the gate towards the entrance. She looked around in appreciation and relief at the well-maintained garden framing the entrance. Bamboo fencing framed sections of the garden, strategically including or excluding manicured decorative trees and hiding windows. She could see a pond running along one fence line. The starkness of the dried bamboo was softened by sculpted azaleas, weeping yamabuki and moss covered rocks all lit by well-placed lamps. *I hope this inn has a masseur. Oh, that would be perfect.* The growing sound of hoof beats broke into her thoughts before they had gone more than a few paces. She turned towards the approaching horsemen. Half a dozen riders, led by a bearded samurai wearing a dark coat over his armour, pulled up outside the gate, dismounting from their huffing horses.

Yatsuhiro walked towards them, raising his hand in salute. 'Tsukino-san!' he called, 'Come, let me introduce you.'

The bearded samurai looked surprised. 'My lord? What are you doing here? We thought you were lost! What happened?'

'All in good time. First I would like you to meet Katsura no Michiru-hime,' he gestured towards Michiru. 'My lady, may I introduce Tsukino Hideki-san, one of Sojiro-sama's best lieutenants.'

Hideki went down onto one knee, head bowed, his men joining him. 'My lady. I am so glad that you made it through. We heard you had been captured on the road.' He looked up and saw Michiru standing there with an arm over Chika's shoulder. His eyes flicked between the two women in confusion.

Michiru laughed, realising that there was no way for him to know who was who. Chika exchanged a smile with her, and backed away. 'Yes, Tsukino-san. I am the Lady Michiru. I am pleased to meet you.' She asked, 'Did you not receive news of my escape from the temple at Kyozuka?'

'No, my lady,' he said. 'We have had no news. The road to Omegura has been blocked by bandits. We were afraid that you had been captured. Patrols were sent out, but they found no sign of you.' He bowed again, 'I am glad to see that you are safe.' He turned and bowed to Yatsuhiro. 'Please forgive me. I should have had more faith in you, my lord.'

'You are right about that, Hideki-san.' Yatsuhiro commented.

'I'm afraid I don't have good news, though,' he admitted. 'The Satake broke into Harashiro castle. I am here to find out what happened to the troops that were here. They are supposed to be in Nagase by now.'

'Yes. I borrowed them for a while. We heard the castle was under attack. Have they taken it already?'

'It gets worse. The Satake emissary says that they have the Lady Michiru as a prisoner in the castle. And if we attack they threaten to burn it with her in it before it falls.' He looked at Michiru, 'They are demanding a large ransom. An emissary is meeting with your uncle at this very moment, and he believes the Lady is their hostage. He will hand over the ransom this very evening.'

Namika is alive! She has done her part well if they still think they have me. What a wonderful girl. She hoped that she had not had to endure too much at the hands of her captors. Michiru would have to ask Shuji how they could get her back.

Yatsuhiro turned to her, steeling himself for action. 'My lady. You are safe now. I must ride to Nagase immediately.'

'No,' she snapped, a smouldering anger narrowing her eyes. Despite how sore and tired she was, this was something she wanted to do. *So close, but still one thing left to do.* To prove the Satake emissary a liar to his face would be a small measure of revenge for everything they had put her through. Michiru declared with firm conviction, 'We will all go.'

'But my lady,' Shuji objected.'Your injuries. It will be most uncomfortable travelling that far, that fast with your injuries.' He thought it would not take much to convince her. She looked worn out. Strands of hair had escaped her ponytail, standing out wildly. Her eyes were red-rimmed from the dust and the crying. The cut on her cheek was already looking angry and inflamed and dark blood stained the leg of her pants. She could barely stand without Chika's support. 'It would be better not to risk it, my lady. Let your samurai take it from here. You need to rest,' he said with genuine concern.

The welcoming glow of the inn and all it promised drew Michiru's eyes. *I would love to rest now.* Resolutely, she turned her back on it. *But not yet.* 'Shuji-san. I appreciate your concern, but this must not be allowed to happen. I will not have my new family tricked and shamed in this way. Let us go and put a stop to this, now.'

Shuji, realising she was truly beyond his control now, bowed to her obstinacy. 'As you command, Michiru-hime.'

Chika helped her back into the kago. As she helped ease her leg into the sling, Michiru looked up at her. 'Chika, you are safe now,' she said. 'Do you want to leave us here and go your own way? Or will you come with me now and discuss the matter later?'

Surprised to be asked at all, she considered her options for a moment, but realised she had already decided. 'I will stay with you awhile longer, if you will have me, my lady. I am still thinking about umbrellas,' she grinned mischievously. Michiru smiled back.

'Let's go,' she said to Shuji, 'But bring a horse along for me. I intend to ride the last part. That way I can make a memorable entrance.' She realised that she wanted to shock them all, riding in to the mansion dressed in armour, bow in hand, surrounded by her own samurai. *That should set the right tone with my future family.* Settling in to the seat, she said to no one in particular, 'After all, my wedding procession was spoiled.'

*　　*　　*

Oseku Toyonari, emissary for the Satake clan, grinned to himself, knowing that he would be welcomed back by Kiyomori. He had achieved everything he had been sent to do. He would be returning with a big fat box of coin and the humiliation of the Arikawa. Even though he was samurai, he had little skill with weapons of war. Toyonari relied on his wit and cunning when concluding agreements. His experience was that many "lords" knew so little it was easy to bluff them.

He sat on a cushion in the audience chamber, sipping on Arikawa Sojiro's best sake. He sampled the delicacies offered while they waited for the chamberlain to return with the strongbox. This gave him time to revel in his enemy's dilemma. Incense curled fragrantly nearby, keeping the insects at bay as he admired the lantern-lit garden beyond the veranda. Toyonari was intelligent, well-read and stylish, and oblivious to the dislike he engendered in others. He had been to the Capital and he considered most of these back-woods samurai as rough buffoons, well below his level.

Hatoyama Toichi, Chamberlain of Nagase, and Sojiro's uncle, sat on the dais in the audience chamber. His face was red and sweating as he tried to think of a way to get out of making the decision. He tried to slow his racing heart and calm down. He picked up the document from the table in front of him and read it through for the third time. Toichi blamed Sojiro for not being here and thus putting the responsibility of responding to these outrageous demands in his lap. He could not bring himself to put a brush to this obscene document. He felt sure that his ancestors would rise up and haunt him if he dared put Their name on it. Yet, his choices were limited.

He looked once again at the folded clothes in front of him. A woman's garment, made from expensive material, the design of the Katsura crest incorporated into the rich blues and grey tones edged with golden thread. On top of the kimono lay a burnished hairpin and a fan, also bearing the same katsura leaf motif. His heart sank, not wanting to imagine what the poor girl was going through at the hands of the enemy.

'You may as well sign it and be done with it, sire,' Toyonari drawled, revelling in Toichi's discomfort. 'You see, time is moving on and I must return with your answer. We would not want Michiru-hime to be ... made to wait, now would we?' An oily grin spread across his face.

Toichi's muscles tensed. He felt a desperate need to get rid of this man. But he could not lay a finger on him. Not without risking the Lady Michiru. 'You have presented me with an important document, Oseku-san,' he said, his lip quivering with the strain of staying polite. 'I must give it my full consideration.'

'What is there to consider,' he goaded him. 'Either sign or do not sign.' He waved a hand vaguely and slurped his sake.

A grey haired Arikawa samurai, tension evident on his face, entered through a side door, eyes downcast and mouth set firm. A pair of samurai bearing strongboxes followed him. After bowing, he directed the samurai to the dais where they placed their loads, opening the lids to display their contents. The old man gave the treasure a mournful look, 'Two thousand koku in gold and silver, my lord, as you ordered.' It was money the Arikawa could ill-afford to lose.

Toyonari's spirit soared. Here was victory. He was set for life. There was a good chance Kiyomori would double his income for bringing him this. His ears picked up the clatter of approaching horses. And the stomp of marching men. He listened with growing annoyance. *Not now! Whoever they are, they are spoiling my moment!* Everyone turned to look out into the flare-lit courtyard as a ragged band flowed in. Toichi welcomed the diversion as Toyonari felt his moment slipping away. 'Sire, we should conclude our business, don't you think?'

Toichi stood and walked out on to the veranda. Toyonari rolled his eyes and breathed a sigh of exasperation as he rose to follow. The courtyard was filling with sweating horsemen, followed by equally sweaty men on foot. Whatever it was that was going on, he felt that it would be prudent to be surrounded by his own guards just now. He turned to the Satake samurai at the back of the audience chamber and beckoned to them.

With a jolt, Toichi recognised his nephew, who dismounted and went to the assistance of another rider. 'You are back!' he called with surprise. Yatsuhiro put out a hand to silence him. He helped the rider off the horse and came to kneel before him at the foot of the steps. The Arikawa samurai and retainers spread out around the courtyard, looking on with curiosity. Horses shook and snorted, the air warm and heavy.

Yatsuhiro strode to the foot of the steps. 'Hatoyama Toichi, I would like you to meet the Lady Katsura no Michiru.'

Toichi looked at the mismatched collection of samurai and ashigaru formed up behind his nephew, looking nothing like the troops that went out as escort, let alone a bridal procession. He could see at least two women in among them, but even they were in armour. Both carried bows and had their hair tied up in similar manner.

He did not know what to think. If one of these women were Michiru-hime, it would make the situation a very different. He peered closer.

'You lie!' Toyonari squealed behind him. With the sudden realisation that his Lord was running a bluff, He knew then that he had been left on a limb. 'The Katsura-hime is being held in Harashiro castle! I have proof,' he declared loudly, gesticulating at the kimono and accessories. 'Look!' He wondered if any of his men had a bow. Could he get away with having her shot? He glanced at his guards.

'It is you, who lie, Satake.' A woman's voice came from among the group. A youthful figure dressed in light armour, shorter than the men around her, limped out from the crowd, bow in hand. A stocky woman dressed in a similarly masculine fashion followed her.

Michiru stood glaring at the overdressed emissary in the veranda. At her back stood samurai sworn to protect her. She had never felt more confident. She understood now what she was, what she represented for them. Survival and safety. Honour and standing among their fellow men. A home. That institution that provides shelter, a place for family, for those who look after and care for each other. For them, for everything they hoped and dreamed for, it was time for her to be what she was. 'I am Katsura Michiru, sister of Katsura Kosei, Lord of Omegura.'

'Hah!' he spat, his scalp prickling as he sensed the danger he was in. 'Sire, this is some kind of ruse. A trick to try and interfere with these negotiations,' he said, gambling for time now. All that was left to him was bluff. His only chance was to work on Toichi. 'I say she is no princess, but rather some harlot or camp follower pretending to be the Katsura-hime!'

The samurai ranked behind Michiru surged forward with a low growl, hands tightening on weapons. The Satake samurai took an involuntary step back from the threatening throng. Shuji barked an order and the movement ceased. She felt a chill in the pit of her stomach, a hard stone of anger as, yet again, she was insulted, as if she could not respond. She started to take a step forward herself when Shuji placed a restraining hand on her arm.

'I am Yoshioka Shuji, Captain of the Katsura clan. I attest to her identity,' he said, standing beside her. 'I have escorted her since she left my master's house. Oseku Toyonari, I call you a liar if you claim to be holding her prisoner.' His pose dared Toyonari to disagree, his chin jutting, hand on his sword. 'She stands before you.'

The Satake samurai tightened around their emissary, the tension drawing all of them in. Toyonari sneered, 'Oh well, excuse me if I don't take the word of my enemy's retainers as truth.'

Yatsuhiro stepped up beside Shuji. In a deep tone Michiru had not heard from him before, he said, 'Enough! I do not care what you claim. I know that this is Katsura no Michiru-hime. I have been with her since she left Omegura domain.' He looked at Michiru with a grim expression. 'I am Lord Sojiro of the Arikawa.'

CHAPTER EIGHTEEN

Lightning flashed through Michiru's mind. Her heart leapt as she realised what his revelation meant. Her eyes were drawn to the man she thought she knew. She saw the expression on his face. Was it reluctance? Embarrassment? Pity? As her mind tumbled through the implications, the rising euphoria in her heart burst into icy shards. *All this time he has been deceiving me. How dare he!* Her eyes narrowed. Michiru was tired, in pain and sick of being insulted. She had endured so much this last week and now, finally, she would tolerate no more.

Her burning eyes snapped around to fix on Toyonari. 'One of your men put an arrow in my leg, before I killed him.' In a smooth movement, she took an arrow from her quiver, nocked it and drew her bow. The arrow whipped through the air with a buzz before anyone realised what was happening, piercing Toyonari's right thigh. Michiru's face was stone as she growled at him, 'Here is one for you to take back to your lord.'

The Satake emissary looked down at his leg, mouth agape in shock. His guards scurried to cover their squealing emissary, swords drawn. 'She shot me!' he blurted, staring wide-eyed at the feathered shaft impaling his leg. Two samurai helped him to stand while the others covered them, retreating into the reception room. What surprised her was that some of the emissary's guards were grinning.

Toichi stood staring in open-mouthed amazement, not a little delighted at the sudden turn of events. He smiled at the gasping Toyonari and said brightly, 'I would imagine that concludes our business then. I will send a doctor to remove that for you,' he said with what might have been sympathy. He waved a servant over to the emissary and turned his attention to Michiru.

Sojiro looked at the chests of coins on the dais and said to the emissary, 'Tell Kiyomori, this one time, I will give him a chance to avoid his karma. He has two days to get out of my castle and off my lands or I will not stop at the border when I come to take it back.' Sojiro knew problems with the Satake would not go away. The problem would have to be resolved, one way or another. *But not to-day.* To the guards he said, 'Take him and go.' With stiff bows, they left, carrying away the whimpering emissary. Lord Sojiro of Nagase turned back to the assemblage in the courtyard.

Michiru glared at him with poorly concealed hostility. Slowly, she lowered herself to one knee, placing her bow on the ground beside her. Her men did likewise, Shuji on her right and Chika to her left, the others ranged behind her. 'I am sorry, my lord, for harming a guest in your house. Please forgive my bad manners.'

He stepped up onto the veranda and bowed. 'Please, lady, forgive me for letting him say such things to you.' He motioned for her to rise, signalling Chika to help her up. 'I would apologise for him, but you have already made him pay. Please do not concern yourself.'

'Thank you ... Sojiro-sama,' came her terse reply, drawing a clearing of the throat from Shuji and a nervous chuckle from Toichi.

Sojiro continued quickly, a little annoyed to be treated this way in front of his own men. He knew she was going to make him regret it later anyway. So he played the part of the better man and continued politely. 'Lady Katsura no Michiru, may I present Hatoyama Toichi, Chamberlain of Nagase, and my uncle.'

'It is a pleasure to meet you at last,' he said with a curious tilt to his head.

'Thank you, Hatoyama-sama. I am glad to finally arrive,' she said with perfect courtesy.

A faint crease formed on Sojiro's forehead. 'My uncle has been ably managing the domain in my absence,' he said, bowing to him in acknowledgement.

'And thank you for putting an arrow into that worm,' he said with growing mirth. 'You brightened up my evening considerably. I would dearly like to hear all about this.' He laughed self-consciously. 'It will obviously be a fascinating tale.' Despite her travel-stained appearance and strange dress, he could see she was as beautiful as she had been described to him. However, he could also see her fatigue, the vicious cut on her cheek and the freshly bandaged leg. He curbed his curiosity and added, 'Tomorrow, maybe?'

'It would be my pleasure, my lord,' liking him immediately. 'Hatoyama-sama, I would like to make a request, if I may.'

Surprised and a little intrigued he replied, 'Certainly, my lady. How can I help?'

'When the Satake claimed to have a hostage, they actually do. My maid, Namika took my place as a decoy and allowed me to escape. I would ask that you make whatever efforts are required to secure her return.'

He stared at her briefly. 'My lady, I will do what can be done.' With a smile at Sojiro, he left to speak to the Satake samurai before they left.

From outside the walls came the growing sound of horses cantering, mixed with the regular tramp of sandaled feet and the clatter of armour and weapons. They all turned to watch as into the courtyard marched a column of samurai, followed by many ashigaru, their long spears flashing in the light of the flares. They marched under the green banners of the Katsura and were led by her brother Kosei, armoured and mounted like a true lord, war fan in hand. He reined in, stopping behind Michiru as the rest of his troops filed into formation. He gave her a broad smile from under his helmet.

Her troops moved aside, making a path between them. She was so happy and proud to see him here. Shuji walked forward to kneel before Kosei as a page ran out to take the horse's reins. 'I see she is still alive, Yoshioka Shuji-san. Well done and thank you,' he said with a brief bow.

'Thank you, my lord, but I was merely doing my duty. I should have foreseen the trap. Please forgive my failure,' he said humbly, as was expected.

'Time enough for that later,' Kosei said, turning towards Michiru, his "Lord" face on display. He surveyed the men kneeling on either side as he strode past. 'Who are these warriors in the company of my sister?' he asked with a sweeping gesture of his war fan.

Michiru spoke up proudly, not caring about decorum, 'They are my samurai, Elder Brother. They are my honour guard,' she said, scanning their ranks, thankful for their dedication. 'They aided Yoshioka-san in getting me here safely.' She saw her men bow a little lower, as she took the opportunity to rebuild some of their pride.

A slight, 'Hmph,' escaped Kosei's lips. 'Time enough for that later, too.' He whispered to Michiru in passing, 'Can't do things the easy way, can you? Oh no.' Approaching the steps in front of Sojiro, he offered a bow, which was returned with equal dignity. 'Lord Sojiro, please forgive the intrusion so late in the day. I hurried here after I heard the news of the Satake attack on Harashiro castle. And, once I reached the Kajigawa bridge, I heard my sister was just ahead of me,' he said, turning to look at her sideways 'So I pushed on to catch up with her.'

'You are most welcome, Lord Kosei,' Sojiro said genially. 'We were about to officially welcome your sister.'

'Well, now that I am here, allow me to present her in person. My lord Arikawa Sojiro-sama, I present Katsura no Michiru-hime, daughter of Katsura Kohiro, Lord of Omegura.' He took her by the hand and led her up the steps to kneel in front of Sojiro. Mustering courage from the spirits of her mother and all her grandmothers, she bowed to her betrothed, the man who would be her husband, the father of her children and her absolute master.

* * *

Utaemon Katsuo ran through the darkened passageways to his lord's rooms, accompanied by four guards and a physician. He could hear Kiyomori raging and shouting over the screams. Faces peaked fearfully from every room and corner as he flew past.

Reaching the last corridor, he came across a scene of horror. The pieces of the screen to Kiyomori's room lay in the hallway, smashed by the bloodied body of the young Katsura maid who had so bravely played the decoy for her mistress. She lay in a crumpled heap in the hallway, an arrow protruding from her forehead. A samurai, still kneeling with his head on the floor, was pinned there by a sword plunged through his back. Kiyomori, half-naked and hair dishevelled like some wild demon, slammed the head of another young woman into the floor repeatedly as he ranted. His face was bright red, spittle flying from his contorted lips.

The guards wrestled Kiyomori off the broken body. Katsuo waved the physician to her side while he carefully approached his lord. Three of the guards held him, still struggling and snarling. 'My lord! My lord, calm yourself,' he pleaded. He looked over his shoulder as the doctor checked the pulse of the battered woman. The physician shook his head. Katsuo nodded again.

'She got away!' Kiyomori screamed. 'She got away! She got away! I'll kill her! I'll rip her eyes out!'

'My lord, you must calm down or you will have another seizure.' He gestured to the guards, 'Sit him down.' His men, disturbed to see their lord this way, forced him down into a sitting position. They had not seen the full range of his behaviour the way Katsuo had. 'Hold him tightly and do not loosen your grip.'

'You're all useless! She dared send me an arrow? Aaahhh!'

Pinned down by the weight of his guards, his ranting subsided into huffs and growls. Katsuo waved the physician forward. 'Tilt his head back,' he ordered. With an arm around his jaw and a hand on the top of his head, the samurai pulled back on the struggling man's head. As Kiyomori opened his mouth to protest, the doctor tipped the contents of a small vial into his mouth and clapped a hand over it, clamping his jaw shut with the other. Kiyomori struggled against them, eyes wide beneath his knotted eyebrows. The doctor's grip muffled the fury of his voice. His eyes threatened death as they flicked between Katsuo and the guards.

Slowly, his struggling began to ebb and the physician removed his hands. Kiyomori gasped for air, his breathing ragged, his eyelids drooping. Tension eased from those present as the doctor's drug began to take effect.

'Much better my lord, much better,' Katsuo said with relief, wiping the sweat from his forehead. He made a decision. 'Let us send everyone away and have some tea, my lord.' He looked at the man pinned to the floor. *A messenger? So that is what set him off. Which idiot sent the messenger straight in?* He sat down with a heavy sigh. *They were always supposed to come to me first.* He signalled the guards to leave. 'Bring tea,' he instructed the doctor.

Kiyomori sat, his breathing still ragged. His half-lidded eyes focussed on the floor in front of him, a string of drool suspended from his bottom lip. 'I can't move, Katsuo,' he said in a small voice. 'Why can't I move?'

'You are just tired, my lord. Do not be concerned. Everything will be fine.' The doctor returned with a terrified maid bearing tea. 'Here we are,' he announced. 'We will share a cup of tea and then get you back to bed.' Katsuo waited until the tea was ready and dismissed the wide-eyed woman. He gave the physician a look and turned back to his lord. 'The doctor will help you drink up.'

With a fixed expression, the doctor added the contents of another vial to the tea and helped Kiyomori drink it. Once the cup was empty, he bowed to the councillor and left him to sit with his lord in the shattered room. Blood pooled under the bodies nearby, soaking into the straw of the tatami matting. Katsuo sipped his tea, welcoming the stirrings of a breeze.

'Katsuo,' came a whisper. 'My eyes keep closing. I'm tired. I want to go to bed.'

'It is alright, my lord. It will all be over soon.' Another puff of breeze fluttered in through the window, stirring the mad tangle of Kiyomori's hair.

'I can't feel my legs.'

'I know.'

'Help me to bed. So...tired.' He wavered from side to side slightly, his head nodding. With a sad groan, he toppled over on to his side.

He watched as the man who was the cause of so much suffering and loss, stopped breathing. Katsuo let go of a shuddering sigh. It was done. He had killed his lord. He struggled momentarily with this crime, this dishonour. One look at the broken body of the woman next to him chased away any guilt. *He would have killed us all.* She had been pretty and vibrant. He remembered she loved to spend nights watching the moon and the stars. *Only nineteen.* A tear rolled down his cheek. *Such a waste.* She had been Katsuo's only niece.

*   *   *

The following morning, Michiru sat contentedly in her reception room enjoying a quiet cup of tea. She shared the welcome calm with Keiko, who reclined beside her on a bed of cushions. They watched the birds flit and play among the camellias as a warm breeze rippled through the tranquil garden outside. Sojiro had given this guest-house over to her, for which she was most grateful. Once she was married, she would move into the Northern Pavilion, the personal domain of the Lady of the Household. She could catch glimpses of it over the fence of the garden. Its timbers dark with age, it was an original part of the estate, dating back some five hundred years. But she could push all thoughts of that aside for the moment.

The doctor had already been to see both of them this morning, replacing the dressings and checking their injuries. He pronounced himself satisfied with the progress of their healing, insisting Keiko in particular move around as little as possible. Michiru requested that everyone leave them in peace to recover, much to the disappointment of Sojiro's relatives, who so far had to make do with the gossip of last night's events. She smiled, satisfied that she was creating some sensation and mystery about herself.

Michiru had just a few more details to settle before the wedding. She called Chika in. The peasant woman entered, knelt and bowed, observing the formalities now they were no longer on the road. Michiru gave her a friendly smile. 'Chika. You served me faithfully on the way here, and fought by my side in battle. I want to offer you something in return. You once expressed a wish to find work or to set up your own business. What can I do for you?'

Chika was intensely aware how out of place she was here. She had never seen such finery or quality of materials. *The whole estate is like something out of a fairy tale. Even the simplest storeroom is better than any house I have ever seen.* She fidgeted as she considered her choice. 'If you don't mind, my lady, I would like to stay on as your maid for a while. I will save money from my wages and start my own business one day. If that meets with your approval, of course,' she bobbed nervously.

'It just so happens that it does,' she said, exchanging a glance with Keiko, smiling broadly. Michiru knew she would be much happier having another familiar face around once her life as Mistress of the House began. 'As a matter of fact I have a task for you to perform for me right now.'

'Anything, hime-sama.'

'Please go to the storehouse and get them to put together a package with clothing, sandals, three days food and some traveling money. Then ask one of the guards to fetch Haru for me.'

'Yes, mistress.' She bowed deeply and left, trying hard to hide her smile.

'My lady,' Keiko queried her. 'If you don't mind me asking, what is it about Haru that has prompted such attention from you? You saved his life, I understand that. But you could have just let him go.'

Michiru frowned uncertainly. 'I don't know for sure. There is just something about his story. The misfortune of it. Especially in the light of our good fortune in making it through safely.'

Keiko winced as she shifted to a more comfortable position. 'We did not make it through unscathed. We very nearly did not make it at all.'

'And yet we did,' she said thoughtfully. 'We are here and we are alive. I feel like I owe something.' She frowned to herself, not sure who, or what, she owed. Reaching a decision, she went to the alcove that housed a large hanging scroll and a vase holding a spray of narcissus blossoms. She opened the panel in the front and slid out the battered rosewood box. She opened it and stared at the gold for a moment. Selecting one of the oval pieces, she closed the box and slid it back into its place again. Seating herself carefully at a low writing table, she took a fresh piece of paper and prepared the ink. After composing herself with a long breath, she wrote a carefully worded letter in her best brushwork. She read it through twice and folded it neatly with the gold coin inside. Wrapping the letter in a cover sheet, she tied a piece of paper ribbon around it, addressing the front of the packet in neat characters. Chika returned with a bundle, placing it by her side. She turned to her with a smile. 'We might have something to eat now, if you please Chika.' She left with a bow.

Before long, Ōmono appeared on the veranda overlooking the garden with Haru in tow. His face scrunched into a fierce grimace, Haru knelt without any prompting, bowing his forehead to the floor. His damp hair was evidence of recent washing and his clothes were new and fresh. She could only imagine what assault on the senses this place must have been for him. Michiru hobbled back to her cushion next to Keiko and smiled. 'Haru. I hope you have been treated well since we arrived.'

He looked up, trying hard not to stare at the unfamiliar surroundings. 'Yes, mistress. They fed me and everything.' He looked sideways at Ōmono.

'I have a task for you, Haru, if you agree,' she continued, ignoring the exchange. 'I would like you to deliver this.' She slid the letter towards him. 'I would like you to take this to the Abbot of the Jokakuzan Monastery, near the Zenkō-ji temple. It is a couple of days travel north of Ueda. I will provide you with food for the journey and money for lodgings.' She indicated the bundle next to her. Ōmono came in and picked up the bundle and the letter, placing them in front of him. Haru's eyes fixed on the bundle, bottom lip between his teeth.

'You do not have to take it, if you do not wish to. You can just walk away,' Michiru reassured him. 'But if you want help,' she indicated with an upturned hand, 'here it is.'

Michiru saw the frozen look on his face and thought that he was going to turn her offer down. After a long pause, he drew the bundle towards himself and bowed from the waist. 'Thank you, mistress. Your offer is most generous.' He picked up the letter with both hands lifting it up and bowing his head. 'I would be happy to deliver this letter for you.'

*   *   *

Chika returned with a light meal for her and Keiko. She also brought yet another request for an audience from Sojiro. Michiru's face hardened. 'Please tell him that I am still recovering from my ordeal and I could not possibly see him today.' Chika gave her a sly grin and left to give him the message.

Keiko gave her a long, expressionless look. Michiru knew her friend was giving her a silent rebuke. 'You don't understand,' she said shortly.

'Oh I understand, my lady. I just don't agree with you. Why are you punishing him like this? Did things not work out for the best? You should be happy.'

'Well I am not happy at all, Keiko-san. He is a liar. I can never trust him again,' she replied bitterly.

'Oh, Hime-sama. Really?'

'Yes. I was mistaken to think so highly of him.'

'But you do love him, don't you?'

Michiru squirmed. 'How could anyone love such a deceiver?'

Keiko grinned gently. 'He did everything he could to keep you safe. Isn't that important?'

She could not think of a reply. Every time she thought of one, it seemed petty and foolish.

'You should forgive him, Michiru-sama. Life is too short and real love so rare to throw it all away just because your pride is hurt.' She looked at her earnestly. 'At least, allow him a chance to explain.'

She frowned, remembering that a part of her had leapt with joy when she heard her Yatsuhiro proclaim his real identity. What had followed was such a maelstrom of feelings in which that joy had been lost, smothered by the hurt of being deceived. *Is it really all that important? What were his reasons?* She realised once again that her serious young friend saw things much clearer than she did. With a sigh, she relented and called in one of the household maids.

*   *   *

Not long after midday there was a fuss in the corridor outside. Michiru's head turned as the screen at the end of the room slid open to reveal a frowning Sojiro, surrounded by escorting samurai and bowing maids. Chika hurried in to kneel in front of her. 'I'm sorry, hime-sama. I asked him to wait, but he just barged in.'

Michiru hurriedly composed herself and waved her aside. 'It is alright, Chika. Please bring us some tea.'

Sojiro stood impatiently, glaring at the bowing maids, waiting for them to depart.

'Would my lord give me the honour of joining me for tea?' she said with an icy bow.

He motioned for his guards to stay and came in, glaring back at one of the maids until she obediently slid the screen shut behind him. He exuded suppressed irritation as he knelt in front of her, placing his long sword next to him.

She sat with a rigid back, hands correctly crossed in her lap. Even though there was a faint smile on her lips, her jaw was clenched hard and her eyes tight at the corners.

'Really, Michiru-san?' he said, looking at her in exasperation. 'Do you have to behave this way? I have tried to see you three times this morning and each time Chika told me that you were indisposed and could not be disturbed.'

'But you came in anyway,' she shot back.

'I am lord here,' he said sardonically.

She inclined her head slightly. 'As my lord wishes.'

He rubbed his temples with both hands. 'Is this how it is going to be?'

'You deceived me,' she hissed at him. 'You lied to me and let me think I was to marry someone else.'

'And I'm sorry.' His shoulders slumped. 'You have no idea how sorry.'

'You tricked me. You made me feel like a fool.'

He sighed. 'Will you at least let me explain?'

She shifted uncomfortably. Her leg was beginning to hurt. But she was unwilling to relax in case he took it as a sign of her acceptance of a possible excuse, a sign of weakness. Her lips hardened into a thin line, but she inclined her head.

He looked at her captivating face and exhaled. 'I expected to be on the road with you for a couple of days. I had planned to tell you who I was when we stopped at the last inn. I thought we would get to know each other better and I could give you the choice, to return home or come here with me.'

Her eyes opened wide. 'What?'

Sojiro's expression softened. 'I thought if I gave you a choice before the wedding, you might be happier about the marriage. First, I wanted to get to know you. I did not want you to marry me just because your father arranged it. I was hoping you might actually like to marry me. And if not, then you could return home without shame. But then,' he waved a hand, 'events changed all of that.'

She thawed a little, but she was certainly not willing to forgive him so quickly. 'You had plenty of opportunities to tell me.'

'In enemy territory?' He shook his head. 'If anyone else had found out...'

'So instead you let me think that I was to lose you.'

A grin spread across Sojiro's face. 'So you did want me?'

She looked away. 'Maybe,' she said softly, not wanting to give him any leverage. She mentally slapped herself for letting it slip. There was still so much she could do to make him pay.

His grin widened into a smile. 'Oh, that changes things does it not?

'No,' she said hurriedly, but she realised it was too late. She was not experienced enough to play such games. With a deep sigh, she let it go. 'I am still angry with you.'

Drawing himself up, trying to stifle his smile, Sojiro adopted a formal air. 'Michiru no Katsura, will you agree to marry me?'

She flinched at his question. Michiru never expected to be asked. No matter what she said to him, she could not fool herself. She did not want to go home. Nor did she want to leave him, whatever name he used. The fragmented memories from their time together only fuelled the fire of her curiosity. Danger had coloured every experience of him. Now she wanted more. She ached to know what it would be like to be held in his arms without fear. To feel his touch without pain. To let her eyes linger on his face without turning away with guilt. She knew now what she wanted. Returning his formality, she placed her fingertips on the floor in front of her and bowed. 'Sojiro-sama, I would be pleased to marry you.'

*   *   *

Muneto fumed silently as he stood on guard outside Michiru's room. All that time the gold had been right under his nose. *She duped me. She duped us all. Sanzo was a fool. He could not see what was right in front of him and we listened to him, like idiots. He was no better than that half-witted Takuro. They should have killed the old man and the rest of them and searched their bodies for the gold. Instead, we listened to that little bitch and let her talk us into serving her. Fools! Idiots!*

His mind went round and round, chewing hatefully over his failure to get his hands on the gold. Soon, a new thought began to emerge. In a way, it worked out better than he first thought. *Sanzo had walked away. All the others had given up on the gold. Nobody was trying to get the gold now. She thinks it is safe.* The only reason he did not leave them at the fort was that he had overheard Michiru and Shuji talking. He had seen the box strapped to Michiru's kago during the escape and watched carefully as it was stored in her room. *And I know exactly where it is right now.*

His pulse slowed. His anger began to dissipate. He started to grin as a plan started to form in his mind. It started with him taking the gold and disappearing from this backwoods shithole. It ended with him living the high life in the big city surrounded by beautiful fawning women. The only thing that made him frown was what went in between. *How am I going to get out of here with the gold? So what is the plan? I can't do this by myself. I need someone else. The other ronin are in such raptures about being samurai again that I wouldn't trust any of them not to turn me in for a pat on the head.* He turned to look at his fellow guard and realised that there was only one person who he could convince to help.

Muneto spent a few minutes in silent contemplation. Then, confident with his newly hatched plan, he whispered to the bored looking man standing on the other side of the corridor. 'I hear Sojiro is talking about sending back all those prisoners that the Lady released. Something about not allowing criminals to get away with their crimes.'

Takuro stuck out his bottom lip and frowned. 'That's not fair. She promised them.'

Muneto smiled. 'Ah, but he didn't, did he?'

'But she promised,' he insisted.

'That's not all. He is going to look into our backgrounds as well.' Muneto looked straight into Takuro's nervous eyes. 'You know what will happen if they find out you were a bandit, don't you? Especially a runaway peasant turned bandit.' He drew a thumb across his throat.

Takuro's eyes flicked to the end of the corridor, as if he expected Sojiro's samurai to burst in and grab him. 'What do I do, Muneto? What do I do?' He licked his lips, his wide forehead wrinkled with worry.

Muneto grabbed him by the wrist. He did not need the man to panic, he needed him calm and co-operative. Afraid that someone might overhear him, he hushed the panicky peasant as best he could. 'Takuro. Takuro, calm down. Look at me,' he whispered. 'Calm down. I am not going to let anything happen to you. Calm down.'

As Muneto's words started to sink in, the frightened man looked at him, his eyes narrowing. 'Why would you help me?' He looked at the bearded samurai, trying to see some sign that he might be lying to him, like so many had done before. 'I didn't think you liked me. You are mean to me sometimes.'

'I know, I know. But it was all for show. I didn't want the others to get jealous. I have never hurt you though, have I?'

Takuro shifted from side to side, trying to remember whether he had. He knew that he had said hurtful things to him. However, he had never hit him like Ichiro had. 'No,' he admitted dolefully.

'Takuro, do you remember the treasure that Ichiro was talking about? The gold?'

'Yeh.' He answered with some hesitation. People were always talking about things that did not make sense to him. He did remember Ichiro saying something about gold, but he had no idea what he meant. But Muneto knew, and that was all that was important.

'Well, I know where it is. And I have a plan.'

'Yeh?'

'And I want you to help me.'

'Yeh? And you will help me get out of trouble?'

'That's right. Smart fellow.'

Takuro snickered because he knew it was not true. He knew he was not smart and that Muneto was just trying to make him feel better. He was his friend after all. He leaned closer, asking in an exaggerated whisper, 'What is it you want me to do?'

'Do you know what a sleeper hold is?'

CHAPTER NINETEEN

Renji rolled over on his futon, missing something important. His mind slowly climbed out from under the weight of sleep. *Just a little while longer. Then I'll get up.* He was next in the rotation for guard duty. Someone would wake him when the time came. Whatever the important thing was, it niggled at the back of his mind, demanding attention. His eyelids rasped open. It made no difference to the light in the room. He could not hear any breathing from the other men who should be asleep around him. *Why was the candle out?*

A shock ran through his body, jerking him up like a puppet. The candle was not lit. The other beds in the room were flat. They should have been back here by now. Something was wrong. Something was happening while he was lying here asleep. He leaped to his feet and rushed for the door, grabbing his swords on the way out. He hurriedly tied on some sandals, his eyes scanning for signs of trouble. His room-mates had been posted in the northern guest house, Michiru-hime's quarters. A chill ran down his spine.

In two quick strides along the veranda he reached the adjoining room and threw the screen open. 'Quick. Get up,' he hissed. 'Something's wrong.' He heard his fellow guardsmen throwing off their covers, but he did not wait for them. He sprinted across to the gate that led into the pavilion compound, his pulse pounding in his ears. *Should I raise the alarm?* If he were wrong, it would cause all sorts of problems and embarrassment. If he were right, he would be warning any villains that they were on to them, giving away the chance to spoil their plan. He opened the gate slowly scanning the outside of the building for any sign of activity. The shutters were up, but light seeped out here and there.

Three more guardsmen ran up behind him, tucking their swords into the sashes. He signalled them to follow him. They sprinted to the steps leading in to the rear of the building. Renji tested the door. It slid open freely. It should be locked. He turned to the man behind him, Misao. 'Go get Sojiro-sama.' Misao nodded and ran off for the Main Pavilion. Renji thought quickly, a dreadful suspicion growing in his mind. He looked at Tendo 'The back gate is the closest. Go alert the guards.' Tendo nodded and left. Renji drew his sword and stepped inside.

The corridor was empty. Lanterns at either end threw their light along the polished timber floorboards. One of the inner screens was ajar, but no light showed. *Where is the guard?* His skin prickled in anticipation of action. He took a few steps and waved the next man, Tano of Kai, in behind him. He signalled for him to go to the end and look around the corner. He kept his eyes fixed on the partially open screen. He was in a dangerous position. With the light behind him, he knew his silhouette would be obvious on the screen inside the room. However, there was nothing he could do about it. The building was designed this way. Tano looked back at Renji from the end of the corridor and shook his head. Two more guards not at their posts.

He motioned silently for Tano to check the corridor on the other side of the building. It also opened into this room. Renji signalled him to enter from the opposite door. Creeping carefully up to the open screen, he peered inside, scanning for shape or movement in the darkened room. Faint light seeped in through the translucent paper. Large privacy screens blocked the light in places, casting dark pools of shadow across the room. He watched Tano's silhouetted progress along the corridor. He tried to control his breathing, keeping as quiet as possible. Tano reached the opposite door. Sweat beaded on Renji's forehead. Silently, Tano slid the door open and they both entered the room, swords poised.

The dark room was empty. 'Get a lantern,' he whispered to Tano, who ducked back out into the corridor to fetch one. In the corner behind a low screen was rumpled bedding, probably Chika's. He went over and moved it aside with his sword. There was no-one there, no sign except that she had got up without putting it away.

Tano returned with a lantern and cast the light around the room. There was nothing unusual except for Chika's bedding and an open sliding door in the panel beneath the alcove housing a large hanging painted scroll and a vase holding a spray of narcissus blossoms.

With a sinking feeling, Renji knelt at Michiru's bedroom door. Tano stood at his back with the lantern. He knocked softly. 'My lady, it's Renji. Are you awake?' There was no answer, no sound at all. He knocked again. 'My lady, I have to come in and check that you are safe.' Fear gripped his heart. Dreading what he would find, he opened the door.

The silent room smelled overwhelmingly feminine, dizzying Renji with its perfume. Two still forms lay under the covers in their beds. To one side would be Keiko. The other, in the centre of the room should be Michiru. At first, Renji was both relieved and horrified, having invaded his mistress's privacy. However, he noticed a strange movement under Michiru's covers, an almost frantic twitching of the feet.

Tendo entered the main room breathing heavily. 'Both gate guards are dead. Throats cut.'

Renji stepped over to Michiru's bed and pulled back the cover. Chika lay there, gagged and bound heavily with rope, one tied around her throat and taut down to her feet. Her face was red and swollen, her eyelids fluttering on the verge of strangulation. He dropped his sword. Drawing his short sword to cut Chika's bonds, he shouted, 'Find Sojiro-sama. He'll be on his way here. The lady has been taken. They escaped through the back gate.' He cut the choke rope and removed her gag. She sucked in a huge gulp of air and panted heavily in relief. With each breathe she groaned hoarsely. 'Muneto. Muneto and Takuro. They took her.'

*   *   *

Muneto checked the stable to make sure no one was in there, before waving Takuro over from the shadows of the nearby alley. The thickset man moved out of the dark with exaggerated stealth dragging a rope behind him. Michiru, bound and gagged, struggled against him, resisting his pull until Takuro simply picked her up and carried her inside. He whispered to her, 'Please, miss. I don't want to hurt you. Just go along with it.' He looked at Muneto's back as he readied the horses. 'Otherwise you might make him angry, and you saw what he did to the guards.'

Takuro was no stranger to killing. He had done his fair share of it. Sometimes he had killed in anger, especially when people taunted or mocked him. Sometimes he had killed because people would not give up their money. However, he tried to avoid killing women. He had to do it once, when a merchant's wife had attacked him. It was something that still disturbed him. He was worried that Muneto might kill the Lady Michiru, which would be bad, because she had been nice to them, and she was pretty. 'Now you just do what he says and everything will be fine.' He smiled and patted her arm.

Muneto lead the first horse out, tying its reins to the door. 'Right,' he whispered. 'Lift her up into the saddle and we'll tie her on.' Takuro did as he was told and held her there while Muneto tied a rope around her waist and secured her to the saddle.

Takuro frowned. 'You shouldn't have killed those guards.' he whispered. 'You said we didn't need to kill anyone.'

'Shhh. Shut up about that,' Muneto hissed in annoyance. 'It's not my fault they stood there talking for so long. We couldn't afford to wait. They already delayed us too long.'

'I just don't think it was right. You said no one would get hurt.'

Muneto finished tying Michiru's bonds and came back around to stand with Takuro. 'Look, we had to get moving or we won't have enough of a head start.'

Takuro was still not happy with the way this was working out. It was much simpler when Muneto had explained his plan earlier. Now it was getting all complicated and Takuro hated it when things got complicated because then he did not know what was going on. 'Why are we taking her to Kiyomori? We don't need the money. We've got the gold.'

Muneto saddled the other horse, tying it reins to the door as well. 'We can talk about this later. We have to get moving now.' He picked up the box and tied it to the back of his saddle.

Takuro watched him for a moment before something occurred to him. 'Muneto. Which horse am I going to ride?'

The bearded ronin turned around, drawing his short sword in the same motion. He slashed Takuro along the side of his neck, staring at his slow friend as he grabbed his neck to try to stop his life from flowing out. Takuro's eyes went wide at the shock of this final betrayal. He sank to his knees and toppled over, his blood mixing with the straw and horse dung. 'You won't need one.'

*　　*　　*

The bearded ronin sat on his horse at the crossroads. The waning moon outlined the landscape with its glow, the details erased by the inky blackness in the shadows. Ahead lay the border between the Satake and Arikawa domains. The road to the right led out of the valley, towards the city of Ueda, and beyond. To the left, Katsura territory and a little used pass down towards the Kanto plains. He looked down each path, wrenching at the horse's reins.

Muneto was torn. He already had the gold. He could afford to leave Michiru here and disappear. However, turning her over to Kiyomori could prove to be lucrative, as long as the famously unstable lord was in a generous mood. It would also give him no small amount of satisfaction to see her humbled and at Kiyomori's mercy.

With a wicked smile, he made his decision. He could be at Kiyomori's mansion in Aoki by midday tomorrow. He would have to stop somewhere first and remove the gold from the box. He might even enjoy Michiru himself for a while. He heeled the horse forward towards the border, so pleased with himself that he almost laughed aloud.

*　　*　　*

Sojiro pulled up at the crossroads, looking helplessly in three directions. There was no way to tell which way he might have gone. Renji and the remaining troopers pulled up beside him. 'Which way would he have gone?' Sojiro asked in frustration.

'If he intended keeping her hostage he could be taking her anywhere.'

'Could he be taking her to Kiyomori? That was his original job.'

'True. But there is really no way to know for sure what he is planning.'

'Very well.' He turned his horse, picking out three troopers. 'You men, head up the western road.' He chose another three. 'You men, take the eastern road. See if you can catch up with them. If you don't find them before midday, turn around and backtrack carefully. Make inquiries along the way and see if there is any sign of them. If you do find them,' he fixed them with a glare, 'you are only to follow them. One of you ride back and find me. The rest of you, follow me.' He kicked the horse into action. He did not know how much of a lead Muneto had, or even if he was still on the road, but Sojiro knew he would do everything he could to get Michiru back. As the horse stretched out into a full gallop, he vowed that nothing and nobody would stand in his way.

*　　*　　*

Michiru's shoulders and upper arms burned from being tied behind her back for so long. The gag pulled at the corners of her mouth so tightly that her teeth had cut the skin inside. Being tied to the saddle at least prevented her from falling off, but without the use of her hands to steady or balance herself, her lower back and abdominal muscles were doing all the work. For the last hour, the arrow wound in her right leg had started to burn instead of just throbbing and she could feel the blood from the freshly opened wound running down her thigh.

Muneto had walked the horses for most of the way so far. They had trotted for short bursts at first but Michiru had howled so fiercely behind her gag that he had to slow down. The first time he cursed her and ignored her protests. However, the next time he slowed down and gave up the idea of moving faster than a walk. Evidently, he was comfortable enough with the head start they had.

All of this discomfort aside, what concerned her most was what would happen if the horse bolted or fell. The panicked animal would not be concerned about the human on its back. She faced a real risk of being broken in half. She supposed Muneto was not particularly concerned about her welfare. She glared at his back hatefully. She knew that, as Shuji had warned her, she must accept responsibility for this situation. While some of the ronin had proved themselves worthy, she should have realised that at least one of them would be a viper in the nest.

Michiru's hearing picked up the unmistakable sounds of the approach of galloping riders. Her eyes flicked to see Muneto's reaction but she saw none. Her heart leapt, fired by the hope that the horsemen rushing up behind them were looking for her. She knew that the closer her rescuers were able to get, the less time the ronin would have to react. If she could distract him and keep him occupied, he may not notice them until it was too late.

She kicked the horse with her heels, as wildly as she could. It responded by trying to obey its rider's commands but Muneto's grip on its reins limited its movement. The horse whinnied in confusion, tugging at the reins and sidestepping away from him. The bearded ronin cursed Michiru roundly as he dragged his horse around to cut off her escape, but it began to protest as well, adding to the confusion.

The thunder of the approaching riders finally intruded into the ronin's attention. He drew his sword and tried to get within reach of Michiru. Sojiro and his samurai had spotted him and were bearing down on him, their own swords drawn. Michiru's horse squealed and danced away. Feeling it all slipping out of his grasp, Muneto howled in frustration. He leaned over and swung wildly at Michiru, but she was well out of reach of his blade. 'Damn you!'

Her horse edged sideways a few more steps and then with an angry shriek of protest it reared up ripping the reins free from Muneto's grip. Daggers of pain shot through Michiru's back and the front of her hips as her body was thrown backwards in the saddle, only to be whiplashed forwards again as the horse came back down. Stars blinded her vision as her body tried to shut down from the pain. The frightened horse shook its head as it launched itself away from all the noise at full speed, Michiru slumped forward over its neck.

The thunder of the approaching riders dragged Muneto's attention back to the samurai focussed on him. If they were so worried about her safety, they might ignore him long enough for him to get away. Accepting the loss of Michiru and any ideas of revenge, he dragged his horse around and urged it into a gallop with a shout.

Sojiro watched in horror as the bound Michiru was tossed around on the back of the terrified horse. His heart leaped into his throat as he saw her subjected to abuse that the human body was not built to withstand. Without a thought for Muneto, solely focussed in the limp form of Michiru trussed to the saddle, he charged after the fleeing horse.

A fire burned in Renji's mind when he saw Muneto turn tail and run. Sojiro was already galloping after Michiru's horse, closely followed by the other riders. Renji swerved his mount to intercept the bearded samurai. *It is my fault that this happened. I knew Muneto could not to be trusted. I knew he was up to something. I should have warned Sojiro-sama. I must be the one to bring him down.* Renji drew his sword and urged his horse on harder. 'Muneto, you festering turd! Stand and fight me!'

The bearded ronin glanced over his shoulder, but his only response was to lean forward and whip his horse with the flat of his blade. After the horse's initial burst of speed, Muneto risked another look, seeing a furious Renji gradually gaining on him. He could hear the snorting breath of the pursuing horse close behind.

Renji spurred his horse to a fresh effort, coming up on Muneto's left. He lunged forward trying to catch him in the back with his sword tip. The fleeing ronin swerved left and spun around in his saddle, swatting the overextended blade aside with a forehand blow. His horse eased its pace, bringing him alongside his pursuer. Muneto made a desperate backhand swing at Renji's head. The younger samurai gripped the frame of his saddle with one hand and leaned over. The blade whistled through the air above him. With Muneto's side now exposed, Renji stabbed out to his full reach with an explosive shout. His blade found its mark and plunged in under the bearded ronin's ribs.

Muneto gasped, stiffening and falling sideways off his horse. The animal cantered on for a short distance before coming to a halt. Renji dragged back on his horse's reins, spinning around in a tight circle to come back to the fallen ronin. He leaped from the horse before it stopped, taking the final steps with the fury still burning in his eyes. The ronin lay, dazed and wracked by pain. His left arm was pinned under his body, bent at an impossible angle. He panted raggedly, his eyes tired as he looked up at the vengeful Renji. 'Kill me and get it over with,' he spat at him.

Renji's chest heaved, holding his sword against Muneto's throat. 'I should leave you here for the crows to feast on. Death is more than you deserve.' He shook with anger. 'Why did you do this? Why spoil everything you had? You had a fresh start. What was worth more than that?'

The broken ronin looked up from the ground and snorted in derision. 'She made fools of all of us.' He winced as a wave of pain coursed through his body. Blood flowed faster from his torn side. 'I would have had to look at her every day and be reminded of that.' Sickened by the man's useless pride, Renji drew back his sword and struck off the ronin's head.

*　　*　　*

After catching the quivering horse, Sojiro and his men cut Michiru loose from the saddle. They lowered her to the ground gently. She was only partially conscious as he removed the gag and cut her arms free. She moaned as they straightened her arms out carefully by her side. Sojiro could not take his worried eyes off her face. 'We can't risk moving her,' he said, licking his lips. He looked up at the concerned faces around him. 'You,' he motioned to one man. 'Ride back and get a doctor and a stretcher here. Go!' The samurai jumped onto his horse and thundered back down the road towards Nagase.

Seeing her lying there, still in her sleeping robes, his heart was clenched with fear. He took off his own kimono and laid it over her. *After everything she has been through. After everything she has survived. To be snatched out of my own house.* He put a hand over his face. *I failed to protect her.* The shame burned in him. Sojiro's fingers gently traced her jawline. A tear ran from the corner of her eye, momentarily clinging to her silken lashes. He tenderly brushed the stray tendrils of hair from her face, her brow delicately frowning from the pain. *She is a rare and delicate thing, yet so strong.* He could not deny the strength of his feelings for this contrary young woman.

Her eyes blinked open, looking up into his face. He smiled at her. She made to sit up, wincing at the pain the simple movement brought. He laid a gentle hand on her chest. 'Shhh. You should not move until the doctor gets here.'

She closed her eyes again briefly, biting her bottom lip as a wave of pain washed over her. After a moment, she stared back up at him, realising that she was safe now. The strange feeling that had troubled her since they met at the inn returned. She knew she did not have to push it away any longer. She let the warm glow fill her up. 'You came after me.'

He grinned. 'I was not going to let anyone take you away from me.'

Though her body ached from the punishment it had taken, she smiled weakly. 'Thank you, Sojiro-sama.'

The clatter of approaching horses drew their attention, drawing a hiss of pain from Michiru as she tried to turn her head. Renji dismounted and knelt beside Michiru. 'My lady,' he said in a sad, tired voice, bowing his head to the ground. 'I put you in danger by not reporting my suspicions about Muneto. I failed you, and you my lord,' he added to Sojiro. He placed a blood soaked bundle in front of him, bowing to the ground again. 'I have brought you the head of the renegade Muneto. Please forgive my failure.'

CHAPTER TWENTY

After three days of rest and recovery, Michiru sent word to Sojiro and Kosei that she felt ready to proceed with the wedding. Servants and family alike bustled with excited preparations. Michiru kept to her rooms, trying desperately to stay calm. She still ached, finding most movement painful but not impossibly so. Slow and deliberate motions were required for the ceremony anyway.

Shortly before midday, a message came from Sojiro, requesting a meeting. Unsure as to what it might portend, Michiru agreed. She changed as quickly as possible, and settled herself in her room facing the garden, breathing deeply in an attempt to calm her imagined fears about why Sojiro would want to see her so close to the wedding ceremony.

She was just starting to lose herself in the tranquillity of the garden when Chika appeared at her elbow to inform her he had arrived. Sojiro walked around the corner onto the veranda followed by Renji, carrying a heavy rectangular package wrapped in green fabric. They were both dressed in fresh crisp kimonos, complete with formal wing-shouldered mantles. Renji, freshly shaved and with his hair trimmed and combed back looked uncomfortable, keeping his gaze nervously fixed on the floor in front of him.

Once seated, with due courtesies satisfied, Michiru saw no sense in drawing things out. 'You requested to see me, my lord?'

He grinned at her manner, knowing it was not all a front. 'My Lady,' he began with a bow. 'Something of yours was taken from under my roof. I only hope that you can forgive me for my failure.' He motioned to Renji, who placed the green wrapped bundle in front of her.

Removing its wrappings, Renji displayed the battered rosewood box that had contained her dowry. He opened the box and backed away a pace, bowing to the floor. 'I am sorry, my lady. I was unable to recover all of the coins.' His voice trembled in shame with the admission. 'One coin has been lost.'

Michiru hid a smile behind her sleeve, struggling to keep it from showing in her eyes as well. *Renji must be feeling terrible!* 'Renji-san. Be at ease. I can account for the missing coin.'

They both looked at her in puzzled silence.

'I sent the coin to the Zenkō-ji temple, as a donation. To ask for a blessing.'

'You sent the coin?' Sojiro looked at her through narrowed eyes. 'I don't suppose that you gave it to Haru to deliver?

His question irritated her. She was not some idiot child without any knowledge of the world. Michiru took a deep breath, savouring the sweet smells wafting in from the garden, letting the irritation slide away. *Then maybe I should stop reacting like a child.* 'Yes, I did,' she replied calmly.

He looked down and shook his head. 'I do not understand why you felt that was necessary. You could have paid him with any coins. Those kokushin are irreplaceable.'

'You are correct, of course. But they are mine. And the gods deserve their share,' she said.

'But now your dowry is incomplete, Michiru-hime.'

She smiled. 'I am sure our family can survive with one less coin.' She took a deep breath. 'I do not hold any of you responsible for the actions of Muneto. He betrayed all of us. The fault is not yours,' she said with a bow. Michiru indicated toward the box of coins with a hand. 'I would be honoured if you would take this for safekeeping.'

Sojiro bowed his assent and Renji closed the box.

'I would like to ask you for a favour though,' she added.

He paused and sat back, one eyebrow rising unconsciously. 'What is that, my lady?'

She bit her lip, knowing that she had no right to ask and he had every right to refuse her. But she felt this was a debt that had to be paid. Shuji, Shigemori, Hirakazu, Ōmono, and countless others, deserved reward and recognition for getting her and the gold to Nagase. However, they had done no more than their duty, for which they should expect no praise. It saddened her to think that their efforts would go unrecognised. But Michiru knew what was owed to them and that she must find a way to repay that somehow. 'I want to form my samurai into a household guard, my Honour Guard. They have earned that distinction. To have the title of Guardsmen. And Renji-san should be their captain.'

Renji's head bowed to the floor, his muffled voice protesting. 'My lady. I do not deserve such an honour.'

'I would not ask this, Renji-san, if I did not think you were the best of them.'

Sojiro was momentarily speechless. He knew many husbands would have laughed in her face and refused. *I am head of the household. The samurai owe their allegiance to me. It is true, though. They had proved themselves worthy and kept her safe. Even Tanzo the farmer has earned his swords in defence of Michiru.* So, he ignored custom and let Michiru have her way. 'Then it shall be so.'

*   *   *

Michiru shivered with the effort of appearing calm and upright. Her pulse thudded behind her ears. She looked down and took a slow breath. Halfway through her exhale the screen in front of her slid open. Bowing heads were lined up on either side of the steps leading out. At the foot of the stairs waited a jet black and gold lacquered norimono, bearing the Arikawa crest. The bearers and their armoured guards all wore the Arikawa red livery. The samurai guard lining the front of the house consisted of her own men, now proudly dressed in new outfits of clan-made armour.

Shuji stood in front of her once more. The cut across his cheek still looked red and gruesome, but his eyes were bright. A smile slipped past her mask briefly as he bowed his head to hide his own grin. He gave her a supporting hand and led her down the steps. She carried the multi-layered burden of her kimonos on her shoulders, dragging the trail behind her. Everyone around her held themselves rigid, only moving in stiff, formal gestures. The chanting of the shrine maidens and the intonations of the priest were the only voices to be heard. It felt strange, going through this process again. She paused in front of the open norimono. She looked around hopefully for a nearby horse, before turning to Shuji in disappointment. He just smiled and bowed, his open hand indicating towards the seat.

She settled onto the cushion and the door closed. *In the box again.* She sighed. *But things are not the same.* She had just spent her first time truly without a proper home. She had left the protection of her family and the world quickly became very real for her. When she fought off the ronin at the derelict house, she had been truly alone. *By myself, I was prey.* She realised how important people were to each other. She began to understand how they needed each other, and the bonds that held them together. *With a new family, friends and a whole Household behind me, I am safer and even stronger now.* She smiled to herself. *It was nice of Sojiro to send the Arikawa norimono for me. Even if it was only for a short trip.* With no one able to see her, she felt comfortable enough to let the smile spread. *I really am quite lucky.*

The procession travelled at a tortuously formal pace from the guesthouse around to the front entrance of the main Pavilion. She shrugged her shoulders at the unaccustomed weight of her clothes, even while seated. Her legs and back still ached no matter which way she leaned to relieve the discomfort. Looking out through the grille of the window, she saw Arikawa samurai, family and retainers lining the courtyard. Her stomach knotted nervously. *I will be glad when this is all over.*

The bearers stopped at the foot of the stairs, where Sojiro and his uncle Toichi stood next to a Shinto priest. The norimono settled down gently and the door opened. Shuji offered her a helping hand as she stood to face Sojiro. Two ranks of red and white clad miko held up branches of katsura with their heart shaped leaves fluttering in the light breeze, to form an archway leading to the groom. Her eyes sought out Kosei, standing to one side, who nodded with a barely suppressed grin. It was a delightful gesture that reminded her of home. Michiru swallowed hard and closed her eyes, walking towards the priest. Everyone bowed as she approached. She took her position to Sojiro's right, to undergo the priest's cleansing ritual.

Michiru did not see anyone else. She kept watch for Sojiro's every move out of the corner of her demurely lowered eyes. She barely noticed the blessings of the priest, who then led them up the stairs into the Main Pavilion. The central chamber now held an altar and accoutrements from the Arikawa family shrine. The air was thick with the spicy incense curling from the smoking bronze incense burners that flanked the altar.

Her heart pounded as they knelt in front of the altar. Prompted by the priest, she followed Sojiro's offering with her own. Her movements were stiff as she struggled to control her trembling limbs. *There is no turning back now.*

Sojiro took the cup offered by a miko, which the priest then filled with sake. Sojiro looked at her and their eyes met. He drank a mouthful and passed the cup to her. Terrified of dropping the cup, she willed herself to be graceful as she sipped the sake. Her concentration was so intense, her nerves so strained, that she neither understood the words that came from Sojiro, or indeed from her own mouth.

The priest smiled. Sojiro smiled. Michiru still bemused, did not register the people gathered around. She only had room in her mind for Sojiro. He took up her whole attention, until a katsura leaf settled on his sleeve, blown in from the courtyard on a gentle puff of breeze. Her eyes were drawn to it, giving her a moment of clarity.

She blinked. *Now that the ceremony is complete, I owe my life and my loyalty to the Arikawa. My home is here in Nagase, as The Mistress in the House of the Arikawa. But I will always be what I was born; a Daughter of the Katsura.*

HAKONE – WINTER OF 1652

Cold seeped down the back of her neck. Michiru blinked and looked around the gloomy room, dimly lit by a small lamp. Night had fallen. The occasional gust of breeze rattled the screens. She had drifted off again. Her hand still rested on the lid of the box. She was alone. Where are they all now, she asked the heavens painfully? *All gone. All dead. None left alive who know what happened. Except me. None left alive who were there. Except me. Why has someone as unworthy as I survived so long, while better people suffered and died?*

Michiru's lips quivered. The sadness began to overwhelm her. As her head drooped, she noticed that the young maid had brought back the tray and poured fresh tea. Thin tendrils of steam still rose from the cup. *She must have been very quiet.* Taking her hand off the box, she found a quilt draped over her shoulders. *Just like Keiko had done for me while she was alive.* With a sad smile she drew it tighter around her.

www.ingramcontent.com/pod-product-compliance
Lightning Source LLC
Chambersburg PA
CBHW050408260626
47156CB00003B/928